He leaned back against his pillows and grinned.

"Of course, if you would care to play piquet for a small stake, I would be happy to oblige."

Eloise laughed. "What sort of stake?"

"A guinea a point."

"You'll beggar me," she said in mock horror. A light-headed exhilaration was taking hold of her; his bantering tone, his quick smile were intoxicating her. "Or rather, you'll beggar yourself. It's your money, after all."

"A kiss, then. Just one, if I win the game."

"And if I win?" she managed, her heart suddenly beating faster.

"You won't," James said with certainty.

It took only two hands for him to claim victory.

"My game, I believe," he said, taking her wrist and drawing her closer.

Hoping he could not feel her trembling, she leaned over and kissed him very quickly on the cheek.

"Try again," he advised. "Kisses on the cheek are not accepted as payment for gambling debts."

She had lowered her eyes, because she did not want him to see her expression. Blindly she bent over the bed. He pulled her head down gently, his hand sliding through her hair. Then he kissed her, a slow, searching kiss.

<u>BOOK YOUR PLACE ON OUR WEBSITE</u> <u>AND MAKE THE</u> <u>READING CONNECTION!</u>

We've created a customized website just for our very special readers, where you can get the inside scoop on everything that's going on with Zebra, Pinnacle and Kensington books.

When you come online, you'll have the exciting opportunity to:

- View covers of upcoming books

- Read sample chapters

- Learn about our future publishing schedule (listed by publication month *and author*)

- Find out when your favorite authors will be visiting a city near you

- Search for and order backlist books from our online catalog

- Check out author bios and background information

- Send e-mail to your favorite authors

- Meet the Kensington staff online

- Join us in weekly chats with authors, readers and other guests

- Get writing guidelines

- AND MUCH MORE!

Visit our website at
http://www.kensingtonbooks.com

THE SPY'S BRIDE

Nita Abrams

ZEBRA BOOKS
Kensington Publishing Corp.
http://www.zebrabooks.com

ZEBRA BOOKS are published by

Kensington Publishing Corp.
850 Third Avenue
New York, NY 10022

All Kensington titles, imprints and distributed lines are available at special quantity discounts for bulk purchases for sales promotions, premiums, fund-raising, educational or institutional use.

Special book excerpts or customized printings can also be created to fit specific needs. For details, write or phone the office of the Kensington Special Sales Manager: Kensington Publishing Corp., 850 Third Avenue, New York, NY 10022. Attn. Special Sales Department. Phone: 1-800-221-2647.

Zebra and the Z logo Reg. U.S. Pat. & TM Off.

First Printing: May 2003

10 9 8 7 6 5 4 3 2 1

Printed in the United States of America

To Mom, Dad, and the Hyde Park Suite

Prologue to a Wedding

November 1813
Roehampton. The bride's family

Samuel Bernal put down the book he had been leafing through and looked again at his watch. He was nervous. His wife was nervous, too. He could tell by the way she was bustling about the small sitting room rearranging china figurines.

"You did send for Eloise?" he asked for the second time.

"She was out walking," his wife reminded him. "But I am sure her maid will help her change very quickly. I sent word that you had come down from London expressly to speak with her."

"Walking." Bernal's tone was a mixture of puzzlement and scorn. He had purchased an estate in Surrey because he had seen that it was expected for a man in his position. That his wife and daughter would prefer it to London—would spend virtually the entire year there—had never occurred to him. Indeed, Eloise sometimes begged to remain at Roehampton even when her mother went in to London. She was a quiet girl who kept herself happily occupied in the country—potting plants in the succession houses, tramping down muddy lanes, driving off in the gig on trumped-up errands to small local markets.

She had dutifully gone off to Miss Myncheon's seminary last year when, in an unheard-of coup, that institution had actually agreed to offer her a place "as a visiting pupil." But she had made few friends there and had been ecstatically grateful to return home at the end of her third term. Her only regret had been the drawing master, who apparently had encouraged her interest in botanical sketching and had even suggested that she might be able to obtain employment producing illustrations for scientific treatises. Bernal had been insulted that the man had supposed his daughter in need of a paying position, but Eloise had been delighted.

He wondered, not for the first time, if it was right to uproot her again so soon—and this time, permanently. She still seemed very young to him: his only child, late and unexpected, with her fine-boned delicacy so unlike his own round face or Reyna's broad, olive-skinned one. Nevertheless, there were many advantages to the match. A good alliance, connections with both Whitehall and the Change, and—not to be discounted—the very tangible approval of his mother-in-law, in the form of a large and securely invested dowry for Eloise.

His eye fell on a Meissen vase. Reyna had just finished adjusting it so that the painting of Diana at the chase would face front instead of half sideways. The slim, bare-breasted figure of the goddess stared out at him accusingly, an arrow half drawn from her quiver. Was it not Diana who had refused to marry, who had begged her father, Jupiter, for perpetual virginity? He suppressed an urge to march over and turn the painting back towards the wall.

"Reyna," he said, giving voice to his qualms, "are you certain we should proceed so quickly?"

"You made the arrangements yourself!" She turned and gave him an indignant stare. "You thought my mother's proposal was very reasonable! Generous, even, you called it!''

Reasonable from a financial point of view, he thought. Was it reasonable to allow his mother-in-law to choose a bridegroom for his daughter? No, not choose: prescribe. Command.

At the sound of light footsteps in the hall, Reyna gave a warning frown and hurried over to perch on one end of a chaise, where she had deposited her work basket.

''Papa!'' called a breathless voice, and his daughter burst in. She was in a plain merino wool gown, presumably the one she had worn for her walk, but her dark hair was neatly coiled back, and she had changed into white silk stockings and thin kid slippers.

''Head and feet repaired,'' she said apologetically, following his eyes to the slippers. ''Danielle told me you had made the trip expressly to speak with me—and in such weather!'' It was raw and misty outside, with a bone-chilling wind. ''I thought you would prefer me in my dirt now, rather than in my finery half an hour later.''

There was, in fact, actual dirt on the hem of her gown, he realized. And a few blackened wisps of straw.

Then she looked at her mother, back at him, and paused, uncertain. ''Is something wrong?'' she said hesitantly.

''Please sit, my dear,'' he said. ''No, there is nothing wrong. Quite the opposite. I have received a visit from Mr. Lobatto.'' He saw that she did not recognize the name, which was not surprising, since she had not spent much time in London and had no friends who had been married at Bevis Marks.

Looking puzzled, she sank down on the chaise beside her mother.

''A *kasamentero*,'' Bernal clarified. ''He has brought us news of a most advantageous match for you. James Meyer. James *Roth* Meyer. A very worthy suitor. It is a great honor for us that you have attracted his interest.''

Even Eloise knew the Roths. ''Eli Roth's nephew? Do

you mean the"—she paused and said carefully—"the young man who is one of Lord Wellington's officers?"

Bernal knew what she had been going to say: *Do you mean the boy who has been the talk of East London for the last three years?*

"Yes," he said, equally careful. "The son of Eli Roth's late sister."

"Papa, I have never met him," said Eloise bluntly. "You know that very well. We have not been used to going to the homes of *Tudescos*."

He coughed. "Apparently he has heard good reports of you from Elena and Isabella Mendez."

"I have spoken with Elena Mendez once. Isabella, never." Eloise was beginning to get that stubborn, wary look he knew well from her childhood. She did not like to argue, but when she took up a cause, she did not relinquish it lightly. "And why would they mention me to James Meyer?"

"He is their cousin by marriage."

"That is not what I meant, Papa."

"Samuel, this is absurd." Reyna spoke in a sharp tone which was unusual for her. "Eloise is not a child. Let us tell her the truth." She turned to her daughter. "Your *nana* has proposed this young man as a husband for you," she said simply. "You know she has been ill recently. She would like to see you married, and his family has agreed to consider it. What do you think? If you say yes, you are not agreeing to marry him. The matchmaker would come to see you, tell you more about him, and then if you both wished it, you could meet."

Eloise considered this question gravely for a minute, as though her father's fictionalized version of the affair had never existed.

"Can we omit the meeting with the *kasamentero*?" she asked.

"No." Her mother's voice was firm. "Mr. Lobatto would

be very offended, as would your grandmother. I will ask him to try to be more plausible than your father.''

Bernal gave an indignant huff.

''Well, then, my answer is yes,'' said Eloise. She stood and brushed off her skirt, which had some of her mother's silk floss clinging to it.

''Yes?'' echoed Bernal weakly. He had anticipated a protracted argument.

Eloise gave one of her rare, clear smiles and kissed him on the cheek.

''I will never understand that girl,'' he muttered as Eloise excused herself to go finish changing her clothes. ''Never.''

''What is the mystery?'' countered his wife. ''Your dreadful friend DaCosta has been sniffing about her for months, hinting that he is a lonely widower. Ever since she came back from Bristol last summer she has been hearing that it was time for her to be married, and she probably believed you would support his suit. Instead, you propose a finelooking young man, wealthy, from a powerful family—''

''Handsome, wealthy, and notorious,'' growled Bernal.

''For a girl Eloise's age, a hint of scandal makes a groom more appealing,'' observed Reyna.

''It's more than a hint,'' he muttered, suddenly feeling renewed anxiety on his daughter's behalf.

''Nonsense,'' said his wife. ''I do not know any of the Meyers, but I know Louisa Roth. She raised the boy after his mother died. And that is enough to satisfy me.''

London. The groom's family

''He's too young.'' Nathan Meyer faced his brother-inlaw across the tiny width of his study, a cramped room at the back of Roth's sprawling City townhouse. Since Meyer was rarely in London, he and his children had gradually abandoned any pretense of maintaining a home of their own and had moved in with the Roths.

Eli Roth waved his hand dismissively. ''James is nearly

three and twenty, Nathan. I was married at nineteen. And *you*"—he jabbed a finger at the taller man—"*you* were married at eighteen. Do you regret the extra years you had with my sister?"

Meyer looked up at the portrait hanging over the fireplace. "No," he conceded. "But don't try to distract me. I did not mean his age when I said he was too young, and well you know it."

"A good wife has helped many a youth become a man," said his brother-in-law sententiously.

"An overyoung groom has made many a good match into a bad marriage," was the sharp retort. "Don't fence with me, Eli. You are very eager to bring this about, perhaps too eager. I know the Bernals are a powerful family. I know they did not treat you well when you first arrived in England. Time was when a German Jew suing for the hand of a Bernal would have been tossed into the street. It was a nine-days' wonder when your sister was allowed to marry Israel Mendez, and his family is as far below the Bernals as a knight is below an earl. Naturally, you are delighted to be sought out by Samuel Bernal. But why James? Yes, your own sons are too young to be betrothed—but what of the French cousins? Or Anthony, in Italy?"

"The Bernals were very evasive with me," said Roth, dropping onto a stool by the tiny fireplace. "But when they insisted on James as the groom, I made some inquiries. This match was not their idea. Reyna Bernal is from the French branch of the Carvallo family, and her mother, who still lives in Paris, has been ill recently. Madame Carvallo became convinced that it was her duty to secure her grandchild's future before her death."

"What does this have to do with James?" asked Meyer impatiently.

"I am coming to that. Madame insisted that her granddaughter must be married at once, to a man of our faith. So the father began to inquire about prospective alliances, and then he received another communication from the grandmother, ordering them to make certain that the bridegroom was English, since she loathes Napoleon and is certain he will bring the entire continent to ruin.''

''I hardly think James is a good choice if religion is in question,'' Meyer remarked. ''Surely there are many eligible bachelors in the Bernals' congregation.''

''But,'' said Roth softly, ''they are not the son of the man who loaned Wellington the gold that financed his first campaign in Portugal. Nor are they acting as couriers for the British Army. Madame Carvallo's second letter named you and James as desirable *partis*. In that order. Next to each of your names she had noted the price on your head set by the French Imperial *Sûreté*. The enemy of her enemy is her friend, it appears.''

Meyer's face, normally impassive, was a study in dismay.

''In fact, my dear brother,'' Roth pointed out maliciously, ''if you truly feel that James is not ready for marriage, there is another way to achieve this very desirable alliance. You could marry Miss Bernal yourself.''

Meyer shot him a warning look, and Roth returned hastily to the subject of his nephew.

''Do you think it better to let James continue on as he is now?'' he asked, getting to the heart of the matter. ''You left Rachel's marriage far too late, and look at the result. She fell in love with one of James's fellow couriers and wed outside our faith. Think of the scandal if her brother also contracts a shocking misalliance.''

''I care nothing for scandal,'' said Meyer, in a tone which warned Roth that this topic, too, was best left alone.

''Very well. Imagine what sort of woman James would pursue if left to his own devices.'' There was a pregnant silence. Neither man needed to exercise his imagination very hard.

''Well,'' Meyer said, wavering. ''Perhaps new responsibilities, new companionship might not be such a bad thing for him. What harm is there in at least bringing the two young people together? They can decide if they will suit.''

Roth broached the difficult question. "Will he consent to visit the Bernals? Will he even consider a marriage contract?"

"I believe so," Meyer said slowly. "He has been eerily compliant of late."

Paris. Other interested parties

The Countess of Brieg was having her hair put up when she heard the news. A junior minister was coming to escort her to a reception, and at first when she heard the bell peal distantly she thought it was Michelet. He was the most attractive—and the most gullible—of the officials she had collected around herself in the three months since she had fled to Paris. But when Josef opened the door, she knew it was not the earnest young Frenchman. No one in her household would ever admit a male visitor to the countess's boudoir while she was having her hair done.

It was her brother. He paused in the doorway, eyeing his delicate, golden sister with a mixture of irritation and admiration.

"Who is it tonight?" he asked, with a slight curl of his lip.

"Michelet."

He snorted. "Small fry."

"Charming small fry," she corrected sweetly. She considered the pile of burnished curls her maid was building atop a small silver tiara. "Not so high," she ordered. Obediently the maid began tweaking the topmost layer of ringlets out into a wider circle.

"Why are you here, Fritz?" she said, her eyes on her image in the mirror. "Do you need money?"

He flushed. He blamed her for their exile, she knew, and he blamed her even more for having had the foresight to deposit a very large chunk of her late husband's fortune in a French bank long before they had been forced to flee Austria. He hated being dependent on her.

"I could use a small sum," he conceded. "Until my rents are forwarded."

The rents were a myth, a fiction both maintained out of courtesy. The chance of any money arriving safely through the war zone between Vienna and Paris was virtually nil. If any rents were even being collected on the estates of a Bonapartist nobleman who had fled his homeland when Austria had declared war on France.

The countess sent Josef for her strongbox and returned to contemplating her curls while the money was counted out. Arranging her hair was a long, tedious process because it was so fine that all the layers had to be done one by one from the bottom to the top, in order.

The maid was finishing up the tendrils at her temples when her brother turned back. He had thanked her already and wished her a pleasant evening with Michelet. His hand had been on the doorknob.

"Oh, by the way," he said casually, swinging around and meeting her eyes in the mirror, "I heard something which might interest you."

She knew at once that this was the real reason he had come. One perfect eyebrow went up inquiringly. "What might that be?"

"Do you remember the English spy? The Jew?"

She would not pretend that she didn't remember. "Captain Nathanson."

"Yes—or Meyer, if you prefer his real name."

"What about him?"

"He's to be married."

"Oh?" she asked. Her maid stepped back and she nodded approval of the coiffure. "Earring box, Magda," she said. The maid disappeared into an adjacent room. Her brother was not fooled; he knew her too well.

"You may as well admit you are not indifferent to my news, Theresa."

She swiveled around on the cushioned stool and gave

him an icy stare until his smirk faded slightly. "Very well, perhaps I am curious. Where did you hear this?"

"The *Sûreté*."

A reliable report, then. French counterintelligence kept very good track of the activities of the top British couriers.

"Don't give up hope," he advised her. "It's an arranged marriage. The family is very wealthy, you know."

"I am sure I wish him every happiness," said the countess, daring her brother to disagree.

He gave a nasty smile. "Perhaps you should write and offer your good wishes."

"Perhaps I shall." She turned back to the mirror. Her maid had returned and was holding out two pairs of earrings for her inspection.

She waited until after she had heard him ushered out the front door by Josef. Then she picked up the nearest breakable object—in this case, a Sèvres rouge pot—and hurled it straight at the wall. It shattered into a dozen pieces.

"That was very careless of you, Magda," she said coldly to her terrified maid. "I am afraid I shall have to dock your wages to replace it."

One

"Not the merriest wedding feast I've ever attended." The speaker, a young man leaning on a cane, had muttered this nearly under his breath, but his companion instantly frowned.

"Mind your manners, Evrett," he reproved in a near-whisper, glancing around quickly to see if anyone had overheard.

"Oh, they can't possibly hear us in all this racket," said the man with the cane. He looked over at the noisy crowd of guests milling around the half-cleared tables in the long gallery at the rear of the house. The two men were standing by one of the floor-to-ceiling windows which looked out towards the Channel. Earlier, there had been a view of gray sea under gray sky, but on this late November day darkness had fallen early, and now the windows revealed only the reflection of the candles on the tables and the sconces on the inner wall. Across from the embrasure where they stood, double doors opened into a large drawing room filled with more tables and an equally unruly company.

"I do feel like a popinjay in a murder of crows," said the second man, an army officer named Michael Southey.

He was slight, with short reddish hair, and his glittering dress regimentals were very conspicuous amid the dark coats and plain breeches of the other male guests.

"Don't be deliberately obtuse, South. I was not lamenting the lack of embroidered waistcoats when I made that complaint, and you know it. I was thinking of our comrade-in-arms. The groom." Evrett nodded towards a tall, dark-haired young man in the center of the drawing room. He had just risen; the bride was retiring upstairs with her mother to prepare for bed. She was appropriately pink-cheeked and confused, but their friend did not look like a nervous bridegroom. Or an eager bridegroom. He looked remote and faintly hostile.

"What about him?" Southey frowned as he considered the distant figure, who was standing frozen in place as his bride moved away.

"Ah, yes, I had forgot. You haven't seen him for a bit."

"Not since the hearings at Whitehall nearly a month ago. I was delighted to hear about the wedding, naturally."

"Are you still delighted?" Evrett asked pointedly. "Or do you perhaps feel a bit uneasy after observing him today? Concerned that this marriage might be a trifle premature?"

"His uncle seems quite enthusiastic," said Southey uncomfortably.

Evrett's dark eyes narrowed as he considered the round figure of Eli Roth, energetically talking and gesturing just beyond the entrance to the drawing room. "He does. He is in the minority, however. The guests have been murmuring all day. Especially when James had to stamp on that goblet. Did you see that?"

"Yes. He can't put his full weight on that foot for very long, can he?"

"The old man standing next to me pronounced it a terrible omen."

"I'll take Eli Roth's judgment over that of a superstitious old grandfather," retorted Southey. "Roth is the most powerful banker in England, and he has known his nephew far longer than we have. I wouldn't dismiss his opinion lightly.''

"Have you looked at James?" demanded his friend furiously, gesturing towards the motionless figure in the next room. "Not just today—yesterday, and the day before, and the day before that. He's like a dead man! His eyes are empty, his color is dreadful, and he moves as though he were sixty, even taking the injured ankle into account. When you speak to him, he barely answers. He's not fit to choose a snuffbox, let alone take a bride!''

There was a brief silence.

"I was hoping he might have recovered a bit," said Southey with a sigh. "Still that bad, eh?"

"Still that bad," confirmed Evrett gloomily.

"Whatever do you suppose his father was about, then, agreeing to this match?" asked Southey, glancing towards the far end of the gallery, where Nathan Meyer was gallantly entertaining some of the bride's great-aunts.

"Well, if it were my son wearing the willow for a vixen who sold him to the French, I might be desperate enough to try a fairly drastic remedy.''

"Seems a bit hard on the bride. I've only caught a few glimpses of her today; have you met her?''

"Yes. Just out of the schoolroom: petite, big dark eyes, rather shy."

Southey snorted. "She won't last a week. He'll have one of his explosions and terrify her out of her wits.''

Evrett shook his head. "No explosions," he said. "Not one. Not since he's come back from Vienna.''

Astonished, Southey swung round. "No challenges? No brawls?"

"None."

"That's not James," said his friend flatly.

"Precisely," said Evrett.

* * *

The old James Meyer had been a paragon of insubordination. He had started out on a small scale at the age of eighteen months with his mother. His first word, and his favorite word, had been ''no.'' The gentle and affectionate Miriam was a poor target, however, and so he had quickly graduated to confronting his father. When his mother died and his father went abroad, leaving James and his sister Rachel with his uncle, he transferred his defiance to Eli Roth. Shortly afterwards, Nathan Meyer had begun taking the children to the continent with him. James was delighted: he could alternate rebellions. Winter in London against his uncle, summer in Spain against his father.

At eighteen he had achieved a masterstroke: he had adopted a false identity as a convert to the Church of England in order to purchase a commission in the infantry. This not only horrified his family but gave him dozens of superior officers to defy. Captain Nathanson, as he was known to Whitehall, held the record for disciplinary hearings in the Ninety-fifth Rifles. He had been demoted (once, but had then been promoted again), reprimanded (twice), fined (once), and confined to quarters (once). During a leave of absence in Lisbon he had fought six duels in ten days, including one against a lieutenant-colonel. Only his considerable skills at reconnaissance work had saved him from being cashiered—that and evidence that several of his opponents had offered insupportable provocation.

The duels continued, more discreetly. But unofficial complaints from senior officers traveling with their families were also received: handsome, devil-may-care subordinates are not popular with the fathers and husbands of the females who fall under the rebel's spell. Eventually, he had been recalled to London and reassigned. He was outraged at his removal from the front lines, even though his duties as a courier were in fact far more dangerous than an infantry command. The old James had demonstrated his displeasure in predictable and familiar ways: storming out of his uncle's home, seeking out increasingly risky assignments, threatening to resign his captaincy.

And then, last summer, he had gone to Vienna. A mere three months, on a mission which appeared to be a luxurious respite from his normal clandestine assignments: he was there in uniform, officially accredited to the Austrian court. A summer of receptions and parades and garden parties. There was one small, ugly incident, with no lasting repercussions beyond an injury to his ankle. Yet he had returned a changed man.

The new James Meyer was submissive and accommodating. He stiffened whenever his father entered the room, but deferred politely to his sire's every request. When his uncle had hesitantly mentioned marriage to him, he had agreed at once to make the acquaintance of Miss Bernal. Two brief and horribly stilted calls upon the Bernals had ensued. Eli Roth had watched with concern as his normally eloquent nephew sat silent for two consecutive half-hour visits. Nevertheless, James announced at once after the second meeting that the match was acceptable to him and proceeded to vanish from London.

He returned a week later, barely in time to approve the proposed marriage contract—but since he agreed to all its provisions without reading it, the time normally required for negotiation was, fortunately, not needed. Emissaries from the Bernal household brought increasingly peculiar demands, none of which troubled him in the least. The wedding would be held at the Bernal house in Ramsgate? He could see no objection to that. He must not wear his uniform or call attention to his military service? Entirely understandable. Eloise and her mother had both been feeling a bit poorly, would he mind if the Bernals canceled the reception planned for the Monday before the wedding? Would he *mind?* He had been unutterably relieved, but had written a brief and scrupulously correct response, expressing his sympathy for the Bernal ladies and his hopes for their speedy recovery. Reyna Bernal was still indisposed, in fact;

he had seen the doctor coming down the stairs this morning before he went up to unveil his bride. Since he himself now seemed to be walking around in a permanent, feverish haze, he sympathized.

The ceremony had gone by him in a blur; he had simply done whatever he was told to do. Stand here; say this; drink that. There had been an awkward moment when, attempting to break the crystal goblet under his foot, his bad ankle had given way and nearly pitched him onto the floor. But the shocked murmurs at this unlucky slip were only louder versions of the murmurs he had been hearing all day: how odd to have the wedding in Ramsgate; how odd that there was no reception in London; how odd that it had all been so hasty; how odd that the Bernals were giving their only daughter to a *Tudesco*. A German. The old James Meyer would have confronted the murmurers. The new James Meyer stored it all away, one more dose of bitterness and humiliation.

Now the new James Meyer had been told to go up to his bride. He had, therefore, obediently risen, taken polite leave of the remaining guests, and gone up the polished oak stairs to the door of the suite where his new wife was waiting. His uncle and his father had asked if he would like their escort, and of course he had said yes, although the old James Meyer would have given them a dry *thank you, no*. He wished suddenly that Evrett and Southey had not left, that they were here to play the traditional role of groomsmen and send him in to his bride with some barracks-room jest.

"Our very best wishes," said his uncle formally, shaking his hand and trying to smile.

His father eyed him thoughtfully.

Gritting his teeth, he raised his chin and gave his father stare for stare.

"Yes, one must hope for the best," said his father in a rather cryptic echo of Roth's blessing.

The door opened, and a group of women emerged—he recognized Reyna Bernal, and one of the bride's aunts. And, of course, his own Aunt Louisa. The women ducked their heads nervously, avoiding his eye, and vanished.

"Good night, Uncle Eli." He gave a respectful nod to Roth. "Good night, sir." This to his father. Then the new James Meyer opened the door and went in.

Louisa Roth had dragged her husband out onto the terrace behind the house, in spite of the bitter cold. There was nowhere else she could be sure of privacy.

"This," she said bluntly, "is a terrible mistake. I think you should put a stop to it right now. For both their sakes."

"Don't be ridiculous." Roth's voice was muffled as he struggled into the greatcoat he had demanded from a puzzled servant.

"A little embarrassment, a little scandal, is of no moment in comparison to a lifetime of misery," she said sternly. "Everyone in that house could feel it. All the women were whispering to each other from the moment James walked in. And that Eloise looked scarcely any better. She didn't taste a single bite of food."

"Wedding nerves," said Roth irritably, buttoning the top buttons of his coat with increasingly numb fingers.

His wife shook a gloved finger at him. "Wedding nerves, my eye! Are you blind, Eli Roth? How many weddings have we attended this past year? Ten? Were there any other grooms who never looked at their bride? Who never smiled? Nathan agrees with me, I am sure."

"Louisa," said Roth, exasperated, "even if Nathan *did* agree with you—which I take leave to doubt—he and I have no right to interfere at this point. James signed the marriage contract. Not me. Not Nathan. The decision belongs to him. To him and the Bernals, and his bride."

"You know perfectly well that you could walk in and talk quietly to Bernal right now and the wedding would be annulled tomorrow."

"Very well. I concede that if some disaster were looming,

I would probably be able to step in and call a halt to the proceedings. But there is no such disaster. I will not make a mockery of our family—for believe me, Louisa, it would not be a 'little' scandal—to placate some vague feminine intuition of yours. Granted, there is some awkwardness between them at the moment, but I believe Eloise Bernal will be a good wife to James.''

His wife shivered and pulled her pelisse closed under her chin with one hand. But she was not ready to go back inside yet. ''What of her?'' she demanded. ''Will James be a good husband to her? Can you really believe that?''

Roth hesitated. ''Yes, I do,'' he said finally. ''It may take some time. But there is something about the Bernal girl. I know''—he held up his hand to forestall her—''I know she was a bit reserved when we called on her, and you thought James might do better with someone more lively. And she has not seen much or done much, rusticating down in that barn of a house in Roehampton. You will simply have to trust me in this, Louisa. I have a feeling.''

''Your feelings,'' she reminded him, ''have frequently proved misleading. Your feeling that Rachel would forget that young officer, for example. And now she is bearing a Gentile's child, and your mother mourns her as dead. Or your feeling that Nathan would get over the loss of your sister and find a new wife. How many times did you try to match him with 'the perfect young widow'? Four?''

''Three,'' grumbled Roth. ''And one does not count, because he was called off to Spain before I could introduce them.'' His tone changed. ''Louisa, I will concede that this marriage is something of a gamble. But James is like a son to me. I know him better than you might think. We must simply trust that he will recover. And there is another consideration as well, little though I like to mention it.''

''An heir,'' his wife sighed.

''You must admit that James has been doing his best to get himself killed for as long as we have known him. And the French are more than eager to assist him. Nathan would never say so, but I am certain that he agreed to the match for precisely this reason."

"No, now you *are* wrong." Louisa Roth had started walking back towards the lighted windows at the far end of the great terrace. "Nathan agreed to this match for one reason and one reason alone: because he couldn't bear watching James brood any longer. And that, in my opinion, is a very poor reason to marry off one's son. It simply transfers the pain from the parent to the bride."

"I wouldn't feel too sorry for Eloise Bernal," commented Roth as he held open the glass doors for his wife. "Do you know who was next on her father's list if James had refused her?"

"Who?" Louisa paused, oblivious of the discomfort of the guests nearest the door to the back hall, who were now treated to a bath of frigid air.

"Rafael DaCosta."

"DaCosta? Her father would give that old tyrant a timid nineteen-year-old?"

"So he said. DaCosta is rich, influential, and the head of the oldest Sephardic family in England."

"Well, then, she is better off with James. Even if he is possessed by a demon, as he is now."

Roth closed the door and relinquished his hat and coat to the hovering servant. "He isn't possessed by a demon," he muttered under his breath. "He's possessed by that accursed countess."

Two

The door closed behind him, and the muted murmur of voices as the last guests took their leave at the foot of the great staircase was suddenly cut off. After hours of noise and celebration, the silence was odd. He stood for a moment, leaning against the door slightly to take the weight off his ankle. It was throbbing viciously.

He looked around the small antechamber. This was the room where he and Eloise had been sent a few hours ago to have the customary bowl of soup after they had said their vows. It was furnished in the latest French style, with sphinxes carved in relief on the panels of a cabinet, and red and gold draperies cascading from the ceiling to frame a black laquered divan. The whole house had been redecorated, Eloise had told him, the furniture and fabrics shipped down from London in the space of three weeks—at what cost, he couldn't begin to imagine.

The door to the bedroom was slightly ajar. Taking a deep breath, he limped over and pushed it open.

In the center of the room, the bed glared at him. It, too, was framed in cascading draperies—red again, surmounted by a gilded eagle high above the headboard. The covers had been turned down, and he glimpsed a bouquet of herbs on one of the pillows. His aunt had presumably put it there, or one of the other women who had come in to help his bride undress. Where was she? He frowned. Shouldn't she be here? He loosened his neckcloth absently, his eyes wandering around the room.

It took him a moment to see her. She was standing behind a small inlaid table on the far side of the room—standing very still, like a rabbit who hopes the hunter will walk on by. The two walnut side chairs which had been beside the table were now drawn up in front of her, blocking access to the far side of the table. In the half-darkness he could see only that her face was averted and that she was wearing a long white wrap with filmy sleeves. It was clear she had heard him come in, equally clear he was not a welcome sight.

"Eloise?" he said tentatively.

She turned then and he saw her face, strikingly pale against the cloud of dark hair unbound around it. She was afraid, he realized. She was clutching one of the chairs as though she might fall without its support. With some effort, she managed a small, apologetic smile.

"What have I done?" he whispered, grasping only now that there was another human being involved in this farce of a marriage. Guilt, an emotion he loathed, rose up from somewhere inside him and twisted his gut. He had moved through the past month in a self-absorbed stupor, assenting to everything his uncle and his father had said, never thinking that there would be a price to pay—or that someone else might have to pay it with him.

She was still watching him, but the smile had faded.

"*Peste*," he swore, sitting down on the bed and putting his head in his hands. "A fine mess I've made of things." He took a deep breath, looked over at the girl. Her dark eyes were anxious, wary. "You did not want to marry me, did you?"

Taken aback, she hesitated.

"Never mind. You need not answer. Your feelings on the subject are not difficult to understand, as they mirror my own." He grimaced. "A nasty tangle, and I must take the blame. I fancy you had little say in the matter, but I had several opportunities to draw back and failed to take them. I will go down at once and speak with your father before he retires for the night." Mechanically he pushed himself to his feet and began to retie his neckcloth. "You need not appear, although I believe most of the guests have gone. This is my fault, and I will try to set it right at once."

"I beg your pardon?" She sounded bewildered.

Was she dull-witted? He had thought her quite intelligent, from the little he had seen of her before the wedding. "I will explain to your father that we have made a mistake," he said impatiently. "That we do not wish to go through with—with the rest of the marriage." He waved his hand awkwardly towards the bed, with its expectant pillows and forlorn-looking posies. She blushed. Her skin was so fair that he could see the color running beneath it like shadows under clear water. Taking her silence as assent, he moved back towards the door.

"Wait! Please—"

He swung around, surprised.

She bit her lip, clearly distressed, then said hesitantly, "Did I give you some reason to think I no longer wished to marry you?"

"Some reason?" He walked over and gestured towards her little fortress of chairs. "You hardly seemed entranced with me when I came in just now. Modesty is all very well, but it does not, I think, impel most brides to blockade themselves off from their grooms with furniture."

"I was afraid, yes. Perhaps I was afraid of something like this—afraid you had changed your mind, did not want me for your wife. You seemed angry. I supposed I had done something wrong, embarrassed you perhaps."

He was angry, it was true, although not with her.

"Did you or did you not wish to marry me?" he asked, suddenly unsure of himself.

"I thought I did," she said stiffly. "Apparently, I was mistaken. I most certainly do not want a husband who calls the marriage a mistake within two hours of the ceremony." She tilted her head up and stared blindly at the ceiling, but because he was so much taller than she, he could see the tears pooling in her eyes, and her valiant efforts to blink them away.

Now it seemed as though she would be devastated if he left. He shook his head, fighting to understand her odd behavior. She *was* afraid of him; that was clear. But she was even more upset at the thought that he might go downstairs and announce that there was no marriage. He had imagined that she would be relieved to have him walk out that door.

And then he paused, frozen in place. Memories were shifting inside his head. Long-dead powers of reasoning were stirring. The numbing fog which had surrounded him for so long was breaking up and drifting away. The events of the past few weeks replayed themselves at lightning speed, and this time he was paying attention.

Why such haste in arranging this marriage? Why had he, with his odd double life as a pseudo-Christian, been acceptable as a bridegroom to the haughty Bernals? Why was the wedding at a rarely used summer home in Ramsgate, and not in London? Why had the bride's devout grandmother, the supposed author of the match, been absent? Why had his wife been unable to eat any of the banquet downstairs? Why did she have that dreadful trapped-rabbit look on her face?

For so many questions, just one answer, seemingly so clear that in retrospect he could not imagine how he had not known. Eloise was with child. The physician he had met this morning had been attending her, not her mother. Her pallor, her lack of appetite were explained. It made sense now; it all made sense. She had refused to name her lover, or the lover was already married, or he was someone completely unacceptable. Of course she was fearful of her bridegroom; he would at best learn at once that she was no maiden and at worst might deduce the whole sordid story. She expected him to be enraged at the deception, possibly to repudiate her publicly. It was amazing that she had managed the ceremony with so much composure even to this point.

He looked at her again, seeing for the first time a hint of resolve behind the anxiety in the dark eyes. *She has her pride*, he decided. *She would not name him; that must be what happened.* He admired her for it. And he could understand the Bernals' decision. After all, a *Tudesco* perjurer was better than no husband at all. This new, logical view of his situation brought with it no sense of injury, no jealousy, no disappointment, but a calm acceptance tinged with relief. He had always preferred explanations to mysteries, even when the explanations were unpleasant.

"I see it now," he said gently. "I understand." He moved around behind the table and took her hand. It was cold and stiff. "Here, sit down." He helped her into one of the chairs beside the table and dropped into the other one with an exhausted sigh.

"You needn't worry," he continued after a moment. "I won't tell anyone your secret. I'll acknowledge the child as mine. And I won't touch you, of course, until you are recovered." He did not look at her at all, feeling that to do so would somehow shame her even more. But he heard her take in a sharp breath. She held it for a very long time. When he dared to glance over, her head was lowered, and the curtain of hair hid even her profile from view.

"We can take a place out in the country if you like," he added desperately, suddenly wanting her to stop shrinking away from him, to be comforted. "If you wish to avoid friends who might ask awkward questions. Or we can go to my sister. She is expecting a baby, also. Whatever you need me to do. Just tell me."

She shook her head.

He touched her wrist gently. "Eloise, listen to me. These things happen. We will make the best of it." Why wouldn't she answer him? He suspected that she was finally crying, but if so she had suppressed all but the barest movement as she sobbed.

He tried again. "Did you love him? The father?"

That finally produced a reaction. She raised her head, her eyes swimming with tears, gave him one furious look, and slapped him across the face.

Just before dawn, James rose and lit a small lamp. He was not certain when morning visitors would arrive, and he could take no chances. Eloise was asleep on the far side of the bed. In the beginning, after his repeated apologies had finally calmed her enough so that she could retire to bed, he had been nearly certain that her sleep was feigned. He had waited a long, long time before getting into bed with her and even so had thought he detected a slight flinch as he lowered himself very gently down beside her. The gentlemanly thing to do would have been to sleep in a chair, or on that divan in the garish red-and-gold anteroom. He would have preferred that, in fact, and he no longer required comfort in order to sleep soundly. Even the floor would have been luxurious compared to many places he had slept in the past few years. But without discussing it, both had understood that it would not do for some servant to come in and discover that all was not well with the newlyweds.

Now he crossed quietly over to his trunk and rummaged through the top layer until he found his riding clothes. Pulling on hose, buckskins, and shirt, he tossed his jacket over his shoulders and picked up his coat. Neckcloth and gloves, he stuffed into his boots. Then with boots in one hand and coat in the other, he stole out of the room, carefully latching the door behind him. He would have to remember to get his hat, which he thought was downstairs in a pile of gentlemen's outerwear abandoned as hopeless by the overworked ser-

vants after the festivities last night. The rest of his things
could come up in the carriage.

Not even in the meanest two-room inn did James ever
fail to make certain that he knew where Silvio was sleeping,
in case of emergencies. He supposed this was an emergency,
of sorts. Counting doors in the central hall, he tentatively
pushed the fourth one open, breathed a sigh of relief as he
saw the small staircase, and climbed swiftly up past the
second floor to the attic. It was very cold up here, and his
stocking feet curled away from the frigid floorboards. Boots
made too much noise, though. His days of walking silently
in shoes were over. As if to confirm this, one of the boards
gave an indignant creak underfoot. Grimacing, he shifted
his weight carefully and stepped sideways. Faint light was
beginning to trickle in from a dormer at the far end of the
narrow corridor.

From behind a door to his left, he heard a rustling noise
and then a slight thump. Slowly the door swung open. A
dark, tousled head peered out, followed by a slim pair of
shoulders, already clad in a crisp white shirt and short jacket.
''Sir?'' said Silvio doubtfully, stepping all the way out
into the hall. Then, taking in the expression on the face of
his half-dressed master, he opened the door all the way and
dragged James into the box room behind him. Darkness
closed in momentarily, dispelled by the flare of light as
Silvio lit a candle. Without saying a word, he took James's
coat and boots and set them on a large brass-bound trunk
next to the cot he had just vacated. Then he held out the
broadcloth jacket and tugged it expertly over his master's
shoulders. Only at this point did he notice the absence of
the neckcloth. Pursing his lips, he shook his head, removed
the jacket, and dove down into the boots.

''Here, I'll tie it,'' said James abruptly. ''No one will see
it under my coat in any case.'' He lifted the white rectangle
out of Silvio's hands and knotted it carelessly.

''Signor is leaving?'' inquired Silvio cautiously, holding
out the jacket once again.

"Yes." James pushed his arms into the sleeves. "I've received an urgent summons from Whitehall."

"You have?" said Silvio, surprised. "No one roused me—" He paused. "I see," he said, scowling, tugging the jacket up with such vehemence that James stumbled forward.

"You see what?"

His servant didn't answer. The weather-beaten face was stiff with disapproval. Instead he gestured James onto the cot and began dusting the boots with a soft leather rag.

"You will escort Mrs. Meyer and her maid to London later this morning," instructed James, helping Silvio tug the boots over the bottom edge of his buckskins. "Pack up the rest of my gear; I will not be taking anything with me. Please convey my apologies to the Bernals and tell them my wife and I will drive down to Roehampton at the earliest opportunity." He stood, wincing slightly as he eased his weight onto both booted feet.

"But, sir," protested Silvio, "I had been told—the dinners . . ."

The thought of the social upheaval which would ensue when a week's worth of dinner parties in honor of the newly-weds were all canceled brought a surge of grim satisfaction. "Ask Mrs. Meyer to send our regrets to the first three hosts. I may be back by Thursday afternoon."

Belatedly, he realized that if he had only just received a summons to the Horse Guards, he would not yet know when he might be returning. Silvio realized it, too, he saw. Not that he had ever imagined that his longtime valet-cum-coachman-cum-bodyguard would believe this improbable tale of an urgent message.

"And what," demanded Silvio, cutting to the heart of the problem, "am I to tell Signor Meyer?"

James narrowed his eyes. "Whose servant are you, Silvio?" he inquired softly. "Mine, or my father's?"

"Yours, Master James," was the hasty reply, belied by the inadvertent use of his childhood title.

"See that you remember it," snapped James. "If you

suspect that my father may ask unpleasant questions about my absence, then it might be prudent to avoid him. Do I make myself clear?''

"Yes, sir." The subdued manservant handed over his gloves and coat. "Your hat is on the table in the rear hall, sir. It is a very cold morning for riding, if I may say so. Did you bring your muffler with you?"

"Perhaps you would like to offer me a sweetmeat before I leave?" said James sarcastically. "Or to button my coat for me?" But when Silvio located the missing item in the pocket of his wool coat, he wound it round his neck without further protest. "Don't let Toby drive down any steep hills," he said gruffly as he headed out the door. "He's still only an assistant coachman. You will take the reins whenever there is any doubt about the state of the road. Mrs. Meyer has a—a delicate constitution." That seemed a safe, vague description which could account for any number of eventualities.

"Signor, one moment!"

He paused, one hand on the latch.

"I beg your pardon, signor. But I did not quite understand your instructions. Where in London am I to take Mrs. Meyer?"

James stared. "To my lodgings, of course. Where else?"

"To your *lodgings*? The rooms off Houndsditch?"

"Yes," he snapped, glaring. "What of it?" He should have had Wolf find him something more suitable, of course, once he had decided to go ahead with the wedding, but somehow he had never managed to find the time or energy to think about life after the ceremony. And now Silvio was looking at him as though he had proposed to house Princess Charlotte in a brothel.

James cursed the long-standing family practice of the Roths and Meyers which decreed that servants were engaged for life and—in his case in particular—were frequently permitted to behave more like parents than hired help. From the bottom of the staircase he heard faint noises; chambermaids were stirring, checking on the guests. Perhaps knocking on the door of the bedroom where his bride was sleeping in an all-too-neat bed. Panic flooded him; it was past time to be gone.

"Tell Wolf to deal with it," he said, yanking open the door. "And stay out of my father's way. This morning, and up in London. Until I get back." He slammed the door behind him.

Silvio listened to his master's steps as they faded down towards the lower floors. He would do his best to avoid Nathan Meyer, but in his opinion, that gentleman would know exactly what was toward the minute he heard about the "urgent summons" from Whitehall. Even under normal circumstances, it was highly unlikely that Colonel White would have disrupted the wedding of one of his junior officers in such a fashion. But the circumstances were not normal. No one in White's office had asked Captain James Nathanson to so much as read a map since he had returned from Vienna. And Silvio couldn't blame them. Who would want a phantom's opinion on a map? Who would send a sleepwalker down to the coast to pick up reports from France? This morning was the first time in weeks he had seen his master with any life in his eyes. In fact, Silvio realized, brightening, James had actually snarled at him. Feeling much more cheerful than he had in many days, the slender manservant began whistling an Italian folk song as he fished under the cot for his shoes.

Three

Eloise lay motionless for a long while in the gilt bed after hearing James leave. At first she persuaded herself that she was doing so in case he returned. But she knew he was not coming back. After a while, as the room grew lighter and lighter, she realized glumly that she was huddled in bed because she did not know what to do. Sooner or later, someone would come in—she could already hear footsteps on the stairs occasionally. And perhaps at first it would only be a girl who would not dare do more than bob her head and stir up the coals or refill the ewer on the washstand.

But then Danielle would come with her sly, too-respectful questions. Had madame slept well? Would madame like her shawl? Did she not think this house rather draftier than the London house? It was another wintry day—and monsieur gone already, in spite of the cold!

Yes, Danielle, monsieur was gone already. Monsieur had never really been here. Monsieur could stay away forever, for all she cared.

She rolled over onto her back and pulled all the covers over herself in a great heap, the way she had done when she was a small child and something had upset her. Lying in the artificial darkness under the heavy tent of fabric, she thought about what had happened last night. Over and over she saw herself sitting there, speechless, while her new husband concluded that she was carrying another man's child. Remaining silent while he nobly offered to protect her from the consequences of her shame. Lying in bed quietly, never contradicting him, the whole night. What a coward she was! And he—he was unspeakable.

All through the wedding supper, she had felt sorry for him because her aunts and uncles and cousins were patronizing him, explaining (sometimes less than diplomatically) what an honor it was for him to be granted a Bernal as a bride. As the evening went on, his angular face grew darker and darker. His deep-set charcoal eyes glittered with some kind of suppressed emotion. He grew ever more silent and remote, until his behavior was out of all proportion to the well-meant insults of her elderly relatives.

Still she had excused him, thinking he was in pain. He had a wound from the war which troubled him, she knew that much. She had noticed that he had a limp—at times barely noticeable, at other times quite pronounced. Only right before she went upstairs with her mother and his aunt did she catch him glancing in her direction and recognize what that suppressed emotion was. It was not pain or annoyance, but anger: full-blown rage, apparently directed at her.

She found it utterly terrifying. A year at a girls' school had taught her many things; she knew about lust, and she had been nervous enough about facing that sort of hunger in the face of her bridegroom. But his expression was far worse than anything she had imagined. It was an instinctive fear of him which had driven her to take refuge behind those chairs. She winced, remembering. Another example of her cowardice.

And then—she frowned. This was the confusing part. At first, after his dreadful allegation, she had assumed that the anger came from his belief that he had been tricked into marrying her. But as she remembered their conversation now in a calmer frame of mind, she recognized clearly that his animosity had in fact vanished at the very moment that he had made his accusation. For the first time since she had met him, he had seemed gentle, even affectionate. When he had touched her arm lightly, told her they would make the best of it, she had heard the warmth in his voice. Why, then, had he been so furious when he had first come up from downstairs? She tried to remember what he had said, but it was all overlaid with a gray cloud of anxiety and bewilderment, and she could only recall dimly that he had claimed the wedding was a mistake.

There was a noise at the door, and she froze. She heard it open, then a stifled giggle, something which sounded like "your pardon," and it quickly closed again. Relief turned into embarrassment as she realized that the maid must have thought there were two people under the tangled heap of bedclothes. Two people lying very close together.

Hastily she threw off the covers and slid out of bed. The room was frigid; the maids had not dared come in to build up the fire. And her thin lawn gown, so appropriate for a bride, let in every draft which swirled across the floor from the windows. Slivers of sunlight were edging around the curtains, and the clock showed nearly eight. More servants would be coming, followed in very short order by her mother and her aunts. She must make up her mind about what she was going to say.

It would be no more than James Meyer deserved, were she to tell her mother exactly what he had said to her last night. The notion was tempting. She knew what the result would be: her family, and all the Bevis Marks families, would flock to defend the virgin of their people who had been insulted by the German barbarian. James would be disgraced; the mighty banking house of Eli Roth would be humiliated. A pleasing picture of herself as the wronged maiden, bearing her distress with chaste dignity, attracted her for a moment.

Of course, she did not have to be quite so vindictive. She could follow James's own plan: tell her mother that it had been a mistake, that both of them had realized it last night, that they should not suit. She was sure the wedding guests had noticed her groom's odd behavior at the supper. No one would be very surprised. She had heard of other marriage contracts which were canceled the day after the wedding; it was not common, but it did happen.

Another possibility: she could use James's wound as an excuse. He had been taken ill, had told her that a decision about whether to proceed with the marriage should be postponed until he knew more about his condition. That was very plausible. A postponement could gradually become an abandonment. No embarrassment for either side. Another sad casualty of the endless war against Bonaparte.

But she was not going to say any of these things. She was not going to reveal that anything was wrong between her and her husband. It was entertaining to fantasize about calling him to account for his boorishness, but she had already made her choice. All this time she had been moving quickly, stripping the sheets off the bed, folding them into compact squares, and stuffing them down into the bottom of her trunk. No servant was going to inspect those sheets and start gossiping about how Miss Eloise was not properly married, not if she could prevent it. In the confusion as all the family and guests packed up to return to London, the missing bed linens would not be noticed—when one maid saw them gone, she would assume another had already come in and taken them off to be washed. Eloise spread the quilts neatly across the bottom of the bed and patted the pillows flat, to complete the illusion. There were still some coals in the grate; she got down on her knees and blew them into a small flame. Now it looked as though a maid had been here.

She moved to the bell and was about to ring when there was a timid knock at the door. "Come in," she called, snatching up a shawl and wrapping herself in it to conceal the unwrinkled purity of her nightgown. She hoped fervently that it was not Danielle. It was not. It was one of the local girls, the one who had helped Danielle pin up her hair yesterday morning.

"Is it Joan?" Eloise tried, stabbing at a vague memory of the name.

The girl's face flushed with pleasure.

"Good morning, miss—I mean ma'am." The maid's glance went over quickly to the bed and seemed to accept what it saw. "I thought I heard you moving about, and ventured to come in to see if your fire was lit."

"Yes, we rose early." Eloise stammered and blushed at the lie, but the maid did not notice. Brides were expected to stammer and blush, she realized. "My husband has been called away unexpectedly. But would you mind going down and seeing if there is hot water now in the kitchen? I should like a bath."

Joan turned even redder. "Of course, miss. Ma'am," she corrected again. "I should have known you'd wish a bath this morning, and had one ready. I'll see to it right away. Shall I send up your maid?"

"Thank you, no," said Eloise firmly. "She had a long day yesterday. Tell her she need not come up until after breakfast. I can dress myself, if you will hook up my gown in the back." Eight hours in the coach with Danielle would be bad enough.

It was not eight hours. It was two days. By the time the Bernal party had started off, in five carriages, it was past eleven, and her father decreed they would stop at an inn just outside of Chilham for the night. Runners were sent ahead to secure rooms and instruct the innkeeper about the dietary requirements of two of the great-aunts, who observed the laws more strictly than the rest of the family. Fortunately, there were few travelers at that time of year, and the White Swan was able to accommodate the Bernal party. Eloise had come down to Ramsgate in a spacious, well-sprung coach

with team changes every two hours; now she found herself
in a lumbering berlin, squeezed between Danielle and her
mother's maid, jolting along at a pace little faster than walking. Opposite her sat her mother and her mother's oldest
sister, Judit, whose outdated but voluminous skirts ensured
that she had more room than anyone else in the coach. Eloise
thought longingly of the elegant vehicle James had provided
for her, which was bringing up the rear of the cavalcade—
empty, save for their luggage. Her mother had declared that
of course Eloise would wish to ride with her and her aunt.
And the two maids. And her mother's cat, who hissed every
time any of the passengers moved.

Conversation was stilted. Every topic in the world was
of interest, it seemed, except the whereabouts of her husband.
Eloise's aunt would occasionally break off in midsentence,
stare at her, and sigh profoundly. Worse were the pitying
glances Danielle gave her when she thought her mistress
was not looking. The minute the vehicle drew up in front
of the White Swan, Eloise announced that she had the headache and would take supper in her room. It was only a small
lie; her neck and back certainly ached.

Even here she could not escape her maid. The inn was
not large, and a trundle bed had been made up for Danielle
right next to the massive old four-poster which took up
most of the bedchamber. The girl fluttered about waving
vinaigrette under her nose and pressing cold cloths onto her
forehead until at length she actually did have a headache.
She lay awake far into the night, listening to Danielle's light
snores and dreading the long day to come.

When the idea came to her she did not know. It still
seemed odd to think of herself as married, as mistress of a
household with servants and horses and a carriage of her
own, especially since it was not at all clear that she was
likely to have even the nominal title of wife for very long.
One moment she was dozing uneasily; the next she was out
of bed, pulling open the shutters to see whether it was light
yet, her plan fully formed in her mind. The sky was just

beginning to show faint streaks of pink—close enough. She pulled on her gown in the dark as best she could. There were some buttons she could not reach, but her shawl covered them. Next she woke her maid and told her to pack; they were leaving shortly. Danielle made the expected objections: What of breakfast? Would she not wait to take leave of her parents? Eloise cut off a lecture on the impropriety of appearing in public without a proper *toilette* by the simple expedient of stalking out of the room.

Downstairs, several of the inn's scrvants were already at work in the kitchen, as she had suspected they would be, and she sent one of them off to find her coachman. One of the kitchen boys hastily built a fire in the coffee room for her, and she was warming her hands when her husband's manservant came in.

She frowned. This was James's valet—or so she had thought. The coachman was a younger, thickset man. She could not remember this one's name, but he had brought her the note from James yesterday morning. She had assumed he would accompany his master to London.

"Your command, signora?" he asked brusquely.

Intimidated, she swallowed and nearly took a step back before she remembered that this man was her servant as well as her husband's.

"What is your name?" she asked, stalling until she could regain her composure.

"Silvio, ma'am." This was less brusque.

"Good morning, Mr. Silvio."

"Just Silvio, signora," he corrected hastily.

She had thought valets were always addressed by their surnames, but apparently this was an exception. "Silvio, then. I sent for the coachman; is he indisposed?"

The servant looked shocked. "Oh, no, signora. Toby is well, so far as I know. But I am in charge of the driving. He is too young to manage by himself." He looked at her now with frank interest, taking in her uncombed hair and the sagging neckline of her partially buttoned gown.

Eloise was taken aback for a moment—servants in the Bernal household rarely raised their eyes, especially male servants in the presence of unaccompanied females. But then she plunged ahead. "How soon could the carriage be ready to leave?"

He thought for a moment. "Three-quarters of an hour. Perhaps less, if the horses are not in an obstinate mood."

"Half an hour," Eloise said in what she hoped was a firm tone. "I will meet you in the yard with my maid. I would prefer that you get the team harnessed without calling too much attention to our departure."

"Very good, signora."

"Did Mr. Meyer give you some funds to cover expenses on the journey?"

She saw his nod with relief. One worry gone. "Settle the bill, then, for your lodging and mine and the stabling."

He gave her an appraising look, nodded again, and left.

What a strange man, she thought, climbing up the stairs again to her room. His overly free manner should have offended her, but she found that in fact she welcomed it. Perhaps some time during the rest of the journey up to London she would summon up the courage to ask him where her husband was.

As it turned out, she had not been able to speak privately with Silvio at all. Danielle had clung to her the entire day like a limpet—a very querulous limpet. All the complaints were on Eloise's behalf, of course. The food at the inn where they stopped to break their fast was too coarse for her. The road was crowded and slow and must be giving her *une migraine*. And why had no one thought to provide hot bricks for her feet when it was so bitterly cold? It occurred to Eloise that perhaps Danielle herself could have gone into the posting house and requested hot bricks—she was, after all, a lady's maid—but apparently Danielle considered this beneath her dignity.

At the last stop, in Farningham, Silvio's proposal that perhaps they should take rooms for the night was rejected indignantly by Danielle before Eloise could even answer. Stay at the Three Crowns! The place was practically a hedge tavern. London was only an hour farther on; the roads were good and well frequented. Who would choose to spend the night in a grubby inn when they might be settled in comfortable surroundings at home with only a little more effort?

Now, as she surveyed her new home, Eloise took a perverse satisfaction in the disaster which faced her. The sight of their "comfortable surroundings" had reduced Danielle, for once, to silence. The silence had been followed by a sudden and violent headache. The maid was presently lying down in the bedroom—the only room whose fireplace was not spewing smoke—dabbing her own face with lavender water.

Eloise hoped Danielle was regretting her remarks about grubby inns. The Three Crowns had not, in fact, looked grubby to Eloise—only small and unfashionable. James's lodgings *were* grubby. The street was grubby, the building was grubby, the narrow unlit stair leading up to the second-floor apartment was grubby, and the rooms themselves were worse than grubby: half-furnished, sour-smelling, and cramped. Two women were frantically scrubbing floors and airing linens in the back rooms; the planks in the front room where she stood were still damp.

"Signora," Silvio said helplessly, "I must apologize. I should have insisted that we stay in Farningham. I sent a message up from Ramsgate yesterday, to see if something more suitable could be found, but on such short notice . . ." His voice trailed off unhappily.

Heavy footsteps came pounding up the stairs, and a stout young man burst in, panting. He was wearing gold-rimmed spectacles, which hung slightly askew at the moment, and clutching a portfolio full of papers.

He stopped dead, clearly surprised to see her, and looked back and forth from her to Silvio in dismay.

"Ah, Mrs. Meyer," he said, recovering and attempting a bright expression. "Wolf, Augustus Wolf. I daresay you don't remember me; I am your husband's man of business." She did remember him; he had been present at the signing of the marriage contract, arguing with James in a low voice right up until the moment her husband had scrawled his signature. "I had not expected you tonight, of course. The rooms are, er, not quite ready for you, but in any case you will prefer to stay at a hotel tonight. I shall send Toby off to Durrant's at once."

He pulled a small black notebook out of the portfolio and cleared his throat importantly. "I have been looking for more commodious quarters ever since I received the letter from Ramsgate. There are two properties available near your parents' home in Kennington; if you prefer to stay north of the river, there is a likely-looking place on Brook Street." He riffled through a few more pages. "Ah, yes. The house on Brook Street is furnished. That might be the easiest solution, although if you prefer to be in Kennington we could probably have either property fitted up fairly quickly. I am sure you will wish to interview servants yourself, of course, and I have arranged an appointment with an agency for tomorrow afternoon—"

"Mr. Wolf," she said, interrupting, "did my husband charge you to find him new lodgings? Or hire new servants?"

The accountant blinked. "Not in so many words," he hedged, uncertain about the direction the conversation was taking.

"What were his instructions, precisely?"

He tugged his spectacles higher up on his nose. "He has not given me any specific instructions on this matter, but it is a matter of common sense, begging your pardon, ma'am."

"I don't think it common sense to move a man's household across the city without consulting him," she retorted. "We will remain here until he returns."

There was a small shriek from the doorway. Danielle, tottering over towards the little group, looked horrified. So did the two men.

"But, Mrs. Meyer—" Wolf was struggling to regain the upper hand. "It could be a week before your husband returns. And I am certain he never intended that you should reside here. He was very preoccupied before the wedding; he must have forgotten that he had not asked me to see to it. For my part, I assumed that he meant to take you to his uncle's house for the moment."

He hadn't forgotten, thought Eloise. He hadn't planned to bring her to the Roths' enormous townhouse. He simply had not believed he was really getting married.

"You must see that it is out of the question for you to reside here," Wolf continued earnestly.

"Why?"

"Why?" His round face looked indignant. "Every reason imaginable! The neighborhood is not genteel; the rooms are not properly furnished; there is no kitchen, no dining room, only one bedchamber—why, your husband himself has scarcely been here for a week out of the last six months. He usually resides with his uncle, Mr. Roth; only when that is inconvenient does he occasionally use this place."

Eloise turned to Silvio. She was beginning to dislike Wolf even more than she had at the betrothal ceremony, where she had overheard him telling James that he had been far too generous with the settlements.

"Could you show me all the rooms, please? Including any storage chambers or servants' quarters?"

Silently, Silvio led her on a tour of the premises. It was a brief tour. On the main floor, there were five rooms: the front room, where they had entered, and four smaller back rooms. One was fitted up as a bedchamber, another as a study, but there was so little in the way of furnishings or possessions in any of the rooms that it would be easy to rearrange things. The last room was little bigger than a cupboard, but it had a window with one broken pane, covered for the moment with a religious tract held in place against the glass by a brick. In here there was a camp bed, which appeared relatively new and clean. A twisting wooden stair, uncarpeted, led up to the third floor, which was also the top floor of the house. Here there were three more rooms. Two were windowless versions of the cupboard downstairs. At the moment, one was bare; the other held a narrow iron bedstead. The third room, to her surprise, was actually quite pleasant. The ceiling was low, and the windows were much smaller than those on the floor below, but the proportions of the room were attractive. There was a rug half unrolled on the hearth, and two reasonably presentable armchairs, which she resolved immediately to move down to the parlor.

Eloise was glad that Danielle had not followed them on the tour, because she knew her fastidious maid was not going to be pleased to hear that she would be sleeping in a cupboard with a broken window. To Silvio she allotted one of the attic cupboards, reserving the last for a box room. She gave Wolf a list of items to be purchased immediately: a bed, for the upper room, to serve as James's bedchamber and study. A small dining table and chairs, for the brightest of the back rooms on the main floor. Fire screens. A linen chest. Another wardrobe—there was one downstairs, which she suspected would need scrubbing before she could put any of her clothing in it, but James would also need one up here. Two glass-fronted cabinets. Candelabras. Lamps. More rugs. She would have her own worktable and desk sent up from Roehampton. The remaining small room downstairs would be converted into a pantry; hot food would have to be ordered in, but they could keep tea and coffee and cheese and bread and preserved meats there.

Wolf was dispatched, looking cowed and uneasy. The two scrubbers, who proved to be large, bovine sisters named Nan and Peg, were engaged to return first thing the next morning, along with a nephew who was said to be "good with chimneys." Danielle, still sniffing, was sent into the bedroom to clean the wardrobe and unpack her mistress's bag. Eloise turned to Silvio, who had not said a word during all this.

"Is there someplace nearby where you might be able to buy us supper?"

"Yes, signora. Loden's tavern. If the signora is not too particular about the menu. The food is good, but plain."

She was starving and exhausted but tried not to let it show on her face. As soon as Silvio left, she collapsed onto the sofa, ignoring the small cloud of dust which flew up as she landed. A little voice in her head was asking her uncomfortable questions. What would her family say when they saw this place? How would she manage, with no kitchen, no proper bath, and no trained servants except for the useless Danielle? Why was she determined to stay in these ugly rooms? She could be comfortably ensconced at Durrant's right now, and established in a proper house of her own within a week.

Even in her weary fog, she could not avoid the answers. Her family would be appalled. She would manage only with great difficulty. And she had decided to stay here for one reason and one reason only: because for a brief moment, in a childish fit of panic, she had imagined James returning late some night—tonight, tomorrow, Friday, a week hence—and finding no one here.

Four

She did not bother to pretend. Callers were received with a perfunctory apology in the spartan parlor. For family she sometimes did not even remove her apron or the cap she wore to protect her hair from the dust. Danielle often looked more elegant than she did, but surprisingly, the maid had complained very little after her initial outburst. Eloise had tried to think of tasks which would not offend her, and had succeeded beyond expectation when she had inquired on the first morning in their new quarters whether Danielle knew of any place which could make up curtains quickly. The sharp, thin face had lit up; within an hour Danielle, armed with measurements, was on her way to Cornhill, and in twenty-four hours every room had damask hangings in muted colors which did not show the grime.

Seeing that Danielle had an eye for color as well as skill with her needle, Eloise turned over all the reupholstering to her as well. In short order the parlor furniture looked new, the walls were hung with plain but serviceable coverings, and drafts did not leak through the draperies at night.

Nan and Peg had been retained indefinitely. She really

only needed one of them, but evidently they came as a pair, and they were good at scrubbing. Even now, in winter, with the windows closed, soot was a constant invader. It settled everywhere, in a tarry black layer which stuck to surfaces and smeared when you tried to wipe it off. Most rooms were dusted twice a day. What little food they were able to keep in the makeshift pantry was stored in covered bins—even things like whole loaves of bread or jars of preserves. Jam with charcoal-colored grime on the lid was not an appetizing sight, and even though Danielle always made up her break-fast tray with newly dusted dishes, she preferred visualizing the jam emerging from a clean jar before it had been ladled into its little china pot.

Her mother called at first every morning. She always made some cheerful remark about the latest alterations—the new draperies were a vast improvement! What a cunning little pantry she had devised, who would have thought one could manage so well without a kitchen! But she also brought, carefully written out in her clumsy round hand, a list of properties for hire. Eloise took them, thanked her politely, and tossed them in the grate after she left. These visits were painful, far more painful than the equally unwelcome visits by her aunts, who left her in no doubt that she had reaped her just reward for marrying an uncouth German. Against direct attack she could rally to her husband's defense: he was busy with his work for the government (this was the Bernal family code for the unmentionable military service); they would think about more permanent quarters when he was not so preoccupied.

On her fourth day in her new home, she was painting the ironwork of a grille she had discovered abandoned in the lower hallway. The door which opened onto the street was a flimsy affair, and after consulting with Silvio she had decided to mount the grille as a locking gate at the base of the stairs which led up to their apartments. She had tied up her hair and put a smock on over her gown, propping the grille up against the wall, with some of the discarded curtains spread out beneath it to catch drips. Danielle was out looking for fabric for cushions, Nan and Peg had vanished to wherever they vanished to between bouts of scrubbing, and their nephew (who had become the household errand boy after a satisfactory battle with the chimneys) was manning the front door in case visitors arrived. She was enjoying her solitude. It was hard to be the only one in the house who was not a servant. At least by herself she could be Eloise for a few moments instead of "signora" or "madame."

When Silvio appeared, looking uncomfortable, she gave an unconscious frown of annoyance. He had been a great help to her, and she was grateful, but the expression on his face led her to expect trouble, and she was getting tired of trouble. Every day brought something to try her—a broken hinge on one of the doors, or a new hole in the carpet, or, worst of all, callers who looked around the apartment with undisguised horror and inquired pointedly when Mr. Meyer might be expected.

"Signora," Silvio said awkwardly, "please excuse me if I seem to be carrying tales against another servant, but in this household we are very careful about certain things. I must tell you that your maid Danielle is deceiving you. She is no more French than Nan or Peg. I would guess she is from Portsmouth, or perhaps Southampton."

Eloise straightened up and laid down her paintbrush. "Oh, I know that," she said calmly. "I realized it almost at once. My French is not fluent, but my grandmother insisted I be taught it from infancy. I am surprised my mother did not hear her errors, but she wanted so badly to engage a fashionable maid for me, I suppose she closed her ears. And Danielle is very careful; she rarely utters more than a word or two of the language. She relies on her pronunciation of English to fool people."

Silvio's jaw dropped. "You knew? And never said anything?"

"It was very important to my mother," Eloise explained. "I thought it would be ungrateful to quibble. Save for not being French, Danielle is precisely what my parents envisioned. She knows just what genteel young ladies should and should not do. She reads all the fashion magazines. She can spot a refurbished gown at twenty paces. If I chose, I could have a new hairstyle every day. And I can be assured that at least one person is always thinking of my consequence: the happiest day of Danielle's life was the day she learned I was to be promoted from mademoiselle to madame.''

"But, signora," protested Silvio, "you know nothing about her. It could be dangerous to have someone in your employ who is a proven liar."

"Nonsense," said Eloise, picking up her brush again. "It is a harmless fib, like a singer calling himself Signor Volante when his real name is Rufus Boodle. Her references were genuine; you may be sure my father saw to that." Then she paused, holding the brush in midair. Turning, she looked at him and asked warily, "What did you mean just now when you said, 'in this household we are very careful'?"

"Nothing," stammered Silvio. "You understand—the war—Signor Meyer's position in the army."

"Ah, yes, the army," muttered Eloise. She dabbed the paint angrily onto the ironwork. A huge drip plopped onto the floor from the end of the brush. Swinging round again, she glared at the increasingly nervous Silvio. "That reminds me," she said, her casual tone belied by the glitter in her eyes. "I had assumed you would be joining Mr. Meyer now that we are settled here in town."

Silvio held a hasty debate with himself. He had been in England a long time. His English was nearly fluent; "sir" came as easily to him as "signor." He knew what was expected of a valet: an imperturbable demeanor, a hint of arrogance (especially when dealing with other servants), an intimate knowledge of all shops, taverns, stews, clubs, and stables in London, a similar knowledge of inns on the post roads, an ability to dress his master creditably under any circumstances, and above all, complete loyalty and discretion. The correct response to his mistress's statement was a wooden "Just so, madam," or perhaps the more conciliatory "I expect to be summoned by Mr. Meyer shortly."

He was not, however, a normal valet. His duties included cooking, driving, stable work, surgery, horse-stealing, knife-fighting, and burglary. Just lately he had become a combination butler, secretary, and assistant upholsterer. He had been with James Meyer since before that young man had been able to dress himself. And he was not English. In fact, he was feeling particularly Italian at the moment. So he elected to tell the truth.

"I would join him," he admitted. "If I knew where he was."

"You do not accompany him on his army work?" She was puzzled.

"I am encouraged to accompany him when he travels on army business," he said grimly. "In fact, in his younger days, it was virtually required. He is not on assignment at the moment."

"Oh," she said in a small voice.

"He will return, signora," he reassured her. He looked around at the room. In three days she had transformed the place. "He will return, and he will be very, very surprised at what he will find."

He came home late that night.

She was in bed, but she must have been listening even in her sleep for noise on the stairs, because the moment she heard his distinctive, uneven tread, she came fully awake. Lamps had been left on in the parlor and at the foot of the stairs, as they had been every night, by her orders. His footsteps paused on the landing and then came slowly into the outer room.

There was a moment of total silence, then a startled exclamation in French. She did not know the word; she assumed it was an oath.

A hasty clatter of footsteps from the floor above announced Silvio's arrival.

"I see that the signor has condescended to return," he announced in cold tones.

"What happened?" Her husband's voice. "I nearly left just now, thought I had stumbled into the wrong building by mistake."

"You got married," snapped the valet. There was no "sir" or "signor."

"So I see," said James. He sounded bemused. "Is she— is she living *here*? Couldn't Wolf find a suitable property to rent?"

"Mrs. Meyer," said Silvio, stressing the words, "did not think it right to move house in your absence."

"It almost looks like a real home," he said. She heard him walk over to the fireplace. "Look at this; the hearth has been cleaned. It's some sort of gray marble. I always thought it was slate." He laid his hand on her door. "Is this still the bedchamber?" Then, in a voice which held a hint of panic, "Is she in there? Am I to sleep in there?"

She froze.

"The front room upstairs has been converted into another bedchamber for you, signor."

"Ah, good." Another pause. "I would not want to disturb her so late."

Heart pounding, she slumped back against her pillow in relief.

He spoke again, hesitantly, "And Mrs. Meyer? Is she well? Eating properly, that sort of thing?"

She had momentarily forgotten that she was pregnant by some cowardly lover who had refused to marry her. Her fists curled.

"As well as can be expected," was the stiff reply. The unfinished sentence hung in the air: *as well as can be expected for a bride whose husband has deserted her the day after the wedding.*

To her horror, his next words, in a subdued tone, were, "I'll just look in on her quietly."

No time to pull up the covers; she shut her eyes and hoped that she looked asleep. Behind her eyelids she could see a faint brightening as the door opened and he came in. He was carrying a candle; she could smell it burning. There was an excruciatingly long pause; then two sets of footsteps receded, and the door closed.

She had to tell him. This was intolerable. She would get up right now and march upstairs. She slid over to the edge of the bed and then paused. What would he think of her, coming up to his room at this hour in her nightgown? It could wait until morning. She rehearsed her speech in her head over and over until the house was silent, and at last fell asleep, every word memorized.

The speech was never delivered. She rose early—very early, the minute she heard movement in the so-called pantry. That would be Silvio, preparing breakfast. Sure enough, she heard water being poured and then the sound of a pot being set over the fire. Not for the first time, she wondered whether there might not be some corner of the "dining room" which could be adapted to hold a small stove.

Without Danielle to help her, she would have to keep her *toilette* simple. She struggled into one of her plainer dresses, rinsed her teeth hastily, and splashed some water on her face. Her hair was still braided; that would have to do. Silvio had gone down to the back courtyard to get more water; if she hurried she could make her speech and retreat before he returned. She nearly ran up the stairs, knocked gently at the door of his room, and pushed it open at his curt "Enter!"

James was sitting by the fire, sipping coffee. He must have been up for some time; he had shaved and was wearing his full uniform, including boots. The dark eyes widened when he saw her, and before he could resume his impassive expression she saw that there was more than surprise there.

She read dismay and even alarm. He stood automatically as she came in, and she noted abstractly that even in his startled haste he managed to balance his cup perfectly. The coffee barely quivered as he rose.

"I did not mean to disturb you," she said, breathless. "Please don't let your coffee get cold." Then she remembered that he could not sit down again unless she did so first. She darted over to the nearest chair and nearly fell into it. He folded neatly back onto his stool.

"Good morning," he said gravely. "I hope I did not wake you when I came in last night."

"No," she lied.

"You are up early. Did Silvio tell you I was here?"

Trapped in her lie, she shook her head, then found a solution. "I heard you moving about," she offered.

"Yes, the limp is very distinctive," he said.

Mortified, she blushed, but he was smiling wryly.

"I must commend you on a miraculous transformation," he went on. "I did not recognize the place when I walked in. I had not expected to find you still here; Wolf was meant to find you something more appropriate."

"And what would you have done when you arrived here and found the rooms empty?" she demanded.

He stared. "Obtained our new direction from the porter in the basement. What did you think?"

She felt very foolish.

"In any case, now that you have seen me you can authorize Wolf to hire a house. Mayfair, perhaps. Or Goodman's Fields if you prefer something nearby."

"I had thought—" She stopped herself. She had not come up to discuss leasing houses. "I need to speak with you," she announced, gathering up her courage. "About what you said on our wedding night."

His face closed. "I apologized several times, but I'm willing to do so again if required. It was unspeakably cruel of me to taunt you."

"That's not it at all," she said, exasperated. Where was her speech?

As if on cue, there was a sharp rap on the door, and Silvio backed in, carrying a large tray. "There were no rolls yet at the bakery," he announced as he turned around. "I've brought a haddock pie from Loden's." Then he caught sight of Eloise and stopped dead.

"It doesn't matter," said James curtly. "I've no time for breakfast." He stood and set his cup of coffee down on his stool. "Have my bag sent over to Colonel White's office when you've repacked it. I'm leaving this afternoon for Norwich."

The valet simply gaped. He was standing in the doorway, which was narrow, and the tray filled the entire width of the door. Eloise could smell the pie from where she was sitting. At another time she would have thought it smelled delicious, but at the moment she felt slightly queasy.

In grim silence, James strode over to the door, took the tray from his servant's hands, set it on the bed, turned Silvio sideways, and marched out the door. He remembered to bow to Eloise. "Good day, Mrs. Meyer. I shall write as soon as I know how long my business will keep me in Norwich."

"Norwich!" Silvio exploded a minute later. "Norwich! Does he think me an idiot? What would he be doing in Norwich?"

This was no way for a servant to behave, Eloise told herself. She should reprimand him. Servants in the Bernal household were held to the most scrupulous observance of proper conduct. Eloise suspected her mother was too scrupulous, that the household would have functioned better without so much formality and deference. But Reyna Bernal did not want her neighbors in Roehampton thinking her uncouth. The result was that Eloise had never, since she was a small child, done in front of a servant what she did now in front of Silvio. She burst into tears and threw herself onto the bed, sobbing.

Silvio managed to rescue the pie dish just before it slid off the tray into her skirt, and handed her a handkerchief.

"Don't give up on him, signora," he said, patting her shoulder. "It will come right. Wait and see."

She shook her head, desolate. "I heard him last night. When he came in, and you were talking. He doesn't want me here. When he thought there was only one bedchamber, it sounded as though he was ready to bolt again. And now he *has* bolted."

"You heard him, yes," said the manservant quietly. "But, signora, you did not see him. You did not see his face when he gazed at you as you lay in the bed."

She struggled back up to a sitting position and wiped her eyes. "Why? What did he do?"

She was prepared to hear that he had looked at her with tenderness, or admiration, or even desire. She had no false modesty; she knew she was held to be a beautiful girl. But she was not prepared for what Silvio said.

"He looked at you," he said quietly, "as a dying man looks at the draft the physician has prepared—the draft which will save his life. And yet he hesitates to drink it, because he has been ill for so long, he is afraid to return to health."

I have an Italian philosopher for a butler, thought Eloise numbly. *A maid who is better dressed than I am. And a husband who thinks I have betrayed him before he has ever touched me.*

"Bring the pie back downstairs," she told Silvio. "You and Danielle and I can eat it before it gets cold."

Silvio grinned triumphantly. He knew what that meant. It meant she was not giving up. Yet.

Five

"You," said Evrett grimly, "are in disgrace." He had run James to earth in a shabby coffeehouse near the stock exchange.

"I know." The stony expression James wore so often at the moment was briefly replaced by a savage smile.

"No one believes that you were called away right after the wedding."

"Naturally not. Though the Bernals and my uncle must pretend to credit the tale, to save face. One of my better schemes, if I do say so myself."

Evrett dropped into an adjacent chair without waiting for an invitation and hooked his cane over the arm.

"Boy!" he called out, waving at a grizzled fellow in a long white apron. "A pot of coffee here for the gentleman. Canary for me. And a plate of anchovy toasts."

"I already have coffee," James pointed out, hefting his cup.

Evrett plunked his index finger into the sludge at the bottom. "Ice cold. How long have you been sitting here? You're a wealthy man; you could at least order a fresh pot of coffee every so often if you intend using Garraway's as your hermit's cave.''

"This place is hardly eremitic in character," James said dryly, looking around at the bustling crowd of stockjobbers and solicitors. Every table was full, and the din of hundreds of conversations echoed around the stone-floored room. The two of them nearly had to shout to hear each other.

Evrett refused to be diverted. "The LeSueurs and I called on your bride yesterday," he said, staring straight at James. "We called last week as well. You were from home both times. Apparently, in fact, you are *never* home." He paused for effect. "Lovely young woman. Married to a selfish poltroon, of course, but what can one do? Eventually, I am sure she will be offered consolation by some gentleman who appreciates her quality."

The other man stiffened, and for a moment Evrett thought he was going to get a face-full of coffee grounds.

"Have a care, my lord," his friend said softly. "I can call you out, remember. I'm lame now, just like you."

"We've been out. And I'll remind you that unlike the rest of the Ninety-fifth, I actually pinked you." Evrett, in fact, had been the first of a long list of officers in the Ninety-fifth who had determined to teach James Nathanson that someone whose real name was Meyer had no business holding a lieutenant's commission. By the third duel, Evrett was seconding him. By the fifth duel, they were sharing quarters.

James smiled reluctantly. "Yes, you would remind me of that, wouldn't you?" he said dryly. "At every opportunity, it seems. Someday I'll demand a chance to even the score. A cripple's duel."

"Don't exaggerate, James," Evrett said sternly. He gestured towards a table on the far side of the room, where an amputee sat stolidly drinking, his empty trouser leg obvious even at this distance. "We're not cripples. We can still walk, ride, drive, climb stairs. You can even manage a few of the slower dances. You've a beautiful bride, a loving father''—

Evrett had lost his own recently—"an important job at Whitehall. What ails you?"

"Ennui," said James lazily, accepting his pot of fresh coffee from the waiter and handing the glass of wine across the table.

"You? Bored?" Evrett looked around for the food and discovered that the waiter was disappearing, still carrying the plate. "Hi! Bring that back!" he shouted, more loudly than he had intended. The startled waiter tripped, went sprawling, and scattered anchovy toast all over an unfortunate clerk at the next table.

"Well, *now* I'm not bored," James said, adroitly reaching over and snaring a piece of bread from the clerk's collar just as the indignant customer rose from his chair, ready to give the waiter a piece of his mind. "Do you suppose the fellow is wearing clean linens? Dare I eat this?"

When order had been restored and a fresh plate brought to their table, Evrett stubbornly returned to this theme. "I've been your friend for nearly five years, Nathanson." He used James's *nom de guerre*. "And it's not an easy job. You've a hair-trigger temper, the arrogance of a prince of the blood, and a mighty sharp tongue."

"Spare me the flattery—friend."

"I *am* your friend, blast it, and you've not got many. Nor like to make new ones, at this rate. I think I deserve a serious reply."

"What ails me," mused James. He grimaced. "I don't know." His face had lost its impenetrable look; he sat still, thinking for a minute. "I can't explain it. Since I returned from Vienna, it's as though the world has lost its color. Food has no taste. Music has no harmony. I wake before dawn every day and lie there, willing the time to pass until night. I dare not drink more than a glass or so of wine; when I let myself go one evening I could not stop until I passed out. Books have no meaning. After three sentences I have lost the thread of the argument. My work—well, Whitehall has given me nothing more than clerical tasks since my return, and I understand why. I cannot be alone unless I am moving: riding or walking. And yet social events are excruciating. Even informal gatherings with my family. My little cousins are tolerable, but I find the company of my father, my aunt, and my uncle irritating beyond words.''

"And your wife?''

"She terrifies me,'' admitted James. He shook his head. "It's nothing she says or does—we barely speak. I'm sorry,'' he said in low tones, looking down at the table. "But now you understand why I've been avoiding you and everyone else. I'm not fit company for anyone at the moment.''

"Never mind about me,'' said Evrett impatiently. "I'm not the one who deserves an apology from you.''

"Eloise.'' His voice had hardened. "Leave it. It's none of your affair.''

He was already regretting those confidences, thought Evrett, who had never heard James admit any sort of weakness before, even right after the French had punched eighteen holes in his leg. But he pressed on. "You say it's none of my affair. I agree. Whose affair is it?'' His index finger shot out. "*Yours.* Stop wallowing in melancholy and wake up. Those rooms off Houndsditch are appalling. The street is noisy, the furnishings cheap and soiled, the prospect a dirty brick wall. Mrs. Meyer has done wonders with the place since my first visit, but she is clearly wretchedly unhappy. You are never home. She cannot complain to her family or yours, lest she seem disloyal to you. While we were there, a cousin called and invited her to accompany her on a visit to mutual friends in Surrey. Of course, she refused. It would be the very thing for her, but she is too proud to abandon your lodgings, precisely because they are so repulsive. I'll wager no one in your family dares speak to you—if they can even find you—for fear of an explosion. Well, I dare. Take better care of your wife, sir, or *I* will call *you* out.''

He drained his glass and stood up, grabbing his cane and

thumping it down on the sawdust to make his point. "Don't you realize that you are notorious? Have been, for years? Fifteen duels in one year in Portugal, a demotion, reassignment to London—every young officer knows all about you. Your marriage has been mentioned at nearly every club in town. There were bets, you know, after your sister's wedding, that you would offer for a Christian girl. Sooner or later someone besides your family will hear how shabbily you are treating your bride. And when they do, I shall be forced to cut you dead the next time I see you."

"Not sure why you haven't already given me up," said his friend with a sigh.

"Don't be an ass." Evrett picked up his hat. "Isn't your sister back in England, by the by? Mrs. Southey told me she was in the family way."

"Yes, I'm to be an uncle." James's face softened; his eyes lit briefly. "And that coward Drayton sent her home from Gibraltar the minute she gave him the news. Rachel's furious. She's down in Kent, refused to come to London. She told me that so long as she could sit a horse she was staying in the country, and Drayton could send his precious London doctors down to Knowlton to find her. She's a bit lonely, but Drayton's sister is nearby."

"If she is in need of some company," said Evrett slowly, "why not take your wife down to visit? I am certain your sister is anxious to meet her."

"She wrote and commanded me to bring Eloise down at once."

"Well, why not do so?"

"Her letter was ... somewhat imperious." He added grudgingly, "I was considering it, even so."

"Consider it further," advised Evrett. "I have met your sister. If she decides to come to London and finds Mrs. Meyer installed in those lodgings, I shudder to think of your fate."

* * *

Danielle, ever eager to relay gossip, had told her that he was back in town. He had been spotted at a coffeehouse, apparently, and Silvio had instructed Nan—or was it Peg?—that the upstairs bedroom should be dusted and a fire laid. "One would think," Danielle had said with a sniff, "that madame might have been informed." Eloise had accepted the news without comment, only wondering whether, as usual, he would be gone again before breakfast. If she wanted to speak with him, she would need to wait up. And so she had obediently let Danielle undress her and comb out her hair and braid it and help her into her nightgown—and then had hastily redressed herself after the maid had retired.

It was not so late when he came in—barely past midnight. His limp was very pronounced; she could hear it on the stairs. She waited a few minutes after he had gone up, but dared not leave it too long. She did not want to find him already in bed. Pulling on an old pair of slippers, she climbed quietly up to the third floor. At the top of the stairs, a sudden draft blew out her candle, but there was light streaming out from the open door of his bedroom, and she simply set it down on the newel post and hurried forward.

The room was brightly illuminated with a fire and two lamps. The effect, looking in from the dark hall, was rather like being in the theater and seeing the curtain come up on a tableau. In the center of the scene was James, head bowed, sitting in an armchair. He was in his shirt and trousers. His green uniform jacket was slung over one side of the chair. Leaning against the chair on the other side was his sword. Silvio was bending over in front of him with a boot in one hand. They had not heard her approach. She paused, hesitating.

Then the tableau came to life, and the actors spoke. Silvio held up the boot and shook it in his master's face. "What did you do, sleep with them on for two days?" he demanded. "Look at the lining of this one!"

"I didn't sleep." James scowled. "Spare me the lectures. Just get the other one off me."

Grumbling, the servant set down the boot, put one hand gently on his master's knee, and lifted the heel of the other foot.

"It's easier if you do it quickly," said James. He was gripping the arms of the chair very hard.

The valet muttered something in Italian and gave a sharp tug. There was a slight tearing sound. The boot came off. A series of mottled stains were visible on the stocking underneath. With another, even more exasperated exclamation, Silvio peeled the woolen sock off, pulling it free where it was sticking to the calf.

She saw the scars at once: rows of odd, round dents stippled across the top of James's ankle, as though someone had been sowing seeds under his skin. Silvio had set the second boot aside and was kneeling again, smearing a black salve on the marks. Many were red and swollen around the edges. James had slumped back in the armchair, eyes closed. Every once in a while he would flinch slightly when the salve hit a particularly tender spot.

Leave, she told herself. *Quietly. Inch back, slowly. They haven't seen you yet.* But she was held there, unable to look away, let alone move. There was something fascinating about the neat pattern of red circles spiraling up across the bottom of his calf in orderly lines. It was very quiet. She could hear James breathing.

Then he opened his eyes.

She could tell exactly when he spotted her; there was a brief flicker of astonishment replaced by stupefied horror. Silvio jerked round an instant later and dropped the jar of salve on the floor. It rolled under the chair and came to a stop against the wall with a small, clear thud.

For one moment, they were all three motionless, silent. Silvio was the first to move. He struggled to his feet, wiping his hands on the bloodstained stocking. James looked as though he were going to be sick. He grabbed instinctively at his jacket and started to throw it over his foot, then thought better of it and stared at her defiantly.

"Please don't get up," she said hastily, and then realized how dreadfully wrong that particular phrase was.

"No," he said, with an odd grimace. "Perhaps not." Silvio was edging in front of the chair, as if to shield his charge from attack. James waved him aside, still staring at her. "Well, now my revolting little secret is out." His voice was flat. "You got a bad bargain, wife. Damaged goods."

"I knew you were wounded," she reminded him.

"Not like this." He nodded towards the mangled ankle.

"I've seen worse." She had, at the naval hospital, but it was not the same when it was someone you knew, someone whose bed you had thought to share, someone you had considered, in that stunned first moment when she walked into her parents' drawing room last month, the most beautiful man she had ever seen. She managed to raise her eyebrows slightly, as though challenging him, and was rewarded by a rueful smile.

"Very well, I'll leave off trying to win the 'most pitiful scar' contest. To what do I owe the honor of this visit?" He took in her fully clothed state for the first time. "You waited up for me?"

She nodded.

"I apologize, then, for coming home so late."

Silvio melted away. Neither one even noticed he was gone.

"At least you came home. For once."

The sharpness in her tone was a relief. James was spoiling for a fight. He wanted her to feel anger, jealousy, scorn, humiliation—anything to clear the miasma of pity out of the room.

"I cannot imagine why you would want me here," he countered. "It is so much easier to sneer at the lowly Meyers in my absence, is it not?"

"I do *not* sneer," she flared. "I have *never* said one word about your family, or the Roths, or these rooms, or your sister's marriage, or your father, or any of the thousand things my aunts cast up at me every time they call.''

''Admit it,'' he said, glaring up at her. ''You enjoy sitting here like Patience on the proverbial monument. Wolf offered to find us better lodgings the night you arrived, and you refused.''

''Because you were nowhere to be found! A fine thing if you were to have come home and found a closed-up house and all of us halfway across London!''

''I returned ten days ago and broached the possibility of moving to Mayfair. You put me off.''

He could see she remembered that particular conversation, which had consisted of his blurting out two sentences and then bolting, leaving his breakfast half finished. He had not thought she would be up so early, or he would have left without letting Silvio bring a tray up to him.

She sat down on the edge of the bed and sighed. ''I don't want to set up housekeeping in Mayfair, or Goodman's Fields, or any of the other places we are supposed to live,'' she acknowledged. ''I detest London. Once we move into a proper home, I shall have to admit that we live here. This''—she gestured at the attic room with the half-painted shutters—''this is like playing house. A game.''

It had never occurred to him that she would not want to live in town. He realized that he had not even asked her what she would prefer, had no idea of her likes and dislikes, what sorts of activities she enjoyed, who her friends were, where they lived.

''Why did you wait up?'' he asked abruptly. ''What did you want to ask me?''

She shook her head. ''It is not important.''

Perhaps she just wanted to see you, he thought. Perhaps she was lonely. The possibility that Evrett might be right— as he usually was—loomed up larger and larger.

''My sister has invited us to visit her in Kent,'' he said slowly. ''Would you be willing to go?''

"Willing? What do you mean by that? Why should I not be willing?"

"Rachel is in disgrace," he reminded her. "That is why she did not attend the wedding. Half the family has disowned her because of her marriage."

"All the more reason for us to visit." She looked at him suspiciously. "You will come with me? Or do you plan to pack me off down there and disappear again and leave me with a woman I have never met?"

"I'll come," he promised. "For at least a week." He could manage a week. Especially if he could get out every morning and ride or walk until he was exhausted.

Her smile hit him like a blow. It lit her face.

"Danielle will *loathe* being in the country," she predicted, with a sparkle in her eye. "And I will be completely safe from my horrid aunts because they will *never* call on your sister, even if they should happen to find themselves in the wilds of Kent."

She got up and nearly danced over to him, bending over and kissing him gaily on the forehead. Her eye fell on the forgotten pot of salve, lodged behind the back leg of the chair. "Shall I finish putting this on?"

He looked up and saw that she was completely serious and had already bent over to pick it up.

"No," he snapped, then flinched as he heard his own tone and saw the brief look of hurt surprise on her face. How many apologies did he owe her now? Had he flown out at her because she had offered to touch his leg, or because she had kissed him?

Maybe he wouldn't be able to manage a week.

Six

She grew increasingly nervous on the drive down to Knowlton. With every mile that went by, she realized more and more that she knew nothing about rural England, nothing about the life of the landed gentry or the proper behavior of guests at a country house. Her parents' home was dwarfed by some of the palatial mansions she glimpsed on distant hilltops through the carriage window. And as they passed acre after acre of brown fields and great sweeps of forest, she came to understand that Roehampton was a fraud, a plaything. *This* was the countryside. She did not belong here, and she was going to spend three weeks with a woman who did.

If James had been in the carriage, she might have summoned up the courage to confess her misgivings and ask for some hints about what would be expected of her at the Drayton home. But he had chosen to ride; it was a dry, mild day, very welcome after the unremitting cold of the past few weeks. He had even offered to mount her for all or part of the trip. She bit her lip, remembering. The Bernals' groom had taught her to drive both the gig and a more stylish phaeton, and she was reasonably competent at handling her father's sleepy pair for small excursions. But she had never really learned how to ride well, and the thought of hours in a sidesaddle on a crowded turnpike had made her feel faint.

Now she realized that her incompetence in the saddle would be yet another black mark against her at Knowlton. James's sister was apparently a notable horsewoman and would no doubt be disappointed to find her guest unable to accompany her on rides. Eloise was gloomily picturing Rachel Drayton offering, with a martyred air, to walk with her again through the grounds—or whatever one did to take the air at Knowlton—when Danielle touched her arm.

"We have arrived, madame."

Eloise blinked. She had forgotten that Danielle was there. The girl had sat silent and stone-faced during the entire five-hour ride. Her guess that Danielle would hate Kent had been correct. She had hated it, in fact, before ever seeing it, and had made that very clear for the past three days. Now her maid was leaning over, packing up various items which had been pulled out of their basket during the ride, her expression sour. *And just where are we?* her expression seemed to say. *No place worth the journey, to be sure.*

The door opened, and James reached up to hand her out.

It was just as she had pictured it: intimidating. The house was not large, but it was mellow with age and beautifully proportioned. Forest rose behind it, setting off the square white building and the small surrounding lawn. Fields stretched out to one side of the lawn, and with a sinking heart she saw horses. Many horses. More horses than people, she thought, realizing that there were no other houses in sight. She had never been anywhere where you could not see at least one other dwelling.

She remembered that James's sister was no longer welcome in the Roth household and had not yet been acknowledged by her husband's titled father. Her own anxiety gave way to sympathy for her hostess, sent off to this isolated spot like some disgraced medieval queen exiled to a nunnery.

She probably had an elderly female companion to lend her countenance. And spent her days embroidering caps for the baby and listening to the old woman read excerpts from the Countess of Carlisle's *Maxims for Young Ladies*. This picture totally contradicted Eloise's earlier fantasy of the intrepid equestrienne, but she dwelt on it lovingly without relinquishing her worries about her horsemanship.

Then the front door swung open—banged open, more accurately—and two small figures burst out. The taller, a fair-haired girl of about eight, tore across the path and skidded to a stop in front of Danielle, who had emerged from the carriage. As always, the maid looked impeccably neat, her light hair coiled in a gleaming roll at the back of her neck.

"I'm Caroline," the girl announced as though conferring a great favor. "You must be my new almost-aunt Eloise."

It was an easy mistake to make if you looked only at hairstyle and posture, and Eloise was wondering whether it was her place to correct her, or Danielle's; but now the second figure had caught up. This proved to be a toddler. He headed with great determination straight for the team, who were snorting and jostling in their eagerness to be unharnessed.

James stepped into his path and was greeted with lifted arms and an imperious command, "Up!" With a quick smile, he obliged, scooping the boy up to his shoulder. "No!" screamed his victim, kicking James hard in the chest.

"He's dreadfully spoilt," Caroline confided to Danielle, loud enough for Eloise to hear. "Because he's an orphan."

"Horse! I want up on horse!"

"Certainly not," said James coolly, swinging the boy off his shoulders and holding him suspended at arm's length, facing the team. "This is a carriage horse, not a saddle horse. Can't you see he's still in the traces?"

To her surprise, the boy seemed to accept this. He twisted his head around to look at James again and said in a different tone, "Up?"

James laughed. "Very well, but don't touch my hat. Your hands are all over jam."

They were, Eloise realized. The boy was reestablished on her husband's shoulders, and had only grabbed the hat once or twice when the next interruption occurred; this time a frantic young woman—a nursemaid, Eloise guessed—who came running around from the side of the house calling, "Master William! Oh, mercy! Oh, sir, don't let him fall!"

The front door was still wide open, and the next player in the drama now emerged. This was a tall young woman who resembled James so strongly they might have been twins: the same flashing dark eyes and aquiline face, though hers was paler and finer-boned. She was wearing a loose gray wool dress with a red stain down one side—jam, Eloise surmised; her dark brown hair was tumbling out of its knot, and she was wringing her hands and laughing and nearly crying, all at the same time. She hurried down the stairs, calling out behind her to someone in the house. Pacing beside her in a dignified fashion quite at odds with her mistress's disarray was a large bitch, who proceeded straight up to the horrified James and thrust her head in his crotch. After an exploratory sniff, she gave a deep, satisfied bark and sat back on her haunches.

"You have a *dog*?" he said in accents of loathing.

"Oh, you're here at last! I did not expect you so soon!" said their hostess in happy self-contradiction, standing on tiptoe to kiss her brother on the cheek. "Yes, of course we have a dog."

Danielle looked as though she might give notice any moment, Eloise thought. The proper welcome for guests arriving by carriage was for a superior servant—a butler or an upper footman—to open the front door, usher the guests inside, and summon a groom to take the carriage and the accompanying maids, coachmen, etc., round to the stables. No sign of a butler or of any servant beyond the nursemaid, who had reclaimed William but still stood staring in rapt admiration at James. No groom; Silvio and Toby had hopped down and were leading the carriage off themselves in a direction which looked like it might take them to invisible stables. Their hostess was not properly dressed, and two children, who should not have been allowed downstairs until teatime, had greeted the party and had nearly (in one case) been stepped on by the right leader.

"Caroline," she said, taking pity on her maid, "I am your Aunt Eloise. That is my abigail, Danielle."

The girl looked over at her. "Well, you didn't look like an Aunt Eloise," she said frankly. "Aunt Rachel said you were very elegant."

"Oh, dear," said Aunt Rachel under her breath.

"Your aunt had not seen me at that time," Eloise explained calmly.

But Caroline had remembered something else she had overheard, and marched up to James, tilting her head back to stare at him. "Aunt Rachel said you have holes in your leg," she announced. "May I see?" She hiked up her frock, revealing a purple scrape on one knee. "Look, I have one, but it's not very deep."

Eloise held her breath, her eyes swinging over to James's face.

There was only a moment's pause. Eloise noticed that Rachel's grip on his arm had tightened. But his tone was faintly amused. "I take it Caroline is between governesses again?"

"How did you guess?" Rachel sighed, and turned belatedly to Eloise. "Welcome to Knowlton," she said. Her tone was rueful. "This might not be quite what you were expecting."

Eloise decided to confess. "I was expecting seventeen footmen, and a house where I couldn't find my bedroom after dinner, and conversation about cruppers and withers and hooks."

"Hocks," corrected Rachel automatically. "We can't supply the footmen, or the endless corridors of guest rooms, but there is Aunt Lucy. She loves to talk about horses, when she isn't lecturing me about my duties as a mother-to-be.''

''Who is that?'' asked James. ''We don't have an Aunt Lucy.''

Rachel pointed down the drive, where a tiny figure was approaching on horseback, rigidly upright in the saddle. ''You don't. I do. It's Richard's aunt, Lady Ingram. Evidently, she comes with The Drayton Baby.''

The rider trotted up and halted just abreast of the new arrivals. Her blue eyes scanned Danielle, then Eloise, and settled finally on James.

''You must be Rachel's good-for-nothing brother,'' she informed him tartly. ''I'd recognize that profile anywhere.''

James claimed afterwards that it was Caroline's remark about his leg which set Rachel off. Rachel argued that she would have spotted his limp at once. The result was indisputable, though: she cornered him in his half of the connecting bedrooms assigned to the newlyweds and began scolding him in full view of both Silvio and her own maid, Maria, who had followed her into the suite.

''You wrote me it was nearly unnoticeable,'' she said angrily.

''It comes and goes,'' he said wearily. ''Right now it's aching a bit. It's all healed up, Rachel; there's nothing to be done.''

''It is not healed,'' muttered Silvio.

''Would you be kind enough to remove my brother's boots?'' Rachel asked the valet, a dangerous glitter in her eye.

James was aghast. ''With everyone watching?'' He shot a glance at the door which led into Eloise's room to make sure that she would not get another view of his ruined leg. It was closed, and Rachel had told him that Eloise was changing out of her traveling clothes, but he was still nervous.

"I am sure that Silvio has already seen your ankle," she pointed out. "That leaves me and Maria. Your sister and a family servant who is nearly your foster mother, respectively. Let us say that Maria and I are curious."

"What am I, a traveling exhibition?" he said furiously.

She folded her arms. "Give me your word that it is indeed fully healed, and I will leave right now."

He had the grace to look embarrassed.

"Sit," she ordered, indicating a massive walnut divan.

He sat. She jerked her head at Silvio, and the boots disappeared. No stains on the stocking this time, he noted, and the wounds were less angry than they had been that dreadful evening Eloise had seen them. But Rachel was appalled.

"How could you neglect him so?" she demanded in shocked tones of Silvio. "Just look at this!" She knelt down and touched the edge of one of the angrier circles. "Maria, could you go down to the kitchen and start a kettle?" she asked, still peering at the scars. The older woman vanished.

"Don't blame Silvio," said James sheepishly. "I've been traveling quite a bit." That wasn't the real reason he had let it go untended, of course. The real reason was he couldn't look at the rows of swollen dots without thinking about the countess.

"This will hurt," Rachel said brusquely without looking at him, turning the leg and examining the back of the calf. It did hurt. He tried not to flinch.

"I suppose you thought it would be a sign of weakness to see a doctor when you arrived back in England," she said, giving him an especially vicious poke. "Or at least Aunt Louisa."

"White had someone from the hospital look at it," he said tersely. "On my first visit, he suggested I would be better off minus the bottom third of my leg. I didn't go back."

"Well," said Rachel, straightening up. "I don't think it's hopeless. Get him undressed, Silvio. And bring me all his clothes; I'll not have him trying to escape before he's been treated properly. He's to rest for at least a week. No weight on that foot at all. We'll start with a poultice of pennyroyal, and I'll send to the apothecary for some basilicum.''

''I'll not be put to bed like a child,'' he said, glaring at her.

Silvio glanced back and forth between brother and sister uneasily.

''Fine,'' snapped Rachel. ''Brood. Nurse your scars. Limp for the rest of your life.''

''Signor,'' said Silvio apologetically, approaching the divan like a martyr approaching the lion, ''I think perhaps—''

He was cut off by a string of French oaths which made Rachel cover her ears and wince. A quick gesture and Silvio prudently retreated, closing the door behind him.

''Oh, go ahead,'' James growled finally, looking a bit ashamed. ''Dose me. Lock me in my chamber. Load me with poultices, if it will make you feel better. I suppose it won't hurt anything.''

She sat down next to him with a small sigh.

He said hesitantly after a minute, ''Don't let me spoil our visit with my tantrums, Rachel. I've been out of sorts lately.''

''So I hear,'' she said dryly. ''And believe me, I would not spoil your visit (as you put it) by confining you to bed did I not think it necessary.'' Very gently, she reached over and traced the rim of one of the puckered dents with the tip of her index finger. It didn't bother him, he discovered. So why had he nearly died of humiliation when Eloise had walked in that night?

Because he did not want Eloise to find him repulsive, he acknowledged.

''Rachel, do you think the scars are ugly?'' he asked suddenly, knowing he would get an honest answer.

''Not as ugly as Richard's,'' she said after considering for a moment. ''Yours make a nice line. He has one in the front and one in the back, much bigger than yours, and the skin is discolored and stiff. Besides, yours are not fully healed yet.'' She gave him a dark look as she rose and moved towards the door. "Although they *would* be had they been properly tended. They'll be much less noticeable once the swelling recedes."

"Eloise came into my room one night unexpectedly and saw them," he said in a low voice.

She looked puzzled, and he realized with a sickening lurch that he had just made it clear that he was not sharing a bedchamber with his bride of less than a month.

"She was going to put the salve on," he said desperately, as though that explained everything. "Silvio dropped the jar."

"James, she's your *wife*," said Rachel, exasperated, opening the door.

She isn't really my wife, he wanted to say. It was all a mistake. But when he looked up and saw Rachel staring at him, still looking troubled, he turned away and beckoned the hesitant Silvio back into the room. He would be a model patient, he decided. Bed might be the best refuge for him. Now he had to contend with his sister as well as with Eloise, and they were both, in his opinion, very dangerous creatures.

Seven

Eloise had thought that with James confined to bed she would have an excuse to remain indoors all day tending him. Perhaps that was what had given her the courage to confess her ineptitude on horseback very frankly when Rachel had inquired the previous evening about mounting her during her visit. But instead, Rachel and James had agreed at once that this would be an ideal opportunity for her to learn.

"Won't you need company?" she had faltered, looking at her husband as he lounged arrogantly back against the headboard of his bed. They had come up to visit with him after dinner.

He looked appalled. "In the morning? I think not. Not at the hours my sister goes riding, at any rate. Try me after ten."

And so she found herself at half past eight in her rarely worn riding habit, staring down at her hostess from the back of a slippery, quivering, massively muscled gelding. It was cold again, though not as bitter as the day of the wedding.

Little puffs of steam came out of her horse's nostrils. It made him look demonic.

"We'll start out walking and take a look at your seat," said Rachel cheerfully. "It will all be very gentle; I promised James not to overtax you." Her breath made puffs of steam as well.

Perched gingerly in the saddle, Eloise tried to remember what she had been told. Sit back, then forward? Forward, then back? Hands up? Hands down?

"I'll help," Caroline offered eagerly as her mare sidled underneath her. "I taught my governess," she explained to Eloise. "But then she fell in love with the vicar and ran off."

"She did *not* run off, Caroline," said Rachel firmly. "I do wish you would stop saying that. It was all perfectly proper, and your Aunt Sara attended the wedding." Eloise had managed to glean some of the muddled history of the Drayton household: Caroline and William were the children of Drayton's late brother, and he was now their guardian. While Rachel and her husband had both been in Gibraltar, the children had stayed with Drayton's sister. Now Rachel was urging the Barretts to leave both children in her care, and Lady Barrett was resisting. "Sara's as bad as my husband," she had told Eloise. "Thinks me too frail to supervise his wards now I'm *enceinte*."

"May I teach her, Aunt Rachel?" pleaded Caroline. "May I?" She was bouncing in her saddle with impatience and had twisted around to look back at the two women. Eloise could not understand why she had not tumbled off.

"Not today, Caroline," said Rachel firmly. She payed out a little more of the line she was using to lead Eloise's horse. "Some grown-ups do not care to be instructed by children, you know."

"Oh, I don't mind," said Eloise hastily.

"You would," predicted Rachel in an undertone. "She has been absolutely insufferable since our crusty old neighbor told her she was the best horsewoman he had seen in fifty years.'' She raised her voice. ''Samuels?''

A groom emerged from the stable adjoining the paddock where Rachel was standing.

''Is Flare saddled? Would you take Miss Caroline out? I fear she will find our lesson rather dull.''

''I would not,'' protested Caroline. By now she was swiveled all the way round and appeared to be mounted backwards on her horse, who was prancing with impatience. ''Look at her right now, Aunt Rachel. Her shoulders are up by her ears.''

Hastily Eloise tried to push her shoulders down.

''And,'' added the little girl, surveying her new almost-aunt with a frown, ''she's holding her arms very stiffly.''

''That will do, Caroline,'' said an exasperated Rachel. As the groom reappeared, mounted on a large chestnut, she waved him over and made urgent motions with one hand in Caroline's direction. He grinned, raised his eyebrows, and trotted off, snaring Caroline's reins with one neat motion as he went by. ''One would never suppose,'' Rachel said gloomily as his charge howled in protest, ''that Caroline actually had very pretty manners after I made my peace with her last spring.''

She stepped back and looked at Eloise critically. Then she gave a rueful smile.

''I know,'' said Eloise, sighing. ''My shoulders are too high and my arms are stiff.''

Rachel nodded.

After two circuits of the paddock, which took what seemed to be an hour each, Eloise was convinced that she was simply not meant to be on the back of a horse. Every five steps Rachel would stop her, rearrange her hands or her feet, or tell her to raise her head, and then a moment later it had vanished.

''I thought from the beginning that we should start you in a man's saddle, and now I am sure of it,'' said Rachel at last. ''You will need to know how to ride with a regular saddle in case of emergencies, and this way you can learn to hold your shoulders and hands properly.''

"I suppose it might help," conceded Eloise. "I have often suspected I might be more comfortable astride."

"Good, we are agreed, then," said Rachel briskly. "For the rest of this lesson I'll keep you on lead. I'll have Maria alter my old boy's riding suit tonight, and tomorrow we'll have you sitting astride."

"I beg your pardon, but do you mean I must wear *breeches?*" Eloise was horrified.

"Well, not breeches, precisely. But boys' riding clothes, yes. Unless you wish to have the skirt of your habit up around your thighs."

She balked for the first time. She had sat on that mountain of a horse; she had obediently put her hands here and there and turned down her heel and glued her elbows to her side and lifted her chin, and striven with all her might not to look at the ground. But this was going too far.

"No," she said stubbornly. "No boys' clothing. I did not realize I would have to dress immodestly to learn to ride on a man's saddle."

Rachel flushed. "Perhaps you have married into the wrong family, then," she said thinly. "I am afraid that I myself have been known to dress 'immodestly,' as you put it. And my father spent six weeks last summer disguised as a Spanish noblewoman. I am sure James will appreciate your decorum when he is languishing in prison or needs a message taken to him at a sailors' tavern, and you cannot help him because you are too nice to don men's clothing."

Eloise stared. "Prison? Taverns? What are you talking about? And what do you mean, your father was a noblewoman?"

Rachel dropped the leading rein and stood motionless for a moment, looking at Eloise in complete dismay. She peered uncertainly into her guest's face, and Eloise was so puzzled that she forgot for one moment that she was about to fall off the horse.

"They didn't tell you," Rachel said, shaking her head in amazement. She was speaking more to herself than to Eloise. "Those cowards, those imbeciles! I should have known; they're both masters of evasion." Her face was tight with anger. "Come on down," she commanded.

Thankfully, Eloise slid awkwardly down to the ground, landing with a thump in spite of Rachel's assistance. Rachel was already stalking angrily towards the house.

"I don't care if he's confined to bed," she said, nearly spitting the words out. "This passes belief. He can tell you himself."

"Tell me what?" asked the bewildered Eloise, stumbling in her haste to catch up with her hostess.

"What he does."

"But—" She touched Rachel's arm. "I know he is in the army," she said earnestly. "I know he changed his name and pretended to convert so as to be able to hold a commission. My parents asked him to try to conceal it at the wedding, but I think it was more in an attempt to feign ignorance than with any expectation of deceiving anyone. It is common knowledge that he is a captain with Wellington's infantry."

Rachel looked at her with pity. "You don't know much about the military, do you?"

"No," Eloise confessed.

"Did you never wonder why James is not with his regiment? The Ninety-fifth are in France right now, in Gascony. And yet James is in London. Or rather, based in London, working for a colonel attached to the adjutant general's office. Does that not strike you as odd?"

"I thought perhaps he was on leave," Eloise stammered. "Medical leave—his wound."

"He has been assigned to Colonel White for two years now. And speaking of his wound, do you know how he injured his leg? A rather unusual pattern of scars, wouldn't you say?"

Eloise felt totally at sea. *Everything about this marriage is odd and unusual,* she wanted to say. *The Roths and Meyers are fabulously wealthy, yet we live in a tenement. My husband's valet has adopted me as a long-lost daughter. The heir to a title ruined my husband's best hat yesterday afternoon. My husband is afraid of me and runs in the opposite direction whenever I approach him.* She cast herself on Rachel's mercy.

"No, I don't know how he hurt his leg," she said, sighing. "I don't know anything about the army or his appointment. No one tells me anything. They all think I'm too young, or too innocent, or too dim-witted."

"He'll tell you now," said Rachel grimly, resuming her march. "Or I'll feed him nothing but gruel for a week." She slammed into the house and up the stairs to the guest bedroom, trailed by the baffled Eloise, and burst in without even knocking. Luckily, James was awake and decently covered by a dressing gown. He looked up from his book with a guilty start as they came in.

"James," said Rachel in awful tones, "why is it that your wife does not know which branch of the service has currently borrowed you from the Ninety-fifth?"

He looked back and forth from one woman to the other and slowly lowered the book to his lap.

"And would you care to tell her," Rachel continued, clipping her words, "about your injury? Or shall I?"

"Go ahead," he said after a moment, lifting his chin. "I shall enjoy hearing your version. I've heard so many already. All vastly entertaining."

Eloise thought that if someone had brought in dueling pistols right now, brother and sister would have seized the guns and shot each other.

But then, to her surprise, Rachel's face crumpled. She sat down on the edge of the bed and started to cry, very quietly. Her brother reached out awkwardly and touched her shoulder, and she shook her head, still in silence, and took out her handkerchief.

"I'm sorry," she said at last, wiping her eyes. "I seem

to weep very easily at the moment. Lady Ingram says that means it is a boy. And it is true that I am very sore on this particular subject, because I believe Richard was wrong to send me back to England. It is all of a piece, this stifling, overprotective behavior you men find so noble.''

She twisted around to face her brother. ''James, you have no idea how hard it is to always be the one who is left waiting and worrying while you and Papa are abroad. There have been times—especially last year—when I thought I would go mad with anxiety. But it would be worse, far worse, not even to know you were in danger. How could I, or any woman, want to be carefree at such a price? I think it is shameful of you to keep Eloise in the dark about your work.''

''I assumed her father would have told her,'' he muttered. ''Everyone in the family knows.''

''Everyone does not know,'' she said sternly. ''And more importantly, Eloise is your wife, and *she* does not know.''

He sighed and looked up at Eloise. ''I'm a spy,'' he said.

''Courier,'' corrected his sister hastily.

''Spy,'' he insisted. ''I slink about in enemy-held territory, paying disgusting Frenchmen who are willing to betray their country for money large sums to pass information and documents on to my government, through me.''

''James!'' said Rachel, shocked.

''I'm not ashamed of it,'' he said stubbornly. ''Someone has to do it. But it is not very heroic. In London I'm a glorified clerk—reading reports, compiling summaries, transcribing coded dispatches. And when I'm in the field, most of it is hiding and bribing people and forging papers. I'm often in disguise, although I'm not as gifted at that as my father.''

''Is he—'' Eloise started to speak, then stopped.

''Yes, he's a spy as well. But he has no official connection to the British Army. I didn't want to be like him. I wanted a commission. I wanted to be in the field, with a regiment. Hence the name change.'' He sighed. ''It didn't work, though. They made me a spy anyway. The only difference is, I have a nice green uniform to wear here in England, and if the French kill me you will get a pension.''

"So." Eloise swallowed. "Your leg—that is not an injury taken in battle.''

He actually smiled for a moment. "I have tried for hours to think of some weapon used by either army which could have inflicted something remotely like this." He nodded towards his leg. "I confess that even my talent for invention has failed me. No, it is not a war wound. I was captured by the French *Sûreté* last summer in Vienna, and they interrogated me, using a medieval iron boot lined with spikes as an incentive to answer their questions. Luckily, Michael Southey came along and rescued me, or I might have a matching set of scars on the other ankle, and who knows what else besides.''

She nearly gagged as she realized what he was describing. "What . . ." she faltered. "What did they want to know?''

"They wanted to know where to find my father." His face closed. "I don't know if I would have told them or not. But as it happens, I had no choice. *Because even though he was also in Vienna for nearly the entire summer, my father never told me where he was or what he was doing.*''

"And you haven't forgiven him for it, have you?" Rachel slid off the bed and stood up. "So how can you justify behaving the same way yourself?''

He grimaced. "Point taken.''

She handed him his book. "Back to your book, then. We'll resume our riding lesson, which was interrupted when Eloise did not understand why she might need to learn to use a man's saddle.''

"Resume?" Eloise was taken aback. She had told herself it was over for the day, and all her muscles had already decided to take her at her word and stiffen up uncomfortably.

"Yes, but don't worry; it will be much easier tomorrow," Rachel reassured her. "When you can wear comfortable clothing and sit properly.''

Eloise took a deep breath and said, "I am very grateful

for the explanations, but ı would still prefer not to wear boys' clothing.''

"Oh, for mercy's sake," said Rachel crossly.

Unexpectedly, James came to her rescue. "Don't bully her, Rachel," he said, looking up over the top of his book. "She has tyrannized me ruthlessly since our mother died," he explained to Eloise.

"Well, no one else seemed to have the least influence on you," said his sister in milder tones. "Save for Papa, and he was never home."

James refused to pursue that topic. "Leave her be," he advised. "I have no immediate plans which will require her to ride *ventre à terre* to rescue me from a French prison."

Rachel blushed at this cruelly accurate mockery of her argument in the paddock.

Eloise blushed as well, for a different reason. She could not imagine any circumstance under which she could rescue anyone from anything.

As they went slowly back downstairs, Danielle came hurrying past with an armful of clean linens. She gave her usual curt nod to both Rachel and Eloise and bustled off importantly towards Eloise's bedchamber.

"I've been meaning to ask you—" Rachel started to say hesitantly, but Eloise forestalled her.

"I know," she said with a sigh. "You're going to tell me Danielle isn't really French. Silvio mentioned it as well. I realized it months ago, shortly after my mother engaged her."

Rachel look surprised. "Why have you not dismissed her, then?"

"I'm used to her," was all Eloise said. How could she explain that Danielle was the only link she had with her old life? That every haughty "madame" reminded her of her mother? That a sympathetic maid would have been an invitation to collapse and surrender?

"And you trust her? Even after she came to you using a false name?"

"I should think using a false name would recommend her to you," said Eloise dryly. "After all, it seems to be a family habit."

The Countess of Brieg had finished her letter and was rereading it with considerable satisfaction.

Paris, at the Hôtel Lis, 17 December

> *My dearest James—*
> *I may call you James, may I not? After all, we were not merely friends, even if the exigencies of the war prevented our acquaintance from developing into something more profound. It pleases me to write "James." Such an English name, and I know you enjoy thinking of yourself as English, although in truth, like all your people, you are a wanderer.*
> *For myself, I am now a wanderer as well. Paris is a more congenial home at the moment for a loyal supporter of Napoleon than Austria. I rather suspect, now that I am residing in France, that we may see each other again. Indeed, I devoutly hope so, for I have much to explain, and much to atone for. I will confess that I wronged you—I, too easily persuaded by those around me rather than by my own judgment and my feelings when we were together. Fate, I trust, will bring us together again, as it brought you to me once before.*
>
> > *Until then, I remain, your most*
> > *devoted and affectionate*
> > *Theresa*

French was such an elegant language, she thought. So courteous, so vague, so well suited for implication and innu-endo. This letter was more florid and formal than her normal style, but the occasion required a certain degree of epistolary bravura.

Her brother's malicious suggestion that she write Nathanson to congratulate him on his marriage had first stung, then festered, and finally born fruit. Poisoned fruit, if all went as planned. Her letter made no reference to the wedding—how should she, an innocent languishing in exile, know of that? Best not to mention something she hoped was as distasteful to him as it was to her.

As for trusting fate, she had learned very young that fate sometimes requires a helping hand. She rang for her manservant.

"Show Monsieur Doucet in."

The slender Frenchman had been waiting in the anteroom; he entered the moment Josef opened the door and then kissed her hand with his usual flourish.

She sealed her note and handed it to him. "Could you see that this reaches London as soon as possible? Via the usual channels?"

He bowed.

"I should also like to know of any letters delivered here in Paris from this man"—she pointed to the superscription on the envelope—"or his wife. These are the most likely recipients." She handed him a half sheet of paper with two addresses.

"Carvallo," he said, looking at the first name. "Yes, I know the house." Then he frowned. "But I am desolated, my dear Theresa. I cannot help you in the second case. Jacob Meyer guards his correspondence very closely."

"I suspected as much," she said. "Let us have both houses watched, nevertheless. Perhaps my quarry will even appear in person. A young man, half a head taller than you, dark hair, cropped short, very dark eyes, pronounced limp."

"Such a man should be easy to spot," was his comment.

"Look first for the limp," she advised. "He is nearly as proficient at avoiding notice as you are, Raoul."

"Should I be jealous?" he asked lightly, laying one hand on her shoulder for a moment.

"Certainly not." Her blue eyes were wide with indignation.

"Not yet, at any rate," she added under her breath as Doucet withdrew.

Eight

"Well, he lasted longer than I thought he would," said Rachel philosophically. "All afternoon and evening yesterday, and most of this morning." They had taken luncheon up to an increasingly restless James, and now the two women had been sent downstairs with the irritable command, "Find me something else to read before I go mad with boredom."

"Are these all the books?" asked Eloise, scanning the two narrow bookcases.

"Yes. I have a few of my own upstairs, but James detests novels and memoirs," Rachel said. "It's a poor excuse for a library," she added gloomily. "I leased this house from a widowed naval officer, and I cherish a secret hope that he took dozens of books with him to sea, because I would hate to think this is all he and his family ever read."

"These are all about horses and hunting," said Eloise, scanning the spines. "Wait, here are some on the bottom—" She bent over to see better and caught her breath. "Oh!" She could not quite suppress her giggle.

"What is it?"

Eloise handed her three large books, one by one.

"*Letters to Young Ladies*," read Rachel. "By a Miss Hannah More. And this is"—she opened it to the title page—"*The female worthies, or, memoirs of the most illustrious ladies, of all ages and nations, who have been eminently distinguished for their magnanimity, learning, genius, virtue, piety, and other excellent endowments.* What a mouthful! No wonder they did not put the title on the binding. I suppose the third is more of the same?"

"*Mrs. Pilkington's Moral and Instructive Examples for Young Ladies.*"

"I don't think James will care for these," said Rachel cautiously. "Or did you wish to borrow them for yourself?"

Eloise jerked upright in horror. "Good heavens, no!"

Rachel looked relieved. "Why did you find them of such interest, then?"

She blushed. "This will sound very silly, but I must confess that I had been picturing you languishing here with an elderly companion who read to you every evening from the Countess of Carlisle's maxims. And then I saw these ..." Her voice trailed off and she looked doubtfully at Rachel, hoping she had not offended her. But to her relief, Rachel burst out laughing.

"I suppose Aunt Lucy is acting as my companion," she conceded. "But it feels more as though I am *her* companion. She has a way of taking charge of affairs which reminds me of my uncle." She stooped down and pushed the three books back into the gaping hole on the bottom shelf. "I am happy to report, however, that she has not yet attempted to read any of those volumes to me. Let's try the other case."

Eloise had already moved over. "Chess," she announced. She tilted her head and looked at the next shelf. "More chess," she said, surprised.

"James might like that," said Rachel. "He used to play quite a bit. At any rate, we've no better fare to offer him. Perhaps I'll send up to London for some histories, if he behaves himself."

They selected four books and trooped back upstairs, where their offering was grudgingly accepted by the invalid.

"Is there a chess set here?" he asked absently, opening the slimmest of the volumes.

"Yes, I think I saw one. Perhaps more than one." Rachel hurried away.

"Would you like to play?" asked Eloise hesitantly.

He looked up, brightening. "I had not thought of that. I meant only to have a board to look at positions while I read, but I would not mind a game. Do you know how to play?" He looked at her intently. "I don't mean knowing the rules, and how the pieces move. Do you know how to *play*?"

She shook her head. "Perhaps Rachel could be your opponent," she offered.

He laughed. "No, we would quarrel dreadfully."

Rachel reappeared with a gleaming set of ebony and white pieces and an elegant board whose white squares were inlaid mother-of-pearl. "There is one pawn missing," she said breathlessly. "I've brought up a small stone to use in its place. Silvio is fetching you the table from my room."

"Have him bring a chair, as well," said James, pushing himself up to a sitting position. "Eloise and I are going to play."

"Better you than me," said Rachel frankly, addressing Eloise. "He always points out every error I make, in the most insufferably patronizing way. And then I lose my temper, and then he loses his temper, and we never finish the game."

"I'll be a model of courtesy and patience," he promised. He looked young and eager, like a schoolboy who had been let out of lessons early, and he set all the pieces out carefully on the board while Silvio fetched the chair. The bed was rather high, so that Eloise found herself looking up at him once she sat down, even when he slid back down onto his side.

They played two games. He gave her a pawn for the first game, and even so, it was a rout. "I didn't think a pawn would be sufficient,'' was his only comment as he set the pieces back up. ''Let's try a rook.''

Eloise watched dispiritedly as he captured piece after piece without appearing to notice the absence of his second rook. She started to imagine that the chessmen were great siege engines, rumbling down the files as they attacked. Her poor king seemed to wince as each warrior fell. At least this time she managed to stage a rudimentary defense.

''Better,'' he said as he swept up the mound of white pieces, then looked at her closely. ''Had enough?''

Her head was spinning with the unfamiliar effort of visualizing move and countermove. She had only played with her father, who had never himself learned more than the rudiments.

''I can go back to my book,'' he said, reading her expression correctly. But he sounded wistful.

''What about a card game?'' was her counterproposal, endorsed immediately. ''Let me see if I can find a deck.'' Five minutes later she returned in triumph. ''It's old and hideously ugly, but they are all here,'' she announced. ''I counted. What would you like to play? Casino? Commerce?''

James had moved the chessboard up onto the other side of the bed, beside the little stack of books, and he watched as she laid the cards out on the table, preparing to shuffle.

''Stop,'' he said suddenly. ''Let me see the cards.''

Puzzled, she scooped them back into a stack and handed them over.

''We can't play,'' he said flatly after inspecting them. ''Not with these, at any rate. Was this the only deck?''

''The only one Rachel and I could find, yes,'' she said, feeling disappointed. She knew she could hold her own better at cards; at school she had been a steady winner during the forbidden late-night games. ''What is wrong with them?''

He picked up two dozen cards, scanned them briefly, and then set them out on the table. It was a well-worn set, probably ten years old or more, with crudely colored wood-block designs. Eloise watched as he flipped each card over. Royalty disappeared, turning their proud faces to the table; red and black pips gave way to torn and yellowing cardboard backs. She surveyed the shabby rows of blank rectangles.

"Move them around without turning them over and point to a card," he said.

She pushed the cards carefully into new rows and then pointed.

"Spade ten."

She turned it over. It was the spade ten.

Silently she pointed again.

"Knave of diamonds." The leering face of the red-headed knave looked up at her when she turned it over.

She looked at him, looked at the deck, then realized that many of the cards were damaged. Both the cards she had selected had small pieces missing from one edge. The knave had a wedge-shaped nick on one short side; the spade ten a slit in one corner. This time she carefully pointed to a card with no obvious defects.

He shook his head. "Not enough undamaged ones left. I can do it by elimination. It is either the spade queen, the club three, or the heart seven."

It was the club three.

"How can you *do* that?" she said, a bit stunned.

"It's a skill like any other. If you are taught it, you learn it." He stared off into space. "My father used to take me to inns, walk me through the stable once, and then take me outside and ask for the colors and markings of every horse. When I was older I was expected to know which horse was in which stall, as well. Third stall from the end on left, chestnut with blaze."

"I could hold my cards under the table."

"I would still see all your discards, and every card you chose from the stack." He leaned back against his pillows and grinned. "Of course, if you would care to play piquet for a small stake, I would be happy to oblige."

She laughed. "What sort of stake?"

"A guinea a point."

"You'll beggar me," she said in mock horror. A light-headed exhilaration was taking hold of her; his bantering tone, his quick smile were intoxicating her. "Or rather, you'll beggar yourself. It's your money, after all."

"A kiss, then. Just one, if I win the game."

"And if I win?" she managed, her heart suddenly beating faster.

"You won't," he said with certainty. "Not at piquet, when I can know so many of the cards."

Her stubborn streak asserted itself. "It's cruel to leave me without any hope at all," she pointed out. "If I cannot win, why should you mind?"

"What would you like then?" He eyed her speculatively. "Earrings? The ones you have on now are quite nice." He reached over and touched one dangling pearl. She had forgotten that she had them on; Danielle had insisted. She realized suddenly that this was the first time she had ever heard him comment on her appearance, and she felt a slow flush climb up her neck.

"No jewels," she said firmly. She thought quickly. She knew that naming any of the things she really wanted would break the delicate truce between them. His escort to a play. Dinner home together two nights running. A promise not to annul the marriage, so that she could tell him she was not pregnant. If those were the stakes, she thought, she would sit up all night and memorize every wrinkle on the back of every card. But those were stakes in a different game, a game she had been losing until this afternoon. "An introduction to Lord Wellington," she said finally.

He looked pleased. "I do have his acquaintance," he said as he pulled the lower cards out of the deck. "Although only through my father and my uncle. But if by some miracle you do win, you will have to wait to collect until he returns to England."

She started off well, mostly thanks to a very fortunate

deal of her initial cards. After that it was all downhill. It only took two hands for him to claim victory.

"You cheated," she said, laughing. He had been calling his tricks before he played them, to prove he knew what she held in her hand.

"You agreed to the game knowing I would cheat," he pointed out. "Come over here, or I'll have to break my word to my sister and get out of bed."

Suddenly very nervous, she got up and went over to the bed.

"I can still introduce you to Wellington, if you like," he said slowly. "You were a good sport. I have a fatal tendency to prove my superiority at the expense of my friends and kinfolk." He took her hand and drew her closer.

Hoping he could not feel her trembling, she leaned over and kissed him very quickly on the cheek.

"Try again," he advised. "Kisses on the cheek are not accepted as payment for gambling debts."

She had lowered her eyes, because she did not want him to see her expression. Blindly she bent over the bed. He pulled her head down gently, his hand sliding through her hair. Then he kissed her, a slow, searching kiss. She heard him take a deep breath.

"Why, James, how *gauche*." It was Rachel's voice, very cheerful and very unwelcome. "Kissing your wife! At half past three in the afternoon! I would not have thought you so unfashionable."

Eloise straightened up at once, and both of them stared at the invader. She seemed to realize that something was wrong, for she said hurriedly, "I came to tell James that Silvio has contrived a pair of crutches for him, and he may come down to dinner." She paused and looked at him sternly. "*If* you are very careful. And no shoes or stockings on the injured leg, just bandages."

"Agreed," he said, with a shade too much heartiness.

The guarded look was back, Eloise saw. And she had seen something else. He had been as surprised as she by

Rachel's interruption. But his reaction had been relief, not disappointment.

Eloise settled into a routine, a rather pleasant one. An early-morning ride with Rachel, Lady Ingram, and sometimes Caroline. She was still nervous, but Rachel kept her word and never pushed her beyond what she was willing to try. Eloise herself did not see much progress, but Rachel assured her that it was there. She had some days off, though, because sometimes it was too cold even for Rachel. On those days Lady Ingram would stomp furiously from the breakfast room muttering about "young women today," but she would not go out, either. Danielle told her the local servants were saying they could not remember such a cold December, and she believed it.

After riding, Rachel would go off to give Caroline lessons, and Eloise would sit with James. Sometimes they played cards, but only games like beggar-my-neighbor, which relied purely on luck. Sometimes she read to him; she had discovered a book they both liked, a description of a voyage to the West Indies. Sometimes they chatted. She was careful to keep the conversation light. He was rarely willing to talk about himself, so the talk was usually about something neutral, like music, or about Eloise. For some reason he was fascinated by her experiences at school in Bristol, and peppered her with questions. Were the other girls friendly? Had anyone mentioned her religion? What happened at chapel? He teased her about the drawing master until she confessed that he was nearly sixty and bald as an egg.

Luncheon with the two other women was followed by a rest, which she needed, and then she and Rachel usually spent some of the afternoon with James and some with Lady Ingram. One day James, with Silvio's assistance, invited all of them (including Caroline and William) to tea in his room. He treated Lady Ingram and Caroline like visiting empresses, to their great delight, addressing them formally as "madame'' and ''mademoiselle'' and apologizing for not rising to greet them.

Dinner was an early, informal affair. James came down on his makeshift crutches and Silvio served, since, as Rachel said candidly, it was Silvio or the kitchen maid, and Silvio did not drop the serving tongs. After dinner James was permitted to join the ladies in the drawing room for a while, and then he and Lady Ingram retired early while Eloise and Rachel sat by the fire and sewed or read. Rachel was, in fact, embroidering a cap for the baby. ''It's evidently a family tradition,'' she explained. ''Aunt Lucy made it clear that a Drayton baby without a cap embroidered by its mother was unthinkable. I decided to start on it right away, because it may take me months to get it right. I rip out more than I stitch.'' This confession gave Eloise a secret and guilty pleasure. At least there was one thing she did better than Rachel.

On the third day, the routine underwent a slight alteration. James had been getting more and more irritable. Books and card games were clearly beginning to pall as compensations for enforced bed rest. The much-tried Silvio had taken to hiding in the cellar, and meals were now sent up with the younger maids in the hope that James's chivalry would prevent attacks on a helpless innocent.

Eloise and Rachel met that morning's innocent coming down with the breakfast tray as they returned from their ride.

''How is Mr. Meyer today, Sally?'' asked Eloise.

''He's—he's a bit cross, ma'am,'' said the girl hesitantly. ''I'm sure it's his wound paining him, of course,'' she added, blushing.

''Of course,'' agreed Rachel blandly.

But after the maid had vanished belowstairs, she looked at Eloise. ''I predict trouble,'' she said. ''James has always been a terrible patient.''

''It cannot be easy for an active, healthy young man to lie in bed all day,'' Eloise pointed out.

Rachel sighed. "You're right. He'll need to fly out at someone, and better us than the poor maid. Shall we beard him in his den now, or later?"

But when they ventured cautiously into the corner bedroom, James did not attack. Whether by instinct or by some calculated plan, he hit on a strategy which was difficult to resist: humility. The dark eyes were pleading, his posture that of a suppliant.

"Rachel, let me go riding with you tomorrow," he begged. "I'll stay back with Eloise. She only goes at a walk; I'll keep my injured foot out of the stirrup."

"I'll have you know I'm trotting *and* cantering, thank you," said Eloise indignantly. She had only cantered once and had held her breath the entire time, but she trusted that by the time James was out of bed her statement would be closer to the truth.

"James, it's only four more days," said Rachel. "You know perfectly well riding is probably worse for your ankle than walking."

"But you might need me," he argued desperately. "Suppose you were attacked by some of Meillet's thugs?"

Eloise thought at first he was jesting, then saw he was in earnest.

"James is exaggerating; pay him no mind," Rachel advised Eloise. "It's true that there is a French official named Claude Meillet who has sworn vengeance on my father and brother, and he used to send men to spy on us, but the sort of greasy tavern-loafer he usually hires would be very conspicuous in rural Kent. I haven't seen anyone here since I arrived."

"That could change," persisted James. "Especially now I am here. It was usually me they were following, after all."

"Even in the unlikely event of a sudden invasion by French hirelings, we still can manage without you on our rides," said Rachel. "We have Samuels. And I have my pistol."

"You have a pistol?" asked Eloise, staring at Rachel in disbelief.

Brother and sister stared back, equally shocked.

"You don't?" James said, astonished.

"Of course not! What would I need with a pistol?" She looked at James, then Rachel, and realized once again that she was now in a different world. Of course the Meyers would have pistols and blunderbusses and heaven knows what else. And would know how to use them.

"Do you know how to fire a gun at all?" he asked bluntly. "Any gun?"

She shook her head.

"Well, there you are, James," said Rachel. "The answer to your pleas for relief from bed rest. You may get up for an hour this afternoon and teach Eloise how to load and fire a gun."

"Anything else you fancy the wife of a spy needs to know?" asked Eloise sarcastically. "Forgery? Poisoning? Burgling?"

To her surprise, they took her seriously.

"Forgery cannot be taught very easily," said James. "One either has the knack or not. But it might be useful for you to know how to pick a lock." Then he saw Eloise's expression. "We'll start with the shooting lessons," he said hastily.

From then on, she and James went out behind the stables every afternoon and practiced loading and firing a small pistol. Eloise did not like loud noises, or sudden noises, or inanimate objects which moved on their own. Firing a pistol unfortunately involved all three of these unpleasant things. But she was beginning to understand that she might in fact need to know how to ride a horse and fire a gun, and she attacked the shooting lessons with the same grim resolve which got her into the saddle every morning. Her one consolation was the stamping of hooves from the stable every time she fired. Rachel had told her that the horses did not like the sound of gunfire, and with each crack of the gun she secretly hoped that she was paying back her gelding for the many anxious moments he gave her.

She said as much one afternoon to James, and he chuckled. At first he had been content simply to be out of doors and upright. But he gradually found himself drawn into the drama from Eloise's point of view, watching the small, determined face frowning in concentration as she measured powder, tamped down ball and wadding, and steeled herself for the recoil. He rejoiced with her the first time she hit the target twice in a row. He advised her on sighting, stance, and hand placement. When the hammer caught her thumb, he wrapped it up tightly in his handkerchief, and they walked back to the house laughing because her hand was so small in comparison to the bulky lump of white linen.

"I shouldn't like to face you with that pistol in your hand," he said as he leaned on one crutch to open the door for her.

She looked up at him. "But my aim is still dreadful."

"There are many women who can shoot more accurately but are far less dangerous than you."

"Why?"

"Because you would actually fire the gun," he said, remembering her expression as she sighted. The determination he had seen there was in fact a little unsettling.

On Wednesday night, the last night of James's enforced rest, Lady Ingram had retired even earlier than usual, and three younger residents of the house were sitting companionably by the fire. James was deep in yet another of the chess books, looking back and forth from the page to the pieces arrayed before him. This was the second set Rachel had remembered—a small table with the chessboard inlaid as parquet on the top.

"Would you like to have another game?" Eloise asked when he closed the book and began to replace the pieces he had removed. "I think I could provide a bit more of a challenge now. In fact, we could try our wager again."

He raised one eyebrow. "Same stakes? And the usual handicap?"

She nodded and held out her hand for his rook. For one moment she toyed with the idea of simply letting herself lose and taking consolation in her enjoyment of the forfeit. But pride won out. Taking her place across the table, she adjusted her pawns so that they were neatly in line, took a deep breath, and made her first move.

It was a very quick game. By the time James realized what she was doing, it was too late; she had doggedly exchanged off piece after piece until she was left with rook and king versus his king. It took her a little while to maneuver him back to the edge of the board, but when she did, he reached out with one finger and toppled his own king.

"Well done," he said, clearly surprised. He looked at her. "That was planned, not blind luck. What happened?"

"I read a bit of one of the books," she admitted. "I only managed a few chapters, but when I found the section describing this strategy I realized it would work perfectly. The book said that once you were up a large piece like a rook or a queen, you should trade captures and take advantage of it."

"Which book?"

She frowned. "Pruitt? Pratt?"

"Yes, Pratt. *Theory of Chess.* I own it. Let's see how far you read." He set up the pieces again and handed over his queen rook.

This time he was aware of her goals and defended grimly, forcing her to exchange her major pieces first and conserving his pawns, hoping to queen one. But with an extra piece she could both guard her king and capture his would-be queens. In the end she pursued him once more down to his end of the board and chased his king into a corner with her two remaining men—a king and a bishop.

He sighed with relief. "Saved. You didn't read this far."

She peered at the board, puzzled. "I shan't win this time? Can I not capture your king after your next move?"

"There is no next move for me," he informed her. "It's stalemate. You've driven my king into the corner, yes, but it's my move and I have no legal moves. Players are not allowed to move their kings into check. And *you* cannot move, because it is not your turn."

"I see," she said slowly, looking at her pieces. It was true: his king could not move. One space forward, and her king would capture; one space sideways and her bishop was waiting. "Do you win the wager then?" She suddenly hoped he did, although with Rachel looking on she doubted whether the result would be as promising as last time.

"No. Neither one of us wins."

"That isn't much fun," she objected.

He laughed. "Greedy girl. We've each won once; can't you accept a draw? You've more than earned your introduction to Old Hookey. I shan't forget to arrange it. And don't be too charming when you do meet him," he added in a tone of mock warning. "He has a partiality for attractive married ladies."

"James!" said Rachel, raising her head from her book. "Isn't that a bit disrespectful, considering—" Then she looked at the clock and gasped. "What a wretched nurse I am! You disobedient boy, you were supposed to be back upstairs two hours ago!"

With a start Eloise realized that their second game had taken over an hour.

The unrepentant James struggled to his feet as Rachel hastily rang for Silvio. "Madam strategist," he said, bowing to Eloise while balancing on the crutches, "I salute you and promise you a return match at the earliest opportunity."

"We should go back to cards," she said frankly. "If we can find a newer deck. I don't think I can absorb much more chess than the bit I tried on you tonight. My head feels like cotton batting. I shall dream of rooks for weeks."

"I'll send Silvio out to buy us some cards tomorrow,"

he promised. "Though you may find that chess indigestion dissipates after a few days, leaving an appetite for more." His smile was so warm that she inadvertently took a step forward and smiled back. That was when she learned that it was possible for someone to walk backwards on crutches. Quickly.

"He loves to play games," Rachel said absently as Silvio led his charge off towards the staircase. "He made me learn chess and draughts and backgammon and every card game in existence, and although he was much younger than I was, he beat me three times out of four at any game which was not pure luck. I hated it. He's very fortunate to have someone like you for his wife." She paused, struck by an idea. "I haven't yet given the two of you a wedding gift. Perhaps I'll order you a chess set. I'm told Lund's, in Cornhill, makes very nice ivory ones."

A chess set would be quite an appropriate wedding gift, thought Eloise as she gathered up her mending and made her way up to her bedchamber. A chess set with the pieces set up as she had last seen them: the black king, cornered, afraid to come out of hiding. The white attacker, unable to move until the king does. Stalemate.

Nine

Twelve hours later she would have settled for stalemate.
James was gone. The carefully nurtured truce between them
was broken. It was as though a giant fist had come down
from the sky, shattering the chessboard and flinging the
pieces out the window.

The day had started innocently enough. To celebrate his
liberation, James had been formally invited downstairs for
breakfast by the three women on their return from their
morning ride with Caroline. Eloise was in high spirits; she
had managed two miles with only a few heart-stopping
moments. She charged out of her room and ran down the
stairs once Danielle had buttoned up her cambric gown,
trailing her shawl down her back and laughing as she saw
James motioning for her to go faster.

"Hungry?" she said as he escorted her into the breakfast
room and pulled her chair out. He was favoring his ankle
slightly but not really limping.

"Ravenous," he said promptly. "What would you like?"

"Just a roll, if you please."

He served her and helped himself liberally to a large slice

of boiled beef, a coddled egg, three rolls, and coffee before taking a chair across from her.

"Are you eating enough?" he asked hesitantly. "You seem to be going on very well at the moment, but you must keep up your strength." It was his first reference in a long time to her supposed condition, and it confirmed her in her resolve to confront him. She had lain awake last night, balancing her fear of what might happen with her guilt at her deception. Even now she was forced to acknowledge that her decision to tell him today was not really a repudiation of her cowardly tactics thus far, but a different form of cowardice: he would realize the truth himself sooner or later, and she had decided she preferred to have Rachel as a possible ally when he learned that he was no longer under any obligation to remain married.

His query was a perfect opening, and she wondered how long Rachel would be upstairs changing. The answer arrived the next moment, as Rachel came in, smiling and carrying a pile of letters. She stopped her brother from rising to greet her by pushing him back into his chair and kissing him affectionately on the top of his head.

"Do you forgive me?" she asked, eyes twinkling, as she settled into her chair with her plate.

"You are absolved," he said gravely. "I must admit the ankle is much improved, and I hereby give my word to take better care of myself until it is truly healed." His eye went to the envelopes. "Is that today's post?"

"Yes. As usual, most of it is for Aunt Lucy." She set a small stack of mail aside. "But there's something for Eloise, and two or three for you." She handed Eloise her letter, which was from her mother. It was the usual mix of determinedly cheerful family news and anxious inquiries about when she and James would return to London. Eloise had been fending off attempts by her mother to bring James out to Roehampton; she knew it would be a disaster. But perhaps now she might broach the possibility. She looked over at James.

He was holding his batch of letters, his face white. "Excuse me," he said. "I need—I will return in a moment." He stood up so quickly, his chair fell over behind him. He did not even seem to notice. Like a sleepwalker, he moved to the door, his eyes on the envelopes. His hands were trembling. They heard him mount the stairs very slowly.

Rachel sat openmouthed in dismay, her own letters forgotten.

"What is wrong?" asked Eloise, alarmed.

"I don't know," said Rachel, biting her lip. "I wonder if something has happened to my father—perhaps I should go upstairs and see. They both hate it when I let on that I am anxious, though." Another thought struck her, and she clenched her hands. "Perhaps it is Richard; perhaps they sent the news to James so that he could break it to me in person." She rose, then sat down again.

Eloise had her first glimpse of what it meant to be the wife of a military courier.

"He'll come and tell us," said Rachel, more to herself than to Eloise. "I'll wait. If it had been Papa or Richard, he would have said something right away." She sat staring down at her plate and shredded her roll into tiny pieces.

Lady Ingram came in. She took one look at the pile of envelopes, James's uneaten breakfast, and the two frozen women and said to Rachel, "I'll be upstairs if you need me." Then she discreetly retreated.

James reappeared ten minutes later. He was wearing his coat and carrying a small cloak bag. "I must leave at once," he said, not looking at either of them.

"James, what is it?" Rachel blurted out. "Is it Papa? Richard?"

He blinked, and frowned at her for a moment in bewilderment. "No," he said at last, slowly, as though only then understanding her question. "No, there is nothing for you to be concerned about." He turned and walked out. They heard the front door slam, and the sound of hooves on the gravel of the drive.

Rachel stared after him. "He didn't even say good-bye," she whispered. "Not even to you."

Eloise was well aware of the omission. She felt frightened, and miserable, and confused. Her only consolation was that Rachel was obviously equally upset.

"I'm going to see whether Silvio is still here," said Rachel with sudden decision. "When James is up to no good, he always leaves him behind. Perhaps you are already aware of this."

"Silvio was kind enough to explain it to me, yes," said Eloise.

Rachel didn't bother to ring the bell; she simply went out into the central hall, trailed by Eloise, and shouted. "Not in the house," she said after a minute. "Let's try the stables." But halfway across the rear courtyard they were met by Silvio himself.

"He ordered me to stay here," he said to Rachel, looking troubled. "Said he had to go up to see Colonel White at once."

"It must have been something in one of the letters; do you know what it was?" Rachel asked. Eloise had only a light shawl and Rachel not even that, but they did not notice the cold.

"A letter? He said nothing of any letter, and I did not see one." The valet frowned. "But he would not let me help him pack his bag or put on his coat. He sent me straight out to the stable."

"If you are to stay here, that means you must report to me or to Mrs. Meyer," she said after thinking for a minute.

"To Mrs. Meyer. He said I was to put myself at her disposal."

Rachel looked at Eloise, hoping she understood what to do.

"Go after him," said Eloise at once. "He won't send you back, will he? If you come up with him and explain that I sent you?"

"Normally, no." He sighed. "But then, this is not normal."

Rachel followed him back into the house and up the stairs. Both waited in silence while they watched a dejected Eloise disappear into her own room. Then, with one accord they pushed open the door to James's bedchamber.

Clothing was strewn over the bed. Books had been pushed hastily to one side on the table, knocking over some of the chess pieces. At one edge of the chessboard lay two letters, unopened. Both envelopes were in a clerk's hand and bore all the marks of the British Army bureaucracy.

"What do you think, Miss Rachel?" he said in a worried voice.

She knew what he was asking. "There were three letters. One was a woman's writing."

"It's her," he said gloomily.

"I think so, yes," said Rachel.

He spat.

Rachel agreed with him, but ladies did not spit.

The offices of Colonel R. H. White, acting commander of the Adjutant General's Courier Services (Home Division), were not easy to find. For one thing, they were unmarked and usually located in back corners of otherwise unoccupied corridors. For another thing, they moved frequently. In 1809, when White had begun supervising the London branch of the courier service, the offices were in the Horse Guards. Eighteen months later they were moved out to Greenwich, to allow certain visitors who wished to arrive discreetly more privacy. Recently they had moved again, to the upper floors of an armory housed inside the Tower. It had been decided that security was more important than privacy.

White was a tall, elderly patrician with a perpetual scowl and very large mustaches. When not consulting with Wellington in Portugal or Spain or (currently) France, he sat in his office appearing to do very little besides read reports and deposit them in piles on chairs, tables, or the floor. Through the open door to the inner room, James could see him now, leafing through a slim packet of papers. A map lay unrolled in front of him.

The lieutenant who had received James knocked loudly on the edge of the door. "Captain Nathanson to see you, sir," he announced, as though White would not have heard James arrive and state his business in the outer chamber, ten feet away.

"Have him wait," White said, not looking up.

James, standing a few paces back, groaned inwardly. White was in one of his moods.

This particular lieutenant had only been with White for a few weeks. He coughed. "Beg pardon, sir, but he said it was very urgent."

"Nathanson always says it is very urgent. Have him wait." The colonel raised his head, looked straight past the lieutenant to James, and gave him a cold stare.

"Yes, sir," said the lieutenant hastily, backing away.

James flung himself into a chair across from the lieutenant's desk and directed a concentrated glare at the half-open door.

After a long interval—far longer, James knew, than the time it would have taken White to finish the document he had been reading—a bell rang from inside White's office. The lieutenant jumped up

"You may show Captain Nathanson in," White called out. The aide looked relieved.

James approached the untidy desk and stood awaiting his commander's greeting, normally a growled "What is it?" But White said nothing; he merely looked him over. The look was not friendly.

"Thank you for seeing me, sir," said James at last, somewhat subdued by the unusual intensity of his commander's scowl.

"I thought you were on leave," snapped White.

"I—I am reporting back in, sir."

White grunted. ''Lieutenant Moore said you had something urgent for me.''

''Yes, sir. I've had word from a contact in France. At the earliest opportunity, I think it would be wise for me to go over there myself.''

''You're in no shape to go to France,'' said White testily. ''And luckily for me and for you, I've no need to send you there at the moment.''

''My ankle is much better, sir. My sister treated it this past week.''

White simply raised his eyebrows, and James flushed. He was well aware that his injury was not the reason his frequent requests for leaves in the past two months had been granted. That he had been given no assignments of any significance since his return from Vienna. Only to Evrett had he put into words what he knew, and what his father and White knew: he was not himself. But now he had a chance, a chance to be whole again, to see her and let her explain.

''What is the nature of this information you have received? Who is your contact? Where in France?''

Normally a fluent liar, James found his mind completely blank. ''I'm sorry, sir,'' he said after a moment. ''I'm not at liberty to say.''

''So,'' White said mildly, ''you storm in here at four in the afternoon two days before Christmas, demanding to be sent over to an unknown destination in France, to speak with an unknown informant about an unspecified matter of great urgency.''

Put like that it sounded rather implausible, he realized with a sinking heart.

White's voice suddenly rose to a roar. ''Who is in command here, *Captain* Nathanson? Do you think the courier service is for your personal amusement? That because you are the nephew of Eli Roth you can do as you please?''

''No, sir,'' he said, swallowing. He raised his eyes to meet White's. ''I understand your concern, sir. I will ask only that you consider me for the next assignment involving travel to northern France.''

''Very well,'' said White after a long pause. ''I will take your request under consideration. But let me make one thing clear: if you make any attempt to go over there without my express permission, I will have you court-martialed.''

He meant it, James realized.

''So long as you are here, however, you can make yourself useful.'' He tossed over a folder. ''Toulouse cipher. We think they are routine, but it never hurts to be sure. Translate them. Give them to Moore when you are done.''

''Yes, sir,'' he said, relieved to have something concrete to do. But when he had retreated down the hall to the cubby he shared with LeSueur, he found that the letters and numbers swam on the page in front of him. It was an easy cipher; he could normally decode it from memory. With a sigh he went back down the hall and signed the codebooks out from the locked cupboard next to Moore's desk. Then he returned to his desk, sat down, and flipped open the book. For one moment he thought longingly back to the past week with Eloise, when his brain had been working again and the black fog had lifted. It had descended again, darker and more paralyzing than ever. If they were playing cards or chess now, she would win every game. He shook himself. Nostalgia would not help. Grimly he pulled out the first dispatch and set himself to concentrate.

White had not missed the significance of the return visit to fetch the codebook. When he had heard Nathanson's voice in the anteroom demanding admission in his usual arrogant manner, he had hoped, for a brief moment, that the marriage had worked a cure. But one glance at the drawn face and feverish eyes had told him that in fact things were worse. Now, after a moment's reflection, he summoned Moore into his office.

''Close the door,'' he ordered.

Puzzled, the lieutenant complied. White rarely closed his door.

"Do you know Nathanson's batman? Italian fellow, name of Silvio."

"Yes, sir. I know the man."

"Did he come in with the captain?"

"No, sir."

"A bad sign," growled White. "Keep an eye out for him. And get him in here to see me without Nathanson's knowledge, if possible."

Two hours later, Silvio had confirmed White's fears. A letter from a woman followed at once by a request to be sent to France—it could only mean one thing. The Countess of Brieg had invited Captain James Nathanson to come and pay her a visit in Paris.

Informed that Monsieur Doucet wished to speak with her briefly, the countess had excused herself from her guests and stepped into the dimly lit small salon.

"You look quite elegant, Raoul," she said. He was dressed all in black, clearly on his way to some formal affair, and his jeweled buckles gleamed in the candlelight.

"My man reports that your letter has been delivered," he said after he had paid her the usual compliments.

"I knew I could count on you," the countess said with approval. "And the apothecary?"

"He awaits word from me."

"Tell him to proceed."

Doucet coughed. "He warned me that he cannot guarantee the results will not be fatal."

"Madame Carvallo is an old woman," she said coldly. "And a well-known agitator against our emperor. You are very nice of a sudden, Raoul."

"I have met her," he said almost apologetically.

"And I have met the captain. Indeed, we enjoyed a charming flirtation last summer. That did not stop me from turning him over to the *Sûreté* when I realized he was a menace to the imperial armies.''

"How very dutiful of you,'' he said dryly.

"Of course, occasionally duty and pleasure run side by side,'' she pointed out with a smile. "As when I was introduced to you, my dear Raoul.''

"*Merci du compliment.*'' He added casually after a moment, "And what are your plans for the poor young man this time? Duty, pleasure, or both?''

Her smile took on a malicious edge. "I haven't decided yet. He is rather straitlaced, like so many of his people. It is quite amusing.''

He was wise enough not to pursue the topic further, but as he was shown out of the ornate hôtel, he muttered between his teeth, "I think I should like to kill this James Meyer.''

Ten

Signora—Signor Meyer is dicoding despacches for Col. White. I remayne here with him. I managed to see the envelaupe and I bilieve it is her writing. The letter itself he guardes closely. S.

Very late in the evening, Rachel finally received this message from Silvio, delivered by a weary and thoroughly chilled runner from her uncle's bank. "He found him," she said in relieved tones.

Eloise looked up from her sketching. She was attempting to copy a color plate of rare birds from the West Indies book. She had been working on it all day and had now discarded ten ruined sheets of very expensive drawing paper. "Who found whom?"

"Silvio found James. He is fine." She peered at the creased page. "I can't quite make this out; Silvio's handwriting is a bit erratic and his English spelling even more so. Oh, wait," she added, sounding surprised. "James actually did go and report to Colonel White. Silvio says—" She broke off. "Never mind," she said hastily, "it doesn't matter. The important thing is, he's safe, and for once he doesn't seem bent on defying orders and doing something he'll regret later."

He already did something he regrets, thought Eloise. *He got married.* She stared down at her drawing. Paradoxically, the knowledge that James was not in danger made her feel even worse. An enormous wave of desolation flooded her, and she suddenly realized that she was about to cry. The tears were pushing forward, unstoppable and impossible to conceal.

"I—I believe I will retire now," she choked, and fled. By the time she reached her room, she was sobbing, so miserable that she did not even care what Danielle thought. But instead of the disdainful looks and disapproving sniffs she was expecting, the maid was unexpectedly quiet. She sat Eloise down by the fire and pressed clean handkerchiefs into her hand. It took three of them. Only after she saw that her mistress was more composed did she say calmly, "I will fetch madame a cold cloth for her face."

When the door opened again, Danielle did not have a wet cloth. She had Rachel. "Madame will excuse me," she said firmly, "but Monsieur Meyer took the liberty of telling Madame Drayton and myself that you were expecting a *petit pacquet*, and charged us to make sure you were well cared for."

Rachel, looking anxious, said in agitated tones as Danielle withdrew, "Please don't be offended. I don't wish to intrude, but we both thought you should not be left alone, and I know how easy it is for women in our condition to become overwrought." She had tears in her own eyes to prove her point.

"Oh, my Lord," gasped Eloise, starting to cry again. "He *told* you?"

"Of course, it is still early," stammered Rachel. "Very early. He said you were not quite certain yet, but that it looked very likely. I am sure he has not told many other people—he was worried about the riding lessons, although he should know those stories are just old wives' tales." She glanced at Eloise, who had rather an odd expression on her face, and continued bravely, "He made me promise there would be no jumping and no galloping. He sounded just like Richard, in fact. I suppose when it is one's own baby in question one cannot be too careful—"

"There *is* no baby," interrupted Eloise. Her voice rose in despair. "*There is no baby*. There has never been a baby." She added bitterly, "At this rate, there never will be a baby. He won't touch me."

"What?" said Rachel faintly. She sat down with a little plop on the other chair.

"On our wedding night," Eloise said, enunciating each word very clearly, "your brother concluded that I was carrying another man's child and that the marriage had been arranged to conceal my disgrace. He generously offered to stand by me and acknowledge the child as his."

There was a long silence.

"It's not true, is it?" asked Rachel hesitantly.

"Of course it isn't!" flared Eloise. "It's the most ridiculous thing I've ever heard. I've never even *kissed* anyone, save your brother! I've never waltzed with a man, or been alone with a man, or sent a letter to a man, or done anything improper whatsoever! I am revoltingly well behaved! I almost despise myself now for not being more adventurous!"

"Why ever did he believe such a thing, if it is not the case?" asked Rachel, bewildered.

"I don't know." Eloise slumped down again, her anger fading back into dejection. "He produced this theory out of thin air the moment he walked into the bedchamber." Then she paused and acknowledged, "Perhaps not completely out of thin air. Some of my relatives treated him dreadfully during the wedding, as much as said that they could not understand why I was marrying beneath me."

"But surely by now you have told him the truth?"

"How can I?" said Eloise wretchedly. "He is never home. He runs away the moment I try to speak with him. The first night I didn't say anything because I didn't quite believe what had happened. And the next morning he left at dawn. It's been like that ever since—every time I summon up the courage to talk with him, he slips off and vanishes for a day or two days or a week. Or he is sitting there brooding over the scars on his ankle, and I daren't speak because he will think the reason I am suddenly agreeing to an annulment is physical repulsion."

Rachel frowned. "Agreeing to what annulment?"

"Ah, yes, I forgot that part of the story." Eloise gave a twisted little smile. "Just before he decided I was soiled goods, he announced that the marriage was a mistake and he wished to have it annulled. The only reason we are still husband and wife is that he believes I need the protection of his name for my bastard."

"Oh, James," said Rachel with a sigh. She looked at Eloise helplessly. "He's not really like that at all."

Two weeks ago, Eloise would have credited that remark to sisterly affection. But the past eight days had given her a glimpse of another person. "I don't know why I've let it go on this long," she said dispiritedly. "I suppose you think me a coward. And I am. I'm afraid to tell James I've deceived him for so long. I'm afraid to face my parents if the marriage fails, after they humbled themselves to your uncle. I'm afraid my father will marry me off next to someone dreadful. So I play along—or at least, I do not contradict him when he tells me to eat more breakfast." She stared down at the sodden handkerchief in her lap. "But of course, now I have spoken with you, I will go up to London tomorrow and put an end to this farce."

"Oh, no!" said Rachel, shocked. "You must not!"

It was Eloise's turn to look bewildered. "You don't want me to tell him the truth?"

Ever since she had received Silvio's note, Rachel had thought about what to say to James's wife. She had asked herself whether, if it were Richard, she would want to know. And she had not been able to answer that question. So she hedged. She would tell her enough to help her understand, at least.

"He won't know what to do with the truth," Rachel said bluntly. "He cannot tell at the moment whether up is up or the sky is blue. Last summer . . ." She hesitated. "When he was captured, it hit him very hard. Not just the injury, or the brutal way he was treated, but something that for him was worse, in a way. You must understand: he was there in uniform, officially accredited to both the Prussian command and the Austrian court. He had Silvio with him, and Captain Southey, another officer in the courier service. So the French could not attack him openly. Instead, someone James admired greatly"—Rachel blessed the absence of masculine and feminine endings on the English indefinite article—"a member of the Austrian nobility, lured him to a remote villa. There interrogators from the *Sûreté* were waiting—including Claude Meillet, his archenemy. And ever since then, he has been like a man walking in darkness."

She paused to let this sink in. "Now, if you tell him the truth," she said, "tell him now, while he is still reeling from that betrayal, that there is no child, what do you expect will happen?"

"I don't know," confessed Eloise. "I haven't wanted to think about it."

"Well, let us consider it logically, as my father would say." Rachel sat back in her chair. "First possibility. Since he returned from Vienna, James has been sometimes better, sometimes worse. Mostly worse. But suppose he has recovered a bit from whatever set him off this morning by the time you see him, and is more like his usual self. Which is to say, often rather arrogant and hot-tempered. He will be very angry that you have made a fool of him, and he might well be tempted to pursue the annulment. Indeed, he might in the heat of the moment say something which will make *you* so angry that you will want nothing better than to be rid of him.''

"Second possibility. James has not only recovered a bit but is in a gentle and reasonable mood—which does happen more than you might think," she added dryly. "He would understand why you acted as you did, and the two of you could decide together if you wanted to remain married. But since he has been so unhappy recently and thinks himself maimed, he might well feel that it would be best for you to be free of him.''

Eloise remembered his reaction to her glimpse of his scars that night in the attic and nodded slowly.

"Third possibility. James is still in his ghostly trance. He seems to be wary of anything or anyone which might break the spell, hence the constant attempts to run away from you and from Silvio. He will seize this excuse to get rid of you, at least, so that he can enjoy his stupor in peace.''

Rachel looked straight at Eloise. "In other words, it is very likely that if you tell him now you will be Miss Bernal again shortly. And that would be a great pity.''

"Why?''

"Because James is falling in love with you. He just doesn't realize it yet.'' Rachel gave a reminiscent little smile. "I should have confined him to bed for a fortnight.''

"And what if I am not in love with him?'' asked Eloise stubbornly, although her heart had given a little leap at Rachel's confident pronouncement.

"You are, though. Otherwise you would have told him by now that you were not pregnant,'' said Rachel. "More logic, you see.''

James sent down a brief note, apologizing for his abrupt departure. But he made no mention of returning to Kent, and Eloise abandoned her notion of going to London. Confronting him seemed to require a force of will that she did not have at the moment. Instead she floated from day to day in a kind of limbo, noting events without really feeling as though they were happening.

There was her first fall from horseback, a sideways tumble which caused more embarrassment than discomfort. In fact, it seemed to mark some sort of milestone in her riding lessons, which went markedly better afterwards. She still gritted her teeth the entire time she was in the saddle, but at least she had learned to confine the tension to her teeth and keep her shoulders and hands loose. "Just don't let any gentlemen who are courting you take you riding," warned Rachel, teasing her. "You look like a Gorgon once you're mounted."

There was Christmas, an awkward and lonely day for Eloise and Rachel. Lady Ingram's normal frankness deserted her. The holiday was barely mentioned, and when she and the servants and children drove off in two carriages and a wagon to church on Christmas morning, she blurted out, "Happy Christmas!" with a scarlet face and then slammed the door to the carriage without waiting for an answer. Rachel looked wretchedly miserable all day.

Then there was the terrifying morning when Rachel suddenly cried out, clutching her stomach. The household came to a standstill; doctors were summoned in frantic haste from Canterbury and Sandwich, and Lady Ingram, white-faced, sat holding Rachel's hand while she lay gasping in pain on a sofa. But then Eloise began to feel ill, and Rachel's maid Maria, and the footman, and by the time the doctors arrived nearly half the household were staggering between their beds and the water closet, doubled over with cramps. The fishmonger was singled out as the culprit, but everyone was so relieved that nothing had happened to the Drayton baby that he was forgiven almost instantly. Moreover, Danielle, who had not been a favorite with the Knowlton servants, had done heroic service during the emergency, and there was a noticeable thaw belowstairs once everyone had recovered.

It was Danielle who came in late one afternoon when Eloise was resting on her bed, feeling dreamy and lazy. She had confided to Rachel that morning that it was almost as though she herself were starting to believe that she was carrying a child. ''Maria has been cosseting me,'' she explained, ''and I suspect someone has hinted to Lady Ingram, because she gives that little satisfied nod of hers sometimes when she thinks I am not looking, that same nod she gives when you put your hand on your stomach.''

''Madame,'' Danielle announced, ''a curricle is coming up the drive, and if I am not mistaken, the driver is monsieur.'' She picked up Eloise's hairbrush, clearly expecting that this news would send her mistress straight to the dressing table for a hasty repair job. But instead Eloise bounced off the bed, her lethargy instantly gone, and ran over to the window. By standing all the way to one side, she could just see the middle section of the drive. There was indeed a curricle coming up towards the house, with a familiar tall figure holding the reins. Next to him was a passenger— Silvio, she decided.

Perhaps it was his tense posture; perhaps it was the sudden, unannounced arrival; perhaps it was just a premonition— but she knew immediately that something was wrong. She did not even stop to pull on her slippers. In stocking feet, without a shawl, hair flying, she ran downstairs, yanked open the heavy front door, and stumbled partway down the steps. James urged his pair on to meet her and jumped out as he drew up by the lower set of stairs.

His face was grave. ''I've bad news,'' he said gently, looking up at her. ''Your grandmother is very ill. Your parents sent a message to me this morning.''

''How ill?'' she asked, frightened by his tone.

''They think it is a matter of days, perhaps a week. I am

sorry; your father told me you were very fond of her.'' He
seemed to notice for the first time that she had no wrap.
"Come inside," he said, concerned. Samuels had appeared
and was helping Silvio with the team. "You should not be
out in the cold in your condition."

Numbly, she let him take her into the house. She was
dimly aware of Rachel, hurrying into the front hall from
the kitchen, of Danielle, running down with her shawl and
slippers, of Silvio, who had now reappeared and was taking
his master's coat and hat. She was led into the small front
parlor. Out in the hall she could hear Rachel giving instructions to Silvio in a low voice.

"Are you all right?" he asked, steering her into a chair
by the fire. One of the maids was hastily building it up.

"She lived with us when I was little, after the Terror,"
she whispered. "But I haven't seen her for years. She writes
me letters twice a month, though. I don't even know how
they get here. Or how mine get back to her. My father sends
them." Then, in a fiercer voice, "I hate this war! It will
never end! We shall go to our graves fighting the French,
hemmed in on this wretched island, friends cut off from
friends, families from families!"

"A bleak picture, and a true one for most Englishmen,"
said James, drawing up another chair next to her and taking
her hand. "But not for everyone. It is not fair, perhaps, but
people with money and influence are able to make special
arrangements under circumstances like these. French officials have offered to issue safe-conducts for your mother
and father. Your parents are en route to Ramsgate, where
they will wait for permission to cross into France." He
looked at her intently. "Would you like to go as well? My
Uncle Jacob lives in Paris, and I have sent a message asking
him to petition on our behalf."

There was a startled exclamation from Rachel, who had
come into the room carrying a large bottle of brandy and a
teacup.

"Good idea," said James, seizing the bottle. He looked around. "Where are the glasses?"

"I don't know," Rachel confessed. "I've been here for six weeks, and I still can't find anything in this house. Maria and Cook are looking for the decanter and proper glasses, but I thought a teacup would be better than nothing."

James poured out a small pool of gold liquid into the teacup and handed it to Eloise. She took an uncertain sip and made a face. It stung, but it did help the hollow ache which had opened up when she had heard the words "they think it is a matter of days."

"James," said Rachel, "stop trying to distract me with the brandy. Did I really hear you say that you propose to escort Eloise to Paris? You cannot imagine the French will give you a *laissez-passer*?"

He raised one eyebrow. "Why not?"

"There's a price on your head of five thousand francs, for one thing," she retorted.

This was news to Eloise, who stared in dismay at her husband.

"The reward is for James Nathanson," he pointed out. "Not James Meyer."

"They are the same person," snapped Rachel. "And many officials in France are well aware of that fact. Your friend Claude Meillet, for example, who is so fond of spiked iron boots and who is now deputy-chief of the *Sûreté*."

"But Meillet does not issue diplomatic passes." James poured more brandy into Eloise's cup and handed it back to her. "The French foreign minister issues them, and he is eager to remain on good terms with Uncle Jacob."

"James, this is madness," said Rachel, her eyes flashing.

Eloise sipped her brandy slowly. She was well aware that there was more here than she was being told, but the brandy was encouraging her to ignore that fact.

"I will leave it up to Eloise," he said, turning to face her. "I take it you wish to go, if it can be arranged?"

She nodded.

"You might be able to travel with your parents, but if you prefer I will go with you. Would you like that?" His dark eyes had a curious gleam in them.

Wine and truth. Or in this case, brandy and truth.

"Yes."

The gleam deepened.

She added hastily, "If you are certain there is no risk."

"The bearer of a diplomatic pass is sacrosanct," he assured her.

Rachel set down the brandy bottle with a crash and stalked out of the room.

James had moved quickly. Grooms, maids, curricle, coach, bandboxes, carriage rugs—everything was assembled and deployed in an urgent blur, with James supervising in person. He knew, Rachel guessed, that if she could get one moment alone with him she would confront him openly about the letter. He had made very sure she did not have that moment. They were gone within two hours, and he had never left Eloise's side the entire time. Rachel had sat through dinner seething with frustration while Lady Ingram had fretted about the dangers of such a trip, and the oddity of an English girl having family in France. She felt as though she were about to explode.

And so, the next morning, when her father stopped by Knowlton on his way back to London from the coast, it all came pouring out. The infected scars. Eloise's naive ignorance about James's military activities. The French maid who was not French. James's odd behavior towards his bride—one moment warm and affectionate, the next remote and standoffish. The tale of the disastrous wedding night. And finally, the letter and its suspicious results.

"That letter was from the countess," she said, agitated. "I know it was. She's in Paris, isn't she?"

"I believe so, yes."

"And now he's deceiving poor Eloise, letting her think

he is concerned for her and her safety when all he wants is to get to Paris and see that horrible Theresa von Brieg.''

Her father said slowly, ''You don't believe it's possible to want two different, somewhat contradictory things at the same time?''

She frowned. ''What do you mean?''

He shook his head. ''Never mind. I think your fears about the dangers of this trip are unwarranted. Many diplomats, including some English officials, have traveled into France on safe-conducts recently.''

''Papa—even if he goes and comes back unharmed, that is not all that worries me.''

He said gravely, ''I take it you are concerned about his wife. And about his obsession with the Austrian woman.''

''Eloise is barely out of the schoolroom! It seems monstrously unfair.''

''I think you are not giving the girl enough credit, Rachel,'' he said after a moment. ''She is quiet, yes, and much younger than you are. But when I met her I did not think her timid or missish, and the stories I hear confirm that. You say James wanted to back out of the marriage contract—which I can certainly believe after seeing James at the wedding. Yet they are still married. Augustus Wolf and her mother apparently both tried to persuade her to move to less spartan lodgings, yet they are still in James's rooms off Houndsditch. Silvio was so concerned about her abigail that he asked me to investigate her, which I did. He tells me he strongly suggested that she dismiss the maid, who is using a false name and is rude and unpleasant to boot. Now I hear that you, too, advised her to get rid of the woman. The maid is still with her.''

Rachel thought back to the riding lessons. It was true, Eloise would yield up to a certain point and then somehow, without making a great show of opposition, she would go no further. By the same token, once she had decided on a course of action, she stuck with it. ''She beat James at chess,'' she said slowly.

"She did?" Her father was startled.

"He let her play up a rook," Rachel explained.

"Well, there you have it," said Meyer. "He underestimated her. I advise you not to make the same mistake."

Eleven

White had explained many times to James why he hated the Foreign Office. They were like a bullying older brother, he said, the kind who constantly snoops through your cupboards, stealing your best toys and books, sending you on errands you do not fully comprehend, blaming you for everything which goes wrong, and never doing anything for you in return. And James could see why he felt that way. Two years ago they had gotten one of White's best officers killed in what turned out to be a vain attempt to curry favor with a minor Russian prince. Last year they had deliberately disgraced and bankrupted another junior courier so that they could send him into exile and lure a foreign minister to confide in him. Both schemes had resulted in closed-chamber hearings at Westminster, and both hearings had resulted in reprimands—to White, of course. The Foreign Office invoked "diplomatic privilege" and "grave breach of international trust" and slithered off scot-free. So when he saw one of Castlereagh's undersecretaries seated across from White, he understood right away why the colonel looked so harassed.

"Ah, Nathanson," White said as his youngest courier paused in the open doorway. "Come in. And close the door behind you."

James looked warily at the visitor.

"Edward Kerr. Foreign Office," the man said, jumping up and offering his hand. "We met last spring, I believe. I hear great things of you, Captain."

James raised one eyebrow, but he took the proffered hand.

"Sit down," growled White. "Both of you." He took a seat himself and opened the folder Kerr had brought over. "Nathanson, I have just been explaining to Mr. Kerr that by some miracle of compassion the French foreign ministry is granting you a safe-conduct so that you may escort your wife to Paris to attend her dying grandmother. I further explained to him that I gave you permission to go with the greatest reluctance, because I do not believe the safe-conduct will protect you, but that is neither here nor there. When are you leaving?"

"Day after next, sir, if the *laissez-passer* has arrived."

"And how long will you stay?"

"That depends on my wife's family, sir. I requested leave for three weeks."

White looked questioningly at Kerr. "When is the meeting?"

"A fortnight from now, I believe," Kerr said, reaching over and flipping pages in the folder. "Yes, the seventeenth."

James began to have an uncomfortable feeling that he knew what was coming.

"You recall the Chevaliers de la Foi?" Kerr asked him.

He grimaced. "Yes." The so-called Knights of the Faith were a secret society of fanatical royalists working to overthrow Napoleon and restore the Bourbons as rulers of France. The Foreign Office made much of them and had been supporting them with money and arms for years. James had met with several of the leaders and quickly concluded they were fools and scoundrels. He had thought White shared this opinion, but perhaps he was wrong.

Kerr leaned forward, his face glowing. "They write us that they have persuaded two high-ranking officials in Bonaparte's government to join their cause. That these two men have pledged themselves to deliver the cities of Bordeaux and Lyons to us—I mean, to the French royalists—within eight weeks. Think of it! Two of the largest cities in France, suddenly declaring for the Bourbons! It will be the final blow for Bonaparte!"

"Familiar promises from the Chevaliers," said James skeptically. "Somehow nothing seems to come of these promises except more English gold in the treasury of the Chevaliers. Or did they not ask for money this time?"

"They did," admitted Kerr. "Quite a bit of money. And a commitment on Wellington's part to advance his troops at a certain time towards Bordeaux."

Startled, James sat up straight and turned to White. "He wouldn't do it, would he?" he asked, dismayed. "Trust our soldiers to the plans of those spiteful bunglers?"

"Captain Nathanson," White said sharply, "you forget yourself."

"The Chevaliers understand that we require some guarantees from them before we can take such a risk," Kerr interjected hastily. "That is why we need you to meet with their representative in Paris."

"I beg your pardon?"

"In return for our military and financial support, the royalists have agreed to deliver to us signed letters from these two officials guaranteeing their commitment to this enterprise. In addition, they engage to remove from the Tuileries the Lesser Seal of the French royal family and send it to Louis Bourbon here in England. Naturally, however, they are reluctant to entrust these items to an ordinary messenger. For our part, we wish to make certain the letters are not forgeries. They will be signed in the presence of our man. The Chevaliers sent us a list of Englishmen known to them by sight who would be acceptable as representatives to this meeting.''

"And I am on the list," said James with a small sigh.

"You are on the list," confirmed White. "I have some qualms about this, Nathanson. Sending Louis the seal is a showy gesture, typical of the Chevaliers, and it casts some doubt on the rest of the proposal. Nevertheless, the chance of gaining Bordeaux or Lyons or both is too big a prize to ignore. It's a godsend that your wife's family has arranged this safe-conduct for you.''

James looked at White. "I'm sorry, sir," he said helplessly. "I can't do it."

"What do you mean, you can't do it?" asked Kerr, frowning.

"I gave my word. That was the condition of the safe-conduct. I pledged to act as a private citizen for the duration of my visit and to take no actions detrimental to the peace of the imperial state.''

"Oh, that." Kerr waved his hand. "Standard phrasing. You need not regard it."

James rose. "May I be excused, sir?" he said, pointedly ignoring Kerr. "I am sure that you understand my position, even if the Foreign Office has forgotten what it means to stand by one's sworn word.''

"You can't be serious!" Kerr twisted around to stare at him.

James turned in appeal to White.

But White looked uncomfortable. "There are times," he said slowly, "when personal honor may have to yield to the national interest.''

"Are there? And then what? Would you ever trust me again? Would anyone? Is that how we govern England, keeping our promises when it is convenient? What of the Carvallos and Meyers living in France, who would pay the price for my deceit?''

"Nathanson," said White, stung, "there are eight names on that list. One man is dead. One is on his way to the colonies with his regiment. And four of the remaining six are my couriers. Who else would the Chevaliers know by sight?'' He leaned forward and slammed his hand down on the folder. ''If you do not go to that meeting, someone else will be sent. Someone without a safe-conduct, who will have to go secretly, at great personal risk. Who should it be? LeSueur, whose two brothers fell last year in Spain? Southey, whose wife is expecting their first child, who had hoped to sell out but has remained on my staff because *you* have not been fit for duty?''

Troubled, James stared down at the floor. But he shook his head.

''I see you value your opinion of yourself above the lives of your comrades,'' said White in cold tones.

''You know perfectly well neither Southey nor LeSueur would agree to this if they had given their pledge!'' James said furiously. ''I wonder if you would even ask them. After all, they are gentlemen. Is my word less valuable because I do not swear on the Gospels? Have Jews no honor? Or do you think that because I was forced to feign allegiance to your church to purchase my colors, all my oaths are false?''

He looked straight at White and added in calmer tones, ''If you wish, I am prepared to resign my commission.''

''That won't be necessary,'' said the colonel slowly. ''I should have anticipated this problem. You may go, Captain.''

''Well,'' said Kerr in disgust as James stiffly withdrew, ''you spend half an hour reassuring me about this young man. Yes, he is besotted with an Austrian *intrigante* who is hand in glove with French counterintelligence. Yes, he is likely to fall at her feet the minute he reaches Paris. But he would not betray our people to her. He can be trusted, you said. He can keep his head when it counts. He has integrity.'' Kerr threw himself back in his chair. ''Too much integrity, apparently.''

''When I was his age I would have said the same thing,'' said White wearily. He pulled the folder back to the center of the desk and sighed. "That still leaves us with the task of selecting someone to send to Paris."

"Oh, I should think it is fairly obvious," said Kerr with an angry titter.

"It is, isn't it?" White closed the folder. "I'll have him in tomorrow."

Eloise was writing out yet another list of things to be packed when there was a rap at the door. "Come in," she called, expecting Silvio. He had been sent to the Roths' bank to get money for the journey.

It was Danielle. She looked odd. It took Eloise a minute to realize why. First, she had on her best dress, which she normally wore only to church. Second, she was carrying a money box. And third, she was not wearing her usual expression of imperturbable superiority. In fact, she seemed nervous.

"Madame, I have come to tell you that I find myself unable to continue in my position here," she announced. "I am leaving this afternoon."

Taken aback, Eloise laid down her pen.

Danielle held out the box. "It was quarter day recently, and I was paid in advance. It's all here." She added stiffly, "I am well aware I am required to give two weeks' notice, and if madame does not choose to give me a reference I will understand, but I won't go to France. No one informed me when I was engaged that my duties might include travel abroad into a war zone."

Eloise knew immediately what was really at issue. Of course Danielle didn't want to go to France. Her masquerade would be uncovered within ten minutes of setting foot in a place where there were actual French-speakers. As an employer she should be outraged. How was she to find a trustworthy servant to accompany her to France in one afternoon? Silvio and Rachel would probably tell her that this was what came of not dismissing Danielle long ago.

She studied Danielle's face. The girl was hardly older than she was, but she had schooled herself so well to show no emotion that Eloise tended to think of her as ageless. The facade was cracking now; she could see anxiety in the hazel eyes.

"Sit down, Danielle," she said after a moment, indicating another chair at the table.

Warily the maid complied, setting the box down in front of her.

"Have you been unhappy here?" Eloise asked hesitantly. "I know these apartments are quite different from my parents' homes."

Danielle looked around the "dining room," which sat four and was used in shifts by both masters and servants. At the curtains, which the maid had picked out and hemmed herself. At the stained floorboards and the always-dirty windows. The facade cracked further and a small, reluctant smile appeared. "I have the greatest admiration for madame," she said, and her voice did not have its usual cool, distant tone.

Two months ago Eloise would have been delighted to hear that Danielle was giving notice. When the maid had first been engaged, upon Eloise's return from Bristol, she had seemed more like another schoolmistress than a servant. Every misstep, every stray lock of hair, every clump of potting soil on her cuff earned an impassive third-person reproof. Mademoiselle must remember to curtsy when her mother enters the room. Mademoiselle should not wear green in the winter; her complexion was too pale. If mademoiselle would remember to put on her smock she would not stain her skirt with the watercolors. Too tenderhearted to send away a servant who had been handpicked by her mother, she endured, telling herself that in some hazy future the maid would look for a more elegant mistress and she would find a more congenial abigail.

But somehow in the weeks since the wedding, things had changed. She thought back to Danielle's behavior the evening she had collapsed in tears. It was worth taking a chance, she decided. The maid had three handkerchiefs' worth of credit in Eloise's bank, after all.

"Danielle, I believe I know why you are giving notice," she said gently. "I know you aren't really French. I've known almost from the first. My grandmother in Paris, the one who is ill, lived with us for years when I was a girl. I had French tutors from the time I was in leading-strings."

She had never before seen Danielle blush, but now she did. The maid turned bright red. "Did everyone know?" she asked in a small voice after a moment.

"No, no," Eloise reassured her. "Not at my parents' home, in any case. But Mr. Meyer's valet noticed right away once we came here."

"I see." Danielle looked down at the table.

"What is your real name?" asked Eloise, curious. "Not Danielle Lebec, presumably."

"Jane." The maid sighed. "Jane Price. I hated being a Jane. My cousin's wife is French; I took her name when I decided I wanted to be a lady's maid. She raised me after my mother died. That's how I learned to speak some French. And how I knew what it sounded like when a Frenchwoman spoke English." She looked up again. "Why didn't you dismiss me?" she asked bluntly.

"Why didn't you tell Mr. Meyer and Mrs. Drayton the truth about me?" countered Eloise. "You know perfectly well by now there's no baby; you help me dress and undress every day. You take my linens to the washerwoman every week."

"If you wish others to think you are with child that is your affair," said the maid. "I'm sure you have your reasons."

There was silence for a moment.

"You could still be Danielle," offered Eloise, pushing the money box back towards her. "I think it is much prettier than Jane. Unless you truly are concerned about traveling in France while the war is on."

Danielle-Jane rose and reclaimed the box. "I am very

grateful for madame's understanding,'' she said in her old manner.

"It may be a difficult trip,'' Eloise warned her. "It looks like snow again tomorrow, and even when we reach the coast I am not sure how one travels to France through the naval blockade.''

"All the more reason for me to go. Madame will need me.''

It was a difficult trip, and it got off to a very bad start. Recent snowstorms had made travel slow, and a few steep hills had been so treacherous that everyone had been forced to get out of the carriages and walk to spare the horses. Eloise's boots were still soaked. Now, after more than fourteen hours on the road, they had finally pulled up to the Bernal house only to find it dark and locked.

"Try again,'' James called to Silvio, who had been knocking at the front door. He was annoyed, Eloise saw, and she could not blame him. He had proposed trying to get passage at Chatham, much closer to London, but she had begged him to take her to Ramsgate in case her parents were still there.

Silvio pounded on the door again.

"I'll go round to the kitchen, sir,'' he said.

But as he came back down the steps, a glimmer of light appeared in one of the front windows. A moment later the door swung open, and a stout older man peered out. With a sinking heart she recognized Murdock, the caretaker. That meant the house had been closed up and the staff sent back to town. She had not really believed she would find her parents still in Ramsgate. If James had his papers, her father surely had his also, and under the circumstances he and her mother would have left the moment the documents arrived. But she had at least hoped for a house with servants, hot food, and warm beds.

"Miss Eloise!'' Murdock cried, spying her as she leaned

out of the carriage. He turned and bellowed back into the house. "Liza!"

"I'm very sorry, sir," he said to James, coming up next to the carriage. "We weren't expecting you. Mr. Bernal left yesterday—sent the servants back to the town house and told us to close the place. He thought sure you would take ship closer to London; the roads are near impassable in some places."

"So we discovered," said James dryly. "Can you put us up, or should we go back down to the Red Lion?"

"We'll make do, sir," the old man assured him. "Just tucked everything away this morning; easy enough to get a few things back out, and there's still a good meal or two in the larder." He looked at the horses, steaming gently in the light of the coach lanterns. "No groom, though. Just myself and Mrs. Murdock. Can your fellows deal with the team?"

Silvio and Toby were already unfastening the traces.

Murdock's wife came hurrying out of the house now, with a shawl wrapped around her. She, too, greeted Eloise effusively and apologetically. What a fortunate chance Miss Eloise had not come an hour later; she and Mr. Murdock would have been back in the gatehouse and might never have heard them arrive! Mr. Murdock would go into town at once and bring back the two girls from the inn who had been helping while her parents were there. A fire had just been lit in the drawing room, and she had put the kettle on. Had they dined yet? Would they fancy a shoulder of mutton? There was no fish, alas, but if they wished, Mr. Murdock could likely pry something loose from the innkeeper—some whiting, perhaps, or some mullet. Miss Eloise was to come into the kitchen right now, where the stove had been going all day, and take off her wet things.

Danielle duly appeared with dry stockings and shoes, but Mrs. Murdock kept chattering. Such a taking as her mother was in! What a pity, but then, Mrs. Carvallo had been ill these many years. If she could have seen English doctors, now, it might have been different. Too late for that, perhaps, though the latest message had been more encouraging. Still talking, she led Eloise into the drawing room.

It seemed very large and dark and empty in comparison to the last time she had seen it, full of wedding guests. James was warming his hands at a feebly sputtering fire, and a few hastily lit candles did little to dispel the shadows. A sofa and two chairs had been uncovered and pushed over near the hearth. Eloise sank down onto the sofa and wondered if it would shock James if she lay down. She had never felt so tired, and she knew the fatigue was more than physical. It was her grandmother, and James, and the conversation with Rachel, and her increasing apprehension about the safety of the trip to France, all rolled up together.

"I'll just put the mutton in, and then I'll pop upstairs and help your maid make up your bedchamber," Mrs. Murdock promised. She beamed at them maternally. "For later."

James suddenly became very interested in the fire. He picked up the poker and tongs and began rearranging the heap of coals, leaning over every now and then to blow into the grate.

There were seven bedrooms in the house, but Eloise knew what was meant by "your bedchamber." "Put us in the back rooms," she said quickly. "They're smaller, easier to heat."

"Are you sure?" The older woman looked at her doubtfully. "It's no trouble to put you in the larger room; your maid has already gone up."

"I'm sure," she said. Out of the corner of her eye she saw James loosen his grip slightly on the fire tongs.

"Very well, Miss Eloise. There's no denying it's a very cold night, and that corner suite has six windows. But don't let on to your mother I put you anywhere else. She had those rooms furnished specially for you and Mr. Meyer, and many an hour she spent looking at patterns and books of furniture and fabrics."

They sat in silence in the drawing room, listening to Danielle run up and down the stairs in accompaniment to a muted clatter from the kitchen. They sat in silence through dinner. One of the village maids was serving, and Eloise was grateful that it wasn't Silvio or Mrs. Murdock. In front of a servant who knew her, she would have felt obliged to make an effort to converse with James. She ate little. She kept remembering the wedding feast, James's remote and inexplicable anger, the odd tension in his face. She kept her eyes on her plate, half afraid that if she looked at him she would see the same expression there now. At the end of the meal, she excused herself immediately, saying that she wished to go straight to bed.

"I may as well come upstairs with you," he said. "I rather suspect Mrs. Murdock and Danielle have made up only one room for us."

"Perhaps Silvio would have told them—" she faltered.

"Silvio is down at the harbor, confirming our arrangements with the ship's master."

There was only one room made up. It contained a cheerful fire, a tray with a pot of tea, a candlestick with a fresh candle, and a bed. One small side chair. One washstand. No chaise, no sofa, no armchair. The bed was one of the new ones, low and narrow.

"I'm sorry," she said. There was a lump in her throat. "I should have been clearer with her. I did say 'rooms,' but she had already made up her mind."

"Yes, she seems the type to coo over newlyweds," he said with a little smile. "No great matter; I'll sleep on the floor."

She shook her head. "It's too cold."

"Eloise, I'm a soldier. This room has a roof and a fire. It's a palace."

"I don't want you to sleep on the floor," she heard herself say. The lump was getting bigger.

There was a knock at the door. It was Danielle, with her night gear. "Should I leave for a bit?" he asked quietly.

She shook her head again.

James relieved Danielle of the pile of clothing and the

little bag of toiletries and then bade the maid a firm good night and shut the door. He dumped everything unceremoniously in a heap on the chair and came over to where she was standing by the fire.

"What is it?" he said. "Your grandmother?"

"I don't want to cry," she said fiercely, but the tears were slipping out. "I hate it when I cry."

"My father taught me how to stop," he said, unfastening the top hook on the back of her dress.

She swung around, startled. "What are you doing?"

"Putting you to bed. You're exhausted. That's one reason you're crying." He looked at her face and said with satisfaction, "Ah, it worked. You've stopped."

"What worked?"

He turned her around again and pulled open the hooks, one by one, down her back. "Distraction. It's the best way to stop yourself from crying. Think about something different, something curious or intriguing." The dress fell open, and he tugged it over her head. "Here." He shook open her nightgown and handed it to her. "Put it on; then take off your petticoat from underneath."

"What about my chemise?" she protested.

"You don't need that much distraction," he said ironically. "And neither do I. If Danielle notices tomorrow, you kept it on because you feared you were taking a chill."

The fire was dying down, but it was indeed warmer with the additional layer under her nightgown. And the sheets had been heated. Drowsily she watched him pinch out the candle. Then she heard a slight thud as he lowered himself to the floor.

"James, I thought we had agreed you were not sleeping on the floor."

"I'm fine," he said patiently.

The drowsiness receded, replaced by the familiar aching lump. She lay there, trying to think of a distraction. Nothing came to her except misery and more misery. Nana was dying.

Her husband wasn't even willing to lie down next to her, and now she was risking his neck dragging him to France. She turned her face into the pillow and let the tears come— silently, she thought, but something gave her away, because the candle flared back into life and he came over and sat down on the bed beside her.

"We don't do very well in the bedrooms in this house," he said. "And I'm afraid I am the responsible party. What do you want me to do?"

"I don't think I can sleep if you are on the floor." She stared bleakly over towards the faint red outline of the coals in the fireplace. "I'll just picture you lying there and feel guilty. It's all my fault; this whole wretched day is my fault. We could have been well on our way across the Channel by now."

He had already taken off his jacket and boots; now he stripped down to his shirt and drawers and slipped in beside her. It was not a large bed. Even when he edged over to the far side of the bed, his elbow was still touching her back. They lay in silence for a while.

"It isn't just your grandmother, is it?" he asked finally.

"No." The lump was choking her. She was sure he must have heard it in her voice.

He sighed and turned back towards her. "Go to sleep," he said softly, drawing her towards him and settling his arm under her head. "We'll be rising early; the tide is at eight."

With her face safely buried, she confided her secret to his shirtsleeve. "I should never have agreed to let you accompany me to France," she whispered, very quietly so that he would not hear her. "I was selfish. It's too dangerous. Your sister was right." Confession helped somewhat; the lump eased its stranglehold. And James was oddly comforting as a pillow. He was so still, he seemed barely to breathe. Eventually, she fell asleep with a faint sense of surprise that her head was resting on something warm.

*   *   *

James was an expert at lying still. And he had excellent hearing. He counted the coals as they winked out in the fireplace while she gradually relaxed in his arms, her head slumping into the hollow of his shoulder. "It is dangerous," he told the sleeping Eloise sadly. "Though not quite in the way you imagine." He stared in guilty fascination at the fine-spun mass of dark hair which partially concealed her face, until the candle guttered and went out. Then he lay in the blackness, imagining what he would do to the man who had seduced and abandoned her if he ever found the scoundrel. Not the best distraction he had ever conjured up, perhaps, but it worked. They all worked. He hadn't cried in years.

Twelve

The Bernal house in Ramsgate was meant to be a summer
home. It was set at the top of a long hill, well away from
the main cluster of houses and shops near the harbor. A
stand of large oaks on the west offered protection from
curious picnickers who had toiled up the road, and on the
east side there was a magnificent view of the sea. In July,
it was cool, private, and sheltered—a delightful retreat. In
the depths of winter, it was not delightful. On its hilltop the
house was isolated and exposed to the full fury of the wind.
Tradesmen were reluctant to bring their carts up the steep
track, and the local girls demanded extra wages when their
services were required. But it still commanded a magnificent
view, and shortly after dawn two guests were taking advantage of a rooftop platform to survey the harbor at the base
of the hill.

"You're right," said James, lowering the field glass. His
voice held a mixture of incredulity and despair. "I didn't
believe you, but it's frozen."

"Murdock told me it happens only once every century,

signor,'' said Silvio in a feeble attempt at consolation. "It will be the talk of the place for years."

"That's all very well, but what are we to do?" demanded James. "Wait for it to thaw? Even supposing it melts by tomorrow, the boats may be severely damaged." He raised the glass again. "Look at them!" The harbor was full of imprisoned boats. Some, the smaller, flat-bottomed ones, were simply resting on the crust of ice which coated the water. Heavier craft were tilted at odd angles; many had layers of ice extending up their hulls nearly to the deck.

"The harbor at Dover is deeper," Silvio offered after a moment's silence.

"You're suggesting we get the carriage out, hire more horses, retrieve our trunks from the dock, and drive through the snow over one of the worst roads in Kent to Dover?"

"It's that or wait for a thaw, signor," Silvio pointed out. "And take our chances that the ship is still seaworthy."

As if in answer, one of the trees behind the house gave a crack which sounded like a pistol shot.

"It won't thaw today," said James gloomily. "Not if the trees are cracking." He assessed the western horizon with a practiced eye. "No snow today. We'll go to Dover. Go break the bad news to Toby. I know his hands are still raw from yesterday, but I won't travel down that Sandwich road in weather like this with only one coach. You'll both have to drive. Tell him I'll put him up in the best inn in Dover and send him back to town post instead of stage."

It was noon before they got underway. A second carriage and team had to be hired, horses carefully checked for signs of incipient lameness, trunks brought back up from the ship-master's office, where Silvio had left them the previous evening. When Eloise heard James muttering about the state of the road, she insisted that both vehicles be furnished with food and blankets. James did not object, but she could see that he was fretting at the delay, torn between his own

concerns about their route and his longing to reach a port—
any port whose ships were afloat—as soon as possible. At
the time she took his impatience as a sign that he sympathized
with her anxiety about her grandmother.

They reached Sandwich, where they stopped to change
horses and eat, without any trouble. James was in an increasingly black mood, and when Eloise remarked innocently
that the road had been surprisingly good thus far, he said
in withering tones, "It's the stretch between here and Dover
which is difficult; any fool knows that."

All through the afternoon the weather remained bitterly
cold—so cold that even James, who strongly preferred to
be outdoors, was riding in the coach with Eloise most of
the time. Occasionally, however, he would take the reins
from Toby or Silvio so that they could warm their hands
and rest inside the second carriage. It was after one of these
turns on the box, when he climbed back into the carriage,
that he set out to pick a fight with Eloise.

At first she thought the little gibes were accidents—complaints about their reception at the house in Ramsgate, conde-
scending remarks reminding her that she had never traveled
abroad, criticism of the provisions she had purchased for
the journey. But when none of these attempts provoked a
response, he stepped up the attack.

It started with a feint to the right. "I suppose I should
lodge with my Uncle Jacob while we are in Paris."

She stared. "Why? Why would you not stay with us in
the Rue St. Honoré?"

He raised one eyebrow and drawled, "Surely in their time
of affliction the Carvallos and Bernals will not wish to be
reminded of this embarrassing *mésalliance*."

"A few of my aunts and uncles made some discourteous
remarks at the wedding, and you insist on making a great
deal more of them than is warranted," she said, trying to
keep her temper.

"Don't forget I speak fluent Spanish," he retorted. "I
understood what your older relatives were saying in that

odd dialect of theirs. I was referred to as 'the German' by nearly everyone there.''

"Not by me, or by my parents."

"Of course not. *Noblesse oblige*."

"I fail to understand why you harp on my family's alleged snobbery so constantly," she said, finally roused to anger. "How long has it been since the Spanish Jews in London expelled the Germans from their synagogue? A century? More? Yes, some of my older relatives sneer at the German Jews. They have been in England for generations, and they see rag peddlers with beards down to their waist who can barely speak English—rag peddlers who then upbraid them for their lack of adherence to the Law—and they are frightened, frightened that Englishmen will think all Jews are like those peddlers. What does that have to do with you and me? So what if the Bevis Marks synagogue lists you as *Tudesco* on the record of our marriage? I have never been in the place! And you are no more observant than I am! The only reason you remain a Jew is sheer, stubborn pride. Otherwise you would have converted long ago and married a Christian, as your sister did."

"Your family's snobbery, as you call it, is self-evident," he said coldly. "You cannot imagine they would have given a ruined girl like you to one of their own kind? At least if I had married a Gentile she would have been a virgin."

Her heart stopped. She stared at him for a moment in disbelief, then, heedless of the motion of the coach, wrenched open the door.

He knew he had gone too far; he was already looking horrified and remorseful. "Eloise, no!" he shouted.

But she was too outraged to listen, or to think of what might happen if she stepped out of a moving coach onto a snow-covered road. Half-standing, half-crouching, she clutched the door frame and, with a strength she had not known she possessed, launched herself out into an icy white nothingness.

She was lucky. The coach was going slightly uphill, and

it was going slowly. When she hit the ground, she stumbled and fell to one knee, but she did not strike her head or break her wrist, as might easily have happened. Behind her she could see James, shouting to Silvio and leaping out after her. Toby, too, was shouting, trying to halt the second team before they ran into the suddenly braking carriage ahead. Scrambling to her feet, she ran towards the nearest haven— a dense stretch of trees bordering the road. Her only thought was to get as far away from James Meyer as possible.

The snow was not deep under the trees, and she dodged frantically between the trunks, yanking her skirts away from bushes, heading deeper into the forest. Her breath was coming in short gasps, and her hands were scraped raw from her fall, but she did not notice. Anger was driving her, and it was an all-consuming force. Her boots filled with clumps of ice, and she stumbled more and more frequently. Once she fell flat, but picked herself up at once and pushed on, looking over her shoulder to see if James was still behind her. He was. He was gaining, in fact. She thought wildly that he ran very fast for someone with an ankle full of holes. The trees thinned ahead of her, and she risked another glance back. That was when the ground suddenly tilted beneath her feet. Too late, she saw the hillside falling steeply away to a little valley below her. She lost her balance and slid helplessly down, her dress tangling around her legs, snow flying into her face, until she thudded into a bank of earth near the bottom.

For a few seconds she lay there, stunned. But she was more surprised than hurt, and after a moment she struggled up onto her elbow and looked back up the hill. James was coming down, leaping in big arcs through the snow and somehow managing to keep his footing. She hated him again for being so graceful. Her own descent had probably resembled the antics of a drunken sailor.

With an irritated sigh she stood up and began brushing snow from her clothes. Her mantle had come off two-thirds of the way down the hill, she discovered. James stopped and picked it up, then approached her hesitantly, as though expecting her to flee again.

"Don't run," he said humbly. "Or at least take your cloak first." He held it out.

In silence she reached for it. The snow was dry and powdery and fell off when she gave it a shake. She put it on. Her anger was fading, and as it died, she recognized how carefully he had stoked its flames. She remembered Rachel's warning: *"in the heat of the moment he might say something which will make you so angry you will want nothing better than to be rid of him."*

"Are you hurt?" he asked urgently.

"No. Are you?" He had lost his hat, she realized. The dark hair was dusted with snow. His coat was ripped, and with a pang she saw that he was favoring one leg as he stood.

"No, of course not." He saw her gazing at his foot and flexed it. "It's fine, just a bit unused to so much activity. I haven't practiced leaping down hills recently."

"That was very childish of me," she said. "It would serve me right if I were hurt."

"Don't you dare apologize to me," he retorted, his eyes suddenly blazing. "Don't you dare pretend you were to blame. I goaded you beyond endurance, and you know it. I should be horsewhipped."

She stared at him, astonished, and then started to laugh.

After a minute his face softened, and the harsh set of his mouth was replaced by a rueful smile. "What is so amusing?" he asked. "Me, I take it."

"You're the only man I know who could be angry at me because I am not angry at you," she told him.

"You're the only woman I know who could forgive me for what I said," he answered gravely, looking at her with a quiet plea in his eyes.

"I'll forgive you," she said, equally grave.

He looked relieved.

". . . if you carry me back up the hill," she finished.

He lifted his gaze to the nearly sheer rise above them and groaned.

She didn't have the heart to hold him to it. Instead she accepted the loan of his coat to serve as a cushion while she sat on a fallen tree trunk and emptied the ice out of her boots.

"I don't think we should go back the way we came down," he said, studying the hill while she retied her laces. "If we follow this valley down a bit farther, we should be able to find an easier route back to the road."

He helped her up. "Are you certain you are able to walk? My offer to carry you still stands."

"I can walk," she assured him. "These are very stout boots. My footwear is the despair of Danielle."

"I was thinking more that you might be shaken up—" He broke off. "Did you hear that?" he asked sharply.

She had the sense not to ask, "Hear what?" Instead she listened. "It's just a cat," she said, relieved, after hearing the faint wail.

"That's no cat." He put his coat on hastily, not bothering to button it up. "Stay close to me, please. There are some very rough characters in the hollows behind the sea cliffs hereabouts." Slowly he began to walk forward, head tilted to catch the noise on the wind. One hand was in the pocket of his greatcoat, and she had the uneasy feeling that it was holding a pistol.

Now they both heard the sound distinctly, a plaintive cry.

"What *is* that?" asked Eloise, shaken.

"I don't know. Sound can be distorted in these valleys." He steered her into the shelter of a large tree. "Stay here. I think I smell wood smoke. Don't move until I return. If you see or hear anyone else coming, try to stay out of sight."

Then he vanished. One minute Eloise saw him moving through the trees; the next minute, no matter where she looked, he was gone. She was strongly tempted to go over to the place where he had disappeared and look for footprints. Perhaps she had married a demon. But then common sense reasserted itself. Demons did not help you scrape ice out of your boots. Demons did not pick fights with you because they had been a bit too affectionate the night before.

It seemed like a very long time before he returned, and when he did he walked like a man weighted down. She did not have to see his face to know that whatever he had found was unpleasant. Uneasy, she stepped out from behind her tree.

"It's very bad," was all he said when he reached her. "Your mother mentioned you had both visited sailors at the naval hospital; did you go onto the invalid wards, or simply sit with the more able-bodied pensioners?"

"I've been in the wards," she said, raising frightened eyes to his face.

"Then you have seen men with lung fever," he said, as he took her arm. "But not this stage, I'd wager. It's a young woman. The wailing you heard was her little girl."

"Shouldn't we hurry?" she asked urgently, trying to increase her pace.

He gave a brief, bleak shake of his head.

The little shack sat tucked into a stand of large pines. One wall—the front—was made of rough planking and had a door set into it; the rest were a hotchpotch of loosely stacked logs filled in with sheets of tin and pieces of canvas. There were no windows. The roof extended over one side to form a lean-to against one wall of the house, and there were clear signs that several horses had been tied up there recently. The chimney was smoking faintly, and the wailing was clearly audible now. It started and stopped at intervals.

Eloise broke into a run. The door of the hut was half open, and at the time she condemned James for his thoughtlessness, letting cold air in when there was someone inside who was ill. Later she realized that he had not wanted to leave mother and child in the dark.

The woman was huddled on her side in a crude bedstead in the corner, her eyes closed, her breathing labored. Opposite her, on a small crate next to the hearth, sat a girl of about six, her arms wrapped about an odd-looking dog, her eyes fixed on her mother's face. She was keening in a high, piercing voice, but the wail stopped abruptly when Eloise came in.

She went straight over to the bed. "Someone's here now," she said gently, taking the woman's hand. It was damp and cold. The woman's eyes did not open, but she turned slightly towards Eloise's voice.

James had come in behind her, and she turned to him frantically. "Can't we do something? Carry her out to the road, take her to a doctor?"

"Eloise, she's dying," he said gently.

The little girl had started to wail again, very quietly, rocking back and forth over her pet. At the sound, the mother lifted her head and clutched Eloise's hand. With a great effort, she managed to open her eyes and look over at the girl, then back to Eloise. She moved her lips, but no sound came out.

"We'll take care of your little girl," Eloise promised, understanding at once what she was asking. An hour went by; the woman lay in a stupor, struggling to breathe. James had brought a bench over by the bed for Eloise to sit on while she held the woman's hand. Twice more she tried to speak, and each time Eloise repeated her reassurance. It grew darker and darker inside the hut. James went out and brought in wood to build up the fire. The little girl had not moved, though her pet had disappeared under a table. There was only firelight; James had found a lamp, but it had no oil.

Eloise had forgotten that Silvio and Danielle and Toby existed, and when she heard a sharp two-note whistle outside the hut, she jumped.

"It's Silvio," James reassured her. He went out, and returned a few minutes later. "The others have gone on to an inn at St. Margaret's, a few miles down the road. Silvio tracked us here. He'll go fetch us blankets and some food." He held out a small flask. "In the meantime, he left us something to fortify ourselves with, although I suspect if we opened that crate we would find much better brandy than this."

Tired and overwrought, Eloise accepted the flask gratefully. It only took a few swallows to put a haze over everything, to make her accept calmly the notion that she was sitting in a smuggler's den, keeping watch over the deathbed of an outlaw's wife. The haze protected her from stiffness as she sat, hour after hour, feeling the fingers clasped in her own grow colder. The haze congratulated her when the little girl finally climbed down from the crate and crawled onto the bench next to Eloise. Eloise put her hand into her mother's and hoped that the slight squeeze was not her imagination.

Silvio returned, and Eloise fed herself and the girl while James took her place at the bedside. She had thought the woman was past noticing the change, but shortly after he sat down, there was movement; the hands began fluttering in a strangely insistent way.

James looked at Silvio. "She thinks I'm a priest," he said. His black wool coat did somewhat resemble a cassock in the dim light. "I suspect she's Catholic."

Silvio nodded.

The dark head bent down over the bed, and Eloise heard a rhythmic murmuring begin. Occasionally she caught a phrase, louder or more distinct than the rest. It was Latin. Then there was silence. At last James straightened up and pulled the blanket over the woman's face. Silvio crossed himself.

"James, you're not a priest," she said stupidly.

"I am when I'm spying in Portugal or Spain," he said. "Or when someone desperately wants me to be one."

* * *

Eloise sat holding the girl while Silvio and James under-took the lengthy business of digging a grave in half-frozen ground. She had finally fallen asleep, and Eloise looked down at the little face and wondered what would become of her, where she belonged. Perhaps in the village someone would know who her people were. She knew she ought to feel tired—it was long past midnight—but instead she felt extraordinarily awake, as though all her senses had been cleansed. Everything seemed strange and new: the smell of the fire, the texture of the girl's fair hair on her neck, the sound of the wind, softer now as dawn approached.

When James returned she stood up and passed the child to him as easily as though she had slept for eight hours in a featherbed instead of falling down a ravine and then sitting all night with a dying woman. Silvio had brought three horses. Now he packed up the blankets and the remains of the food on the largest animal, then swung up and took the girl from James.

They stood and watched him trot off, but made no move to mount their own horses. Behind the trees the sky was growing lighter.

"It's very humbling, isn't it?" he said, watching the new day outline the treetops in a fiery copper halo.

She wasn't sure what he meant. Death? Grief? The sun-rise? All three?

"I think I should tell you something," he said abruptly. "I allowed you to believe that I agreed to go to France for your sake, but that is not the true reason. The truth is, I have unfinished business in Paris."

"Army business?" she said, frightened.

"No." He looked down at her. "A personal matter. Once it is behind me, perhaps we can make a fresh start."

Thirteen

No one in the village of St. Margaret's had any notion where the little girl's family might be. At the first mention of a hut in the woods behind the cliffs, faces closed. One woman actually made the sign against the evil eye as she backed away. That last incident persuaded Eloise that she could not simply leave the child with someone.

"James, I promised her mother," she said obstinately, when he proposed they should pay a village woman to take her in. "A deathbed promise. Those are sacred. Can you imagine what sort of treatment she'll receive here?"

Danielle emerged from the inn at this point with the girl, who looked much cleaner. The moment she saw Eloise, she broke away from the maid and ran into Eloise's skirts, where she hid.

"What did you do to her?" demanded Eloise, putting a protective arm around her charge.

"Marie did not care to have her hair brushed, madame," Danielle explained. "It was very tangled. I believe that is the reason for her present fear of me."

"Marie? Is that her name?" Eloise brightened. "Did she talk to you, then? She wouldn't say a word to me."

"No, madame, she did not speak. I ascertained her name by trying various possibilities until she nodded."

Eloise suspected that the choice of Marie was Danielle's rather than the girl's, but a name of some sort was certainly necessary, and Marie would do until the child recovered enough from her grief to speak to them. "You see?" she said to James, looking down at the fair head peering out from behind her hip. "She is terrified, poor thing. Can you really tell me we should leave her here?"

"I know some boatmen's families in Dover," he said, capitulating. "We'll find something there."

But that was not the end of the arguing, because Eloise next realized that in the confusion at the hut they had left Marie's pet behind. This became clear when the child saw one of the maids come out of the inn's stable carrying a large tabby cat. Tugging at Eloise's skirt, she pointed at the maid, then pointed to herself and made rocking motions with her arms. Round blue eyes looked up pleadingly at Eloise.

The softhearted Eloise melted instantly. "We forgot Marie's pet," she said contritely to James. "I can't think how I could have been so careless. It's all she has left. We'll have to go back and fetch it."

James stared. "What pet?"

"The little dog. She was holding it on her lap when we first came in. And then it ran under the table. She was rocking it, don't you remember? Like a baby."

Totally nonplussed, James looked at her.

"What dog?" he said, frowning. "There was no dog." Then his face cleared, and he started laughing. "You thought that was a dog?"

"Why? What was it?"

"A goat. A very small goat." He said this as though it were the end of the matter.

"But it's her pet," protested Eloise.

"It's not a pet; it's a *goat*. Believe me, there is an unbridgeable gap between those two words."

"I don't see why you are so determined to rob this poor girl of the only living creature she knows in the world," she retorted.

"Eloise," he said patiently, "you obviously have no experience with goats. I do. I have slept in barns with goats. I have tried to herd goats. I have milked goats. And I can tell you right now, that goat could be St. Francis in disguise and I would still not go fetch it for her."

He was back at the little hut a short time later, with Silvio riding escort and trying to conceal his amusement.

"Perhaps it has run away, signor," Silvio said hopefully.

"It won't run away from that hut," growled James. "Goats are not stupid. Perverse, revolting, filthy, yes. Stupid, no. It's sheltered there and it can eat the straw in the mattress."

Sure enough, when they went into the hut, the goat was placidly chewing on a corner of the bed. It made no objection to being picked up, and James grudgingly admitted that this did suggest it had been treated as a pet. It did object, strenuously, to being confined in a cloth sack. Both men had bruises before the squirming bundle was secured behind the saddle on one of the horses.

"Well, so long as we're here," James said, panting a bit, "how about some of the brandy from that crate?"

Silvio disappeared into the hut, only to reappear a moment later. "It's gone," he said tersely. "The crate is gone. I could have sworn it was there when we first went in, but I was occupied with other things." He gave the bundle on his horse a malevolent glance. "And there is a trapdoor, hidden behind the bed."

All thoughts of goat-bruises vanished. James knelt by the far end of the lean-to. "Horses," he said. "No, one horse." He got up and walked around the perimeter of the hut. "There." He pointed. There were fresh hoofprints in the snow, and fresh footprints as well.

"Let's go, signor," Silvio urged. "This is a smuggler's place; I am sure of it. They do not like trespassers."

James did not argue. They rode out of the valley with pistols loaded and drawn. Their progress was slow; the horses could not do much better than a walk in most places, and James kept stopping and turning around.

"I feel as though we're being followed," he said tensely. "Do you hear anything?"

"No, signor, but this accursed goat is making my horse nervous. It would be difficult for me to hear over his snorts."

They picked their way up the hill, and James looked back again and again, certain that he had heard some noise or seen a flicker of movement out of the corner of his eye. Nothing, no one.

At the edge of the wood, James turned and faced the valley defiantly. "She died peacefully," he shouted. "But you are a brute to have left her there alone when she was so ill." His voice echoed through the trees. There was no reply.

"Come on," he said to Silvio resignedly, spurring his horse up onto the road. "Let's bring Mrs. Meyer her new pet."

Eloise admitted when the goat emerged from the sack that it looked nothing like a dog. Marie, however, was overjoyed to see it. She knelt and embraced it, looking up at Eloise and James with shining eyes.

"Now, how can you say we should have left him behind?" she challenged him.

"Her," he corrected. "It's a she-goat, or I wouldn't have let things go this far. And we'll see who has the last word." He looked at the two fully loaded coaches. "How do you plan to convey this, er, 'pet' of Marie's to Dover?"

"In the carriage with us, of course," she said.

"Not with me," he retorted. "You and Danielle and the

girl can have the big coach. I shall ride in lonely and un-goated splendor in the rear vehicle.''

Eloise and Danielle emptied a large basket and repacked the items in a cloth bag. Then they lined the bottom of the basket with blankets and put in some hay for the goat to eat. They were very pleased with themselves when they were done, and Marie was enchanted. She climbed into the coach happily and put the goat into its nest as carefully as a mother tucking her baby into a cradle. The goat did not seem to mind. It stared around the inside of the carriage with an amiable expression, and only blinked once or twice when the vehicle jerked into motion. Soon it bent its head, and they heard occasional munching sounds as it investigated the hay they had provided.

It was not a long ride to Dover—perhaps an hour or less. The road from St. Margaret's soon joined the turnpike, and the horses were able to trot along very quickly on the wider surface. Eloise and Danielle were happily occupied with Marie. They realized very quickly that she could understand when they spoke, although she would not speak in return.

At first the conversation was very one-sided, with Eloise explaining and Marie nodding. She looked solemn but not frightened when Eloise told her they would go on a boat to France to visit Eloise's grandmother, and smiled when they promised to buy some sweetmeats in Dover. But then they realized they could ask her questions, so long as the questions required only yes or no answers. It became a game, thinking of things to ask and watching the little head nod up and down or shake back and forth. In this way they discovered that she had only come to the shack in the woods recently, that her mother had been ill for a long time, that she had taken care of her mother—she made little gestures of making up the fire, sweeping, and stirring something in a pot. Questioned about her father, she would only shake her head and frown.

On the outskirts of the town, the carriage pulled up and James opened the door. After a hasty glance at the basket on the floor, he carefully averted his eyes and addressed Eloise.

"This is where Robin Noakes lives, a boatman I know. I believe his wife would take Marie in. She is a respectable woman, very kindly."

But Eloise took one look at the cluster of dingy houses and said no.

"You realize that our papers do not mention a child," he said, exasperated. "Surely you are not proposing to take her with us to France?"

"No French official will be concerned about a little girl," she retorted. "She has just lost her mother. Have you no compassion? Have you forgotten our vow? I won't leave her here with strangers while she is still so frightened she cannot even speak."

"Who will tend her? Do you suppose you can hire a nursemaid here in Dover and then take her with you? Surely the nursemaid at least would need papers?"

"Danielle and I will take care of her," said Eloise. "If need be we can engage someone once we reach France."

"Have it your way," he said in disgust. And with another hasty glance at the basket, he closed the door and ordered Silvio to drive on down to the docks.

"We're to take the little one with us, then?" she heard Silvio say.

"I'll see if Mrs. Robey is down at the dock, and we'll try again there," was the reply.

"And the goat?"

"I shall win that one," he said, and she heard satisfaction in his voice. Marie had scrambled down onto the floor and was bending over the basket and crooning.

"No, you won't," Eloise muttered.

But when they rattled to a stop in the cobblestone lane adjoining the harbor, she looked down and discovered that the goat had not only been eating hay. It had eaten most of the blanket, a large chunk of the flounce of Marie's dress, and the rim of one side of the basket.

"Don't gloat," she told James in a fierce whisper as the horrified Danielle tried to repair Marie's frock. The culprit had been tied temporarily to the back wheel of the carriage. "Help me! What am I to tell Marie? We shall be the greatest villains in creation if we take that creature away now after making such a fuss about fetching it for her."

"So, you no longer insist on conveying it with us?" he inquired sardonically.

"Must I grovel?" she said. "Very well. I fully and freely admit that you were right and I was wrong. I solemnly swear I shall never again propose transporting a goat in any vehicle belonging to you. But *you* must tell her. I haven't the nerve."

"Don't fret," James told her. "The solution to your problem is coming right now." He pointed to a stocky older man wearing a weather-beaten tricorn hat who was approaching the carriages. "That is Master Robey, who for a very large sum will take us to France in a very small and uncomfortable boat. You say Marie understands when you speak?"

She nodded.

"Then I suggest you take Marie over to Master Robey right now and ask him in her hearing if he would be willing to have a pet goat as a passenger."

She looked at him doubtfully.

"Trust me," he said. "The answer will be no. And then Robey can be the villain."

Dutifully she took Marie by the hand and led her over to the approaching seaman.

"Master Robey?" she asked.

He snatched off his hat and gave a little bow.

"I am Mrs. Meyer," she said. "And this is Marie, who will be traveling with us."

"So Mr. Silvio said, ma'am," he ventured, eyeing Marie warily.

"Marie has a pet goat," she continued, "and I was wondering if the goat could be accommodated."

His horrified expression reassured her at once that the

answer would be as James had predicted. "No, ma'am," he said vehemently. "Begging your pardon, but no. Not on a ship." He looked down at Marie's woebegone face and clarified matters. "Goats eat rope," he explained. "And a creature as eats rope on a ship is not to be thought of, as you might well imagine. I've seen goats in iron cages reach their lips out through the bars and eat halyards. Goats are all very well in their place," he added hastily. "In a nice pen in the yard, for example. But not on a ship. I'll not have it, ma'am, not even to please the young miss here."

Mrs. Robey took custody of the goat—just in time. It was indeed eating rope, the rope which fastened it to the carriage. But Mrs. Robey did not get Marie, not even when Marie was told that if she allowed Mrs. Robey to take her home she would be able to stay with her pet. She clung to Eloise's hand and watched the goat being led off without shedding a single tear.

"Congratulations," said James ironically to Eloise. "You are preferred to a goat." He was not pleased at his failure to persuade Marie to trust herself to Robey's wife.

"I'm sure she'll be no trouble on the journey," said Eloise. "She seems a very well behaved child." She thought of Caroline and sighed to herself, wishing that Marie were a little less well behaved. It was a bit unsettling.

James must have been thinking very much the same thing, because he frowned as he studied Marie's solemn little face and said slowly, "Yes, she is well behaved. I'll give her that. I suspect it was too dangerous for her to be anything else." Then he narrowed his eyes, surveying the harbor. Even in the relative shelter of Dover's great bay, the boats were jerking at the moorings as icy gusts swept across the water. "Let's hope she is a good sailor. This may be a rough ride."

Eloise was the one who was not a good sailor—the only one. Marie was in her element on board the little fishing boat—clearly she had been on craft like this many times, confirming James's guess that her parents had been involved in smuggling. Danielle sat stoically on a bench in the tiny cabin, sewing by lanternlight. She had purchased several ells of cloth in Dover and was determined to have Marie in new garments as soon as possible. James was on deck. He, too, had clearly made this trip many times. Ostensibly, he had remained above to make sure that Robey would not be molested by British naval craft enforcing the blockade. But when Danielle went out to make sure Marie was not underfoot, she reported on her return that he and Silvio were helping Robey and his mate man the sails.

Eloise lay in misery on the lone berth and wondered why anyone would ever travel by sea. Danielle's offers of vinaigrette- and cologne-soaked handkerchiefs were rejected, as was James's suggestion of brandy. She hadn't the heart to dismiss Marie, however, and the little girl would fly in every quarter hour or so, pat her arm sympathetically, and offer her some watered wine out of a chipped mug. Eloise sipped and fought to keep it down. Usually she lost.

The worst moments were when they were ordered to heave to by patrol frigates. The boat would wallow sluggishly, an even more unpleasant motion than the normal rolling thump, and she could not even console herself with the thought that they were moving forward. They were stopped three times, and James grew more irate each time. "Do they think we are complete fools?" he asked her in exasperation after the third time. "Would we be sailing in daylight, right through the patrol lines, if we had no papers?" He did not expect an answer, which was just as well, because she was not up to speaking at that moment. The light faded, and the little cabin grew darker and darker. At last she fell into an uneasy, drifting sleep, punctuated with bangs and thuds as the boat hit an especially rough patch or the sails were hauled about.

She woke to find Danielle shaking her. "We are tied up safely, madame," she said with satisfaction, offering Eloise a damp cloth and a basin of water. Eloise tidied herself as best she could. She felt hollow inside, and when she tried to stand up, her legs did not seem to be working properly. James lowered himself into the cramped hold. He didn't even ask—simply picked her up and carried her out onto the deck. The breeze whipped her hair out from beneath her bonnet, and through the strands she saw the lights of the little harbor town, dotted up the hillside, and the familiar, unutterably welcome sight of trees and houses and churches etched against the nighttime sky. Land.

"Do we have to go back the same way?" she asked faintly as he stepped carefully down onto the dock, still carrying her.

"Last time I inquired, England was still an island," he said, amused. Then he took pity on her. "We'll be on a proper ship going back," he promised, setting her gently on her feet. "It won't pitch about so violently. I would never have taken you on Robey's boat if it hadn't been for the harbor freezing at Ramsgate."

A crowd had started to gather, curious to hear English spoken and to see a lady emerging from the hold of a fishing boat. Was it her imagination, Eloise wondered, or did several of them look startled at the sight of James? One man certainly scuttled back into the shadows of a warehouse the moment he saw him. Then the crowd was pushed aside, and a loud voice was heard shouting in French, "Make way!" A portly official appeared, clearly enjoying himself.

"Your papers, madame, monsieur," he demanded, drawing himself up to his full and not very impressive height. He scanned the documents, then turned to the crowd.

"This lady and her party are expected," he shouted. "There is nothing to see. Go home!"

"I suspect they were hoping to watch all of us being led off in irons," James said to her in a low voice charged with laughter. He was enjoying himself even more than the official was. She realized suddenly how bizarre this must be for him—to sail across in daylight instead of in darkness, to step onto the dock and hand a French harbormaster papers instead of landing on a lonely beach, praying no one was nearby.

"I'll send someone ahead to bespeak rooms for us," he told her as the crowd dispersed. "There's a reasonable inn about two leagues on if you think you can stand a short carriage ride."

She was feeling more herself every minute. "I'll do," she told him.

He squeezed her arm. "Good girl." He looked across at the road winding up the hill out of town towards the southeast—towards Paris. There was an odd, suppressed excitement in his face. "Welcome to France," he said.

More than an hour after the excitement at the waterfront had faded, a lone figure sat smoking his pipe on the damp wooden steps of a chandler's shop adjacent to the docks. He was not exactly hidden—and in any case, the pungent smoke would have given him away—but he did not seek the better-lit areas where guards patrolled in front of the naval store sheds, nor did he take refuge from the cold in the Trois Cochons, an aptly named hostelry which catered to sailors and fishermen. He seemed to be keeping some sort of vigil, and when a rowboat pulled quietly up to the wharf, he peered keenly into the darkness but then grunted quietly and kept his seat when he saw a stranger disembark.

To his surprise, the new arrival did not head for the tavern but wandered, apparently randomly, until he came to a stop right in front of him.

"Good evening, Grandfather," said the stranger respectfully.

Sizing up the younger man, the watcher decided to accord him the favor of a return greeting.

"Perhaps you have been here for some time?" the stranger asked casually.

"Perhaps."

A small coin appeared. "I am seeking a family—an

English couple, with a child, and two or three servants. Did they by chance land here?''

"You are in luck." The pipe-smoker gestured vaguely towards the road which led up the hill. "They disembarked an hour since."

"And there was no trouble with the officials?"

"No, their papers were in order." The older man shook his head. "It is a long while since I saw an Englishman step openly onto the dock here, hire a carriage, rent rooms at an inn."

"Oh?" said the younger man softly. He produced another coin. "Did you hear where they are staying?"

"I might have heard something." There was a pause. Yet another coin appeared. "You aren't with the *Sûreté*, by any chance?" the pipe-smoker inquired cautiously.

"Those dogs? No," said the stranger with undisguised contempt.

"Well, then," said the old man grudgingly, "I believe they lie tonight at Abbéville."

The stranger added an extra coin, handed both over, and pulled his hat down even lower over his face. "Thanks for your help, Grandfather. Wish me luck."

"Good luck!" called the old man obligingly as his questioner strode away. Then he sat down on his step and puffed away on his pipe, stowing the money he had received very carefully away in an inner pocket. "You'll need some luck," he muttered, "if you plan to shadow a British courier. That was Rover's son, or I miss my guess. Looks just like his father. And neither one of them takes kindly to folk trailing after them asking questions."

Fourteen

The morning fog had finally lifted, and the coach stood sharply silhouetted against a wintry blue sky. James drew Silvio aside as the valet emerged from the stable. Glancing over towards the inn to make sure the women were still inside, he said in a low voice, "We're being followed."

"So I think, signor." Silvio, too, kept a wary eye on the inn. "Perhaps we should stop here for the night? I know you had hoped to make Beauvais, but this is not a bad spot, if there is any trouble."

James surveyed the old stone building. The ground-floor windows were small and grilled, those on the first floor all had stout shutters, and no trees gave access to the roof. An easily secured spot. Still, if they remained here they would not reach Paris until day after next. It was difficult enough as it was to restrain himself from seizing the nearest horse and galloping off by himself towards the city.

"No," he said. "Let's push on. We'll see how skilled our pursuer may be. How long until the new team is hitched up?"

Silvio peered into the stable, where two grooms were preparing to bring out fresh horses. "Now."

"Delay them for just a moment," said James. "And send one of them ahead to the wood beyond the old mill with two horses."

"You think we are dealing with such an amateur?" asked Silvio scornfully.

"It was like pea soup all morning," James pointed out. "And we both noticed him." He had actually enjoyed the fog. It was a small price to pay for the milder temperatures and snow-free roads here in France. And, he suspected, it had made their pursuer careless.

"You're risking a bullet in the back of the head," said Silvio bluntly.

"Nonsense, I've—" He broke off and laid a warning hand on Silvio's shoulder, jerking his head towards the inn, where Eloise and Marie were framed in the doorway. Eloise was laughing at Marie's attempts to show how full her stomach was; her cheeks were flushed from sitting by the fire. She looked over and saw James watching her and her face grew still.

"Has the little one spoken yet?" asked Silvio hurriedly.

"No." James's face had grown equally still. "Get going."

Muttering to himself, Silvio disappeared into the stable.

"Are we too early?" asked Eloise politely, bringing Marie up to the carriage. "I can take her back inside. Danielle will be out in a moment; the innkeeper's wife offered us some warm things for Marie that her own daughter had outgrown." Marie's story and the silent, wide-eyed face had inspired similar gifts at every halt so far.

"No, stay out here. We should be hitched up in a few minutes." Out of the corner of his eye he saw a groom bring two saddled horses out of the stable and mount up. Eloise did not notice them; she was watching Silvio and the other stableboy lead out the new team.

"Where is your horse?" she asked.

"I'll ride in the carriage with you this afternoon."

She looked surprised, as well she might. He had taken great care to avoid riding with her since the quarrel on the road to Dover. He handed her in, then lifted Marie to her. Danielle, laden with an armful of donated clothing, scurried over and hopped in without waiting for assistance. James took advantage of the distraction offered by a pair of bright-red stockings and a rather lumpy rabbit-fur muff to give Silvio a quick raised eyebrow. There was a small nod in response.

It was clear the moment he climbed into the carriage that Danielle and Marie had not expected him to accompany them any more than Eloise had. An uncomfortable silence fell, and Marie shrank so far into the corner that she and Eloise together took up less than a third of the seat.

"Perhaps the child could sit by your maid?" he suggested to Eloise, wishing they still had two carriages.

The only response to this remark was a fierce glare from the aforementioned child. Hastily he sat down next to the maid himself, but this meant looking straight at both Marie and Eloise.

"Is she afraid of me?" he asked in a low voice, leaning towards Eloise.

"Marie understands when we speak," she reminded him pointedly. Sure enough, the glare intensified. "And yes, I fancy she is afraid of you. She has been traveling with us for nearly three days, and unless you were more cheerful on the boat than on land, she has yet to see you smile."

Mortified, he looked away and occupied himself with studying the view out the window. Eloise and Danielle began to converse in low voices, occasionally asking Marie some question or other. He refused to turn his head. He needed to keep watching for the curve in any case, he told himself. But as they wound down the long hill and turned into the woods, he suddenly realized that Eloise might misinterpret what he was about to do. After all, she had done it herself under similar circumstances.

"I'm not—this isn't because of what you said," he blurted

as he grabbed the handle. "Silvio and I planned it. Shut the door after me, will you?" Then he opened the door and swung himself quickly out, dropping onto the road with only a slight thud as the carriage rumbled on without him. A quick glance behind told him that the pursuer—for he was certain there was one—had not been close enough to see or hear him, and in another instant he was deep in the shadows of a thicket, waiting. After only two or three minutes, he heard the sound of hoofbeats, and a rider came into view.

An amateur, he thought at once. The rider was muffled against the cold in well-worn garments which offered neither anonymity nor freedom of movement should their wearer need to flee—a bright-green muffler, an equally garish hat, clumsy round-toed boots which probably offended the horse even more than they surprised James. But then he reconsidered as the rider passed by. His posture was alert and cautious; his eyes swept the road on both sides. One hand hovered suggestively over the far edge of the saddle, and James knew the man had a pistol holstered there. And after all, the muffler and hat were easy to discard, and concealed the man's face well without looking as though that was their intended purpose. Not completely unskilled, then, although—here he recalled both the boots and the rider's seat—not used to conducting his business on horseback.

Thoughtfully James walked back a hundred yards to a little side trail which led off the road. There at the bottom of a streambed was the groom with the horses, looking rather sullen. His mood brightened when he saw the color of the coin James tossed him, and he rode off back towards the inn, apparently well satisfied with the tale of a wager Silvio had fed him. James had found the reputed fondness of the English aristocracy for absurd bets useful more than once in his work.

Once the sound of the groom's horse had died away, James led his own up to the road and set off on the trail of his pursuer. This ridge was one of the few areas near the

inn with any place of concealment near the road; that was
why he had chosen it. Otherwise the road ran over a series
of open hills. It should be easy to keep his man in sight.
Sure enough, as he came over the top of the next rise he
saw both carriage and solitary rider strung out ahead of him,
the carriage little more than a fat dot on the horizon. He
estimated distances with his eye. He would need to come
up fairly quickly; he had decided that the safest plan was
to ride past his quarry at an even pace and then waylay him
in the next valley. The man would be on guard when he
heard someone coming up behind, but would relax once the
stranger went on by.

Timing his approach as best he could, James rode past at
a steady canter, schooling himself to give his victim no more
than a passing glance, the glance any traveler in these times
would give another man he met on an isolated road. The
carriage disappeared over the next hilltop in front of him,
and he set his horse to a faster pace. He needed enough time
to dismount while still out of sight. Now he, too, crested
the rise. There at the bottom of the hill was the bridge, an
old one with lichen-covered stone walls on both sides. The
road narrowed perceptibly to pass over it. Even now the
carriage ahead of him was slowing, the cautious Silvio
unwilling to risk grazing one side of the vehicle.

He tore down the hill, chancing the gallop to make certain
of arriving in time, and was rewarded by the sight of an
empty horizon behind him as he dismounted. Then he posi-
tioned himself carefully. When the rider appeared against
the skyline, James was studiously bent over the back right
leg of his horse, feeling the hock and gradually (as though
by accident) wheeling the animal until it stood right across
the entrance to the bridge.

Apparently absorbed in his examination, James gave a
credible start at the sound of hooves and straightened partially, keeping his face well concealed under his hat. "But,
my apologies, monsieur!" he exclaimed, aiming for a Belgian accent. It must have worked; the rider seemed totally

uninterested in anything except getting onto the bridge. "It is my horse; he is going lame," James continued garrulously. "Hired horses these days are miserable creatures, of course; all the decent ones have been drafted for the cavalry." He had grabbed the bridle of his horse and was backing it slowly as he spoke, and now there was just enough of an opening for the rider to push through onto the bridge. He did, with one wary eye on James's horse, in case it was inclined to bite another animal which came alongside. He did not have a wary eye on James, and that is how he found himself, a moment later, on the ground on his back with his own pistol pointed at him.

"Get up," James said, still with an overlay of Flemish in his speech. "We're going to have a little conversation underneath the bridge, where we can be private."

From under the muffler, pale-blue eyes glared at him, and James had a disconcerting memory of Marie. He stepped back, and the prisoner struggled painfully to his feet. Still wrapped in the muffler, he picked up his horse's rein and led the animal around the wall and down into the damp hollow beneath the bridge. James followed, keeping the pistol trained on the stranger while he tied up the horses. Then he motioned him back towards the light.

"Let's see your face," he ordered.

Defiantly the rider unwound the scarf. He was a young man, not much older than James, with light-brown hair and a hawklike nose, which would certainly explain the need for a covering. No one would forget that nose quickly. "You can drop the Belgian accent," said his enemy coolly. "I recognize you now. You're from that party in the carriage. You're British."

"Who are you? Why are you following us?" asked James, ignoring this comment.

"I saw you in St. Valery. I don't trust any Englishmen, no matter how many papers they show the harbormaster."

It came out without hesitation and sounded plausible, but James was having a hard time judging this strange young man who was shadowing them. He had assumed, as had Silvio, that it was one of Meillet's hirelings, that in spite of the safe-conduct, the *Sûreté* had decided to keep him under observation. It was only natural; he would do the same in their shoes. But Claude Meillet had changed suppliers if this man was his. The usual lot were dock rats from Calais and Boulogne: dirty, uneducated louts who never met your eyes and were happy to be paid by the *Sûreté* for the bullying and extortion they were already practicing in the rough neighborhoods by the wharves. Whatever this man was, he was no bully and no coward.

"Turn around," James ordered.

"Going to shoot me in the back, English?"

"No, search you," said James. He should have done it straightway, but the blue-eyed glare under the muffler had distracted him. He found nothing. A small pistol and a knife, but that was to be expected. No papers. None. One of Meillet's crew would have had some—perhaps several sets, in fact. "Give me your saddlebags," he ordered. Still no papers. Some food, a spare shirt, two flasks of brandy with dark wax seals, a purse with a modest sum, and a woman's bracelet. James frowned at this last item. Perhaps the man was a robber? That would explain the lack of papers, certainly. But the bracelet was a plain affair, well worn, without even a stone to make it precious. And this man did not appear shabby or desperate enough to risk hanging for such a trinket.

He frowned. "Let me see your hands," he said slowly. He had lowered the pistol, but his prisoner complied anyway, stripping off his coarse wool gloves and silently offering his hands for inspection. They were calloused and chapped, the fingers laced with dozens of tiny cuts. The face was bronzed, too.

"I hope you're not a robber," James said, stowing the pistol in his greatcoat and handing the man back his saddlebags. "I've given my parole in exchange for the safe-conduct, and I believe the wording would require me to turn you in."

"Me? I'm no robber," answered the other composedly. He extended an ungloved hand. "Denis Bourciez."

"James Meyer." He offered his hand in return, but he was watching the eyes, and saw a slight flicker. In the next instant, he stepped aside just in time to avoid a vicious elbow to the gut, and once again the Frenchman ended up on the ground. This time James was lying on top of him pinning both arms over his head.

"*Sacré con Anglais*," swore Bourciez, struggling in vain. He was short and slight; James outweighed him by two stone. Then he looked up at James and sighed. "Let me go. No more tricks. I swear it."

Telling himself he was a fool, James stood up and watched Bourciez stiffly get to his feet.

"You're no robber, you say?" he said. "What was that about, then?"

"It was my turn to search you," said the Frenchman. "See if you were a spy."

"How very patriotic of you," said James dryly. "Believing that the Ministry of Foreign Affairs has been duped, you nobly sacrifice your own livelihood—fishing, is it?—and set forth on a long and dangerous journey to protect the Empire from an evil party of British agitators. Would you like to search my carriage, too? Perhaps terrorize my wife, who is en route to the sickbed of her grandmother, or the little girl we have with us, who just watched her mother die and is still so overcome that she has not spoken one word?"

Bourciez started, then flushed.

"I'll let you go this time," James said. "But if I catch you sneaking about again, I'll turn you in to the police. Something tells me you are not a simple, honest fisherman. They don't know that elbow-to-the-gut maneuver."

"How do you know it, then, if you are a simple, honest English gentleman?" Bourciez challenged him.

"I never said I was a gentleman," James said mildly.

The blue eyes measured him for a long moment. "I never said I was a fisherman."

"Your hands did."

"I've caught my share of fish. That doesn't make me a fisherman." Bourciez reached into his saddlebag and tossed James the smaller of the two flasks of brandy. "Here. With my compliments."

And that, James realized, was all the thanks he was going to get for giving Denis Bourciez back his weapons and letting him ride away.

"You let him go?" Silvio was incredulous.

"What did you want me to do? Strangle him and dump his body in the river?"

"You could have tied him up. Or taken his horse. That would slow him down."

"What's the point? He knows we're headed to Paris. He's not one of Meillet's; I'm certain of that. And until I know who sent him after us and why, I'd just as soon be pursued by someone I can recognize and outmaneuver. If they send in someone new I might not fare so well."

"If it's not the *Sûreté*, who is it?" asked Silvio, troubled.

"An interesting question." James stared moodily down at the trough of water. His horse had long ago stopped drinking, but he hadn't noticed. "There are so many factions in Paris right now who might have gotten wind of my safe-conduct and decided to make trouble, I could speculate from now to next week and still miss half of them. The Chevaliers. The police. The deputy foreign minister." He didn't name the two most likely suspects: the countess and her father. Conversations with Silvio about either of those individuals were fraught with peril at the moment. "We'd best push on," he said abruptly. He handed Silvio the reins of his horse. "Have them send this nag back to Amiens."

"Do you need a fresh mount already?" Silvio was puzzled; they were barely five miles beyond the inn where the horse had been hired. He had stopped the carriage in a small village square and waited for James to come up with them.

"I don't need any mount," James said. "I'm riding with the women." At the look of surprise on Silvio's face, he stiffened. "It's cold out, in case you hadn't noticed," he snapped. "And there's a very unhappy little girl in that carriage who is probably wondering why I jumped out the door earlier. I think I owe her an explanation, don't you?"

He didn't wait for a response but wrenched open the door of the carriage and climbed inside.

Marie was asleep, stretched across one seat with her head in Eloise's lap. On the other seat a child's dress was spread out, and the maid's head was bent over it, taking stitches in one sleeve. Eloise was peering anxiously out the window on the other side but turned as he came in. He crouched awkwardly, on the point of retreating. He could explain himself and leave—ride up on the box, hire another horse.

But her face brightened when she saw him. "Where were you? What happened?" she asked, lifting Marie into her arms so that there was room for James to sit.

"I thought we were being followed." He lowered himself onto the cushions, careful not to touch the child. "So I arranged a little ambush."

Even the maid looked up at that.

"I was mistaken," he added hastily. "I gave a poor fisherman who merely hoped we knew the route better than he did some very bad moments, I'm afraid, but I made it worth his while."

"Oh." Eloise, satisfied, sank back against the squabs. Then she frowned. "You didn't hurt him, did you?"

"No, not at all," he assured her. "We parted friends." He pulled the little bottle out of his pocket. "A farewell gift from Monsieur Bourciez. Care for some?"

Eloise laughed and shook her head. "What is it?"

"Brandy." He pulled out the stopper and sniffed cautiously, then closed his eyes and inhaled again more appreciatively. He took a small sip, then another. "Very, very good brandy,'' he said, surprised, corking it up again. He opened his eyes. Marie was sitting up, looking straight at him and reaching for the bottle.

"Eloise," he said helplessly as the girl started to crawl across the seat towards him. "I think it's a cognac, a royal reserve, from before the revolution. The recipe supposedly goes back to Henry the Second. Twenty guineas a bottle, if you can even find it."

"Just tell her no," Eloise said primly. He had a dark suspicion that she was enjoying herself.

Marie was in his lap and reaching for the flask. He lifted his arm up into the air.

"No," he said. His hand was touching the roof of the carriage. Marie stood up on the seat and reached again. He remembered Eloise's comment earlier and gave the girl a tentative smile. "No," he said again, but gently. "Spirits are not good for children."

She smiled back, a sweet, clear smile which made her look like an angel in an old painting. Then she grabbed the bottle, made a little gesture which resembled a curtsy, and went back to Eloise's lap clutching her prize. She would not give it up, not for Eloise, not for Eloise and Danielle together. When Eloise tried to pull it out of her hand by force, she screamed so piercingly that Silvio stopped the carriage and rushed back to see what was wrong.

In the end it was James who found a solution. With a dim memory of his sister's successful tactics in the case of a spoiled four-year-old cousin, he proposed a trade. "Look," he said coaxingly to Marie, showing her his own flask. "This one is silver, and it's bigger." She shook her head, holding her treasure tightly against her chest.

"Marie, we cannot allow you to drink that," he said, beginning to lose patience. "It would make you very ill."

She gave him a look of utter contempt. And that was when he finally understood. "You don't want to drink it, do you?" he asked, leaning forward. "You just want the bottle. Is that right?"

She gave a single, grave nod of her head.

"May I pour the brandy from your bottle into my bottle, then?"

Another nod.

Without a thought for the waste, he emptied his entire flask out the window and held it out to the child. "I'll help you pour," he said. He put his hand over her little one and tilted the smaller flask to just the right angle. The other three adults held their breath and watched the golden stream spiral neatly from one bottle into the other. Only at the very end did a few drops spill, filling the coach with a fiery aroma.

For an hour afterwards James could close his eyes as the carriage bumped along and imagine that he sat in a tapestried chair in the royal bedroom at Chambord, sipping from a crystal goblet. In the great velvet-hung bed a beautiful woman was sleeping—perhaps the queen, perhaps Diane de Poitiers. He did not have to choose. Because he was a king it was perfectly understood that he had the right to be in love with two women at once.

Fifteen

He had told himself that it was too risky. Paris was not as familiar to him as Lille or Bordeaux; it was foolish to try to find her house in the dark—and so late at night that any pedestrian was suspicious. That had made no impression. When had he ever counted the risk where she was involved? Then he had told himself it was callous to be concerned with his own affairs when the Bernals were in such distress. The Carvallo house, when they arrived, had been as tense as field headquarters before a battle. An overwrought Reyna Bernal had greeted them at the door with a whispered command to be as quiet as possible and dismissed them to their rooms. While Madame Carvallo was on the mend, her condition was evidently still very grave. That argument, too, had failed. Finally, he had forced himself to think about Eloise. Hadn't she endured enough at his hands already? What if she woke and realized he was gone? He had thought she was asleep when he left, but he had been too impatient to wait and be certain. Too impatient and too guilt-ridden.

But of course, it didn't matter what he thought, or said, or feared, or hoped. What mattered was what he did. And what he did was always the same. Summer in Vienna, winter in Paris. Dazzled, unattached Captain Nathanson. Embittered, married James Meyer. He couldn't stay away from her. So here he was in the middle of the night, standing in the street below her hôtel and wondering whether she was at home, which room was hers, what she was wearing, who was with her. Especially who was with her.

He had managed to collect some information before he left London. She was here with her brother, ostensibly visiting family friends, although she had hired a very expensive house (the former residence of a duke) the moment she had arrived. Already in the short time she had been here, a court of admirers had collected, including (according to the reports) several ministers, two ambassadors, and even a marshal. One name which appeared frequently was that of Raoul Doucet, whose half-brother was head of the army's counterintelligence service.

The rational part of him reminded him that this was just the sort of thing he had seen in Vienna. She cultivated men who could bring her information, power, or money. She sold the first two items to those with the largest quantity of the last item. She was utterly heartless and completely untrustworthy.

And then another part of him would rise hotly to her defense. She was so young, had been used so cruelly by her ambitious family, married off at sixteen to a roué of sixty-five. Once she was widowed, her brother, that bully, had decided to exploit her beauty and her money to further his own ends. Had she not herself confessed that she had been misled? Did he not owe her a chance to explain?

Explanations? jeered the rational voice. *What sort of explanations are you seeking here at midnight under her window? Admit it, you fool, she could tell you that she was commanded to betray you by the ghost of Joan of Arc and you would believe her.*

"No," he whispered, his eyes on the shuttered windows of the hôtel. "No, I wouldn't believe her." That was the worst part. He had never trusted her. He had never believed her. He did not, in truth, expect her to give him any plausible justification for her treachery last summer, in spite of what she had written, in spite of what he had told himself over and over during the sleepless nights and the wretched days. Now that he was here, now that he might, at any moment, see her again, he was able to be more truthful with himself: that letter had been nothing more than an elaborately constructed lure to draw him back to her.

So why was he here?

He couldn't answer that question.

Very well, said the rational little voice. *How long do you plan to stand in the street? Can you answer that one? You do realize you are being watched?*

He had noticed the man almost at once, an automatic reflex, as a hunter notes the flight of birds or a dressmaker the line of a seam. It did not surprise him or even alarm him. It was probably Bourciez, and he hoped that one of the two of them would have the sense to leave before dawn. Otherwise he would have to make good on his threat and turn the man over to the police, which for some reason was not an appealing prospect.

An hour later, he was bitterly concluding that he, at least, might not have enough sense to leave before dawn, when he heard the sound of a carriage. Brilliantly lit by four lanterns mounted on the corners of the roof, a black-and-gold coach rounded the turn from the avenue and rolled up to the front door. The dark, silent house sprang to life. Lights flared behind the ground-floor windows; footmen appeared in the doorway with flambeaux; an older manservant hastened over to the carriage and put down the steps.

Out jumped a black-clad young man. James hated him on sight, even before he heard a familiar, clear voice calling him her dear Raoul as she thanked him and bade him good night. So this was the infamous Doucet. He told himself it could have been worse; she could have been consorting with

Claude Meillet. Luckily, the blond Frenchman was hundreds of miles away in Bayonne.

Her voice dropped to a murmur, a murmur which suggested intimacy, or conspiracy, or both. It was torture to force himself to remain still. Doucet was blocking his view, and he did not actually see her until she was in the doorway, her head turned back for one more laughing retort to the man by the carriage.

She was just as he had remembered her: perfect features, etched on a porcelain face; gold curls tumbling out of her fur-lined hood. One tiny gloved hand reached up to tuck them back in. He waited for the jolt, the heady rush he had always felt at the sight of her. A pale imitation, a dim moment of awareness, flickered and died in his chest, leaving a bewildering impression of loss in its place.

He felt as though his senses were abandoning him. Had he not longed to hear her voice for months? Yearned to see her face? Why did the sound of her and the sight of her not give him the same thrill he had sought out every day last summer? After a moment of near-panic he realized what must have happened: it had been so long, he could scarcely believe it was really her. When he saw her face to face, when he could speak to her, *then* he could expect to recapture those ecstatic feelings.

For ten minutes after she had gone inside, he stood there, unmoving. Then the nagging voice prodded him. *Well, there she is. You have seen her. Do you plan to celebrate your good fortune by remaining here until that skulker across the way can get a good look at you in daylight?* Sighing, he folded his collar up higher over his face and walked quietly back towards the river. He did not really care if he was being followed or not, but out of habit he ducked into a colonnade, went round a corner, halted, and then doubled back around the outside of the column.

Facing him, knife in hand, was Silvio.

"Getting a bit sloppy," said the Italian contemptuously. "I could see that coming from forty paces back."

"Was that you spying on me at the Hôtel Lis?" James demanded, trying to forestall the tongue-lashing he knew was coming.

"No." Silvio gave him a dark look. "Unlike some people, I try to remember my professional skills even when someone I care for is behaving like a madman. The man across the street, if that is who you mean, was there well before you got there."

"How do you know that?" asked James, nonplussed.

"Because *I* was there well before you got there. I went over as soon as I had unpacked your valise. I knew you would be coming, and I wanted to make certain you didn't run into any unpleasant surprises when you arrived. Iron boots, for example. Gangs of French thugs. The usual entertainments the lady provides for you."

"And where did you obtain her direction?" James had kept the letter on his person night and day since he had received it.

"From Colonel White."

There was a moment of icy silence.

"Your concern on my behalf is very gratifying," said James softly. "But let me remind you—and Colonel White, when next you see him—that the office of father to James Meyer is not, at present, vacant."

"Yes, sir," was the wooden response.

James sighed. He wasn't going to reform Silvio at this late date. "Did you bring a key to the back door of the Carvallo house?" he asked. "Or do we have to break in?"

Silvio held up the key.

"Some servants may be awake; Eloise's mother implied that they have been nursing Madame Carvallo around the clock. Where have we been?"

The valet thought for a moment.

"We received an urgent message from your uncle?"

"That will do, I suppose." James started walking again, with Silvio dropping behind in mock subservience. He wondered what he would say if it turned out that Eloise was

awake when he slipped back into their suite. For some reason
he was finding it increasingly difficult to lie to her. In fact,
he was more and more tempted to confess the whole sordid
story to her and throw himself on her mercy.

Marie's presence was proving to be an unexpected blessing, thought Eloise. She was sitting in the huge gilt-framed
bed which had been originally intended for her and James,
her knees drawn up to her chest, arms clasping her lower
legs, looking down at the slumbering child. Because Marie
would not sleep unless Eloise was with her, she had been
able to avoid another fiasco like the night at the house in
Ramsgate. She and Marie were in a large bedchamber which
had two adjoining rooms: a dressing room, where Danielle
was sleeping, and a smaller bedroom, which had hastily
been made up for James. The only entrance to the three
rooms was through the bedchamber where she and Marie
were ensconced. That was how she knew James had gone
back out shortly after she had blown out her candle. But
since she did not want to disturb the child, she had pretended
not to notice. And now, when after two fruitless hours of
trying every combination of pillows she had finally admitted
that she could not fall asleep, she could pretend she was
worrying about Marie instead of about him.

She had lit her candle again, and the light pooled around
the hollows of the child's face, making her lashes glow
against her cheeks. Another glow came from the brandy
flask, firmly tucked under one little hand. Marie had not
relinquished it for one instant since snatching it away from
James. Eloise smiled. Her mother had been horrified when
she had realized what Marie was carrying. And that, of
course, was another advantage of having Marie attached to
her: her mother had not been able to speak to her privately.
Eloise knew that in the morning, when Danielle would take
charge of the girl, she would have to face her parents'
interrogation. Why had she traveled to Paris with James and

not with them? Why had she and James refused all the invitations to Roehampton? Why had she not relocated to a more suitable address in London? How could she have been so thoughtless of her own reputation as to spend two weeks with Rachel Drayton? Didn't she realize it was best not to call attention to the more unsavory aspects of this marriage alliance?

Absorbed in these reflections, she did not notice at first when James slipped into the room. Only the shifting of the candle flame as the door closed alerted her. He had paused halfway across the room, dark eyes guarded, expression wary, clearly expecting her to look up and challenge him.

"You're back," she said, surprised. Somehow she had assumed he would disappear for days, as he had in London. And perhaps because she herself had been fretting about the questions her mother would ask her, she decided that for her part she would forgo the obvious sequel: *Where have you been? What were you doing?*

He came over to the bed. "Did I wake you when I left?" he asked softly. "Or has Marie been crying? Or"—an even more plausible explanation had occurred to him—"did your grandmother suffer another attack while I was gone?"

She shook her head. "Nothing untoward has happened here. I feel wakeful, that is all. Perhaps I dozed too much in the carriage."

"I couldn't sleep, either," he said, offering her another chance to ask her questions.

But instead she looked down at Marie, resolving that she would let him escape in peace.

Again he surprised her. "Come into the other room for a moment," he said abruptly. He held out his hand.

Wondering why he was seeking her company when she had given him every opportunity to retreat to his normal solitude, she let him help her out of bed and followed him into the darkness of the side room. Here he proceeded to bustle about like some country innkeeper, offering her a chair, putting a quilt over her, building up the fire, and lighting two small lamps. It was so unlike him that she couldn't help staring at him, bewildered. Then he pulled another chair over near hers and sat down across from her.

"I—I wanted to talk to you," he said awkwardly. "I would like to ask—" He broke off and fell silent.

A frightening thought struck her: he had discovered her deception. But no, he didn't look angry. He looked as puzzled as she was. Indeed, he was giving her very odd little glances, as though he were not quite sure who she was.

There was a long silence. He looked at the fire, back at her, back at the fire. Finally, hoping that she was not precipitating her own doom, she said tentatively, "Yes?"

He jumped up. "It's late. You should go back to bed."

"You wanted to ask me something," she reminded him, curiosity overcoming her anxiety that he might confront her about the nonexistent baby.

"Yes." He sat back down, stole another glance at her. What was the matter? She had never seen him at a loss like this. "Tell me about your grandmother," he said finally.

She was quite certain that he had not brought her in here to talk about her grandmother. But she treated his question seriously and thought for a minute. "She's rather stout, and fond of expensive gowns, and she dyes her hair black—at least she used to when she lived with us. She seems a bit frail and speaks very softly. Indeed, she *is* frail. She has been ill off and on ever since I can remember. The result is, people think her merely a vain old woman and then they are bewildered when she tramples them into the dust."

"What do you mean, she tramples them into the dust? Does she lose her temper? Shout? Threaten to disinherit them?"

Eloise shook her head. "She doesn't need to be so crude. Somehow she always ends up in command, without ever getting up from her couch. Everyone listens to her; everyone obeys her. Even when she is only writing, from Paris, she gets her way. She made my parents buy the house in Ramsgate, for example. She wanted something easily accessible by boat from France. She decided I should go to school, and gave my mother no peace until she arranged it. My father had picked out a husband for me——'' She stopped, realizing that this particular example was an unfortunate choice.

"But your grandmother insisted on me," he finished for her. "Remarkably poor judgment."

"You haven't met Raphael DaCosta," she said bitterly.

He was startled. "Yes, I have. Was he your father's candidate?"

"I believe so."

"No wonder you are so patient with me," he muttered. Again he gave her one of those strange, assessing stares.

Suddenly flustered, she rose, still wrapped in the quilt. "Was that all you wanted to ask me?"

"Yes." He had risen automatically. "No—that is, it can wait."

She took a step towards him, half expecting him to back away. Instead he swallowed and took a breath, as though he was finally going to tell her what he had really wished to ask her.

"Will your grandmother be able to receive us tomorrow, do you think?"

That wasn't it, either, she thought. But she answered him. "My mother thought so, yes. In the morning. That is her best time at the moment."

"I need to pay a call on someone," he said. "But I will wait until the afternoon. I am sure your grandmother will want to see the results of her matchmaking for herself." There was a bitter edge to his voice, directed, she assumed, at what he believed to be the Bernal family plot to ensnare him into marrying her. But she was wrong. Reading her face, he put out his hand and held her arm, as though afraid she would run away from him again as she had in the woods. "That wasn't meant as a reflection on you," he said quickly. "I've said far too much about your predicament. I give you my word I won't mention it again."

And suddenly, acting on a reckless impulse, she decided to tell him the truth. "James," she blurted out, "you don't need to stay married to me. It's not necessary. I'm—I don't need a husband. You're under a misapprehension." She stopped, aghast at what she had said.

But he did not seem to have heard, or comprehended. He gave her another of those searching stares, as though some secret knowledge was hidden in her appearance—behind her eyelids, in the set of her chin, underneath the dark braid which fell over her shoulders.

Under that piercing scrutiny she lost her nerve and fled back to the safety of Marie and the gilt bed. Huddled under the covers, she lay there, wondering if he had understood her confession, hoping one minute that he had and the next that he had not.

If she could have seen through the door into his room, she would not have been reassured. For a long, long time after she had disappeared, he simply stood where she had left him, eyes closed, leaning his head against the wall. Then he methodically extinguished the lamps, stripped off his clothing, and climbed into bed. "Are you still in love with the father of your child?" he asked the headboard. "Do you think—is it possible that you feel something for me as well? If I am in love with another woman, does that preclude a true marriage between us?" The headboard did not answer. But silence from his wooden confidante was preferable, he thought, to the response he would likely have gotten from Eloise.

The countess was still in bed sipping chocolate when her maid brought her a note from Doucet. "Have Josef show him up," she told the girl. "And make me presentable at once." Five minutes later she was sitting up in bed, her hair concealed under a lace cap, with a matching lace shawl over her shoulders.

"You are early abroad," she greeted him.

"My apologies for disturbing you at this hour," he said politely, leaning over to kiss her cheek. "I am called out of town, but I thought I would give you the news in person before I left. Your English Jew is here. Evidently, the limp is no longer so conspicuous; my man at the Carvallos' missed him. But he was seen here, last night, quite late. He watched you get out of my carriage and go into the house."

"Then he saw you with me!" she exclaimed, opening her eyes very wide.

"Theresa, I am certain he knows quite well that you and I have been keeping company," he said calmly. "He has access not only to the reports collected for Whitehall, but to his uncle's private messenger service."

She was well aware of that, but with Doucet she occasionally feigned moments of flustered naïveté. He enjoyed soothing her. And he also enjoyed the notion that she imagined their relationship as a secret liaison, concealed from dupes such as Captain James Nathanson.

"How long will you be gone?" she asked anxiously. "I don't think I should try to see him if you are not here to help me should something go wrong."

This was just the right thing to say. His shoulders relaxed slightly, and he gave her another quick kiss. "Two days, no more," he promised. "I shall call the minute I return. My men will report to Josef every morning; will that suffice?"

She thanked him prettily, and clung to his hand for a moment as he took his leave. But her thoughts were black. She had not missed the implications of his careless report on the captain's movements. Doucet was having *her* house watched, as well as the Carvallo and Meyer houses. She supposed she should be flattered; it was proof of his jealousy—as if she needed further proof. But she did not like surprises. Unless, of course, she herself arranged them.

Fortunately, an instrument of retribution was right at hand. Ignoring her chocolate and roll, she called for pen and paper. When she was finished, she summoned Josef.

"Close the door," she told him.

Impassively he obeyed.

"Monsieur Doucet is having the house watched. I wish to know by whom. If possible, I would like the men bribed to report to you first. Also, I suspect he may have some of my servants in his pay. If necessary, dismiss all of them and hire new ones."

He bowed. It would not be the first time she had dismissed her entire staff, but Josef was an old hand at ferreting out the guilty parties and terrorizing the remaining servants into absolute obedience.

"Oh." She held out the letter, as if it were an afterthought. "Deliver this. In person, and discreetly. You do remember the captain?"

"Yes, madame."

Of course Josef would remember him. He was the only man she had ever tried to seduce who had turned her down.

Sixteen

Madame Carvallo was exactly as Eloise had described her: short and plump, with improbably black hair, a soft voice, and calculating olive-colored eyes which looked as though they could bore right through him. It was clear this morning that her health was much improved from the previous day. He had pictured a brief interview with a feeble, bedridden invalid. Instead he was facing a shrewd-looking matriarch who was reclining quite comfortably on a chaise. He had a brief moment of hope when the sick woman dismissed her granddaughter after only a few minutes, ordering her to return again in the afternoon. But when he rose to accompany Eloise out of the sitting room, a deceptively gentle voice stopped him halfway to the door.

"If it is not too much trouble, Monsieur Meyer, I would enjoy a chance to speak further with you privately." She added the familiar, dreaded words: "I am acquainted with your father, as you may know."

He hadn't known, but he should have guessed. His world seemed at times to be one vast collection of people acquainted with his father, half of whom wondered why

James was so disappointingly unlike him, and the other half of whom—consisting largely of French counterintelligence officers—pursued James vindictively in the hope that he would lead them to the elusive Nathan.

"Sit over here," she commanded, pointing to a chair drawn up near her couch. "Where I can see you better."

He sat stiffly and waited as she examined him for what seemed like a very long time.

"You have quite the look of him," she pronounced at last, leaning back against the cushions piled behind her. "Although the last time I saw him, he was masquerading as a Spanish noblewoman. June, I think it was. You are both unutterably foolish to come to Paris, of course." Then, recollecting the presence of her nurse, she beckoned the woman over from her post by the door. "You may leave us, my dear. I will send for you when Monsieur Meyer and I have finished our conversation."

James watched disconsolately as his one remaining hope of protection curtsied and closed the door behind her.

"Well, then," she said briskly. She did not sound ill at all. "What do you think of my granddaughter?"

"I admire her more than I can say, madame," he said sincerely.

"She is a very dutiful and affectionate girl," she commented. "And I am happy to see she has turned out rather well. I had a hand in forming her character myself, you know. Her mother was inclined to spoil Eloise as a small child, but fortunately I was residing with them at the time." She paused and gestured delicately towards a small glass of cordial on a side table, which James handed her. After taking a sip, she continued. "I would say that her one fault is that she is too softhearted. Not an unusual fault in a woman, of course, and preferable to its opposite. I was not surprised to hear that she had an orphaned little girl in tow."

James was gradually relaxing, anticipating a long lecture on Eloise and her upbringing. He was, in fact, curious about his bride, and not at all averse to learning more about her.

But Madame Carvallo's next words jerked him out of his comfortable role as passive listener.

"I *was*, however, surprised to hear that she found this child because she ran away from you—jumped out of the carriage in the middle of nowhere and ran into the woods. Or am I misinformed?"

"No, madame," he managed to say, his mouth dry.

"And why was my granddaughter running away from you?"

His face was burning. "I insulted her."

"To the point where she jumped out of a moving coach?"

"Yes."

She eyed him coldly, clearly waiting for him to explain, to offer an excuse. But since, in fact, his behavior had been inexcusable and entirely unwarranted, he said nothing.

"You lost your temper?" she suggested at last.

He frowned, trying to reconstruct that black day. "I think it is fairer to say that I deliberately goaded Eloise into losing hers," he said slowly. "Which was not easy." With some effort he met Madame Carvallo's scornful green eyes. "It won't happen again."

"Let me tell you something, young man," she hissed, leaning forward and pinning him to his seat with a fierce glare. "I made this marriage. I made it in some haste, yes; I wished to see her settled before her bungler of a father did something irreparable. But I know your father, and your Uncle Jacob. I had heard enough about you, as I thought, to consider you a suitable husband for my Eloise, in spite of your German heritage. And unlike some people—my apothecary, for example, who apparently has been grossly negligent—I do not make many mistakes. Eloise's father was one of my mistakes. A small mistake, but a mistake. If you are a mistake, I do not think you will be a small one. Are you?"

"I don't know," he admitted, shaken by her vehemence. "I'm afraid I might be."

"Well, you are honest, at least," she commented. Her

Get 4 FREE Books!

We created our convenient Home Subscription Service so you'll be sure to have the hottest new romances delivered each month right to your doorstep—usually before they are available in book stores. Just to show you how convenient the Zebra Home Subscription Service is, we would like to send you 4 FREE Kensington Choice Historical Romances. The books are worth up to $24.96, but you only pay $1.99 for shipping and handling. There's no obligation to buy additional books—ever!

Save Up To 30% With Home Delivery!

Accept your FREE books and each month we'll deliver 4 brand new titles as soon as they are published. They'll be yours to examine FREE for 10 days. Then if you decide to keep the books, you'll pay the preferred subscriber's price (up to 30% off the cover price!), plus shipping and handling. Remember, you are under no obligation to buy any of these books at any time! If you are not delighted with them, simply return them and owe nothing. But if you enjoy Kensington Choice Historical Romances as much as we think you will, pay the special preferred subscriber rate and save over $8.00 off the cover price!

We have 4 FREE BOOKS for you as your
introduction to
KENSINGTON CHOICE!
To get your FREE BOOKS, worth up to $24.96, mail
the card below or call TOLL-FREE 1-800-770-1963.
Visit our website at www.kensingtonbooks.com.

Get 4 FREE Kensington Choice Historical Romances!

YES! Please send me my 4 FREE KENSINGTON CHOICE HISTORICAL ROMANCES (without obligation to purchase other books). I only pay $1.99 for shipping and handling. Unless you hear from me after I receive my 4 FREE BOOKS, you may send me 4 new novels—as soon as they are published—to preview each month FREE for 10 days. If I am not satisfied, I may return them and owe nothing. Otherwise, I will pay the money-saving preferred subscriber's price (over $8.00 off the cover price), plus shipping and handling. I may return any shipment within 10 days and owe nothing, and I may cancel any time I wish. In any case the 4 FREE books will be mine to keep.

Name_____

Address_____Apt._____

City_____State_____Zip_____

Telephone (____)_____

Signature_____

(If under 18, parent or guardian must sign)

Offer limited to one per household and not to current subscribers. Terms, offer and prices subject to change. Orders subject to acceptance by Kensington Choice Book Club. Offer Valid in the U.S. only.

KN053A

4 FREE

Kensington
Choice
Historical
Romances
(worth up to
$24.96)
are waiting
for you to
claim them!

See details
inside...

Il..l..lll....lll.l.l.l..ll..ll..l.l..ll..l

KENSINGTON CHOICE

Zebra Home Subscription Service, Inc.

P.O. Box 5214

Clifton NJ 07015-5214

expression softened slightly, and now he could see that in fact she had been ill. Lines of fatigue were etched around her temples, and her skin was puffy and sallow, but underneath the swelling and the wrinkles he suddenly glimpsed the lines of what had once been a very beautiful face. And as she watched him acknowledge that other, vanished self, she softened further. "We shall see," she said, patting his hand gently. "We shall see. Perhaps you give yourself too little credit. Ring for my nurse, if you please. You may wait on me again this evening."

The moment she nodded in dismissal, he fled from the sitting room, barely remembering to hold the door open for the returning nurse. He felt utterly drained, as though he had been scoured from the inside out with dredging hooks. His one thought was to find Eloise and tell her that her description of her grandmother had paled beside the real thing.

She was sitting with Marie at a table in their suite when he burst in.

"Oh, dear," she said, reading his expression correctly. She set down the book she had been reading to the girl.

"Your grandmother," he said, breathing hard, "is not ill. Or if she is, I tremble at the thought of what she is like when she is in health."

"Was it very bad?" she asked timidly.

"Someone had told her about the quarrel in the carriage." She winced.

"I'm sure you were not the one who spoke of it," he said hastily. "And I certainly deserved the trimming she gave me."

"She has an ancient maidservant." Eloise made a face. "Mademoiselle Lucille. Lucille collects all the servants' gossip and reports to my grandmother every morning. So far as I know, she has no other duties whatsoever. When I was little I used to hide from her; I was convinced my grandmother had set her to spy on me. She must have spoken with Danielle. Everyone has been very curious about Marie, of course, and perhaps that is how word of our disagreement reached my grandmother.''

James suspected that it had been more straightforward. This Lucille had probably simply asked Eloise's maid what sort of a master he was. The abigail had no great love for him; he could sense that. She avoided him whenever possible and turned up her nose in silence when it wasn't. Danielle would not have missed an opportunity to pass on the tale of how her mistress had jumped out of the carriage in terror of her husband.

He collapsed into a chair next to Marie, who eyed him warily and clutched the ever-present brandy bottle more firmly to her chest.

"Has she spoken yet?" he asked Eloise.

"No, not yet. But you can ask her questions, you know."

He looked down at the watchful little face. "Marie, why do you want that bottle?" he asked slowly.

"It's easier if it's yes or no questions," Eloise said. She leaned over. "Marie, do you like the bottle because it had brandy in it?"

A quick shake of the head.

"Because it's pretty?" suggested James, although the bottle was fairly ordinary.

Another negative and a small smile, directed, for once, at him.

"Is there something special you like about the bottle?" he asked, beginning to be intrigued.

This time he got a nod.

"Can you show me what it is?"

Scrambling over closer to him in the wide chair, she held out the bottle and pointed to the seal.

"May I see? I promise to give it back."

She bit her lip but finally handed him the bottle.

He studied the seal intently and then burst out laughing. "Take a look," he said, handing the bottle to Eloise. "No wonder she wanted it so badly. And here I thought she was some depraved street urchin, nursed on gin. She simply wanted a reminder of her lost pet.'' Etched faintly on the seal was the unmistakable image of a goat's head. ''Monsieur Bourciez's vintner has a droll notion of how to mark his wares,'' he added.

Eloise looked up from her study of the wax disk. ''Oh,'' she said, remembering, ''I forgot to tell you last night. When Danielle was bringing the luggage in, she met him. Bourciez, that is. He introduced himself to her while she was unloading the coach.''

He stiffened, then forced himself to relax. Eloise had enough to worry her without Bourciez and his clumsy surveillance operation.

She continued cheerfully, unaware of his reaction, ''He sent you his regards, said he was greatly in your debt and hoped to find some way to repay you.''

''How very obliging of him,'' said James smoothly. ''I shall be sure to keep an eye out for him while we are here.''

More as penance than anything else, James accompanied Eloise back down to the sitting room when she returned to her grandmother's side after lunch. But Madame Carvallo informed him tartly that his presence was not required and that she trusted he could occupy himself for an hour or so while she spent some time with her granddaughter. He withdrew, relieved, and in the circular hall outside the sitting room nearly ran into a man wearing an old-fashioned tie wig and carrying a leather case. The doctor, James deduced.

''Ah!'' His face brightened. ''You are Monsieur Meyer?'' James bowed.

The doctor pumped his hand energetically. ''René Laën-nec,'' he said, beaming. ''I am delighted you and your wife were able to arrange this visit, and even more delighted that it has proved merely a visit rather than a funeral.''

James attempted to make some polite reply, but Laënnec swept on. ''This was a very near thing, you know.'' He nodded in the direction of the sitting room. ''I congratulate myself on some rather nice diagnostic work. These dropsical patients can be quite difficult.''

Madame Carvallo might indeed be a difficult patient, James agreed silently.

Laënnec stepped closer and said impressively, ''You realize, of course, that the accidental increase in the dosage created symptoms identical to the disease itself? Until I realized what was happening, I myself was poisoning Madame Carvallo! I had naturally concluded that her sudden weakness and increased swelling meant that she required more of the drug! Only when she complained of stomach pains did I think to examine the color and taste of the drops she was taking!'' Then, seeing James's bewildered look, he paused. ''Your wife did tell you, did she not, that her grandmother's attack was the result of an error by the apothecary? He did not dilute her medicine properly; it was nearly a double dose.''

''Madame Carvallo said something of the sort, I believe,'' James said slowly.

The physician lowered his voice even further. ''I can ill afford to lose her, both as a friend and a client. I am an avowed royalist. Madame Carvallo is one of my few remaining patients who can pay her bills. The cloud of official disapproval has driven most of the others away.'' He sighed. ''I must be fair, though. She, too, is a well-known critic of the present regime, and yet the Ministry was most accommodating when they heard of her illness. They realized that the Carvallos might feel awkward about approaching them, given their opposition to the government, and they wrote of their own accord, offered to arrange safe-conducts for the Bernals and for you and your wife immediately.''

James had thought that his uncle had arranged for their papers, but the talkative Laënnec was back to the treatment of dropsy, and he found himself hopelessly at sea. Because his aunt was the daughter of one of the royal physicians, he had been an unwilling auditor of many similar discussions

in England. He spent another ten minutes hearing about the
wonders that could now be accomplished in cases like that
of Madame Carvallo, before he escaped and fled, for the
second time that day, back to the safety of the second floor
and his suite.

This time there was no one there. Marie, he remembered
vaguely, had been taken for a walk by Danielle. Eloise was
still with her grandmother. It was silly to lurk in his room
like a shy girl at her first house party, but his other options
were not appealing. He did not want to go down to the
drawing room or the library and encounter the Bernals—he
acknowledged now to himself that he had treated them very
badly in the past weeks. He did not want to go out, because
he was afraid that if he did he would end up once again at
the Hôtel Lis. After pacing aimlessly around Eloise's larger
room, he at last gave up and went into his own chamber.
He would find his card case and send a message over to his
Uncle Jacob. Presumably his uncle knew he was here—the
private Roth-Meyer courier system was as efficient, in its
own way, as the military version James served—but it was
just as well to observe the niceties.

The note was lying folded underneath his hairbrush, only
one small corner showing. It was unsigned, but he recognized
the handwriting at once. The imperious manner was familiar
as well; there was no greeting, no closing, just one sentence:
Meet me at five at the south gate of the Palais-Royal. His
heart gave a little leap—she knew he was here. She wanted
to see him.

Then he froze. It hit him, suddenly, that someone had
come into the suite to deliver this note. This someone had
walked right through the room where Eloise and the child
slept, where they had been reading a picture book not three
hours before. And the someones employed by the countess
were usually very unsavory characters indeed. He reached
the bell rope in one stride and pulled it so hard it tore slightly.

Then he marched out to the main room and waited, fum-
ing, by the door, until Silvio appeared. At least it was Silvio,

and not some unknown Carvallo footman. He dragged Silvio into the smaller bedroom and thrust the note at him.

"I found this just now under my hairbrush," he said intensely. "Did you put it there?"

Dumbfounded, Silvio read the note, looked at the hairbrush, looked back at the note.

"Did you?"

"Of course not!" snapped the valet.

"I want to know who did," said James, looking grim. "One of the Carvallo servants? Someone who came into the house unobserved? I don't much fancy either possibility." He could see from Silvio's face that he didn't, either. "I want you to go to my uncle's," he continued, looking around for the card case again. Only this time he wasn't concerned about observing the niceties. He found the case, pulled out a card, and scribbled a few lines on the back. "Have him find me some reliable types who can watch this house. Then talk to the other servants. See if you can find out who brought this into my room. And I want you, personally, to check the locks. All of them. Every door, every window. Cellar to attic."

He slung on his coat, dropped the card case in his pocket, and picked up his hat.

"Where are you going?" asked Silvio. His eye fell on the note again. "Never mind," he said in disgust. "I need not have asked."

"I'm going to ask her," said James, "how this note was delivered. And we'll see if her answer matches the answers you come up with on this end." He paused, then added bitterly, "If she makes an appearance, of course. She rarely did when she arranged meetings like this in Vienna."

Silvio watched him go with mixed feelings. The last time his master had answered a summons from the countess, she had kidnapped him and turned him over to the *Sûreté*. But the Palais-Royal was a very crowded, very public place. And James had been more and more like himself recently. Silvio could have sworn there was even a trace of anger in his voice when he promised to ask the countess how the note was delivered. He closed his eyes and said a small prayer to St. Lucia. Her intervention was said to be efficacious for victims of blindness.

At half-past five, heavily veiled, the countess made her way unobtrusively through the crowds around the shop windows, towards the archway at the southern end of the Palais-Royal. This was her favorite part of these assignations: watching him wait for her. Sometimes in various gardens in Vienna she had spied on him from behind hedges for forty-five minutes or more and then left without ever keeping the appointment. Once she had kept him waiting for nearly two hours. But this was January, not July. It would be cruel to keep him outside for two hours. Besides, she had to confess that she felt a certain eagerness to see him, to see his eyes fix painfully on her, to see his normal address and poise fall away from him, to see the lean face grow pale and bewildered. He was so delightfully young and malleable. She smiled reminiscently. A refreshing change from cynical, paunchy French ministers. They were malleable as well, of course. But it took much more work, and the work was not nearly as enjoyable.

She scanned the throng around the archway from under her veil, carelessly at first. It was not usually difficult to spot James Nathanson—his height took care of that. She frowned. Perhaps she had remembered him as taller than he really was, because she saw no one resembling him near the gate. Her maid was trailing behind her, and she beckoned her forward.

"Walk all the way out through the gate," the countess told her. "There will be a tall, dark-haired young man somewhere nearby. Find him, without letting him see you, and come back and tell me where he is." Five minutes later, her maid returned to report failure. "You fool," said the countess angrily. "I suppose I will have to look for myself."

And she did, very thoroughly. Inside the gate, next to the gate, in the shops adjacent to the gate. He was nowhere to be seen. Even then it did not occur to her that he would not come. He always came. Perhaps, given how often she had been late in Vienna, he had decided to arrive late himself. She stationed herself next to a pillar and scanned every male over six feet who approached from either direction. Not until the palace clock struck the hour did she think to send her maid to make inquiries. The first few tries yielded nothing. But at last her maid found a chestnut-seller who had seen a tall young man lingering near the gate. Abandoning discretion, the countess hurried over to the cart and interrogated its owner. Did the young man have a limp? He could not say. Had he spoken with anyone? Gone into any of the shops? The man grunted and pointed to a shop about halfway down the western side of the arcade.

Reassured, the countess hurried down to the indicated doorway. He must have decided to wait indoors, where it was warmer. But when she peered into the little shop, it was empty save for a wizened old man. He was up on a stepladder, dusting the glass-fronted cases. Once again the maid was pressed into service.

"Someone answering your description was in the shop, madame," she reported a few minutes later. "He bought a small china figurine." Perhaps he could not wait, she reasoned. He had appearances to keep up, now that he was married. But he had purchased something for her, to apologize for his failure to keep their appointment. She went into the shop and smiled at the proprietor.

"My maid was just here," she said sweetly, "inquiring about my fiancé."

"Yes, mademoiselle," he said, bowing awkwardly as he climbed down once again from the ladder. "How may I help you?"

"Would you know what time it was when he left?"

"Just after quarter past the hour, mademoiselle. I have

many clocks in my shop; it is very noisy when they chime!"
He gave a little chuckle.

She looked around. He did have quite a few clocks, mostly
china, like the figurines in the cases. "And where did he
go? Did you see?"

"Why, yes, mademoiselle, I held the door for him, as I
do for all my customers," he said reproachfully. "He went
off towards the Rue St. Honoré." His face grew sentimental.
"I suppose he was wounded at the front? You are to be
congratulated, to have one of the emperor's fine soldiers for
your husband."

He had only waited fifteen minutes! Now she was angry.
Angry and worried. She had promised Meillet that
Nathanson was still hers to command. Then she remembered
that he had bought her a gift. Her spirits lifted again as she
looked around the little shop. She was very fond of china.

"May I ask what he bought?" she said to the shopkeeper.
"Or did he mean it to be a surprise for me?"

"Oh, no," he assured her. "He said it was for a little girl
he knew. It was a very fine piece, Dresden-ware. A goatherd
with his flock, playing the panpipes."

Seventeen

Danielle had persuaded Eloise to let her go down to the Rue des Petits Champs to buy fabric and trimmings for more frocks for Marie. The expedition had been very successful— so successful that she was returning without any parcels. They had been too bulky to carry and were being delivered. Thus she was able to stroll along (not too slowly, for she was conscious that duties awaited her) and pretend for once to be a young lady of leisure. Peering into the occasional shop window was permissible as well, for she was still scheming to refurbish not only Marie's wardrobe but her mistress's. Was that not part of her job as a lady's maid?

Studying the lace fichus tacked up in the window of À la Belle Anglaise, she was not at first aware of anyone behind her. But she had a slightly guilty conscience—the Rue St. Denis was not, after all, on her way home from La Veilleuse, where she had made her original purchases—and perhaps she was uneasy. When she sensed someone looming at her shoulder, instead of turning around she peered farther into the window, hoping to see something in the reflections at the edge of the glass.

She did see something. A hand, in a rough woolen glove, planted on the edge of the shop window and cutting off her escape.

"Good morning, mademoiselle," Bourciez said politely as she turned.

"Good morning, monsieur," she said warily. The hawk-like face was studying her with an intensity which did not at all match his casual greeting.

"The child is not with you?" he said abruptly.

She drew back, although she could not go back far. The shop window was right behind her.

"No," she answered stiffly. "I was shopping."

He looked pointedly at her empty hands.

"The parcels are being sent," she said, beginning to grow angry. What business was it of his where she had been, or where Marie was? Her initial impression of a friendly rustic was rapidly fading. "Good day, monsieur."

But when she tried to move around him, he blocked her by stepping sideways. "Just one moment, mademoiselle." He took her arm. "I introduced myself the other night, but I did not hear your name."

Now she was frightened. "Let me go," she said. "My name is no affair of yours."

"Isn't it?" he said softly. "You don't remember me, do you?"

"I most certainly do not! Let me pass at once, or I will hail a policeman!"

The blue eyes looked at her reproachfully. "That would not be wise," he said. "Because I remember you, Jane Price. And I understand that at the moment you are using the name Danielle Lebec. Perhaps the police would find it interesting that an Englishwoman was in Paris attempting to pass herself off as French."

She stared at him, shocked into silence.

"I don't mean you any harm," he said quickly. "I merely wanted to ask you to deliver this to your master." Reaching into his coat, he extracted a small, sealed paper.

She scowled. "There is a very efficient Imperial postal service," she pointed out.

"This is highly confidential."

"Well, then, deliver it yourself," she snapped. "So far as I know, the Carvallos' porter is still answering the door."

He shook his head. "The house is being watched, front and back. And I suspect the guards have been instructed to look for me."

She shook off his arm. "I won't be a party to such clandestine dealings. If you have something to say to Monsieur Meyer, he is not difficult to find. I believe he is at the Carvallos' at this very moment."

"Please," he said. "Please. It's urgent. I truly mean no harm." He held out the note. "You can read it for yourself; I'll reseal it."

She drew herself up to her full five feet and four inches and glared at him. "How could you *possibly* imagine that I would read a letter intended for monsieur or madame? What do you think me?"

He colored. "My apologies. I wanted you to know I trusted you. Sometimes it is dangerous for a man to work openly. That does not mean he is a villain." He sighed and put the folded paper back inside his coat. "Never mind."

Something about his expression made her reconsider. Finally, she held out her hand. "I will deliver it after all," she said haughtily. "I suppose it is not my place to decide what messages monsieur should and should not receive."

He thanked her effusively. But when she turned to go, he stopped her once more. "And the little girl? She is well?" He must have seen that the question alarmed her, because he added lamely, "She—she reminds me of my niece."

"Yes, she is well," she said, adding pointedly, "Of course, she is now forbidden to leave the house, because monsieur is concerned for her safety. Most probably because of *you* and your attentions."

He winced.

She glared at him and waved the square of paper in his

face. "As though she was not frightened and confused enough, poor little thing! Do you know she has not said one word since we took her in? Madame had the doctor examine her yesterday afternoon, and he told us that she was perfectly healthy. It was simply nerves, he said."

"Nerves, my eye!" he said hotly. "*Tonnerre de Dieu*, woman, you of all people should know why she won't talk!" He looked down at the note he had given her. "Put that thing somewhere safe," he said brusquely. "It's important." Then he pushed himself away from the wall of the shop and walked angrily off toward Les Halles.

"My grandmother is better," said Eloise happily, tossing her shawl onto a chair. James looked up from his study of the newspaper. According to the *Moniteur,* Lord Castlereagh (the paper called him "the infamous Castlereagh," an assessment which did not differ much from James's own opinion) was en route to Allied headquarters on the Rhine. And Napoleon, he knew, had left Paris ten days ago to join his armies. An enormous clash was brewing; it was a good thing Madame Carvallo was recovered. He wanted Eloise back in England. Probably he could stay on by himself at his uncle's for a day or so to take care of his own affairs. After all, calling on an old acquaintance did not violate the terms of his parole.

"Did you see the doctor?" he asked, folding up the paper.

"No, but there are certain infallible signs," she said. "First, she quarreled with my father. My parents are therefore leaving tomorrow. It's nothing serious," she added hastily. "Papa and Nana have never gotten on well."

"So I gathered," he said, recalling Madame Carvallo's disparaging remarks about her son-in-law.

"This morning," she continued, "she hired her old chef back."

He looked puzzled, and she explained. "When she is ill, she alters her diet drastically. No meat, no butter, only the plainest sauces. Which infuriates her chef; he usually only lasts a few days before he resigns. It has happened three or four times now.'' Her eyes twinkled. "She announced that she was well enough to dine with us tonight, and you should hear the menu. Nine courses.''

James pictured nine courses with Madame Carvallo as hostess and gave a silent groan. If she had indeed quarreled with Bernal, he might even be seated next to her. He gave Eloise a weak smile. "How nice," he said.

She wasn't fooled. "I'm relying on you to keep my grand-mother entertained, so that she won't scold Papa," she said, with a hint of pleading in her eyes.

"I'll do my best," he promised.

"She likes you; she told me so. In fact, she is hoping we could stay on for a few more days. We need not leave at the same time as my parents." The pleading look was quite obvious now.

It was tempting. The safe-conduct was for *Monsieur et Madame Meyer;* it might not remain in force if Eloise left. If both of them stayed, he would have no difficulties. And yet it was appalling to think that he was willing to compromise Eloise's safety so that he could satisfy his curiosity about the countess.

"Just for a day or so," she coaxed. "I shan't let her plague you. She can be very charming, you know, when she is in a good mood."

He was weakening. A day or two should not matter; it was unlikely that either army would move without some diplomatic feints and parries first.

"I'll consider it," he said finally. "But you know, Eloise, this is an illusion." He nodded out the drawing room window at the pleasant street below, with its immaculately kept stone houses and cheerful pedestrians. "France is at war, and we are the enemy. The sooner we leave, the better."

There was a knock at the door, and Danielle put her head into the room. "I beg your pardon, madame," she said breathlessly, "but I believe I know why Marie will not speak.'' She disappeared for a moment, and then the door swung open and she edged in, Marie clinging to her hand.

''There's nothing to be afraid of,'' she said to the girl, in a gentle voice quite different from her usual stiff, impersonal tone. Then she caught sight of James. ''Oh! I will return later, madame,'' she said, stepping back. ''I did not know monsieur was with you.''

''No, come in; don't mind me,'' said James, trying another smile on Marie. It worked. She smiled back. The figurine had been an instant success, although it did not travel everywhere with her as the bottle did. He could see the flask tucked under one arm now. ''I'm curious as well.''

Danielle brought Marie over to Eloise, who sat down on a sofa and took the girl on her lap.

''What is it?'' said Eloise, looking up at the maid.

''May I ask her a few questions, madame? I should perhaps have spoken with her before I brought her downstairs, but I thought madame would wish to see her answers for herself.''

Both Eloise and James assured her that they were anxious to have her try her theory.

Kneeling on the floor next to the little girl, Danielle reverted to the gentle voice. ''Marie, when I was a little girl, my mother died, just as yours did. And my cousin's family took me in. They had two other girls and a little boy, all younger than I was. I was eight. I missed my mother, but my cousin's wife was very fond of me. She treated me like her own daughter.'' She paused to let this sink in. ''When we get back to England, we will find your family, and you will have someone to be like my cousins, your new family.''

James wondered what all this had to do with the girl's silence, but he kept still. Marie's blue eyes were riveted on Danielle's face.

''Shortly after I joined my cousin's family, my new mother came up to the bed where we all slept one night. She told us that there might be times when it was not safe

for us to speak. She asked us to practice remaining silent.
I was the oldest, so I was in charge of helping the little ones
learn.''

Now the eyes were so wide, the fair little eyebrows had
nearly disappeared.

To James's surprise, Danielle suddenly switched to
French—good French, but not, he realized at once, the
French of a native speaker. "Is that what happened, Marie?
Did your mother tell you not to speak to anyone?"

Slowly the little girl nodded.

"Because they might realize you were French when they
heard you speak English? And that might put your family
in danger?"

She nodded again.

"If I tell you that it is safe to speak again, will that do?"

Looking down, Marie shook her head.

"What about madame?" coaxed Danielle.

James saw Eloise bite her lip. Marie curled her hand
around Eloise's, but her answer was the same. *Please don't
ask about me,* he prayed. *She'll say no, and Eloise will
think I've done something dreadful to her.* He broke in on
Danielle's interrogation.

"Marie," he said, leaning forward and still speaking in
French, "is there anyone besides your mother who can give
you permission to speak?"

She nodded.

"Your father?" That brought a hasty and vehement
denial. "Some other relative?"

A decisive nod this time.

"Well," he said wearily, "we could list all possible relatives, starting with great-grandfathers."

"James, she's shaking," said Eloise, whispering in
English. "Let's stop for now. Danielle is right; when we
get back to England we should be able to find her family.
It's of no use to discover that her aunt can lift the ban, when
her aunt is not here." She picked up Marie and set her on
her feet. "Go with Danielle," she said firmly. "She's going

to measure you again. When she was out this morning she bought material for more frocks for you.''

At this news the girl's face brightened a bit, and she went off with the maid docilely enough.

''Your abigail is not French,'' said James flatly after the door had closed behind them. ''She's a fraud.''

''Congratulations, master spy,'' said Eloise, folding her arms and glaring at him. ''I myself, though not trained in military intelligence, spotted her the moment she was hired. Silvio noticed within three days. Your sister in two. You, however, with your superior skills, took two months to see something right under your nose.''

He was taken aback not only by her unusual vehemence but by the truth of what she had said. Had he really spent week after week in the same household with the woman and not noticed her mispronunciations? Had the black fog made him deaf as well as thick-headed, sleepless, and self-centered? Apparently so.

''You did not dismiss her when you discovered she was using a false name,'' he said after a minute.

''No,'' said Eloise crossly, ''I didn't. I *like* her. She is a very good maid. And her pretense is an innocent one. Danielle Lebec is—is—her *nom de travail*, as James Nathanson is yours. Good ladies' maids are French. Danielle is a good lady's maid. Ergo, she needs to be French. Just as you need to be Christian to hold your captaincy.''

''It sounds very logical when you put it like that,'' he admitted.

''Good,'' she said. ''Then it's settled.''

''Just a moment,'' he protested. ''You do understand that I cannot simply allow a servant in my household to tell lies unchallenged.''

''I have already discussed the matter with her,'' said Eloise. ''And she is *my* maid.''

There was another knock at the door, and the bone of contention came back in. ''I am sorry, monsieur,'' she said to James. ''I forgot to deliver this note. Monsieur Bourciez approached me this morning when I was returning from the cloth-sellers and asked me to convey it here. His manner awakened certain misgivings in me, but I thought it best to honor his request. I hope I did not judge wrongly.'' She handed him a small sheet of coarse paper, folded over and sealed.

''No, that's quite all right,'' James said absently, staring down at the note. The problem of Danielle and her false name suddenly receded in importance. He broke the seal.

The first shock was to see that it was in English. The second shock was the contents—thirteen words, unsigned: *In my trade one hears gossip. Ask your uncle who paid Théophile Emmert.* He shook his head, frowning. The name meant nothing to him, but Bourciez clearly knew who he was and who Uncle Jacob was. That was not good news. The third shock was the seal. A saturnine goat's head stared up at him, twin to the one on the brandy bottle which Marie carried everywhere in her arms. Apparently, Denis Bourciez bottled his own liquor.

Scowling, James contemplated the two-line note. A fisherman who spoke English, who had access to fine cognac and was sending cryptic messages about his uncle was no fisherman. He was a smuggler, and he had been hired by someone to follow James. Not by Claude Meillet—the smugglers hated the *Sûreté* with a passion. No, the most likely employer was his father. Bourciez was probably Nathan Meyer's equivalent of Mademoiselle Lucille. That gave him an idea.

''Danielle!'' he called as the maid was closing the door.

Surprised, she came back in.

''Do you take your supper with Madame Carvallo's staff?'' he said.

''Yes, monsieur.''

''I would like you, as discreetly as possible, to ask the upper servants if they recognize the name Théophile Emmert,'' he said.

''Oh, I know the name, monsieur,'' she said calmly. ''It

is Madame Carvallo's apothecary. His carelessness has been the talk of the kitchen since I arrived.''

"My dear boy!" said his uncle, rising from behind his desk. "How very nice to see you!" Jacob Meyer was a short, wiry man with thinning salt-and-pepper hair and keen black eyes. Next to his nephew he looked tiny, but an objective observer would ignore the difference in height and note instead the aquiline profiles and high foreheads both shared. "Your aunt is hoping that now Madame Carvallo is recovered, you and your wife might join us tomorrow night," he continued, showing James to a chair. "We are giving a small reception in honor of your Roth cousins, Anselm and Elena."

Then, seeing James's grim expression, he sat back down himself and sighed. "I take it you are not here to pay a friendly call? Your message yesterday was not a false alarm, then?"

"No, it wasn't a false alarm." James pulled Bourciez's note out of his pocket and shoved it over to his uncle.

Meyer read it and raised his eyebrows. "Who is this man Emmert?"

"An apothecary. Who nearly killed Madame Carvallo a fortnight since by mismeasuring her medicine."

"And have you spoken with him?"

"Silvio and I went by his shop on the way here." James crossed his legs and leaned back in his chair. "It was closed. There was a placard on the door directing customers to an *épicier-droguiste* in the next street. Silvio managed to find out that Emmert left last week, telling his neighbors that he was retiring to the country. Somewhere in the Dordogne."

"Well," said his uncle, tapping his fingers absently on the note, "that does offer some possibilities. The easiest way to pay someone discreetly, of course, is to give them coin. Not that there is a surplus of ready money in Paris at the moment. But it looks as though your apothecary was paid in land, and the imperial bureaucracy is very useful

sometimes when transactions of this nature are involved. I
can look into this for you and send a message over to the
Carvallo house tomorrow.''

James shook his head. "I'll wait," he said. "Or I'll go
myself. I need to know now." Something was making him
very anxious. The conversation with Laënnec yesterday,
combined with Bourciez's note, seemed to fit together in a
disturbing pattern.

His uncle did not argue. He reached over and rang a small
bell on his desk. A smartly dressed young man materialized
instantly. "Bloch, find Ruebell for me," he said. A few
minutes later an older man appeared, and huddled in confer-
ence with his uncle for several minutes.

"You're in luck," said his uncle dryly. "Today is not
one of the seventy-five official holidays for the staff of
the Central Tax Registry for Departments, Townships, and
Cities. Ruebell is well known there; he handles many mort-
gages for our bank." He looked at James. "This may take
quite some time."

"I'll wait," James repeated. "You can stick me in some
unused storeroom if I'm in your way here."

"That's quite all right," his uncle assured him. "I have
a meeting in a few moments next door, but I'll tell Bloch
to have Ruebell come straight in if he returns before I do.
Have you had lunch?"

James tried to remember if he had even had breakfast.

"I'll send for something," said his uncle amiably. He
patted James on the shoulder before he left.

There was time for an ample meal. His uncle returned,
then went out again. More food was sent up, and a stack of
recent newspapers in case he needed some entertainment.
His uncle reappeared and began working methodically on
a large pile of correspondence on his desk, ignoring James.

Five hours after Ruebell had left the office, he came back,
looking very pleased with himself. "Not the Dordogne,"
he announced. "Perigord. A farm of thirty-five hectares
outside of Cahors, including house, barn, two unspecified

outbuildings, and a blacksmith's shop, which has a ninety-nine-year lease automatically transferred to the new owner of the property. I found it through the lease.''

"Were you able to discover who arranged for the purchase of the land?" asked James tensely. He had sprung to his feet the moment Ruebell had come in.

"Yes. A man named Pierre-Adolphe Duchenne."

His uncle nodded, and Ruebell withdrew. "Private secretary to the Chevalier Raoul-Marie Doucet," said Meyer in answer to James's unspoken question. His voice sharpened. "What is going on, James? Doucet is an acquaintance of Madame Carvallo. He offered to help me arrange for your safe-conduct, cleared it with his half-brother, who is a colonel in the army. You cannot imagine it was easy to persuade the French to allow an officer in the British courier service a free pass to Paris.''

"I'll wager he did more than clear it," said James bitterly. "The two Doucets planned it, start to finish. They made her sick, and then they invited her British kin over to attend her deathbed. Her kin, of course, now including one Captain James Nathanson." He closed his eyes, seeing a neatly ordered stream of events unfolding. If only he had paid more attention to Laënnec yesterday. He would not even have needed Bourciez's note if he had put it all together. The countess's letter. That was to ensure that he would accompany Eloise. Madame Carvallo's artificially induced illness. The conveniently available safe-conducts. White's proposal that he meet with the royalists . . .

His eyes flew open. "Has the bag gone yet?" he asked.

His uncle knew what he meant. Every day the Roth-Meyer banks sent private dispatch bags to their other branches. The bags for Italy and Austria left Paris in the morning, but the bag for London left in the late afternoon. Longer documents went by ship—illegally. Short, urgent messages were sent after dark by carrier pigeon.

"Bloch!" called his uncle. He stepped out into the anteroom for a moment to find his assistant. "It's gone," he said, returning and closing the door.

"Then you'll have to send a special messenger," said James. "My colonel is about to send one of my colleagues into a very elaborate trap. It was designed for me, but they'll take anyone they can get."

There was no point concealing what had happened; his uncle was privy to everything he and his father did, and James needed his help. "The Chevaliers de la Foi invited us to send over a British representative to meet with two potential defectors from Napoleon's government," he said crisply. "In fact, they specifically requested one of White's couriers as the representative. Me, for example. An obvious choice, when my wife's grandmother lay dying and the French minister had generously issued me a safe-conduct. And"—he forced himself not to lower his eyes—"not content with poisoning my wife's grandmother, they made sure there were additional incentives for me to come here." His uncle's expression left no doubt that he knew perfectly well what (or who) those incentives were. "Someone has infiltrated the royalists and woven a net to catch both a British courier and the would-be defectors. London must know of this at once."

"I think," said his uncle cautiously, "that it might be fastest and safest to send the message to your Uncle Eli. He can see that it reaches your colonel."

The last thing James wanted was to reveal to Eli Roth—and, thus, of course, to his father—the whole sordid story of how he had been lured to France by the countess, who was herself (he assumed) the victim of some clever manipulations by Doucet. But he knew his Uncle Jacob was right. Messages sent by carrier pigeon could usually find Roth within half a day, and although the birds sometimes got lost or were captured, multiple copies of ciphered messages were fairly reliable. Conventional dispatches to addressees unconnected with the bank were risky and far slower. His pride was not worth Michael Southey's life.

"I'll try to be concise," he said, sitting down at his uncle's desk without even asking permission. "But this may require every bird you have available. We'll send two sets: three birds with an immediate warning, and then an explanation. I just hope White can reach the French participants in this little tragedy."

"Do you need the cipher book?" asked his uncle. "Or should I have Bloch transcribe it?"

"I remember it," said James tersely. He realized, with a pleasant shock, that he did in fact remember it. And it was far more difficult than the French cipher he had blanked on in White's office. "The fewer people who see this, the better."

It took him twenty minutes, and his uncle waited patiently through the whole process, continuing to work on his correspondence in the side chair where James had been sitting. When the messages had been sent off, he hovered solicitously over the weary and anxious James while the latter destroyed all the rough copies.

"Don't forget the reception tomorrow," Meyer reminded him as he rose and collected his coat and hat from the dutiful Bloch.

James grimaced in distaste. How could his uncle speak of receptions when his own carelessness had probably just doomed one of his friends to a firing squad at Vincennes?

"If you are correct about the French plot," his uncle pointed out, reading his expression accurately, "it is all the more important to appear unconcerned and ignorant. It is only for a few days; no one will expect you to remain here long now that Madame Carvallo is well again. Buy your wife trinkets. Stroll in the park. Be seen at receptions, at concerts, at dinners."

"Dinner!" James gasped. He looked at the clock on top of his uncle's bookcase and groaned.

"Now what?" asked his uncle, startled.

"I've just missed at least three courses of Madame Carvallo's first proper meal in weeks," he said gloomily. "I don't know who will be angrier: Eloise or her grandmother. And I can't explain why I'm late.''

"I suppose not," agreed his uncle. Then he paused, struck by an idea. "I could tear your jacket, smear your face with dust," he offered hopefully. "We could pretend you were attacked by footpads.'' He looked around the office in search of a source of dust, but the bank employed an army of charwomen and no dust seemed to be available.

James hid a smile. His Uncle Jacob had always harbored a tiny kernel of envy for his brother, who after the death of James's mother had suddenly transformed himself from a quiet bank administrator into an unofficial spy for Wellington.

It was his turn to pat his uncle's shoulder. "I am sorry to tell you," he said, "that in view of my behavior in recent weeks no one will be surprised if I am late. On the contrary, it will give everyone except my wife great satisfaction to see that I am just as ill-mannered and thoughtless as they predicted I would be.''

Eighteen

Parisians who wanted to sneer at Jacob Meyer said that he was just like any bourgeois: he lived over his shop. And it was true that his hôtel, off the Rue de Provence, was attached to the offices of the bank. But it was hardly accurate to describe the Meyer residence as "living over a shop." The bank and hôtel together encircled a substantial courtyard with a garden, and the hôtel had three stories (not including attic and basement), fourteen bedrooms, three drawing rooms, two dining rooms, a small and large ballroom, a library, and a conservatory. Since the reception for the newly married Roths was a private, informal affair, it was held in the small ballroom, which accommodated a mere fifty couples.

Eloise surveyed the crowded room and clutched James's arm a bit more tightly. "I thought you said it was only family and close friends," she hissed urgently.

"We have a large family," James reminded her. "And you would be amazed at how many close friends bankers have." He squeezed her arm. "You look very elegant. Stop fretting."

She did look lovely, he thought, in an amber-colored silk gown which somehow made her dark hair darker and her fair skin fairer. He had forgiven the maid completely for her sins when she had remade the dress from one of Madame Carvallo's in six hours flat. Eloise had not packed any evening clothes, thinking she would be in mourning. He himself felt oddly vulnerable in his knee breeches and dark silk jacket. Normally he would have been in uniform. And normally, he would know more than one or two people in the room.

He tried to look around unobtrusively. His uncle had buttonholed him for one moment with the reassuring news that his message had been received in London and all was well; then he had disappeared. His aunt was still receiving guests. His cousin Charlotte, like Rachel, had married a Christian and was not usually invited to large family gatherings. Her younger sister was still in the schoolroom—no, wait, there she was, looking much older than he had remembered her and flirting clumsily with a young man in a very ugly lilac waistcoat. His gaze moved beyond her, passed over several men in uniform, a small clutch of older women, and finally found a familiar face: Anselm Roth, one of the guests of honor, looking just as lost as James was. A few yards away from him, a huge knot of people, mostly male, surrounded someone who was invisible even from James's height. He knew who it was: Anselm's wife, Elena, the other guest of honor.

"Let's go rescue my cousin," he told Eloise. "He's very nearsighted, and he isn't wearing his spectacles. Probably standing still in that corner lest he trip over someone."

Roth greeted them with relief. "I thought you were never coming," he told James after Eloise had been presented. "Elena, of course, abandoned me the moment the first guests arrived, and I don't know a soul. Your uncle didn't invite anyone from the Academy."

"Professors do not hobnob with financiers," James pointed out.

"Well, they should," grumbled Anselm. "My colleagues are desperate for funds, and all the money is going to the confounded war."

"You could ask Elena to introduce you to some of the bankers she has collected," said James dryly, looking over at the crowd which encircled her. "I see marriage has not dulled her skills."

Anselm laughed. "Don't try to bait me, James," he said. "I'm a happily married man, and I intend to stay that way. Asking Elena not to flirt would be like asking a fish not to swim."

Just then the crowd parted, and a petite young woman with lively green eyes caught sight of the three of them.

"James!" she cried. Abandoning all her admirers, she ran over, tripping slightly over her skirts, and threw herself into his arms.

"Well," he drawled, a bit embarrassed. "This is a warmer greeting than I received when I saw you in July."

"You can't lecture me now," she said, looking up at him with a mocking smile. "As you did so frequently and so insufferably last summer. I have a protector." She gave her husband a quick, affectionate glance which did much to reassure James about the flirting. Elena had always been the wildest of his cousins—except for James himself, of course. You never knew what she would say or do next.

Now Elena looked at Eloise. "You must be James's wife," she said, smiling warmly. "Come away for a moment; we cannot talk properly here, and I've been so anxious to meet you. I was with him in Austria last summer, and if you had told me then he would be married six months later I would have been *astounded*."

James watched helplessly as the two women went off, arms entwined. Elena talked without pause as they vanished into the crowd. He caught only a few words, which sounded innocent enough: "Gibraltar," "Isabella" (Elena's sister), and his name, followed by a burst of laughter.

"I don't suppose you can stop her," he said to Anselm

with a sigh. He hoped fervently that Elena would refrain from
going into too much detail about his activities in Vienna.

"They're probably tracing family trees," said his cousin.
"Elena's father's family and the Bernals meet somewhere
back in Portugal a few hundred years ago. One of the Mendez
grandmothers told me so when your wedding was announced."

That was a cheering thought, and he clung to it when ten
minutes went by and neither woman reappeared. What on
earth could Elena be telling her? Hadn't his aunt finished
greeting the late arrivals yet? Shouldn't she be making sure
that Elena met the other guests? He looked over towards
the double doors which led into the ballroom from the main
staircase. His aunt was turning—she had seen him, had seen
Anselm.

He relaxed. She was clearly looking for Elena. Now she
had apparently found her, in one of the alcoves (he inferred
this, since the crowd blocked his view). She was moving
away from the door. No, there was one last pair of guests
to greet. A man and a woman. The man was some sort of
official, his chest covered in medals and ribbons. The woman
was wearing a low-cut dress in an unusual shade of sapphire
blue. With a horrible sense of fatalism he recognized the
matching blue eyes, the carefully spun gold ringlets, the
delicate features, the gleaming shoulders curving down with
the mathematical precision of a Greek statue to the tiny
piece of fabric which pretended to be a sleeve.

And Elena was not in an alcove. She was standing about
ten feet away from him, clutching Eloise's arm and staring
in horror at the door. "My God, that's her!" he heard her
say. Everyone around him heard her as well, her shocked
tones falling into an unfortunate pause in the music. "That's
the woman I was telling you about. That's the Countess of
Brieg."

* * *

She looked straight at him from all the way across the room, as though there were no one else there. And smiled. That same impossible, perfect smile which never failed to stun him. It worked now. He was paralyzed. Anselm, who could not see across the table, let alone across that ballroom, sensed only that something was wrong. And as the other guests repeated Elena's tactless remark, a murmur went around the room.

"What is it?" asked his cousin, peering uncertainly around.

James couldn't answer.

The room had fallen nearly silent. Even the musicians had stopped playing. His aunt had not moved to greet the new guests. But the murmurers had told him who her escort was. He was a senior finance minister, and James's uncle could not afford to insult the man. So James set his feet in motion, one slightly uneven step after the other, and dragged himself across the endless expanse of parquet floor. To his relief, he saw his uncle hurrying back in from the drawing room, which had been opened to accommodate guests who wanted to play cards. Meyer drew the minister aside, beckoned over a servant with a tray, offered him a glass of wine.

The countess had not moved. He had wanted to see her, yes, but privately. Not like this, with half of Paris watching. With Eloise wondering who this woman was and what claim she had on her husband. Or worse, not wondering. What had Elena said to her? He turned anxiously. She had vanished from Elena's side. Perhaps he could take the countess into another room before someone told her what was causing such a stir.

"Captain Nathanson," the countess said in her clear, carrying voice as he came up to her. The whole room could hear her. "What a surprise to find one of France's deadliest enemies here in the heart of Paris."

"It is James Meyer," he corrected. "And I am here as a private citizen, visiting my wife's family."

"And calling on old friends," she said, challenging him.

"A few, yes," he said coolly, but his heart was pounding.

"Old friends from the Faubourg St.-Germain?" Since the district was a royalist stronghold, this was virtually an accusation of treason in Napoleon's Paris, and she had not lowered her voice.

"No, I was to meet an old friend from Vienna," he retorted. "But unaccountably, my friend failed to keep the appointment."

For the first time she dropped her eyes. He felt as though he had just been released from a blue vise.

"You did not wait very long," she said with a small pout. She had finally lowered her voice.

His one thought was to get her out of that ballroom and away from Eloise. Out of the corner of his eye he spotted a potential refuge: the drawing room. He offered her his arm and she laid her hand over it, taking two steps to his one as they walked slowly through the crowd. The unnatural quiet was terrifying, and people drew back as they approached. The doors were nearer now; there were fewer people. He was not certain what he was going to do or say when they did reach the shelter of the smaller room, but at least he would be through this gauntlet of narrowed eyes and whispers.

And then, of course, just as he had feared she would, Eloise materialized. Had she followed him, curious to see the countess for herself? Or had she supposed he would *want* to introduce her? He looked longingly at the elusive doorway with its promise of safety. But she was too close to him; he could not possibly pretend he had not seen her. From somewhere he summoned up the willpower to stop, to turn politely to his companion, drawing her forward just the right amount.

"Countess," he heard himself say, "may I present my wife, Madame Meyer. My love, this is an old acquaintance from Vienna, the Countess of Brieg." He had never called Eloise "my love," but for some reason he did not want the countess to hear her name.

Eloise curtsied gracefully, and the countess gave her a regal nod.

"I had not heard you were married," she said to James. She had raised her voice again. "My felicitations." She gave Eloise a patronizing smile and turned her blue eyes back up to James. "But, my dear James, she is quite charming."

This time her voice was pitched to suggest that only James was meant to hear her, while carrying to Eloise. It was the first time she had ever used his given name to his face, and he knew it was meant not as an endearment but as an insult to his wife. He was disgusted to realize that part of him still counted it as a victory.

Desperate to escape, he stammered an incoherent excuse and nearly shoved the countess through the doors into the drawing room. A few cardplayers looked up, startled. He spotted another set of doors. It could be the water closet and he would not care. He headed for it single-mindedly, praying there was no one in there.

It was a square anteroom between the two smaller salons, and it was empty. He closed the door behind him so quickly that he nearly caught the countess's skirt in it. Unfortunately, there was no lock.

"This is very indiscreet, James," she pointed out with a malicious little smile. "Quite unlike you, to drag me off behind closed doors with everyone watching."

He collapsed into a chair, not caring that she was still standing. His legs couldn't support him another minute.

"Why did you come here?" he asked, trying not to look at her face, or her half-exposed breasts, or her shoulders, or her impossibly tiny feet in their sapphire-blue sandals. He concentrated on the elbows of her gloves. That seemed relatively safe.

She moved closer. "To see you, of course."

"You could have seen me yesterday, if you had kept your own appointment at the Palais-Royal."

"I was delayed," she said. She wandered in a small circle around him, tracing her finger on the back of his chair.

"Won't you offer me a seat? I had not thought you so boorish."

"Think again," he advised her.

She made an exasperated moue and settled gracefully into a chair across from him. "So, tell me," she said. "What *are* you doing in Paris?"

"Visiting my wife's family," he answered wearily. "As I told you before."

"You cannot expect me to believe that," she said scornfully. "You are spying. Visiting the Carvallos! A tale for children."

"Nevertheless, it's the truth." It wasn't, of course. Perhaps she would not press him.

No such luck. She leaned towards him. "Didn't you also hope to see me?" Now her voice was very, very low.

He thought of denying it, then gave up. "Yes." He risked a glance at her face. "You made some mention of explanations. I was curious."

"Ah, you did receive my letter." The blue eyes clouded. "Perhaps it was wrong of me to write, but I could not bear the thought that you hated me now, that you supposed I was a party to what Monsieur Meillet did to you in Vienna."

"It was your villa," he reminded her. "You asked me to come and meet you. You stood there and watched them drag that boot out of your cellar."

"But I didn't know," she pleaded. "I thought they would just frighten you. I never imagined—" Her voice faltered, and her eyes went to his ankle. "Can I see?" she asked softly. This was yet another level of soft, one which suggested unimaginable secrets.

He leaped to his feet, horrified.

"It's nothing to be ashamed of," she said, her eyes filling with tears. She looked up at him. "If anyone should be ashamed, it's me. I believed what Claude Meillet told me, and you paid the price. You cannot imagine how relieved I was to see that you were no longer limping so badly. As for the scars, many women find them attractive."

"No one," he said savagely, "would find these scars attractive." He strode to the door and jerked it open. "This was a mistake," he said, forcing out the words. He didn't turn to look at her, because the sight of her in tears was agony. She had been crying, he remembered, when he first met her. "I wasn't thinking clearly. My wife is out there, wondering what her husband is doing with the most beautiful woman in Paris in a secluded anteroom. And the rest of the guests are not wondering. They know, or think they know. If I leave now, at least they'll conclude we had no time do more than snatch a few kisses. I won't stay here any longer, and I won't see you again. Whatever explanation you could give, whatever you could tell me—it's not worth it. I don't care. I forgive you. I forgive you for Vienna; I forgive you for letting Doucet use you to lure me to Paris. Now please leave me in peace."

He closed the door behind him. The extent of the disaster began to come home to him as he saw the cardplayers hastily ducking their heads to avoid looking at him. Forcing himself to appear calm, he crossed the room slowly, as though he had nothing to hide. The doors to the ballroom stood open. He stepped through and looked around for Eloise. Once again conversation came to a dead halt as the other guests saw him standing in the doorway, sweeping the room with his stare. The musicians, at least, continued to play this time. He was thankful for that.

Nodding awkwardly to strangers whose eyes slid away from his, he dodged across the room, trying frantically to spot Eloise without appearing to look for her. Finally, a glint of gold appeared, and to his immense relief he saw his aunt and Anselm Roth making very determined conversation with an equally determined Eloise. She seemed miraculously poised and unruffled, although on closer inspection he could see that her back was rigidly straight. The dark head was turned towards his cousin, tilted slightly as though listening to an anecdote. Now she made a gesture with her fan, and Anselm matched it with a shrug. James vowed innumerable donations to Anselm Roth's laboratory as he made his way towards them. And when he saw Eloise acknowledge him with a brave little smile, he decided he was not going to let Theresa von Brieg scar his wife the way she had scarred him. Even better, he would pay his debt to Anselm right now.

He produced what he hoped was a confident grin which he scattered liberally around to various groups of guests, crossed over to the musicians, and asked them to stop playing. Then he returned to Eloise and put his arm around her, kissing her lightly on the forehead. "I have an announcement to make," he said loudly. Just in time, the countess appeared in the doorway to the drawing room. The guests whispered, turned from him to the countess, whispered again.

"The Countess of Brieg and I have been embroiled in a dispute concerning a financial transaction in Austria for some months now," he said. "The sum involved is approximately ten thousand florins." The figure produced a startled buzz from the crowd.

"After conferring with me just now, the countess has graciously consented to a proposal which will resolve our difficulties. In honor of Monsieur Roth, who is an old friend of hers from Vienna, she agrees to donate whatever share of the monies may rightly belong to her to the Academy here in Paris, where Monsieur Roth is at present conducting research." More excited murmurs greeted this.

The next part was the delicate bit. Luckily, this was not London, where public mention of childbearing was frowned upon in polite society.

"For my part," he said, raising his voice to be heard over the no-longer silent crowd, "I have agreed to donate my share to the same cause, in celebration of my cousins' marriage and of some very welcome news I have received tonight from my wife." And he bent down and kissed the startled Eloise full on the mouth. Her blush, that amazing blush which ran under her skin, her confusion, her lowered eyes were perfect. He couldn't have asked for more if she had been a professional actress.

And the audience, of course, loved it. Shouts and applause erupted as he beckoned the countess over, kissed her hand, and shook hands with Anselm. He held on to Eloise the whole time, curling his arm protectively around her shoulder. "I'll pay your share," he said between his teeth to the countess as she smiled sweetly at Anselm. For once, he was profoundly grateful for his family's enormous wealth.

"I expected as much," she whispered back. "A very nice solution to our problem. I congratulate you." She was all gaiety and charm as she took her leave. She had only stopped in for a moment, she told his aunt earnestly, hoping to resolve the dispute without further acrimony. She was delighted at the outcome and planned to visit the Academy in person to see what sort of experiments Monsieur Roth was conducting. What a pity other quarrels could not be resolved so easily— the quarrels of nations, for example. The minister who had come in with her was now deep in conversation with some other officials and accepted her excuses with an absent smile.

James escorted her personally to her carriage, accompanied by the unexpectedly resourceful Anselm, who made a very eloquent little speech of thanks.

"That was a near thing," said James when the carriage had rattled out into the street.

"I am in awe," said Anselm. "If I were wearing a hat I would take it off. James, that is the most brilliant lie you have ever concocted."

"It doesn't quite make up for my idiocy in going off with her in the first place, but I hope it will serve," he said. "Do you think most people believed it?"

"Absolutely," was the emphatic reply. "It explained everything—why she appeared uninvited, why she insulted you, why the two of you went off alone so blatantly. And no one, of course, could be so despicable as to have an assignation with his mistress in front of his wife on the night she had told him she was carrying his first child. That was the pièce de résistance.'' He added after a moment, ''Is it true? Is Eloise expecting?''

''Yes,'' said James. ''She didn't tell me tonight, though. Does that make me less despicable?''

''No,'' said Anselm bluntly. ''But at least your little drama spared her public humiliation. You're despicable but not cruel.''

Two streets beyond the Rue de Provence, the countess rapped on the ceiling of her carriage. The little window popped open, and the startled face of her coachman appeared.

''Turn around, Hans,'' she ordered. ''We're going to the Place Vendôme, not the hôtel.''

''But, madame—'' he protested.

''Place Vendôme,'' she repeated inexorably. ''Number Seven.''

She saw the driver cross himself before he closed the window again and turned the carriage south. This would not be the first time she had gone to the Paris garrison, although she normally went during the day. There were ghoulish stories about what happened in that building at night. She wasn't frightened. It was one of her gifts that she was never frightened when she was angry. And at the moment, she was very, very angry.

An hour later, a detachment of soldiers appeared at the reception and arrested James Meyer. They had received reliable information that he was in fact none other than Captain James Nathanson, a notorious British spy. With apologies to the terrified guests, they marched off, forming a square around their prisoner until they reached a massive black carriage. Then the square became two neat lines, a tall figure was handed forward into the carriage, and a mounted guard formed up behind the vehicle. The soldiers saluted and turned south, back towards the garrison. The carriage and its escort headed east.

Nineteen

Danielle was supervising two of the Carvallo footmen as they loaded trunks and boxes onto a cart, when she heard a familiar voice raised in protest behind her.

"Let me pass. Let me pass, I say."

It was Bourciez, and a huge, rough-looking man in a frieze coat was physically blocking him from entering the rear courtyard, where they had brought up the cart. She remembered that he had told her the house was being watched. Comparing the watcher to the intruder, she was not sure she did not prefer the latter.

"No solicitation," said the large man rapidly, grabbing Bourciez by the arm. "Petitions and benevolent societies on second Tuesdays. Tradesmen by appointment."

"Mademoiselle Lebec!" called Bourciez, straining to catch her eye over the other man's shoulder. "I must speak with you."

Against her better judgment she walked slowly over to the back gate. "Monsieur Bourciez is delivering a message to me," she told the guard, hardly believing that she was saying it.

"I regret, mademoiselle, but I have my orders. No one admitted without express authorization." He gave Bourciez a malevolent look which said, *especially him.*

"Then I will step out for a moment," she said calmly. "I trust that is permitted?"

Nonplussed, the guard stepped back. "Certainly," he said, shooting a suspicious glance at his captive. Grudgingly, he released his grip on Bourciez and let her through the gate.

"There is a cemetery a few streets away," she said. "We can talk there without attracting too much attention."

The short walk was accomplished in silence. Danielle kept her head down and did not look at her companion, who eventually fell a few steps behind her. But when they had entered the little graveyard and she had selected a battered headstone for contemplation, he came up beside her.

"I am very grateful," he said quietly in accented but comprehensible English.

"I am a fool," she shot back. "What do you want?"

"The cart, the luggage—you are leaving? Leaving Paris?"

Her suspicions returned. "What is it to you?"

"I need to see your mistress." He sensed her outrage and caught her arm. "I know what happened last night; all Paris knows. I was very sorry to hear the news. But I must see her before she leaves." He looked very earnest.

"We are not leaving," she said reluctantly, not sure why she was telling him the truth. "Madame has refused to leave, although she was advised to do so."

"Good advice," he said bluntly. "Though for me it is easier if you remain. Where do you lodge, then, if not at the Rue St. Honoré?"

She pulled away. "I've said too much already. I must be mad."

He shook his head. "No, not mad. You recognize a kindred soul, that is all."

"We are not kindred souls," she hissed, glaring at him and pulling her shawl closer around her.

"Oh?" He pulled out a small piece of yellowed paper, covered with British excise stamps. "Recognize this?"

Her eyes widened. "Where did you get that?"

"My father made the stamps," he said dryly. "As a favor for your adoptive mother, who is, I believe, my third cousin. I have dozens of these. You say you don't remember me, but the two of us spent a day inking the engraving plates in a shed near the Swanage quarries."

She shook her head. "I don't remember," she insisted, with a hint of panic in her voice.

"You were ten," he said. "I was thirteen." He gave a wry smile. "Covered with spots, sullen, scrawny, and not very fluent yet in English. Perhaps it's a blessing you don't remember. I remember you quite well, though. And you cannot possibly pretend you didn't recognize those stamps."

"So, you are telling me that if I do not assist you in— in whatever it is you are planning, you will tell my mistress that I was raised by smugglers and counterfeiters?"

"That is not what I am telling you," he said, exasperated. "I'm telling you to trust me."

"I *left*," she said, her eyes flashing in anger. "I'm *respectable*. I don't need to hide my face under hoods, or go down in the cellar when I hear horses coming towards the house, or sew things into the hem of my skirt, or smear dirt on myself and pretend I am hurt to distract a kindhearted Riding Officer."

"I see," he said flatly. "I'm not respectable. Therefore, not to be trusted."

She folded her arms. "Very well," she said, her jaw set. "If you want me to trust you, tell me why you need to see madame."

It was nearly midnight, but Eloise had not undressed. Since the arrest twenty-four hours earlier, in fact, she could not remember eating, or drinking, or washing, or sleeping. She was no longer wearing her evening gown, so at some point Danielle must have helped her change. And she knew they had left her grandmother's house and come here to the Meyers' hôtel. But she could not have said whether she had gone back to the Rue St. Honoré last night or had simply stayed here while Danielle and Silvio brought the luggage over and settled her in one of the fourteen bedrooms with Marie.

Jacob Meyer had left the house at dawn, sent one message announcing that James was still alive—there had been false rumors of an immediate firing squad—and then another message summoning Silvio. Other than that, there had been nothing. She had asked to see the newspapers, but James's aunt had told her gently that they would only distress her needlessly. Finally, she had extracted a promise from her hostess and Danielle and every other servant she could find that Meyer would come to see her immediately when he returned, no matter what the hour.

Elena Roth had called, and had sat with her telling her stories of James's miraculous escapes from various calamities. It didn't help. She was overwhelmed with guilt and anger—guilt because James had come to France partly on her account; anger, because he had also come for other reasons, which had become painfully obvious last night. For every story of ingenuity or courage or luck Elena offered as consolation, she remembered what Elena had told her, what she had seen, and responded silently: *but that was before. Before he met that woman and turned into a shadow.* Marie's feelings were less complicated. She was asleep in Eloise's bed, one hand on the brandy bottle and the other on the figurine, which she had not let out of her sight since Eloise had told her the terrible news.

There was a gentle tap at the door, and she started to her feet, but it was only Danielle, with a tea tray. "Would madame care to change into her nightclothes?" she asked politely. She had asked the same question at ten and at eleven. Two other tea trays had come and gone untouched.

"Thank you, no," said Eloise. "I thought I told you to go to bed, Danielle."

"You did, madame. I will do so once Monsieur Meyer has returned and spoken with you."

"It might be very late," she pointed out. "There is no need for both of us to wait up."

Danielle looked shocked. "Madame cannot imagine it would be proper to receive monsieur's uncle in her bedchamber without a companion present?"

The thought of Jacob Meyer making advances to his nephew's wife not even twenty-four hours after the nephew had been arrested—and this in full view of a six-year-old, a china figurine, and an empty brandy bottle—was so absurd it actually made Eloise smile.

Seizing her momentary advantage, the maid poured her a cup of tea. Absently Eloise accepted it and took a sip. She choked. "What is in here?" she said, staring down at the cup.

"I believe it is a black currant cordial, madame. Monsieur's aunt suggested it might help calm you."

"I *am* calm," said Eloise angrily. She held out her hand. It did not shake. "See?"

Then they both heard it, the unmistakable sound of voices in the hall below. Eloise jumped up instantly, white-faced, and the china cup crashed to the floor.

"My dear?" called Meyer from the staircase. "Are you awake?"

Danielle opened the door, and James's uncle came in, turning to give some last instructions to someone in the hall. He studiously ignored the broken teacup, which Danielle was quickly scooping up in a towel. The maid retreated to the dressing room but gave Eloise a very speaking look and left the door slightly ajar.

"Please sit down," he said, taking her hand and guiding her back to her chair. "I am sure you will wish to hear a full report."

"Would you like some tea?" she said, her voice trembling a little.

"I hope you do not mind, but I sent my man down to fetch me something a bit stronger. It has been a very long day. First, James is well and in no immediate danger. That is the good news. The bad news is that he is being held at the Château de Vincennes." The name meant nothing to Eloise. "He is not, however, in the donjon—at least, not at the moment. The wardens of the castle have granted permission for his servant to attend him at certain times, and have also said that you may visit for one half hour each day."

"But that is wonderful!" She got up, unable to sit still, and poured him a cup of the tea, forgetting that he had refused it. "If he is allowed servants and visitors and is not in the prison itself, that must mean they do not regard him as a real criminal. More as a prisoner of war." She handed him the cup.

"It means," said Meyer flatly, "that I spent a great deal of money. Nothing more, nothing less. If he were considered a prisoner of war, he would be at Verdun. Not at Vincennes, which is for prisoners of state."

"Oh," she said in a small voice, and sat back down.

"Now, there is no reason to despair, either," he added hastily. "The situation is very delicate. I have been calling on various officials this evening; that is why I am so late returning home. Let me put it this way: I do not think there will be any immediate move to try James, let alone execute him. On the other hand, it will not be easy to get him released. We will have to be very patient and careful."

"I don't understand," said Eloise painfully. "He's innocent. He came here in good faith, under the aegis of an official government safe-conduct. How can they even contemplate—" She broke off.

"Because it's not about James," explained Meyer. "It is not even, in fact, about the war. It's about Paris, and newspapers, and bungling field marshals, and feuding ministers.

And luckily, three of those four items are things I can influence. We shall have to pray there are no major military reverses while I work to get him out." He took a sip of his tea, coughed violently, and put the cup back in the saucer.

"Did you see him?" asked Eloise.

"No, but his valet was allowed to take him clean linens and some personal items. James sent a message back for you with the servant." He looked at her. "You won't like it."

"Go back to England," guessed Eloise.

He nodded.

"He already told me that last night, when he was arrested," she said. "My answer is unchanged."

"He's right, you know," said Meyer gently. "It's not safe for you to remain here. You could find yourself in a cell in St.-Lazare. Your grandmother has been considered a harmless agitator, but you will be assumed to share her opinions, and with James's arrest some may decide it is not a question of opinions in your case, but actions."

There was a knock at the door, and a manservant appeared with a decanter and two glasses. Meyer looked at his teacup, grimaced, and waved the man away.

"I'm not going," said Eloise stubbornly when the servant had withdrawn. "So I may as well be useful. There must be something I can do to help him."

Meyer sighed. "I'll take you to visit him tomorrow morning," he said. "Perhaps he can be more persuasive." His eye fell on the sleeping figure of Marie. "This is the little orphaned girl, is it not? Is she fond of him?"

"Yes," said Eloise. She was surprised to realize it was true. "Yes, she is."

"Dress in black," he told her. "But no veil, and a bonnet which shows your face. And take the child with you. We will try making some stories of our own for the newspapers. At the very least we can create enough sympathy for you to keep you out of prison."

* * *

"The reports said it was an arranged marriage!" The countess was pacing back and forth—stamping back and forth, in fact—between the map cabinet and the window in Doucet's office at the garrison. She turned and pointed an accusing finger at him. "You deceived me! You misled me! I saw her for myself! I saw the way he looked at her!"

"My dear Theresa, do sit down," said Doucet, amused. "So far as I know, it *was* an arranged marriage. Occasionally, it does happen that the participants find they have some affection for each other. In any case, I am not the one who needs to provide explanations to Claude Meillet. *You* are the one who lost your temper and had Nathanson arrested. Do you think the *Sûreté* will find Madame Meyer's unexpected loveliness an excuse for throwing months of planning out the window?"

"You told me just now that the English had apparently become suspicious and postponed the meetings with the royalists," she retorted. "So there is no harm done." Sullenly she dropped into the chair he was patiently holding out for her.

"No harm done, so far as we know," he corrected. "Our man in the Chevaliers de la Foi has his eye on the likely traitor in Bordeaux. But the identity of the official who offered to surrender Lyons is still unknown to us. This arrest will make him all the more cautious."

She waved her hand scornfully. "No great matter."

"I don't think you quite understand," he said, his amusement giving way to irritation. "You asked me to assist you in bringing the man to Paris. I agreed, after consulting with my superiors. They told me you were a trusted associate of Meillet and that the *Sûreté* was engaged in a confidential counterintelligence operation which had been approved at the highest levels. I would hardly call your behavior that of a 'trusted associate.' You seem to think that your whims are more important than foiling a dangerous and very wide-reaching plot against the emperor.''

"It wasn't a whim," she muttered, stretching out one kid-booted foot and examining the toes for scuff marks. "He is a spy. Everyone knows it. He should be shot."

"Most likely he will be," he said calmly. "But his uncle is a very powerful man in France. He will point out, quite correctly, that his nephew was here on an official safe-conduct and that there is not a shred of evidence that he violated the terms of that safe-conduct. Nor will there be—now. Thanks to your ill-judged, impetuous actions, he is safely locked up in Vincennes where he cannot possibly meet anyone or steal anything."

She looked thoughtful. "I could have him released," she offered.

"No, you cannot," he said, thoroughly exasperated. "The arrest was very public, and the newspapers have trumpeted it everywhere as a great coup. Hundreds of people have a stake in this now—ministers and deputies and colonels and aldermen. Even *you* cannot twist that many men around your finger at once."

"Well, then," she said after a moment, "I shall go and visit him. Perhaps I can persuade him to tell me something incriminating."

"Theresa, I do not think that is a good idea," he said. Normally, prisoners at Vincennes were under observation during all visits, but somehow he suspected she would manage to get rid of the guard. The picture of a handsome, despairing Nathanson alone in his cell with the countess was not a pleasant one. "I do not think that is a good idea at all."

She rose and smiled at him. "You are always so anxious, so serious," she said, reaching up and patting his cheek gently. "I can take care of myself, I promise you. I will write to Meillet. He will understand. We will contrive something."

Twenty

Until you reached it, the Château de Vincennes looked charming, thought Eloise. First she had seen only glimpses of pale stone through the buildings and trees which surrounded the castle. Then, as the carriage drew closer, a corner of the circuit wall appeared, capped by a little square tower. Finally, the entire west face of the wall came into view, with the ancient keep soaring up behind it, and the chapel just visible over the top. The Gothic windows in the chapel glittered in the morning light, and a classically proportioned stone pavilion appeared like a seventeenth-century surprise at the end of the enormous courtyard as the carriage drove through the gates.

The minute Eloise stepped out of the carriage, though, the Château revealed its true nature. The former palace was a war machine. There were soldiers everywhere—drilling, hauling gun carriages, clearing rubble away from a partially dismantled sentry tower. Most of the windows in the chapel were broken, and carts were being pushed in and out of what should have been the nave through a large hole in the wall. Clearly, the chapel was currently consecrated to the army rather than to God. Just in front of the pavilion an outdoor furnace was smoking, and teams of soot-covered soldiers were stoking it with coal. The sound of metal pounding on metal echoed brutally against the stone towers. Marie, who had just climbed down from the carriage, covered her ears and shrank back against Danielle.

"Your pass, madame," demanded a soldier. The Meyers' coachman produced it again. They had shown it twice on the road, at the bridge over the moat, and at the gate inside the wall. "Just one moment," the soldier said, frowning down at the paper. He hurried off. "Children are not permitted inside the castle walls," he announced when he returned, stamping the pass and handing it back. "The munitions works are not fenced." Eloise had suspected that children would be denied admission to the castle, but she had followed Jacob Meyer's instructions to the letter. Marie, looking appropriately fragile and woebegone, was carried back to the carriage by Danielle.

She had to take charge of her own papers now, for the footman who had remained with her when the carriage left was, it turned out, also barred from proceeding any further. A sour-looking lieutenant escorted her into the pavilion, where a clerk put another stamp on the pass, and then up a stone staircase to a corridor lined with sturdy wooden doors. "This way, if you please," said the officer, unlocking one of the doors. It led into an anteroom, where a sentry sprang to attention. Behind him was yet another door; the officer unlocked this one also and held it open for her.

The room was spartan, but one glimpse of the massive donjon had made her profoundly thankful James was in here. There was a cot, a chair and table, a washstand, and, incongruously, a prie-dieu, pushed into the corner as though someone had forgotten to remove it. There was even a window—she had seen very few in the walls of the donjon. It was barred, and James was leaning against it, looking out towards the half-ruined sentry tower and the teams of workmen. He had not heard the door open; the clang of the hammers from the courtyard was too loud.

"Captain Nathanson," said her escort sharply. "You have a visitor."

Startled, he turned. She saw him raise one eyebrow as he took in her severe black dress and matching bonnet.

"I'm not dead yet," he said after a moment. "Although that dress was probably a good investment. I suspect you'll need it shortly." He looked at the officer who had admitted her. "Might I beg the favor of a few minutes alone with my wife?"

The man shook his head. "I am sorry, Captain, but I must remain in the room whenever anyone else is present. Those are the regulations. No exceptions."

"Come over by the window, then," he told her, reaching out his hand. "Admire the view."

"Enchanting," she managed to say, staring sightlessly at the bars across the bottom of the glass. Her hand was curled around two of his fingers as though she were a child clinging to its mother.

"Noisy," he said softly into her ear. "Covers our voices. Not that I have anything confidential to say to you. But I'm not going to give that smug piece of *saleté* over there the satisfaction of hearing me tell you to go back to England. He'll think it means I've given up hope."

"Have you?" she asked, searching his face.

"No, of course not," he said hastily. "Uncle Jacob is very influential, and there is no evidence against me."

"On this visit," she reminded him.

"I have a safe-conduct for this visit. That is what matters. I keep my side of the bargain, the French keep theirs."

She indicated the barred window. "They don't seem to have remembered that."

"Don't try to distract me; we were discussing your return to England."

"No, we weren't," she said firmly. She glanced around the room. "What do you want me to bring when I come tomorrow? Some books? A chess set? Pen and paper? Are they feeding you decent food? I can pack a basket—''

He interrupted impatiently. ''You are not coming tomorrow. You are leaving France.''

''Your uncle said you would try to persuade me to go home,'' she said, beginning to grow angry. ''It appears he was wrong.''

''Wrong?'' he said, stepping back and staring down at her. ''What do you think I've been saying just now?''

''You're not persuading, you're ordering.''

''Do you want me to beg? I'll beg.'' His tone changed, his eyes held hers. ''Please leave. As soon as possible. It's too dangerous for you to stay here. If anything happened to you because of my folly and selfishness, I'd never forgive myself.''

''Did you know that Marie and I are a very pitiable sight— I in my black, and Marie with her little bottle?''

He looked at her as though she had gone mad. ''What does that have to do with anything?''

''The newspapers have devoted quite a lot of attention to your case,'' she explained. ''A man came to sketch me and Marie this morning before we left to visit you. My bonnet, in particular, made quite an impression.'' She tilted her head first to one side, then the other, so that he could admire it. ''Danielle made it for me late last night. It makes my eyes look very large and my face look very pale.''

Forgetting about concealing their conversation from the guard, he shouted, ''I don't care about your maid's talents as a milliner! Why won't you listen to me?''

''Because,'' she said, suddenly very stern, ''if anything happened to you because I cravenly went home instead of trying to win public opinion over to get you released, I would never forgive myself.''

He was silent for a minute. ''It's not worth the risk,'' he said in a low voice. ''*I'm* not worth the risk.''

It was her turn to beg. ''Let me try for a few days. Just

until the end of the week. Your uncle thinks it could make a difference.''

He was weakening, she could tell. And in any case, he could not force her to leave, and he knew it.

''I'll play piquet with you,'' she offered, trying to smile. ''The usual stakes.''

''Two days,'' he said at last.

''Two days, and then we shall see,'' she amended.

There was a sharp rap at the door. ''Madame, I am afraid you must go now,'' said the officer from across the room, opening the door to reveal two guards.

''It has not been nearly half an hour,'' she said indignantly.

''Your visit is timed from the first stamp on your pass,'' he said in a cold voice. ''Please say your farewells.''

''Good-bye, then,'' she said lightly to James, producing a better smile this time. ''Until tomorrow. I'll bring playing cards with me.''

''Speaking of piquet,'' he said slowly, ''I think that if the newspapers interview my jailers we should make certain they have something interesting to report.''

''What do you mean?'' she said, flustered. She felt a tug under her chin. He was untying her bonnet strings. ''What are you doing?''

''Claiming my winnings in advance.'' He tossed the bonnet onto the table and drew her towards him.

She flushed and turned away slightly in embarrassment as she realized he truly did mean to kiss her with three strange men watching.

''Not on the cheek, remember?'' he reminded her. He set one hand lightly under her jaw and turned her head back to face him. For a long moment they stood there without moving. Then he leaned over and covered her mouth with his.

It was nothing like the ceremonial kiss at the reception. It was not even like the kiss he had given her after the game of cards. It was not brief, it was not gentle, and she was quite certain that both of them had forgotten all about both the guards and the newspapers long before it was over.

"That's good-bye," he whispered as he let her go. "In case—in case you come to your senses and go back to England."

It doesn't mean anything, she told herself as she walked along next to her escort, mechanically picking up her skirts as they stepped over heaps of soot-covered debris. *He's frightened, and he's feeling guilty about that scene at his uncle's. He's trying to make both of us feel better.* But in his eyes as she had stepped back from the window she had seen regret, and this time she didn't think he was regretting the kiss.

Just before sunset, James was surprised to see his door rattle as though someone was unlocking it. Silvio had come and gone at noon, and his supper had been served at an hour that would be scorned even by rustics. The work crews had laid down their tools; the parade ground was empty. He had expected a long, silent night with nothing to distract him from the contemplation of his sins. The rattle turned into a thump, and the door swung open. It was the sour-faced lieutenant.

"Another visitor, Captain," he announced, stepping aside to admit someone. Someone tiny, and blond, and very agitated. He had been sitting at the table; now he rose, astonished and uneasy.

"My dear James!" she cried, stepping all the way into the room. "I came as soon as I could. I only heard the news late this morning. I was devastated." She pushed the hood of her cloak back, and he saw that she looked drawn and anxious. Still perfect, of course, but it was a strained, compassionate perfection. Now she was taking off her cloak and her gloves and handing them to her escort.

The officer was leaving, he realized, incredulous. The man was about to close the door behind him, like some valet carrying off his master's hat and walking stick.

"Here, you!" he said sharply. "Where are you going?"

The lieutenant muttered something about special circumstances.

"Regulations," James reminded him. "No exceptions."

Red-faced, the man draped the cloak over the prie-dieu and took up a position as far away from his two charges as possible.

"Don't you want to be alone with me?" the countess asked reproachfully, stepping closer.

"No," he found himself saying. "You are too careless of your reputation," he added hastily to excuse himself.

"But I have important information for you," she said in a low voice.

"Speak in German," he suggested, following his own advice. "I doubt whether your friend understands it." He pulled out the lone chair and offered it to her. "Here. I will make up for my lack of chivalry the other night."

"I don't want to sit down," she said impatiently. "I want to help you."

"Do you?" he said.

"You sound skeptical," she said sadly, settling into the chair.

He pulled the cot over and sat down across from her. "Isn't it an odd coincidence that I should be arrested just after our little conversation at my uncle's home?"

She clenched her fists. "I knew you would think that," she said. "I deserve it. But it isn't true."

He wanted to believe her.

"Do you know who ordered your arrest?" she asked, lowering her voice and leaning towards him. "Doucet. Raoul Doucet. I am sorry to say that he is a friend of mine. In fact, in a small way, I am to blame for this. Apparently he became violently jealous of you and decided to remove you by any means, fair or foul."

Perhaps she truly did want to help him. Perhaps it had not, after all, been her idea to have him arrested. On the surface her accusation against Doucet was perfectly plausible. He had heard her call the man her "dear Raoul"; clearly they were on terms of some intimacy. It was not unthinkable that Doucet might have decided that luring him here was a mistake, once the countess began to flirt with him.

"I am going to find a way to have you released," she was saying, her blue eyes very earnest. "But you must be patient. Promise me you will do nothing rash."

He looked around the room. "What were you picturing?" he asked ironically. "Smashing the furniture? Throwing my dinner out the window? My options for rash behavior are limited at the moment."

"I was referring to *confessing*," she said in a near-whisper, as though the German was not enough protection. "Don't let them bully you. Hold firm, give nothing away."

His uneasiness returned. "Confessing what?" he asked, looking at her suspiciously.

"You don't have to pretend with me," she said, drawing herself up as though offended. "I am trying to help you."

"There is nothing to confess," he said. "I have observed the terms of the safe-conduct to the letter."

She jumped up. "I can't help you if you won't trust me," she said. "I should not have come." She bit her lip, clearly on the verge of tears.

And then just for a moment, for an infinitesimal fraction of a second, he saw her gaze flicker, sharpen. She was watching for his reaction.

He felt as though a mask had slipped, as though he had seen an act which was not quite properly rehearsed. The entire conversation was tilting sideways; everything she had said began to seem false and artificial. He did not respond to her last statement. It was true; he didn't trust her. At least, when his powers of reasoning were working. But he had the sinking feeling that within a day he would have persuaded himself that the fallen mask was his imagination. He would be caught again in the endless round of suspicion and extenuation, repulsion and desire.

Without speaking, he walked over to the prie-dieu and retrieved her cloak and gloves, praying she would not be crying when he looked at her again. She wasn't. Her new expression was sympathetic, understanding.

He found himself watching for the flicker, for the little observer behind the mask.

"I'll return as soon as I have some news," she promised, squeezing his hand. "I'll prove I mean well. I won't ask you to confide in me until you are sure I am your friend."

The lieutenant returned a few minutes later. "Do you have a redhead coming later, then?" he asked in a tone which was almost friendly.

"No," said James shortly. He suddenly wanted very badly to be alone.

"Then why, *mon ami*, did you turn down my very generous offer to withdraw to the corridor?"

"Make me that offer tomorrow when my wife comes," James said promptly.

"I cannot." He shook his head sadly. "Your wife is not an *amie particulière* of the warden."

James wondered for a moment if there were any powerful men in Paris aside from his uncle who did not consider the countess an *amie particulière*. "Do you suppose I could request that no one save family be allowed to visit?" he asked.

"I do not believe so, but I will ask," said the other man. He looked at him doubtfully. "You do not wish to receive the *comtesse*?"

"It upsets my wife," said James, seizing on the first explanation he could think of.

The lieutenant snorted. "Now, that I can imagine. Your wife is a lovely woman, of course, but compared to—" He stopped, for the simple reason that James was choking him and he couldn't breathe, let alone speak. The next minute the two sentries were in the room and James was slammed against the wall.

"Let him go," said the lieutenant stiffly, rubbing his neck. "He thought I was insulting his wife."

That was foolish, James thought wearily as the locks

clicked home on the door. If he had jollied the man along he might have allowed Eloise more time with him, or permitted Silvio to come in more frequently. Now he had a beating in his future. He had seen the promise of it in the man's eyes. And after all, Theresa von Brieg *was* more beautiful than his wife. It was a simple fact. Maybe he had been wrong when he told the countess his options for rash behavior were limited.

The countess's letter, attached to a copy of the *Moniteur* reporting the arrest of Captain James Nathanson, reached Claude Meillet at midnight on January 16. He was just outside Poitiers, already en route to Paris, but what he read changed the pace and purpose of his journey north immediately. The letter consisted of two lines, scrawled above her distinctive signature: *I wash my hands of him. Come at once; there is some risk his uncle may be able to engineer his release.*

Twenty-one

Two days stretched into three, and then four. James no longer spoke of her going home. It had become clear that she was in no danger. His uncle had calculated correctly: no one was going to threaten a lovely young matron with prison—not only lovely but a mother-to-be, and the protector of a mute and helpless orphan girl. "The sacred trio," James called it sardonically: beauty, fertility, charity. His cell began to look almost like a normal room. Silvio brought something new in every day. There were several chairs now, a clock, a small bookcase, a carpet, and proper quilts on the cot. Eloise noted each addition with mixed feelings. She wanted James to be comfortable, but every new item was a reminder that Jacob Meyer's initial guess was right: James might be there a very long time. No one dared make a move to try him, but no one dared argue for his release, either. She tried not to think about the British prisoners at Verdun, some of whom had been there for more than a dozen years.

It was on the fourth day that everything fell apart.

The first sign that something was wrong was the presence of a senior officer when Eloise arrived at Vincennes for her daily visit. Instead of the usual lieutenant, a colonel greeted her the moment she stepped out of the carriage.

"I offer my most profound apologies, Madame Meyer," he said. "It will not be possible to visit your husband today."

At once the nightmares she had been keeping at bay flooded in: tribunals, interrogation sessions, firing squads. "May I ask why not?" she said, trying to keep her voice steady.

"He is . . . unwell." Seeing her face, he added reassuringly, "I am sure he will be able to see visitors tomorrow. It is nothing serious."

"Might I speak with his servant, then? Make certain he does not need anything?" She gestured to a large basket one of her footmen was unloading from the back of the carriage. She had taken to bringing food for both him and Silvio every morning.

"Certainly," he said, appearing relieved that she had accepted his decree without further questions or objections. "You may wait at the bottom of the staircase; his servant should be coming down shortly."

This was another surprise; usually Silvio did not attend James until noon, after she left. James had joked several times about his inability to shave and dress himself elegantly enough to receive her under the circumstances.

"Puzac," the colonel said, turning to a young aide, "escort Madame Meyer into the west guard room." The aide, all obliging smiles, left her at the now-familiar clerk's desk. She held out her pass tentatively, not certain whether it needed to be stamped, but he was leafing through a notebook of what looked like receipts and paid no attention to her whatsoever.

Ten minutes went by. She stood patiently in front of the desk, listening for some sound from the floor above, but she heard nothing. At last a soldier came in—one of the sentries from the outer room, she realized.

"Madame!" he exclaimed. "My apologies. The lieutenant has been called away. I will escort you upstairs. I hope you have not been waiting long.'' He picked up her basket.

Delighted at his misunderstanding, she followed him upstairs and through the two locked doors.

The first thing which hit her when she walked into James's room was the mess. One chair was smashed; another was missing one leg. The clock was broken, bedding was strewn on the floor, and a pile of shards was all that remained of the stoneware pitcher and basin which had been on the washstand. But then she saw James. He was seated in the only remaining chair with four legs, holding a pad of cloth over a cut on his forehead. There was an ugly bruise on one cheek and more bruises on his chest, which was visible because Silvio had pulled open his shirt and was dabbing at several scrapes with a towel dipped in water. James saw her come in and gripped Silvio's shoulder.

''Company,'' she heard him say. ''Leave me for later and get the room back in order, won't you?''

Hastily the servant scrambled to his feet and began righting furniture and folding quilts as James rose to greet her.

''What happened?'' she said, horrified, letting the basket slide out of her hands. ''James, what is it?''

''Nothing much,'' he said, embarrassed. He pulled his shirt closed. ''I was expecting it sooner or later. This is pretty mild; I think Uncle Jacob has the warden under his thumb. I'm surprised they let you in to visit me, though. I assumed you would be told I was ill.''

''They cannot simply *beat* you for no reason!'' she said, outraged. ''You haven't even been charged with a crime yet!''

''Oh, they had a reason,'' he assured her. ''I refused to eat my breakfast. This was against regulations, and three soldiers came in to make certain that I swallowed every bite.''

''I don't understand,'' she said, looking at Silvio and then back at him. ''Why should they force you to eat the prison food? You've been eating the meals I bring you." She nodded at the basket.

"It was pork," he explained. "A nice pork stew. Rather unusual breakfast item, don't you think? I am sure they cooked it especially for me. The lieutenant recalled that I was a Jew."

"But, James," she said, bewildered, "you eat pork. We both do."

"They didn't know that," he said. "And I don't eat pork when someone is pushing the fork down my throat." He gave a contented little smile. "I don't think my breakfast attendants will enjoy their meals very much for a few days. I broke one fellow's jaw, and the other two had a collection of bruises just as colorful as these."

She realized that he was actually in a very good mood. And when she thought about it, it made sense. Days of anxiety and inactivity made a brawl very satisfying. Apparently, it did not bother James that the fight had been three against one, or that all of his opponents were in a position to make his life utterly wretched from then on. She shuddered, picturing an endless series of escalating beatings until James was back on crutches.

"I am going to lodge a protest," she announced stormily.

He sighed. "That is why I thought they wouldn't allow you in today," he said. "Too much paperwork. Women always want to lodge protests."

"They didn't allow me in," she admitted. "I slipped in without getting my pass stamped."

He brightened. "Then you can stay for a bit. And there's no one observing us. I think they were too embarrassed to send someone in to watch Silvio mop up the blood."

Silvio had restored the leg to the second chair, and now she sat down, testing it gingerly.

"It will hold, signora," he assured her. "The peg had slipped out, that is all." He began unpacking items from the basket. "Excuse me for remaining while you are visiting," he added apologetically, "but if I ask the sentry to let me out I am afraid someone will realize you are here illegally and force you to leave with me.''

Eloise nearly had to sit on her hands to keep herself from dabbing at James's cuts. But something told her he would not take kindly to being fussed over. ''What would you like?'' she said, scanning the items Silvio was setting on the table. ''Shall I read to you? Serve you some proper food?'' She colored. ''I still haven't brought playing cards, have I?''

''Never mind,'' he said, looking over at Silvio as he sat back down. ''They'd be no fun at the moment in any case. Too crowded in here. Talk to me. Tell me the news.''

''Your uncle has an appointment today with the foreign minister,'' she said obediently. ''He claims Caulaincourt has promised—''

He broke in. ''Not that sort of news,'' he said impatiently. ''News from the front. Or family news. I don't want to hear about my uncle's endless negotiations. Anything but that.''

She frowned. ''I can't recall any details,'' she said, ''but apparently Wellington is still moving up the Nive towards Bayonne, and the French don't seem to be able to stop him.'' She was silent for a moment. ''There is good news in our household, as well,'' she said finally, trying to sound pleased. ''Danielle says she has located Marie's family. Her name really is Marie. Marie-Josephe Simons. They are coming to your uncle's house this evening.''

Evidently her attempt to sound pleased failed. ''Eloise, it is for the best,'' he said softly. ''Even if we had never found her kin, you would not have been allowed to adopt her. She is Christian.''

''I know,'' she said miserably. A familiar ache settled under her throat, and she felt the tears rising. She had done so well. Not one French officer had seen her with a red nose or moist eyelashes. She had visited every day without ever breaking down. And now it was all crumbling, like the ruined towers outside, under the assault of James's beating and Marie's departure and the unending, relentless anxiety.

"Any distractions available?" she asked forlornly, only half in jest.

"With Silvio here?" he sounded scandalized. That helped.

But more help was at hand. Like a tree toppling sideways under a skilled woodcutter's hand, her chair suddenly tilted slowly to the left. The defective leg slid apologetically out of its socket and clattered to the floor. For a moment she sat, startled, not quite understanding what had happened. And then, with a cheerful little creak, the chair tilted over the rest of the way and deposited her neatly at James's feet.

He bent over and helped her up. "The god of cabinetry has answered your prayers," he said solemnly.

Silvio had rushed over, apologizing profusely.

"I'm all right," she said, dusting off her skirts. The distraction theory appeared to have some merit. The tears had vanished. When the lieutenant appeared a few moments later, scolding her for coming up without a properly stamped pass, she was able to look him in the eye as he led her back down the stairs.

"I am very shocked at what happened this morning," she told him.

"A regrettable misunderstanding," he said quickly. "It will be investigated, I assure you. Do you wish to file a formal grievance?"

"No." She stopped and looked at him. "But if it happens again, I am going to the newspapers. With this." She opened the lid of her basket and showed him the clock, two large pieces of broken pottery, and the chair leg. "One of the chairs collapsed when I was sitting in it," she added significantly. "And as you may have heard, I am *enceinte*."

She treasured the look of horror on his face all the way back to Paris.

"Didn't you say that—that our visitors were arriving tonight?" Eloise asked Danielle. It was nearly time for her

to go down for dinner, and they were putting Marie to bed.
In her presence, the two women were using the vague term
"visitors." Eloise did not want to raise any false hopes.
Danielle had not been able to give her much information.
The newspaper stories had come to the attention of Marie's
family; they had not wanted to trouble Eloise, which was
understandable, and instead had approached Danielle.

Danielle, who was brushing the little girl's hair, looked
up. "I believe so, yes." She looked uncomfortable. "They
may arrive quite late."

"Be sure to send for me, even if they arrive during dinner," Eloise told her. "The Meyers will understand."

But they did not arrive during dinner. By ten o'clock,
she could not make polite conversation with Charlotte and
Sabine Meyer any longer, and she excused herself.

"Not yet, madame," said Danielle as she opened the door
of the suite.

"I suppose they will not come tonight, then," said Eloise.
"Strangers do not call this late, even in Paris."

"You may be right," was all Danielle said. She was oddly
slow and evasive, and at eleven Eloise actually had to ring
for her and tell her she wanted to retire. And she did. She
was looking forward to climbing into bed. She was tired,
and she also admitted to herself that she was pleased to have
one more night with the little girl reaching for her whenever
she had a bad dream.

"Would madame like a *tisane* first?" said Danielle.

"No," said Eloise, irritated. "I want to go to bed."

The maid looked even more uncomfortable. "Yes,
madame." She helped Eloise out of her dress and into her
nightgown, taking two or three minutes to do tasks which
normally took her seconds. The sheets were growing cold;
she would fetch a new warming pan. That took fifteen minutes. Madame's hair was not braided properly. She undid
and redid it twice before Eloise told her in exasperation to
leave it loose. It was nearly midnight before the bed was at
last turned down and the lamps dimmed.

"Madame," said Danielle, taking Eloise's wrap, "if you had to guess, what sort of trade would you say Marie's father was engaged in?"

"James said they were smugglers," said Eloise, startled. "But Marie's father is dead, I think. She shakes her head whenever we mention him."

"He is dead, yes," said Danielle. "But supposing—supposing it was not just her father who was a smuggler. Supposing it was a family business, so to speak."

Eloise climbed into bed and pulled up the coverlet. "It's no use speculating," she said, settling in and stretching out her feet to the warm spot where Danielle had reheated the sheets. She added, yawning, "We'll find out soon enough. Put out the lamps, please."

"Just one moment," said the maid, disappearing again out into the hall.

"Well!" said Eloise, astonished. But she had never had any trouble falling asleep with the lamps lit, and she was dozing off comfortably when she heard a noise at the door.

"In here," said Danielle's voice. She heard the door open. "She is in bed; you were much later than I expected."

"Lamps," she reminded the maid sleepily, not really taking in what she was saying. "Good night, Danielle."

"I am afraid you must get up again, madame."

And a different voice, a male voice, said very apologetically in accented English, "Mrs. Meyer, I am sorry for the lateness of the hour, but it is not safe for me to be seen by daylight near your house. Your husband has set guards to keep me away and threatened to turn me over to the police if he catches me."

Eloise sat bolt upright, her heart pounding. A slight young man with a jutting nose and pale-blue eyes was standing next to her bed. Danielle stood beside him, holding a ring of keys.

"Madame, please understand that ordinarily I would *never* bring a man to your bedchamber," said Danielle, her voice trembling. "This is Marie's uncle, Monsieur Bourciez. I am sorry to have misled you slightly, but I was afraid that if you knew he was not entirely respectable you would refuse to see him. And he is her closest kin. Her mother's brother.''

"He's not!" she said desperately. "He's not her uncle. This is the man who was following us; don't you remember? The one who gave us the brandy? It's a trick. He's a thief, or a smuggler, or a deserter. You heard him; he's afraid of the police. My husband wouldn't have guards posted if he did not think he was dangerous.''

"Your husband thought I was following him," Bourciez said. His eyes rested on the bed, where Marie still slept, her two talismans carefully tucked in beside her. "I wasn't. I was following her." He bent over and shook her gently. "Marie," he said, "wake up. It's me."

The girl rolled over onto her back, yawned, and turned sideways again.

"Marie," he insisted. She opened one eye.

"Not too loud," he warned, just in time. Both eyes shot open, the covers flew off, and she had catapulted herself out of bed and into his arms with only a small scream of joy.

"Didi," she said happily. "Uncle Didi." She looked at him anxiously. "I can talk now, yes?" Her English pronunciation was better than his, but the accent was still audible.

He nodded.

"*Maman* got much sicker and died," she said rapidly, "and madame held her hand, and she has been taking care of me, and we couldn't bring the goat because it eats rope and it ate part of my dress, but a lady has her, and she wanted me, but I stayed with madame and Danielle, and I knew you were trying to find me because I saw the bottle''— she wriggled out of his arms, still talking, and fetched it from beneath the covers—"and monsieur-signor is in prison, but before he went to prison he gave me a present''—another expedition beneath the covers—"and Danielle made me four dresses and this nightgown—'' She stopped. "You're crying," she said accusingly. "You should be happy you found me.''

"I am," he assured her. Danielle silently handed him one of her never-failing supply of handkerchiefs.

Eloise's first thought had been to rouse the household and call the police. Her second, more moderate reaction was to tell Bourciez firmly that she would never, ever let Marie go with him, family or no. Now she felt herself melting. For the second time that day, she was on the verge of tears. And there were no French officers, no angry husbands to see her. She let them spill out.

"What happened to Marie's father?" asked Eloise. All of them were seated around the fireplace, keeping their voices low. Marie was asleep again in Bourciez's lap, clutching a silver bracelet her uncle had given her. Eloise thought it would be much easier to carry around than the bottle.

"His boat foundered off the Dover coast," Bourciez said. "I didn't get the news for ten days. The English smugglers don't meet with the French ones all that often, and he was an Englishman, of course. I raced over to Kent as fast as I could—I knew Mireille had been ill—but by the time I got there you had just buried her." He shifted the sleeping girl slightly in his arms. "Then I followed you across the Channel, but your husband spotted me and ambushed me near Amiens. And that was where I made my first mistake. I didn't tell him right away who I was. I was angry; I didn't much fancy being hauled off my own horse and slammed into the dirt. And I was afraid he might turn me over to the Sûreté. He had already figured out that Marie's father was a smuggler. By the time I changed my mind it was too late; he had threatened to report me if he saw me again, and he had your quarters watched to keep me out. Luckily, Miss Price took pity on me."

Eloise was only dimly surprised that he knew Danielle's real name. She was still coming to grips with the idea of relinquishing Marie to a man who could not show his face in public.

"What do we do now?" she said. "I suppose you will want to take Marie away with you tonight." The idea horrified her, but she kept remembering Marie's little scream of joy and the tears running down Bourciez's face.

"Of course not," he said sharply. "That would be foolish. Miss Price and I have been talking about what would be best."

"I could keep her with me for the present," Eloise offered at once.

"That would be very painful in the long run, I think. For both of you. But I am not a suitable father for Marie at the moment. I am unmarried, and engaged in a very risky profession." His eyes met Danielle's for a moment. "Miss Price has offered to take Marie to my parents' home, if you are willing to do without her services. My mother is somewhat frail, so it would be best to have a younger woman to help take care of Marie. And Marie would have a familiar face to help her adjust to her new home."

"How long would you remain there?" Eloise asked, turning to Danielle.

She colored. "Indefinitely," she said, looking down at her lap. "I would have to resign my position."

"I see," said Eloise, looking back and forth from Bourciez to Danielle. Or was it Jane again? She felt some of her anxiety easing. Instead of a future as a smuggler's waif, Marie could have a stable home with her grandparents and Danielle. She couldn't possibly consider a well-trained lady's maid more important than that. "That seems—that seems a very attractive proposal. I take it your father is more settled than you are?"

"He's a counterfeiter," said Bourciez bluntly. "But he only did excise stamps, never money," he added hastily, seeing Eloise's face. "And he's retired now. Lives in a nice cottage about an hour south of Paris. Keeps bees."

He rose and carried Marie back to bed, shushing her sleepy protest with a promise that she would see him again tomorrow.

"I'll let you out," said Danielle, accompanying him to the door.

He looked back at Eloise. "Mrs. Meyer, is there any hope your husband might be released soon?"

"I don't think so," she said. "Mr. Meyer's uncle is negotiating with various officials, but nothing seems to have come of it so far. James is in no immediate danger, though. There has been no talk of putting him on trial."

He hesitated, clearly debating with himself. "I don't want to alarm you," he said at last, "but I think he is in danger. My associates and I keep close track of the activities of the *Sûreté*, as you can imagine, and the word is that one of their chiefs is heading north to Paris at a pretty fast clip. A man named Meillet. And he has been inquiring, at every stop, for reports about your husband."

"I'll ask about it tomorrow," she promised.

"Don't forget I'm in your debt," he said. "Forever. If I can help, send for me." He handed her a little square sheet of paper. "I usually operate out of Dieppe; these are the inns my men frequent. Or send down to my parents' house. I will be visiting them more often now."

Twenty-two

When Eloise mentioned Bourciez's report in vague terms to Jacob Meyer the next morning, he was inclined to dismiss it. "Imagine life as a smuggler," he pointed out. "They become habituated to watching everywhere for signs of surveillance or pursuit. Of course this official is interested in the stories about James; the papers are still full of them."

A nagging sense of uneasiness persisted, however, especially since she was beginning to think that she recognized the name Meillet, and she had forgotten to mention that name to Meyer. She said nothing to James during her visit. He was paying the price for yesterday's melee, complaining of a headache and sore ribs and generally feeling very sorry for himself. No use adding to his misery, she decided. Instead she waited outside the fortress gate and waylaid Silvio as he rode up from the nearby inn where he was lodging.

"How is Signor James?" he greeted her, swinging down from his horse. "Is something wrong?"

"I don't know," she said. She repeated what Bourciez had told her, nearly word for word, hoping his reaction would be the same as that of James's uncle. It wasn't.

"That is very bad news." The weather-beaten face looked grim. "This time Meillet won't stop with a few holes in his ankle. He'll kill him."

Now she remembered where she had heard the name. A little tendril of fear sprouted. Still, one official might not make that much difference in the careful balance of factions which was keeping James both imprisoned and untried. "Mr. Meyer saw the foreign minister yesterday," she said, hoping her news would reassure Silvio. "He said that his impression is that it would be politically impossible to force a trial right now, that the man who issued the safe-conducts is too powerful."

"Politics!" Silvio made a rude gesture. "The *Sûreté* cares nothing for politics. They answer to no one. They were created during the revolution to patrol the coasts and hunt down escaping *aristos*, and all France has been terrified of them ever since. They do not need a trial. There will be an accident while the signor is in the exercise yard, or he will fall from his window."

"But he hasn't been allowed in the exercise yard," objected Eloise. "And his window has bars on it."

"Then he will hang himself in despair or will be shot attempting to escape," said Silvio, exasperated. "Besides, if Claude Meillet wants him in the exercise yard, he will be there. With a large wagon of heavy stones conveniently nearby. If Meillet wants the window unbarred, it will be unbarred. Unbarred and open, no matter how cold the night."

"What can we do?" asked Eloise, frightened. It had never occurred to her that James could be in danger before he had even been tried.

Silvio stared despondently at the massive walls rising in front of them. "Even I can't get him out of this place," he said. "I can deal with a locked door or two, but not with an entire garrison. I think we need some help. Go back to Paris. Go to the Roth-Meyer bank, and ask to see the uncle privately. Then tell him you must send an urgent message to the signor's father. And don't let him talk you out of it."

"What should I say?" she asked, completely forgetting that he was the servant and she the mistress.

"Try 'Meillet en route to Vincennes,' " he said after a moment. "Let's hope he has some ideas."

Meyer had not objected to sending the message. When Eloise told him the name of the official, he had turned pale and risen from his chair. "If only you had mentioned it this morning," he said, stricken. "The message could have gone out four hours ago. And now it has started to snow." But after he had gone into the outer office to arrange for a special courier, he had returned in a much more cheerful mood. "We are in luck," he announced. "The reply may come more quickly than I had thought."

That was why Eloise was sitting in the library of the Meyer hôtel instead of driving down to Meudon with Danielle and Marie. The parting had been tearful, but Eloise was so distracted with anxiety that she was actually relieved when they were gone. She did not bother to pretend to read, or sew. She occupied herself with trying to decide which was worse: the day after the arrest, when there had been nothing but uncertainty, or now, when certainty was driving towards Paris in a coach-and-four.

James's aunt knew only that her husband and Eloise were awaiting an urgent message, but she must have sensed that this particular urgent message was more important than most, because she kindly arranged for a servant to go through to the bank every half hour to inquire if any couriers had arrived. The servant then came and reported to Eloise. There was a little ritual, which took at least two minutes of the endless minutes which were marching by. The servant would knock. Eloise would bid him come in. The servant would enter and announce that there was not yet word from the London office. Eloise would thank him. The servant would ask if she required anything else. Eloise would say no and thank him again. The servant would scan the room, looking for empty teacups or lamps which needed trimming—it was a very dark day, and the lamps had been lit at half past three. Then the servant would bow and remind Eloise that she had only to ring if she needed assistance. Eloise would thank him again, he would bow again, and then he would leave until another thirty minutes had gone by.

The clock struck seven. Eloise pictured what was happening now: the footman was putting on his hat. He was going through the back hall to the servants' entrance. He was crossing the courtyard, entering the bank. She had seen the inside of the bank for the first and only time this morning, so the next part of the picture was hazy; it involved some stairs and a suite of offices. No courier had arrived, some faceless man was telling the footman; now he hurried back down the stairs, across the courtyard, into the back hall (she thought he would have to wipe his feet; perhaps he had even worn boots and would now change his shoes as well as removing the hat), through the two drawing rooms, into the front hall, and now he was knocking at the library door.

It was eight minutes past seven, and her calculations had been exact. There was a knock at the door.

"Enter," called Eloise.

The servant opened the door. But it was Jacob Meyer who entered.

"My brother has sent a very odd reply," he said, breathless. There were flakes of snow in his hair, and she realized he had come over without his hat or coat. "But I am hopeful, perhaps because it is so odd. He recommends that you go without me."

"Go where?" said Eloise.

"To the Chevalier Doucet."

She shook her head. "I don't know him," she confessed. She had tried to pay attention when Meyer described the opinion of this minister or that colonel about James's chances, had tried to remember names and faces when sympathetic friends of the Meyers had called. But she had not been very successful.

Meyer looked very uncomfortable. "I am surprised Nathan suggested that you approach him," he admitted. "James and I found evidence that he was part of a plot to lure James to Paris. He is the current lover of the Countess of Brieg."

There was a strained silence for perhaps five seconds.

"I'll go at once," she said, standing up. "Do you know where I might find him?"

"Right now he is probably still at the garrison," said Meyer. "But you must wait until you can see him at home, alone."

"How long will that be?" asked Eloise, looking despairingly at her enemy, the clock.

"I'll send a man over to watch his house, and let you know the minute he returns," promised her uncle. "And I've sent to Vincennes for James's servant, in case you need him."

"What is it, Emil?" Doucet asked, looking up from the remains of his dinner. He had eaten sparingly, since he anticipated that he might need to return to his office later in the evening. It would not do to fall asleep over surveillance reports he might well be asked to summarize tomorrow morning for his half-brother.

His butler coughed. "A young lady to see you, monsieur. She would not give her name. A very well dressed young lady. Unaccompanied. Not a Frenchwoman. I would say Dutch, perhaps."

"Is she attractive?" asked Doucet bluntly.

"She is veiled, monsieur."

They always were, he thought.

"And she says it is very urgent."

Another cliché.

"I am not at home," he said, picking up his wineglass.

"Please," said a woman's voice from the doorway. "I will only take a moment of your time."

Startled, he looked up. She raised the veil and put it back over her head, and he recognized her at once. That face had been staring out of the more sensational broadsheets in Paris for three days. The artist hadn't done her justice, he thought.

"Emil," he said slowly, getting to his feet, "this lady has not been here. And tell the porter that he did not admit anyone this evening."

"Yes, monsieur," said his butler, who had been the recipient of similar instructions before. The door closed behind him with a little click.

"This is a surprise," he said dryly after a moment. "I could have guessed the possible identities of female visitors until next year and I would not have gotten it right. Won't you sit down?"

"I truly will not be very long," she said, coming forward and taking the chair. "But if you don't mind, I think I should sit. I am feeling a bit faint."

"Of course," he said, recollecting that the newspapers had made great play of her condition.

She blushed. "It—it isn't that," she said. "I haven't had anything to eat today. And I am not in the habit of visiting gentlemen in the evening unaccompanied."

"And you are very worried about your husband," he added, handing her a glass of wine. "That still does not explain why you are here."

"I don't know why I am here," she admitted. "That is, I know what I want, but not why you would be willing to help me. Someone told me to come here."

"Who?"

She looked uncomfortable. "I am not at liberty to say."

"Well, what did they suggest I could do for you?" he asked, intrigued.

"Help me get my husband out of Vincennes," she said.

He raised his eyebrows. "I think your husband's uncle is doing a fine job there," he said. "He is far better connected politically than I am."

"You don't understand," she said, a note of desperation

in her voice. "I need to get him out *now*. Not next month or next week. Now. Tomorrow."

"Impossible," he said flatly.

She looked down at her untouched glass of wine. "Then he is a dead man," she said. He saw her hands trembling slightly. She hesitated, as though unsure whether to continue, and then said, "An official from the *Sûreté* is on his way here, a longtime enemy of my husband."

"Meillet," he said instantly, beginning to understand her desperation.

"I have been told that he can . . . arrange accidents."

He sat silently for several minutes, trying not to look at her clenched hands or her carefully lowered eyes.

"Why should I help you?" he said at last.

"I don't know," she said helplessly. "Monsieur, I have never even met you before tonight. But you are my only hope."

He knew why he should help her. Because the "accident" would be laid at the feet of his half-brother, whose counterintelligence unit had already been accused (correctly) of killing another prisoner at Vincennes in October. Because his own name was on the request for the safe-conduct. Because a little prying would disclose some very ugly dealings on his part. The bribing of an elderly apothecary, for example. And there would be prying. He thought of the havoc certain journalists could wreak brandishing this woman as a widow and shuddered. Then, too, there was Theresa. He did not fancy playing second fiddle to the ghost of a martyred James Nathanson.

"Very well," he said. "Perhaps it is not impossible. Merely almost impossible." He pushed his chair back. "Wait here." He went to the door, summoned a footman, and sent him off with a note to the Place Vendôme.

"I understand your husband got into an altercation with his guards yesterday," he said when he returned.

She looked startled.

"It was in the newspaper," he said, deciding not to tell

her that he had other sources of information. "Vague reports only. Was he badly hurt?"

She shook her head. "Bruises. A few cuts on his face."

"You are wrong," he corrected her. "He was badly injured. His pride sustained him through one day, but by tomorrow afternoon he will be gravely ill."

"He will?"

"You will have to poison him, of course," he said calmly. "Do you know a reliable physician?"

She thought for a moment. "Yes. Dr. Laënnec, my grandmother's doctor."

"Excellent," he said with satisfaction. "A fanatical royalist. He will certainly not betray you. Once your husband begins to exhibit symptoms, you must go to the warden of the prison and ask to have your husband released, or at least transferred to a location where he will not be abused by the guards. He will refuse, of course, and you will tell him that you are taking your petition to—" He paused, thinking of the police officials in Paris he disliked. "To Baron Pasquier," he decided.

He got up and rang the bell. "Pen and paper," he ordered when the servant appeared. Once they were furnished, he jotted down the name and pushed the paper over to her.

"Who is he? Where do I find him?" she asked.

"He is the prefect of police," was the answer. "And you don't find him. You merely say you are going to do so. That way, when you return a few hours later with an order signed by Pasquier authorizing the temporary release of Captain Nathanson for medical treatment, under the auspices of the Paris police, no one will be surprised."

"Will they honor such an order?"

"Probably," he said. "I happen to know that the beating is considered an embarrassment in certain quarters. The warden might well be relieved to hand the sick man over to someone else, in case he dies."

Now she asked the important question. "How do I obtain this order?"

"That is what makes this scheme almost impossible," he told her. "The rest is risky but feasible. The bureaucrats of France, however, have made seals and stamps into an art form. Orders from high officials like Pasquier are loaded with them. You will have to forge something plausible, and it will not be easy. The officers at Vincennes have seen too many genuine orders from the Paris police to be fooled by a clumsy imitation. I have sent to my office for a dossier containing documents from Pasquier's office so that you can see what they look like."

There was more color in her cheeks now, and she took a tentative sip of her wine.

"Are you hungry?" he asked. He sent for some food and watched her eat it. He had forgotten all about the reports waiting at his office.

He was almost sorry when the breathless footman came in with the material he had requested. He knew what the pink cheeks meant, and the sudden appetite. It meant that hope had revived, and when she saw these papers it might disappear again.

"I cannot let you have these," he warned, opening the folder. "I have taken something of a risk by abstracting them for a few hours as it is."

She leaned over, studying the documents, turning them over again and again. "May I use the pen and paper?" she said.

"Certainly," he said, but he felt sorry for her, deluding herself that she could copy the fine lines of the elaborate stamps. He was almost tempted to tell her the scheme was not workable after all. The chances of success were so small, and the price for failure was going to be very high.

After he had watched her work for ten minutes, he no longer felt sorry for her. "Call me when you are finished," he said at last.

An hour and a half later, he was looking at an excellent copy of the seal of the Paris police, a passable copy of the stamp of the recording secretary of the prefect's office, and a marginally passable copy of Pasquier's signature. "Try the signature again," he said.

After two more attempts, she produced something fairly creditable.

"Very impressive," he said, pushing the papers back into the folder and handing her her copies.

"Botanical drawing was my best subject in school," she explained. "I pretended they were plants."

He escorted her to the door. "Do you have some means of getting back across the river safely?"

She nodded. "My servant is just across the street, and a carriage is waiting for me around the corner." She put out her hand. "Thank you. I am more grateful than I can say."

His qualms returned. "You realize, of course, that once you go to this sort of effort to free him, it will be taken as evidence that he did in fact violate the terms of his safe-conduct."

She nodded.

"If something goes wrong, therefore, he will be executed. And most likely you will be, also."

"I understand that."

"Good luck, then," he said, taking her hand and kissing it. He felt a sudden stab of envy for James Nathanson. And this time it was not because he had attracted the interest of Theresa von Brieg.

Jean-Martin Bourciez was a wiry man of about fifty who looked remarkably like an older male version of Marie. Eloise suspected that he was not as fully retired as his son had said, because when they had explained what they needed it had only taken him a minute to vanish into an adjacent storeroom and return with a rectangular wooden chest full of tools and metal plates and molds. Nor had he been surprised to find strangers knocking at the door of his house at one in the morning, although the rest of the little village near Meudon looked as though it barred its doors at sunset.

"I'll have to make the seal out of plaster," he said, studying her drawings. "We don't have time to cast metal. Even the plaster will barely have time to dry. Still, I think it will work. Denis will bring the papers to you by noon. Or you could sleep here, take them with you in the morning."

"No, we must get back," said Eloise, dragging herself to her feet. "We still have to find Dr. Laënnec."

From the doorway where he had been listening, Bourciez spoke. "If this comes off," he said, "if they let him go, what are you going to do with him?"

He had addressed Eloise, but Silvio answered. "Get him out of Paris. Out of France."

"How?"

"What business is it of yours?" said Silvio suspiciously.

"I was offering to help," said Bourciez mildly. "I'm a smuggler, remember?"

"I thought you smuggled brandy."

"Brandy, silk, wool, rifles, people. It's all the same. One goal, two rules."

Eloise was watching the confrontation between the two men, puzzled at Silvio's antagonism.

"What is the goal?" she asked.

"Convey goods—or people—secretly from one place to another," Bourciez replied promptly.

"And what are the two rules?"

"Fast by night, slow by day."

"I don't understand," she said.

"I do," said Silvio. He was looking less hostile. "Travel fast at night, when all travelers are suspect. Travel slowly during the day, so as not to attract attention. What do you have in mind?"

"I could arrange for two wagons to go out just before dawn day after tomorrow. Porte St.-Denis."

"And what would be in the wagon, besides us?"

"Goats. Or perhaps chickens. But usually goats." And at Silvio's instinctive recoil, he added, "I use them all the time. You would be surprised how seldom even the most suspicious inspector or patrol captain insists on unloading and searching a wagon full of goats.''

Eloise noticed that even though Silvio gave Bourciez another black look as he helped her put on her mantle and veil, he did not actually reject the proposal.

''Why don't you like Monsieur Bourciez?'' Eloise asked in a low voice when they were back outside the house.

''He's a criminal,'' he said resentfully.

''So are you,'' she reminded him. ''In France. I don't think we can afford to turn down any offers of help.''

''No, signora, I suppose not.'' He shook his head. ''Goats. I might have known.''

Twenty-three

Just before dawn the next morning, Silvio presented himself at the main gate of the Château de Vincennes and requested permission to attend his master. Madame Meyer, he explained, had been concerned about his condition the day before.

Every day the regulations limiting visits to the prisoner had eased slightly more, and in the wake of the beating there seemed to be a guilty impulse to demonstrate concern for Captain Nathanson's well-being. No one seemed to find Silvio's request unusual, and no one made any difficulties about signing him in and escorting him up to the locked room.

"Good morning, signor," Silvio announced loudly as the sentry opened the door for him and the lieutenant. "How are you feeling?"

James sat halfway up on his cot and looked at the window, where the blackness was barely giving way to gray, and then disbelievingly back at the valet. He had never been an early riser, and Silvio was banking on this fact. "Go away," he growled. "I feel terrible, if you must know. My head is splitting open. Can't a man have his sleep in peace?"

"You'll feel better when you've had this gruel," Silvio said soothingly, bending over the fireplace and fanning the embers into life underneath the small kettle. He shot a glance back over his shoulder at the lieutenant standing in the doorway. "It's all prepared; just needs to be heated for a minute."

"*Gruel?*" said James, incredulous, sitting up the rest of the way.

"More like a broth," said Silvio hastily. He moved over to the table, where the food and drink Eloise had sent in was laid out, keeping his body between the guard and the bowls and cups on the table. "No need to get up, I can bring it to you over there." He took out a stoppered jar, mixed it with something in the bowl, and then added hot water from the kettle.

"You can't possibly imagine I'm going to eat that," said James flatly when Silvio brought the bowl over. "It looks revolting and smells worse."

"I'm sorry you don't care for it, sir," said Silvio stiffly. He handed James a mug of sweetened tea and took the bowl back. "Perhaps you will have more of an appetite later."

"Not for that stuff," said James darkly, sipping his tea. "Isn't there any coffee?"

Silvio looked at the jars on the table. "I'm afraid not." He had just emptied it into the "gruel" a minute before. "You don't look at all well," he added, counting sips of tea out of the corner of his eye. "Are you sure you wouldn't try just a bit of this broth?"

"Quite sure," said James between his teeth.

"I'll return in an hour or so," said Silvio, taking the mug and backing away. "With some coffee."

"Make it two hours," said James grumpily.

"Yes, signor," said Silvio, emptying the rest of the mug surreptitiously into the rejected gruel. James didn't like tea, but he couldn't take a chance that he might decide to finish it. "I'll clear away these dishes later."

Silvio was fairly certain the lieutenant understood some English, but just in case, he said to him as they returned to the desk at the foot of the stairs, "He seemed very peevish. I am afraid his head is bothering him. Would it be possible to have a doctor see him?"

"He does not look unwell to me," said the lieutenant haughtily.

"So long as no one decides that he has broken regulations again by refusing his breakfast," said Silvio pointedly. And having established that James had a headache, was irritable, and had no appetite, he left, very well satisfied with his visit.

Laënnec had warned her that the drug worked fast, but Eloise was still totally unprepared for the results. A messenger from the warden arrived at the Meyer hôtel twenty minutes before she would normally have left for her morning visit, with an official escort to convey her back to the prison. At his urging, the journey to Vincennes was made at top speed, and the swaying and lurching of her carriage did not help the hollow in the pit of her stomach which had opened when she had seen the expression on his face. As she hurried through the courtyard into the pavilion there were no stamps, no inspections of her pass—a frightening omission after days of reassuring routine. Even more ominous was the pitying glance of the sentry as he held open the doors.

She thought for a moment there was another brawl in progress when she walked into the room. The cot was tilted on its side in a corner, one boot lay toppled near the prie-dieu, and there were three men struggling in front of the fireplace. Then she realized who they were. Silvio and a man she assumed was the prison doctor were holding a writhing body down on quilts spread on the floor. It was James.

Oh, my God, she thought numbly as she watched the

spasms shudder through his legs. He was covered with sweat. *I've killed him. Meillet didn't have to cause an accident. I've done it for him.*

"A very bad sign," the doctor said to Silvio as James finally went limp. "A very bad sign." He looked up and spotted Eloise. "This is the wife?"

"What is it?" she asked, dropping down on her knees. "Is he—is he dead?"

"No, no," he assured her. "Merely swooning. He suffered a small seizure." Now she could see that James was breathing. "Apparently, the injuries your husband received the other day are more serious than they appeared at first. Sometimes this happens with blows to the head—a day goes by, or two days, and then you see this." He indicated the unconscious James.

"What will happen?" She had forgotten she was playing a part; she really wanted to know.

He shrugged. "It varies. Some recover fully; some are plagued with seizures occasionally for years afterwards; some die."

James groaned and opened his eyes. They were impossibly, intensely black. "Water," he said hoarsely. Silvio propped him up and put a cup to his lips. Most of it dribbled back out, and then he gave another groan and turned away.

Panic flooded her. She had no need to feign hysteria; it was real. She whirled on the lieutenant. "I want to see the warden," she said frantically. "At once. He's dying. I want my own doctor to see him. I want him home, where he can be tended properly."

"The warden has already been here, madame," said the harassed lieutenant. "He is very concerned."

She was trembling with rage and fear. "I want him to see this," she said, pointing to James. "Fetch him at once."

Cowed, the lieutenant sent one of the sentries off to try to find him.

"You've killed him," she shouted at the silver-haired official when he hurried in. "You couldn't put him on trial, because he hadn't done anything wrong, so you sent your men in and brutalized him.''

He looked horrified as he took in the condition of his prisoner. Clearly James had not been this bad when he had sent for her two hours ago.

"I assure you, madame—" he began, but she cut him off.

"You cannot keep him here! I demand that you release him immediately! It is clear that you have no control over the soldiers who guard your prisoners!''

He looked so alarmed and anxious that she almost thought he was going to agree to let her take James then and there. But he recovered his poise quickly and gave her the answers they had expected. It was most regrettable; the physician was an excellent doctor; he would receive every care and attention.

"I've seen your care and attention," she said furiously. "I'll go to someone in Paris. To the police, to"—she had to grope for the name, try to remember her task—"to Baron Pasquier. I shall take this to the highest levels. I won't have him here another night." She turned to Silvio. "Don't leave him alone for one instant. Not one. I'll be back, with help."

"Too bright," croaked James. He was staring sightlessly at the window. Silvio carefully turned him so that he faced the other way. *I can't go; I can't abandon him when he's so ill*, she thought wildly, but underneath the wildness was a grim taskmaster who moved her to the door, pushed her down the stairs, walked her across the rubble-filled courtyard. The warden followed her back to her carriage, mingling attempts to reassure her with excuses for what had happened. It was meant to calm her, but she was still so agitated when she got in that she nearly forgot to tell the driver loudly to take her to the prefecture of police.

Only when she was safely inside did she collapse onto the cushions in hysterical tears, praying that Silvio had started giving him the antidote in time, that he could swallow it and keep it down. It was a delicate balance, Laënnec had told her. Belladonna produced violent, immediate effects. Left untreated too long, James could suffer irreversible damage, could even die. Small doses of laudanum reversed the actions of the poison, but if the symptoms abated too soon, James would no longer be ill enough for her scheme to work. And the worst part was that James did not know what was really happening. They had not been able to tell him. Silvio had not been left alone with him this morning. She closed her eyes, remembering the look of bewildered anguish on James's face. If he didn't die, he would probably kill her when he found out she had done this to him deliberately.

At precisely one o'clock, two carriages arrived at the main gate of the Château de Vincennes. One was the Meyer family carriage. The other was a square black vehicle which any resident of Paris would immediately recognize as a type frequently used by the police. The guards stopped the first carriage, prepared to wave it through when the coachman showed them the expected visitor's pass. Instead, the window opened, and the woman in the carriage handed them a folded set of papers, stiff with seals. They looked at the documents, at the escorting vehicle, with its four uniformed outriders, and sent for the captain of the guard.

The captain read the documents and requested that the occupant of the first carriage accompany him to the office of the warden. The carriages sat unmoving just inside the gate for nearly an hour. Then a procession emerged from the pavilion, heading for the carriages. First came two soldiers. Then the warden, escorting the woman. Then two more soldiers, flanked by a lieutenant, who was looking over his shoulder. Behind him four orderlies were carrying a man on a litter. The rear of the procession was brought up by a liveried footman, a servant in a dark jacket carrying a valise, and two more soldiers.

When the procession reached its destination, the soldiers fell back into a row of six facing their lieutenant. The orderlies carefully lifted the man on the litter into the carriage, and the warden handed the woman in after him. Finally, the servant climbed in and closed the door. The footman was just putting up the steps and getting ready to mount the box on the rear when the warden approached the second vehicle. He leaned over and spoke through the window to the occupant, who had remained invisible throughout the whole process.

The footman froze.

Everything was still for a moment except the gesticulating arm of the warden.

Then he nodded and stepped back, the carriages wheeled in a great arc until they faced west, and first one, then the other disappeared under the stone archway. Inside the second carriage, a man in the uniform of a senior inspector of police sat back against the squabs and took a deep breath.

"What did he say to you?" Jacob Meyer asked Ruebell later.

"He asked me to give Baron Pasquier his regards. I have never been so frightened in my life."

"I always thought you had a slightly military air," said his employer. "Where did you find those uniforms in such a short space of time?"

"In the warehouse. Ordered but never paid for," said Ruebell. "Like so many other things in the French government these days."

Twenty-four

There had been an anxious debate about where to take James once they left Vincennes. Eloise had thought they would drive to some secluded spot immediately. But Silvio and Jacob Meyer had raised objections. If someone from Vincennes grew suspicious, the failure of the coach to return to the Meyer home would immediately raise the alarm. James might not be well enough to leave until dawn; what if by then every road out of the city was being watched? No, better to maintain the charade. The "policemen" were posted outside the house, and the invalid was ostentatiously carried inside. Eloise could only hope that Baron Pasquier had taken the afternoon off and was conveniently unavailable to answer questions about his intervention in the Nathanson affair.

When James began to recover that evening, the whole argument was rehearsed again. "I should never have been brought here," he told his uncle. He was propped up on a sofa in the small drawing room, and his voice was hoarse but firm. "Now you and my aunt are implicated."

"Nonsense," said Meyer. "We were deceived by your

wife and your servant. How were we to know that the police escorts were frauds?''

"Two of them are your footmen, and the rest are tellers at the bank," James pointed out.

"Italian brigands," insisted Meyer. "Hired by the nefarious Silvio." He looked at the flushed face of his nephew. "You're in no condition to go anywhere at the moment, so this argument is pointless."

James moved restlessly against the cushions. "I'm much better."

Eloise, with a shudder at the memory of his condition nine hours earlier, agreed wholeheartedly. On the other hand, "much better than nearly dead" did not mean "ready for a grueling journey to the coast." She handed James his dandelion tea. "Drink more," she ordered.

He grimaced.

"It purges the drug," she reminded him.

"Drugs, you mean," he said bitterly. "The laudanum was almost worse than the first lot."

"You're alive," said his uncle tartly. "And out of Vincennes."

James looked embarrassed. "I don't mean to sound ungrateful," he said. "But I'm appalled at the risks that were taken. I find it hard to believe there will be no repercussions for you."

Meyer sighed. "Your Uncle Eli and I have been smuggling gold into France for three years now, including gold which is destined for Wellington's troops. I believe I know how to protect myself and my family, and how to judge which risks are worthwhile."

"You sound like my father," grumbled James.

"Not surprising, since he is my brother." Meyer rose from the chair he had pulled over to the bed. "I'll leave you to your rest."

"Wait!" croaked James as Eloise and his uncle got up and moved away. "You still haven't told me how you thought of all this, how you got the papers—"

"Later," said his uncle firmly, ushering Eloise out and closing the door.

Laënnec had been very satisfied with the patient's condition when he called earlier in the evening. He had warned James that he might be dizzy for several more hours, might have spells of forgetfulness or confusion, and that his voice would likely not return for a day or so. It was all very well, thought James, for the doctor to warn him. What if he forgot the warning? He had huge gaps in his memories of the day. For example, he could not remember Silvio's visit in the morning at all, or the carriage ride back to Paris, or being carried into this room. He did remember some of the terrifying moments with the prison doctor, including being held down on the floor, although he would have preferred not to. He remembered refusing to go up the stairs here in the hôtel because he was afraid he couldn't make it up them on his own and he did not want to be carried any farther. And he remembered Eloise leaning over him after they had settled him here and asking him to forgive her.

"For what?" he had said in his raw voice.

"For almost killing you," she answered, her face white.

"Better you than Meillet," he had jested grimly. She had not found this amusing.

He hated being ill; he hated being helpless. And, he admitted to himself, he hated not being in charge. The notion of leaving Paris in wagons made sense; their pursuers would be looking for speeding coaches or fleeing horsemen, not carts full of livestock. But he wanted the wagons to be *his* wagons, with *his* people as drivers. He didn't want to trust Eloise's safety to some chance-met smuggler who might or might not sell them to the authorities at the first opportunity.

The door opened, and a maid poked her head in. "Ah!" she said, her face brightening. "Monsieur is awake." She nodded to Silvio, who was keeping watch from a corner of the room, and bustled over to the sofa and cleared away the dandelion tea and the vials Laënnec had left behind. They still smelled of camphor, even empty. James wondered bitterly if he would ever eat again. At the moment he could not even contemplate food. But of course, here came the maid again, with a small tray of toasts and calf's-foot jelly.

"No," he said, too hoarse and wretched to be polite.

"Monsieur could at least try a few bites," she suggested. He shook his head.

"One or two bites," she said, very insistently. "Of toast." And she nodded significantly at the little pile of triangular crusts at the edge of the plate. There was a tiny line of white peeping out from underneath one of the pieces of bread. He could only think of one person who would send him clandestine messages which had to be concealed from Silvio. Sighing, he took the plate and nodded in acknowledgment as the maid pulled the doors closed behind her. Then he drew out the note, unfolded it, and read it. It was just like all the other notes, melodramatic and imperious.

I must see you. I am in desperate trouble. Doucet has discovered that I helped plan your escape this afternoon. I know you are ill; I will come to you—to the conservatory, at an hour past midnight.

"What is that?" Silvio asked, seeing him staring down at the wrinkled paper.

"Another note from Her Highness." He tore it into shreds and watched them flutter down onto the plate of jelly. "Burn it. And find that maid and make sure she is dismissed, immediately."

Silvio nearly beamed at him, whisked away the plate, and disappeared, presumably to track down the traitorous maid.

So. He set himself to reason the problem out. Was it possible Theresa von Brieg had indeed helped plan his escape? It would certainly explain why no one had been willing, so far, to tell him more than the sketchiest details of what must have been an elaborate affair. Instead they had wanted to talk about goats and chickens and hollowed-out wagon bottoms. She had even promised him, when she had visited his cell, that she would get him out. Of course, she had also lied to him every time she had seen him. He might not be able to remember what had happened this morning, but he certainly did still remember that sickening moment when he had seen her watching from behind her mask, waiting for his applause for her performance. He wouldn't see her, he decided.

An hour later he thought about it again and came to the same conclusion. But he began to have a nagging sense of guilt.

At eleven, Eloise, who had been sitting with him for the latter part of the evening, announced that she was going up to bed. She and Silvio urged him to come up and go to bed in his bedroom, and he found himself debating which location would make it easier to creep out and go to the library. If he slept upstairs, he would have to go out through Eloise's room. But if he slept down here, Silvio might well insist on having a pallet right in the room with him. He decided to go upstairs, but he was still resolved that he would not come down. After all, the likelihood was that she would not appear. She might not realize that "policemen" were guarding the house. They would make it too difficult for her to gain entrance to the courtyard which offered access to the conservatory.

He went upstairs but refused to undress, pointing out that they would be getting up again in a few hours to make their way out to the Porte St.-Denis. Eloise thought this very sensible and decided to follow his example, to the horror of the aunt's maid.

"It feels quite like old times," Eloise said cheerfully as she climbed into bed. "My maid is sneering at me."

"Where is Danielle?" he asked, frowning. It was odd that she was not here, and all oddities grated on him at the moment.

She stared at him. "I told you. She took Marie to Meudon, to her grandparents."

He had forgotten. For a moment he could not even remember who Marie was, and his brain reeled wildly until it settled on the little figure clutching a brandy bottle.

"That's right," he managed. "So you did. Good night, then."

She hesitated. "Should you sleep with me? In case you have a bad turn?"

He shook his head. "I'm fine. Just a bit disoriented. And I fear I may be a bit restless. I slept off and on for nearly eight hours this afternoon and evening, don't forget. Whereas you probably had very little sleep last night."

"None," she confessed.

"Get some rest, then," he advised her. "I've traveled in this sort of vehicle before. It's very uncomfortable. Not conducive to dozing en route."

He retreated into his room and lay on the bed, on top of the counterpane. He had turned down the lamp, but he could still see the clock. Not that he would normally need the lamp, or the clock. He could rise at any hour by simply willing himself to wake at that time—when he was well. It didn't matter. He had told Eloise the truth: he was not sleepy.

Midnight, and the faint echo of clocks tolling the hour came through the window. Supposing she really was in danger? In danger because she had helped him? He couldn't live with himself if it turned out that for once she was telling the truth. And he realized suddenly that he had to see her precisely because, for the first time, he dreaded seeing her more than he longed to see her. The balance had tilted, and there was a real danger that his disgust might mislead him now in the same way that his desire had misled him so many times earlier.

Just before one, he went quietly out through Eloise's bedroom. He took no candle, relying on the tiny stream of light edging in from the lamp he had left on in his own room. Eloise was asleep. He could read it in her body, flung partly sideways across the bed. He wished for the hundredth time that he could make the journey to the coast alone, leave her safe in Paris with her grandmother. But she was as deeply implicated as he was now. More deeply; his role in the escape had been a passive one thus far.

He moved silently past the bed, out into the hall, down the stairs. For the first time in a long while, his ankle was aching. A premonition, he thought. A reminder that the Countess of Brieg had caused him nothing but pain. He stepped cautiously through the darkened rooms, making his way through the library to the baize doors which led into the conservatory. He opened the doors and went in. It, too, was dark. Leaves brushed his hair as he circled the rows of potted trees. She wasn't here. He felt an instant surge of relief. Not yet the appointed time, he reminded himself. He would wait until exactly one o'clock, and then he would leave. He shivered, recalling how he had waited sometimes for hours just for a glimpse of her.

Somewhere outside, a clock chimed a single note, and he gave a sigh of contentment. He had honored his obligation, if he had even had one, and now he could go. He stepped softly back into the library and came to a dead halt. It was no longer dark. Someone had lit a brace of candles on a table near the door he had just opened. And just at the edge of the candlelight, halfway across the room, he could see the gleam of a small but very deadly-looking pistol. Pointed at him.

"How nice to see you, Captain," said the countess's voice. "I was very disappointed when I called at Vincennes this afternoon and discovered you had gone. Surely you were not planning to leave without saying good-bye?"

Nathan Meyer had been in France for a fortnight. He had traveled first to Bordeaux, then made his way east to the French army encampments east of the Moselle. He had in fact concluded his affairs nearly a week ago and was headed home when the news of his son's arrest reached him in the form of a newspaper sporting the unmistakable likeness of his new daughter. The picture, with the black dress and bonnet, had given him one moment of heart-stopping terror, but he had soon read enough to come to the same conclusion as his brother: James was in no immediate danger. Nevertheless, he did not take his usual route back to the coast but headed toward Paris and sent a coded message to his brother letting him know that he was in France. The reply had been Eloise's desperate message. And at that point he had been very grateful—not for the first time—that he had never accepted any official role in Wellington's army. Officers were not allowed to stop on the way home from secret diplomatic missions to make certain their children were safe.

He smiled grimly. His motives might have been tainted, but he suspected Whitehall would be very grateful that he had made this particular detour. From his position outside the library window he saw the shadows flicker as his son moved carefully towards the doors which led to the conservatory. The countess, he knew, was behind one of the thick marble pedestals supporting busts of philosophers which lined the far side of the room. He had followed her here from the street and watched her slip in through the unlocked window where he was now standing, watched her step behind the pedestal and wait while James crossed into the conservatory. He had to admit that she was very, very good at her job. He had not seen even a flicker of movement until just now, when she had emerged to light the candles.

When she got out the pistol, he shook his head sadly, reached into the top of his boot, and took out a knife. He inched the window open a fraction more, hoping that she would not notice any additional draft. She walked over towards the baize doors. She hadn't yet cocked the hammer, so he gave her the benefit of the doubt. Nevertheless, he eased himself silently into the room. Just in case. The doors swung open, and James appeared.

"How nice to see you, Captain," Nathan heard her say.

The candles were perfectly placed; James was outlined against the doors as neatly as a clay target at a shooting gallery. Then, slowly, she leveled the gun and started to pull the hammer back. Luckily, his knife did not wait to see if he was going to give her the benefit of the doubt again. It flew out of his hand the minute her thumb moved. The pistol clattered to the carpet; the countess gave a small cry, clutched her shoulder, and staggered backwards into the row of philosophers. There was a sharp crack as her head met the corner of a pedestal. He realized as she fell that he was actually hoping, for the first time in his life, that he had killed someone.

James picked up one candle and stepped forward, his expression a mixture of horror and disbelief. He took in the red seeping out at the hollow of her shoulder, the dull metal hilt of the knife gleaming above the wound. "What . . .?" he whispered.

Meyer moved out of the shadows by the window and saw his son's face harden as he realized what had happened.

"You! You did that? Why?" he burst out looking at the limp form under the pedestal. "You monster, you've killed her! She wasn't going to shoot me!"

Meyer knelt by the countess and felt for a pulse. "Stunned," he said briefly, tucking a small leather bag under his arm and getting to his feet. "It's only a flesh wound. And she was going to shoot you, James."

"That's absurd!" James was frantically fishing in his pocket for a handkerchief which wasn't there. He snatched the one Meyer offered him, without a word, and dropped onto the floor, pressing the folded linen against the red as he drew out the tiny blade. "What are you doing here?" he demanded, glaring at him.

"Someone had to come meet with the men recruited by the Chevaliers," Meyer reminded him. "We couldn't leave the poor royalist conspirators dangling."

Now he finally saw something besides anger: consternation. "You didn't get my message?"

"I had persuaded White to cancel the formal meeting long before I received your message. Did you think I would miss the implications of her invitation to you"—he nodded at the figure on the floor—"in conjunction with the safe-conduct? I went and spoke privately with a few individuals who might or might not help us in Bordeaux and Lyons. If the Foreign Office won't take my word for what was said, that is their affair. Witnessed signatures, royal seals! It reeked of stagecraft." He added after a moment, "I am headed back to London now. Do you need any assistance leaving Paris?"

It was a mistake; he knew it as soon as the words were uttered.

"No," said James stiffly. He stared down at the still, white face of the countess. "Perhaps you should leave. She might come to herself at any moment."

"Very well. You are right, she must not know I have been here." He moved back towards the window. "What did she tell you?" he couldn't help asking. "That her brother had threatened her? That Doucet forced her to write to you? That she loved you and had to see you one more time?"

Without looking up, James muttered, "She said she had helped plan my escape, and that she had been discovered."

"And did you believe her?"

His son sighed. "Not really. But I don't believe she was going to fire that gun, either."

His father held up the leather pouch. "I do. It makes a nice, loud noise, you see. And then she was going to scream, and the four men I saw waiting behind the bank were going to rush up to the house, demand entrance (as concerned citizens), and find you in possession of the items in here. You, of course, would no longer be in any condition to defend yourself. A nice case of *de mortuis nil nisi malum*. Would you care to see what is in this bag? Something incriminating, I'd wager."

James shook his head. "Leave," he said wearily. "You don't want her to know you were here, remember?"

It didn't look to Nathan as though the unconscious woman was going to revive any time soon, but it also didn't look as though his son was ready to hear any more unwelcome truths. Suppressing a sigh, he went back out the window, closing it carefully behind him, and made his way to a carriage stationed a quarter-mile away on the Rue Le Pelletier.

"Any luck?" asked his manservant, Rodrigo, as he climbed in. His olive-skinned face was anxious; he had known his son since James was eight years old.

"Well, he isn't dead," said Meyer. "I knocked that Jezebel unconscious before she could shoot him. But he didn't want to hear about her plans. I left him staring at a flesh wound on her shoulder as though it was a mortal blow."

The carriage jerked into motion.

"What were her plans?" asked Rodrigo.

"Light the lantern and let's see what she meant to plant on him," he said, untying the laces around the pouch.

As the wheels rumbled over the cobblestones, he extracted two folded documents. "What an ungrateful young woman," he said, amused, perusing them. "Apparently, she was growing tired of Monsieur Doucet. I believe I will forward a copy of this interesting concoction of lies to him. I am feeling very kindly towards him at the moment." He stuffed them back into the pouch, then froze as his hand met a hard lump at the very bottom.

"What is it?" Rodrigo had seen his expression.

"If I didn't know better . . ." He fished the lump out and unwrapped the velvet cloth. There was a moment of silence. "Well, well," said Meyer. "It seems Louis Bourbon will get his lesser seal back after all."

Twenty-five

Eloise was dreaming. With a sense of dread, she recognized the dream. It was the same one she had had last night, in the two hours of sleep which was all she had managed after consulting Laënnec. The dream began in her parents' London house, a tall, narrow building which her mother had remodeled and added onto several times, so that no two floors had the same layout. She was looking for Marie, and once again she found herself running from room to room, searching frantically, each room more unfamiliar than the last. When she reached the top floor, she was suddenly in the little antechamber to James's cell at Vincennes. This, too, was the same as last night.

"No," she told the dream, panicking. "We got him out. He's safe."

The dream ignored her. The door opened, and she saw James spring up from a chair, his face lighting as she stepped into the room. For one brief moment she was allowed to enjoy his expression and the way he reached his hand towards her. Then, as before, he vanished, and she found herself on top of the fortress wall, looking down at the moat.

His body, riddled with bullet wounds, was floating facedown below her.

"No," she said again in a faint voice, and then, with a surge of triumph, she cried to the dream, "There is no water in the moat at Vincennes!"

"It doesn't matter," the dream told her. "He's still dead." And now she saw that the moat had reverted to its familiar muddy, weed-infested reality. The body was gone. She woke, heart pounding, with a terrible sense of loss.

She was so groggy from lack of sleep that for a minute she was frightened when she realized there was no small body curled trustingly against her. Then she remembered: Marie was gone. Marie was gone, and James was safe—for the moment—and she needed her rest. She should go back to sleep. She forced herself to breathe slowly and close her eyes. "He's dead," the part of her still under the dream spell insisted. She tried to argue it away, but it gave her no peace, and at last she got up and stole over to the door which led into the adjoining room. Lamplight was glinting behind the partly open door. Carefully she peered around into the room.

Ten minutes later Silvio was reassuring her that the signor was often restless at night, as they hurried from floor to floor, from room to room. Both were remembering very clearly the doctor's warnings about dizziness and memory loss. It felt like her nightmare, only this was real. Not in the other guest bedrooms. Not in his uncle's study. Not in the kitchen, where a sleepy scullery maid stared at them, owl-eyed. The reception rooms were all dark, but they walked through them anyway, peering into corners as though searching for an errant child.

"Stop," she said suddenly, laying her hand on Silvio's arm. "I heard something." It was faint, but unmistakable: the sound of voices. "What's through this passage?" she asked, pushing open a set of paneled doors which seemed to lead towards the sound.

He frowned, holding their candle up to examine the furniture. "Another drawing room," he decided. "Then the library, on the other side of that."

"He's just come down to get a book, then," she said, relieved. "And one of the servants is with him."

Silvio headed across the chamber towards the far set of doors, an action he would shortly regret very, very bitterly. "Let's just look in on him," he said, opening the right-hand door and holding it for her. "I don't believe he is quite recovered yet."

James had sat numbly on the floor next to the countess, holding the bandage over the knife wound and waiting for her to wake. He had tried shaking her, and even slapping her, but she had only moaned slightly. Since he was dreading what she would say when she did finally rouse herself, he did not persist. He himself had been knocked unconscious several times—once by the countess's own men, in fact— and he knew it could take some time to come to. About half an hour had gone by. He had stopped looking at her; instead he was staring out the window, brooding about his father, when he heard a soft intake of breath and felt her chest move under his hand. He whirled around to see her frowning down at the lump of cloth pressed across her collarbone. She moved her arm slightly and winced. He winced with her. Then he saw her expression change as she registered fully the meaning of the bandage, and the telltale knife, still lying on the floor by her side.

"You stabbed me," she whispered, raising her eyes to his stricken face. They were clear, blue, and burning with some intense emotion he assumed was anger. She put her fingertips to her shoulder and moved aside the makeshift bandage. "You stabbed me," she repeated, and her voice held wonder.

"No! It wasn't—" He started to deny it and then remembered that he could not do so without exposing his father.

"I—I did not stab you, precisely," he finished lamely. "I threw my dagger. An old rifleman's trick."

She was not listening. As if in a trance, she dipped her fingertips into the thin pool of blood under the cloth and brought them up to her face. His heart twisted inside him when he saw her looking back and forth, from the dark fingertips to him, back to the red, back to him. Her deceit and her faithlessness didn't soften the bitterness of seeing a woman he had once cherished lying in pain she thought he had inflicted.

"I would never hurt you!" he burst out, anguished. "It was a mistake—you cannot believe it!" But the evidence to the contrary was stealing down her fingers and dripping into the hollow of her palm.

Then she reached out and cupped his face with her bloody hand.

He froze.

"Look at me," she said in a low voice, breathing hard.

He had never stopped looking, but something about her tone made him realize that he had misinterpreted her expression. It was not anger that she was feeling. Her lips were half parted. Her hand slid, slick with blood, across his cheek, over his ear. The stained fingers curled behind his head and pulled it down, gently, inexorably.

"Don't," he whispered, suddenly afraid. The mask of delicate helplessness was totally gone now. Her gaze was hypnotic, feral. But he didn't move away quickly enough. She was embracing him, wrapping her arms around his neck.

"I thought you were a boy," she murmured into his mouth. "But perhaps you are a man."

No, he thought wildly. This wasn't his dream any longer. Last summer he would have given everything he owned to see that fierce, possessive passion directed at him. Now it was dust and ashes. He wrenched himself away from her.

She pushed herself up to a half-sitting position against the pedestal. The mask was back: the blue eyes were filled with bewildered reproach. Her gold hair spilled down over her cloak, over the cream-colored silk of her gown. The bandage had fallen unheeded to the floor, and one long curl brushed against the matted red dampness at one side of her neckline. Blue, gold, white, red. She was impossibly beautiful. She was hurt. She was waiting for him to rescue her. And she was a monster. He had worshipped a monster for six months.

Something must have shown in his face. The bewildered look vanished, replaced by scorn. "You little bourgeois fool," she whispered viciously. "I was right the first time. You are a boy. A boy-husband in love with his girl-wife." She gestured back towards the doors which led into the drawing room. "Why don't you tell her of your undying affection? She's right there behind you. I'm sure she had an excellent view of our little embrace just now."

Even Theresa von Brieg told the truth occasionally. He knew with a horrible sense of dread that this was one of those occasions. And as he came stiffly to his feet and turned around, he could already picture what he was going to see. Eloise, in her plainest traveling dress, standing in the doorway and watching him throw her devotion to him into the gutter and spit on it.

She was there, of course. It was worse than he thought. Silvio was right behind her as a witness to her humiliation. The phrase "I can explain" came to his lips, and he rejected it. He looked at her helplessly. Her face was still in the shadow of the doorway.

"You were not in your room," Silvio said nervously. "The signora and I were anxious . . ." His voice died. Why wasn't Silvio reviling him? James wondered. Then he knew: he was too frightened.

"We have a visitor; she has had an accident," he heard himself say. "Make sure she is properly bandaged and then have her escorted home."

He took one step. Then another.

Silvio pulled himself together and hurried past him to see to the countess.

A third step. A fourth. A fifth. He could see her face very clearly now. It was like stone. Wisps of braided hair were escaping around the edges of her forehead. Her eyes were shadowed with strain; her gown was wrinkled; she was weary and untidy and utterly unlike the porcelain-and-enamel vision watching from under the pedestal on the other side of the room. He looked at her and thought that she had never seemed more beautiful to him.

"Eloise," he tried. He made a despairing gesture.

"I want an annulment," she said. "Do you hear me? I want an annulment." She turned and retreated into the darkness of the drawing room, walking very slowly, like an old woman.

He stood rooted to the spot for a long moment. Then he stumbled after her.

There was nowhere to go but up to their suite, so he did. She was sitting facing the door, her hands gripping the arms of the chair. He had rarely even seen her angry. Now she was beyond anger, so far away he couldn't imagine ever reaching her.

"Eloise, I'm sorry," he said desperately. "I didn't mean for that to happen. I didn't mean to hurt you." What was he saying? He was condemning himself with every word.

Her mouth tightened infinitesimally. Otherwise there was no reaction.

He tried again. "Would you believe me if I told you that what you saw was innocent?"

No, of course not. Why should she? At this very moment he was covered with blood the countess had daubed on him like a Druid queen anointing her consort. And in any case, even if he could explain the scene in the library to Eloise—when he scarcely understood it himself—surely in her eyes it was simply the last in a long series of insults. Over and over again he had abandoned her, humiliated her. On their wedding night. In London. In Kent. In the carriage. At the reception. Now, at last, it was her turn to abandon him.

Wearily he walked over to the washstand. The water was

ice-cold, but it didn't even occur to him to ring for someone to bring hot water. She watched in silence while he stripped off his stained shirt and washed the blood from his face and neck. Still silence while he put on a clean shirt—a cold, hostile silence.

He buttoned it carefully, tugged down the sleeves and fastened his cuffs, picked up a neckcloth, tied it—all without taking his eyes from her.

She did not move, did not speak.

It wasn't every man, he reflected bitterly, who could grievously wound two women he thought he loved in the same night. And he knew, with a black certainty which opened before him like a road stretching into emptiness, that Eloise would not react as the countess had. She would not find pain an aphrodisiac.

"Let me tell you a story," he said to the closed face.

She did not look as though she was listening, but she did not turn away, so he pressed on. "Once there was a young officer, a rather angry young man, who had been sent on a mission to Vienna. And one evening in a garden he met a young woman. A very beautiful young woman, a damsel in distress. She was crying; she had quarreled with her brother. The young officer escorted her back to the house. He was curious about her, and later that night he learned that she had been married as a schoolgirl to a man of sixty. Now, as a widow of twenty, she was (as he thought) under the thumb of her oafish brother.

"By the time he learned more about her—and he did, because he could not stay away from her, could not rest until he had collected every scrap of gossip he could—he had fixed that initial image of the lovely, tear-stained girl so firmly it could not be displaced. She spied for the secret police? So did everyone in Vienna. She had lovers? Her grotesque marriage had temporarily corrupted her. She collected incriminating letters and used them to threaten Austrian nobles opposed to Napoleon? Her brother compelled her to do it.

"Then she lured the young officer to a lonely spot where he could be captured and interrogated by the French." He paused, then added grimly, "I'll give her this: she didn't stay and watch while they screwed the boot shut." He gave a quick shiver and resumed. "Even then, he couldn't give up his fantasy. He persuaded himself that she was naive, that she had been manipulated by the clever Frenchman who was pursuing him."

He was still watching her face. The more painful it became to see no reaction whatsoever, the more he hoped that the pain itself would count for something, give his words more weight.

"He returned to England, but he could not stop brooding about her. It was as though he had been bewitched. He couldn't sleep, couldn't eat, couldn't think." He groped for words to describe the black fog. "It was like a shutter, a shutter over the windows which looked out to the future. There was no future. And the present was unbearable. He thought about suicide, but he was too arrogant. That was for cowards. Instead he simply retreated. He vanished. He appeared every day, did whatever he was told to do: nodded, bowed, ate, drank." He swallowed. "Got married."

Her face flickered slightly from indifference to contempt, then back to indifference.

"And then gradually, his vision began to clear. His family, his friends, began to take shape around him again—" He stopped. He took a step towards her. "It was you," he said, abandoning the third person. "When I was with you I was myself again—for whatever that may be worth. Not much, I suspect."

The indifference was replaced by skepticism. "And yet you came to Paris," she said scornfully, "risking your safety and possibly mine as well, simply to be with her."

He was so startled to hear her speak that he nearly forgot to answer. "Yes, I did. I had to. I felt as though I couldn't go forward, couldn't be alive again, unless I cured myself.

And to do that I needed to see her.'' That wasn't the whole story. He knew it, and he could see that she knew it, too.

''A fine cure. The sot takes brandy in the morning for his headache and calls it a cure as well.''

''Eloise, I admit it. Part of it. I thought I was in love with her, yes. It seemed like love to me—she was dazzling; she was fascinating. She tried to seduce me in Vienna. I walked away, not because I didn't love her, but because I idolized her so much that a tawdry affair seemed like sacrilege. Tonight, when I was bandaging her, she tried again and I had a very different reason for pushing her away.''

He tried to think of a way to explain it better. ''You know the old tales of the knight who meets a sorceress by a spring? A sorceress in the guise of a lovely woman? The knight offers her his heart, and in the morning he wakes to find beside him not a woman but a snake. Here in Paris I finally saw the snake. I had been in love with an illusion. *You* are real.''

''So, you are now free from the spell?'' she asked. She sounded almost friendly.

''Yes,'' he stammered. ''Yes, I am.''

''Are you not forgetting something about those legends?'' she said. ''Is it not true that when the hero wakes and discovers how he has been deceived, he returns to his home only to find his castle crumbled into dust, his family and comrades long dead?''

He looked at her in mute appeal.

''It's too late.'' Her voice was implacable. ''You can't come back. What is there to come back to, after all? We were never married. Best to acknowledge it and be done.''

He had thought that her threat downstairs had been made in the heat of anger, without thinking. Now he had his first hint of the full extent of the disaster.

''But—there is the child,'' he reminded her. ''Surely you wouldn't subject yourself to that sort of notoriety? Ruin the child's life? Disgrace your family?''

''I don't believe much of this story of yours,'' she said

with contempt, "but I certainly can believe you were unable to think." She pulled her skirt taut across her stomach. It was flat, a curved hollow between her hipbones. "Look!" she commanded. "According to your version of our marriage, I must have discovered I needed a husband before my father approached your uncle in October. It is now late January. I should be nearly five months along. Do you see any sign of a child?" Her anger mounting, she ripped at her neckline and pulled the shoulder of her dress down to the top of one small, pale breast. "Do you see any sign of a child here?" She tore off the other shoulder. "Or here?" Pushing it down farther, modesty forgotten in her rage, she said furiously, "Are you blind? Are these the breasts of a woman who is breeding? How could you spend a week with your sister and not understand that my body should have changed between November and now?"

"There is no child?" he asked slowly, stupidly. Her skin glittered in the lamplight like polished marble.

"No!" she shouted.

"Why didn't you tell me?" He was so bewildered he could barely comprehend what she was saying.

"Because," she said bitterly, "I thought you would set me aside once you realized I no longer needed a husband. Because I had the ridiculous delusion that I wanted to be your wife. But I have come to better knowledge, like the knight in your story. And I am going to take you up on the proposal you made on our wedding night."

She pulled her dress together and repeated the terrifying words she had uttered downstairs. "I will have our marriage annulled."

Twenty-six

It was goats *and* chickens. Also five rabbits, in a cage which looked as though a six-year-old had put it together, and a mangy dog who growled at anyone within three feet of the driver's box. The animals had the luxury accommodations, in crates stacked in the backs of the wagons. Eloise and James were in cylindrical hollows underneath, one to each wagon. The spaces were clearly designed to hold barrels, and even with some hastily contrived padding made of layers of sacks they were uncomfortably hard and round. And dark. And very, very noisy: every bleat, every bark, every thunk of a horse's hoof seemed to pierce right through the wood. James was no stranger to wagons with false bottoms, but he found himself seeing it all through Eloise's eyes. The stifling compartment would be terrifying for her, he thought. And if it hadn't been for him, she could be traveling now in a coach, with a fire and a clean bed awaiting her in Beauvais.

Silvio and Bourciez were driving. From somewhere—his father, presumably—the smuggler had obtained papers identifying himself as a farmer from a village west of Arras who had come south to collect his widowed sister's livestock. Silvio was his hired hand, a discharged veteran originally from Valberg, near the Italian border.

"That is unnecessary," Silvio had told Bourciez, offended. "I do not speak French with an Italian accent."

The only reply he got was a skeptical grunt.

"And furthermore," Silvio had added, "these papers force us to go to Arras. It's twenty leagues out of our way. We should be headed west, towards the coast."

"Those are today's papers," Bourciez said pointedly. "In my opinion, any vehicle driving west out of Paris this morning will be searched. Thoroughly. North looks more innocuous. I even considered heading east and then doubling back, but there are too many troops headed that way. The roads east are jammed with them."

"Well, what do tomorrow's papers say?" demanded Silvio, not at all mollified.

"Tomorrow we are from Lille, and we are traveling north again," said Bourciez. "We are *never* traveling west. During the day, at any rate. Tonight we will abandon these wagons, ride cross-country towards Rouen, and then pick up new wagons before dawn. By tomorrow night we should be within an easy ride of the northwest coast."

"A crack-brained scheme," the Italian objected. "Why not simply go a bit out of town, hide somewhere until dark, and head for Dieppe straightway? Why must we nurse these goats and chickens all day?"

"Because," said Bourciez between his teeth, "the first place they will think to look is the road to Dieppe."

And at this point, with the two men glaring at each other like cocks in a pit, James had been forced to intervene. At least they would make a good master and hired hand, he thought as he pushed himself gloomily into his coffinlike compartment. Silvio looked plausibly disgruntled and uncooperative; Bourciez, impatient and exasperated.

As they jolted along through St. Denis and northwards towards Auvers, James lay staring at the tiny slivers of light outlining the cracks in the false floor of the wagon. Eloise hadn't spoken to him since pronouncing sentence late last night. Their furtive exit from his uncle's house had been accomplished without so much as a nod or glance from her. Silvio had functioned as an intermediary when communication was necessary.

But after all, how much communication was required? Bourciez was in charge. He and Eloise were cargo. Cargo did not hold conversations. Of course, cargo also did not get down on its knees in an alley near the Porte St.-Denis and beg for forgiveness. He tried to envision scenes which ended with Eloise forgiving him. The only ones which were remotely credible had as their prologue various violent and martyrlike episodes in which the perfidious James Meyer redeemed himself by dying. He didn't want to be dead. He wanted to be alive, and married to his wife. And that, unfortunately, did not seem a likely outcome.

At midday there was a brief stop in a ruined church. Eloise looked shaken and weary but still unapproachable. "Is she all right?" he asked Silvio in a low voice. "She could have some extra sacking from my wagon."

"She won't take it if it's you who offer," Silvio said bluntly. He went over and spoke to Bourciez, who was rearranging the wicker chicken crates to protect them from attacks by the goats. After a suitable interval, the latter then approached Eloise, but she shook her head vehemently and gave James a withering glance.

"So much for diplomacy," said James gloomily. "Could you at least tell her she should try to sleep? We'll be riding all night."

"At the moment, with what is weighing on her mind, I don't think she could sleep in a featherbed," the valet retorted. "Let alone in that jouncing case of squawks."

"Perhaps she could ride next to you, now that we are out of Paris, then. It's me they are looking for, after all."

"It would be very risky," his servant said. "I take it you never saw the newspapers while you were in prison. A very well drawn picture of your wife and Marie has circulated all over northern France at this point, with the inaccurate but touching caption *The English Widow and Her Orphan*.''

"She probably wishes she *were* a widow." With a sigh he crawled back into his cylinder. "How far are we going?" he asked as Silvio lowered the wooden cover.

"I'm not sure. *He*"—Silvio jerked his head in the general direction of their guide—"has not seen fit to confide in me."

"Perhaps if you were more polite, he would respond in kind." James pushed a lump of burlap out from under his neck.

"You're a fine one to give advice on courtesy," snapped the valet. He slammed down the cover, and James resigned himself to another long session of penitential meditation.

Claude Meillet pushed aside the maps on his desk and surveyed his visitor. Perhaps *visitor* was not quite the right word. Errant pupil? Defendant? "I would never have thought you could be quite so incompetent, Theresa," he said coldly. "First you lose your temper and have the man locked up in Vincennes when we want him out and about. When you discover he has been removed from his cell, instead of informing the proper authorities you arrange a midnight assignation and attempt to kill him. This, too, misfires. *You* are wounded and packed off, nicely bandaged, onto the Orléans road in a locked coach. Fine news to greet me on my arrival."

The countess dismissed this indictment with an airy wave of her hand and moved over to the window. The morning light revealed, for once, signs of fatigue and pain on her normally flawless face. "I did escape from the coach," she pointed out. "And then I came to you at once. It is still early. They can't have gone far. You can call out the militia to go after them."

"The militia," he reminded her, "is under the command

of Raoul Doucet's half-brother. Luckily, it is unlikely either one of them knows about your adventures last night. If I were Raoul Doucet I would not be inclined to assist anyone connected with you. He will not be pleased to discover that his mistress had planned to incriminate him by planting false documents on a dead British spy. Especially when she doesn't even manage to kill her victim.''

''If you were Raoul Doucet it wouldn't have happened,'' she said, smiling at him. ''I would never dare trifle with *you*.''

''No, you wouldn't,'' he agreed grimly.

''In any case,'' she continued, ''there's no great harm done. It's true, I shouldn't have had him put in prison, but as it happens he was not the messenger we were looking for.''

No harm done? he thought as he summoned a sleepy aide from the outer office. He had lost his chance to identify the traitors in Bordeaux and Lyons, and France would shortly be littered with more Bourbon propoganda—now sporting the newly recovered royal seal. Nor would Theresa von Brieg be blamed. Instead *he* would be reprimanded if he failed to catch the fugitives. And his chances of catching a veteran British courier who had several hours' start on him were virtually nil. Although—he stopped, suddenly more hopeful. There was the wife. *She* was not a courier. She could not gallop cross-country in the dark, or speak French with six different local accents, or swim across fast-flowing rivers. He beckoned the man over to his desk.

''Send an express out to all northern ports,'' he told him. ''Have our patrols close down the harbors, search every outgoing boat. Circulate descriptions of Nathanson and his wife. Then take this over to Colonel Doucet.'' He was writing as he spoke. ''Ask him to get his men out onto the routes to the coast. Every road, no matter how small.''

The aide had seized a notebook and was scribbling rapidly. ''And if the patrols come up with the spies?'' he asked respectfully. The countess was listening avidly.

"Take the wife into custody," he said. "As for Nathanson, he is now a prisoner attempting to escape. Even the Minister can't dispute that. Shoot him on sight."

Eloise came to life for the first time that night, when Bourciez produced four horses sporting crude military saddles which looked as though they dated back to the Seven Years' War.

"Best I could do," said Bourciez apologetically. "It would attract attention were I to go off to the Croix d'Or in Auvers and demand a ladies' saddle. It was hard enough to get a horse tall enough for Monsieur Meyer." He indicated the lead animal, a bay gelding nearly seventeen hands high.

Reading Eloise's face and recalling the painful lessons at Knowlton, James decided to risk another rebuff. "It will be cross-country, will it not?" he asked Bourciez.

"Yes." Their guide gestured vaguely towards the farmhouse where the wagons were being unloaded. "Our host tells me there are patrols stopping everyone on the roads between here and Rouen. Putting quite a crimp in his business; he had a delivery going out tonight." He looked at James. "Someone at the *Sûreté* wants you very badly."

James shuddered to think what the coast would be like if the *Sûreté* had brought out this much manpower inland on what he hoped was a guess rather than any certain knowledge of their route. But before confronting the harbor patrols, there were still two nights' hard riding ahead of them.

"Hedges?" he asked. "Stone walls? Or lanes through the fields with gates?"

"Mostly the latter," said Bourciez. "But several hedges, yes."

"Then you'll need to ride with me," James said, addressing Eloise.

"I can manage," she said stiffly.

"You've never ridden this sort of horse," he replied, keeping his tone carefully neutral. They were some sort of cross: draft horses bred with Iberians for speed. Their thickly muscled legs promised rough gaits and powerful jumps. "You've never jumped a low stile, let alone a hedge in the dark."

"I'll ride with someone else, then," she said desperately. But in the silence which met her proposal, he saw her look at his horse and understand that only the largest animal could safely carry two riders.

"I won't speak to you," he promised, not caring that Bourciez could hear. "I won't take advantage of the situation in any way."

He had a hard time keeping that promise when she was up behind him, her arms wound around his waist. She was holding herself rigidly upright, trying not to lean against him, but he hoped that would change.

"Relax," he said softly over his shoulder.

"You engaged to keep silent," she reminded him.

"Instructions don't count."

"I don't recall your mentioning any exceptions," she said icily. They were trotting along a rutted path, and she seemed comfortable enough in spite of her attempts to hold her chest away from his back, so he let it drop.

For forty minutes they dodged around farmhouses, through gaps in thickets, along the edges of fields, still at a steady trot which shook James's teeth. His mount had not been chosen for his smoothness, that was certain. But he showed no concern at the extra weight, and that was far more important. They had to jump a small hedge, and he heard Eloise gasp, but she said nothing and ostentatiously loosened her grip afterwards.

"Ford," said Bourciez laconically, looming up beside them as they descended a gentle slope. "I daren't risk the bridge, even though there's no patrol there at the moment. The hooves make an infernal racket, and there's a *mairie* just by the bridge, which houses a unit of guards."

They were splashing into the water as he spoke, and he heard another little gasp from Eloise.

"Keep to the right," called the Frenchman. "It drops off to the left."

James struggled to keep his horse moving forward. The animal was decidedly nervous, backing and sidling. Sidling left. James tried to ease the horse over to the right. Then one foot slipped, and the horse panicked. Snorting and tossing his head, he wheeled and scrambled back out onto the near bank.

"I'll have to lead him," James told Eloise, peering through the darkness. He unwound her hands and slid off.

Bourciez was splashing back across. "I was afraid of this," he admitted. "His owner told me Brutus doesn't like water."

James was stripping off his boots and stockings.

"Couldn't Monsieur Bourciez lead him across?" Eloise said hesitantly. "On his horse?"

"Brutus doesn't like other horses, either," said Bourciez, who had been keeping his distance. "That's why he's been leading."

James was still peeling off clothing. He bundled it all up and handed it to Bourciez, trying not to care that he was undoubtedly a pathetic figure, shivering and nearly naked, as he inched his way into the freezing water.

"Can I help?" Eloise's voice was very small.

"Sit still," he answered roughly. "Hold on to the mane if you need to grab something."

Bourciez was just ahead of him, trying to pick out the easiest route. The rocks under his feet were so slick, he was amazed he was able to keep his footing. Several times his weak ankle buckled, but he managed to recover. Halfway across. Two-thirds. His body had gone completely numb below the waist. He emerged onto the far bank and turned to their guide. "How many more of these?"

"Two." Guessing what James was muttering, Bourciez added brightly, "Perhaps he'll be more cooperative next time."

James's teeth were chattering as he pulled his clothing

back on and swung up in front of Eloise. He had unscrewed the top of his brandy flask and was lifting it to his mouth when Bourciez caught a tendril of the powerful fragrance and said in horror, ''Here, don't waste that! It's only for special occasions!'' The smuggler hastily pulled out a container of his own and tossed it over to James.

''I thought running for my life might be a special occasion,'' he said dryly, closing the cognac up and tucking it away again in his coat pocket. The substitute was crude stuff, but it warmed him. He handed the bottle over his shoulder to Eloise. ''Take a sip or two,'' he told her. ''It might ease the pain of that trot.'' Obediently she took two small swallows.

A few minutes later her arms softened their rigid grip and settled gently around his waist. He told himself that it was probably the brandy. Or nervousness; that little drama at the ford must have been terrifying for a novice rider. Or pity. Pity for a half-frozen lunatic who had stripped down to his drawers and staggered in front of her across a stream full of ice-water. Whatever the cause, the result was as sweet as it was unexpected: she gave a little sigh and leaned her head against the hollow between his shoulders.

''We could avoid the next ford,'' said a very unwelcome Bourciez, popping up again beside him. ''It would be longer, though.''

''No, no,'' said James hastily. ''I don't mind.'' Perhaps after three fords' worth of frozen humiliation, Eloise would consider retracting her edict.

By dawn they had covered more than twenty miles and had even been able to snatch a few hours' sleep. James, thoroughly chilled from three successive dunkings, was nevertheless so relieved to feel the last traces of the drugs dissipating that he faced the new set of wagons without a qualm.

Not so Eloise. She shuddered perceptibly as the two vehicles drew up in front of the barn where they had been resting. "Perhaps today I could sit with one of the drivers?" she asked hesitantly. "Now that we are so far from Paris?"

Looking at her white face and clenched hands, James was tempted to say yes. Today's false cargo was limestone blocks, and the noise and choking dust from the shifting stones would make yesterday's goats seem delightful. But he remembered all too well the warning about the newspapers. Probably it would have gone no further than that tentative query—Eloise was already moving towards the back of her wagon—when Bourciez chose to answer, addressing Silvio.

"Out of the question," he said curtly.

"And why is that?" fired back Silvio, bristling, apparently forgetting his own reasoning of the previous morning.

"Too risky." The Frenchman glared at the valet.

"Surely we are better qualified to make those judgments than a two-penny smuggler," retorted Silvio scornfully.

Bourciez shrugged. "As you wish," he said, and turned back to supervise the placing of the stones.

At the look of relief on Eloise's face, James stifled his own qualms. If Silvio, who had actually seen the illustrations, felt it was reasonable to let her ride outside, he would not object. In any case, she would probably take his opposition the wrong way and return to her terrible walled silence. The three fords had thawed her appreciably; she was actually speaking to him—so long as he was careful to limit the conversation to practical matters.

And that was how he came to add yet another mistake to the long series of mistakes which had begun in Vienna.

He had been enclosed in his compartment, of course, when the man driving in the opposite direction had courteously raised his hat to Eloise and then stiffened in amazed recognition. The grinding noise of the rocks had made it impossible for him to hear Silvio's frantic whispered commands—she should sit up as though nothing had happened, and above all make no move to conceal her face with her shawl (her first instinctive reaction) while the rider might yet be able to see her if he turned around. James did feel them turn off the road, though, and bump to a halt. When the panel was torn off two hours too early and he saw their faces, he knew.

"Perhaps it won't matter," faltered Eloise, looking utterly wretched. "Perhaps he won't tell anyone. He might decide he was mistaken."

Silvio, abjectly repentant, shook his head. "A traveling salesman of patent medicines," he told James. "He was driving a painted cart advertising Les Remèdes de St.-Amand. He'll be in the next tavern telling everyone he sees of this encounter, whether he thinks he was mistaken or not. It will sell thirty bottles of tonic for him."

Bourciez was pulling the teams and wagons farther into the little wood. But there was no way to hide their wheel-ruts. Limestone blocks were heavy. "Should have used goats again," he said wearily as he came back with the four unharnessed horses, glancing at the telltale lines scored in the frosty earth. "Let me go look around a bit. We can't stay here—too easy to follow the tracks from the road. We'll be very conspicuous on four unsaddled cart horses, so it's best to know where we're going and get there as quickly as possible." He strode off towards the edge of the wood.

"This is my fault," Eloise said miserably, sinking down onto the pile of sacking Bourciez had put down for her.

"No, it's mine," said an equally miserable Silvio. "And he didn't even say, 'I told you so.' "

They sat in depressed silence, waiting for the Frenchman to return.

"Take heart," Bourciez told Eloise breathlessly when he reappeared nearly an hour later. "You can stop feeling guilty. They were on our trail even before your friend the tonic vendor spotted you. That is the bad news. The good news is, the loyal folk of Aumale didn't want some stranger to get all the credit for finding you, and several of them claimed to have seen you. On the road to Dieppe, of course—

our expected route. So the *Sûreté* men and the troops with them tore out of town, headed west.''

''And we go east,'' said James.

''Northeast,'' corrected Bourciez. ''We'll have to emerge from the trees separately at intervals and hope no one sees first one, then two, then three, then four riders go by on these rather unusual mounts.''

Eloise's apprehensive glance at the massive draft horse was all the excuse James needed. ''My wife and I will go first on one horse,'' he said firmly. ''While the troops are still racing west.''

''Now, that will certainly be inconspicuous,'' said Bourciez sarcastically. ''A gentleman and a lady mounted double on a cart horse.''

But he looked less skeptical when he saw them set off. James had smeared mud on his boots and pantaloons to disguise their quality and had exchanged his coat for Bourciez's rougher one. For her part, Eloise had discarded her telltale black bonnet and her mantle. In her shawl, perched in front of James, she could pass at a distance for a country girl whose beau had taken her up for a few stolen moments on his field animal.

''Are you comfortable?'' he asked her softly as they emerged from the wood and set off through an orchard towards the distant hill Bourciez had designated as their meeting place.

''I suppose so,'' she said. Her hair, in a loose braid, was swinging gently to the rhythm of the horse's plodding walk. ''If I can ever be comfortable on a horse.''

''You've been an Amazon,'' he told her. ''A credit to my sister.''

''I have not.'' She scowled at the gelding's mane. ''I know I'm slowing us down. Those lessons don't seem to have helped much.''

''Don't underestimate the progress you made at Knowlton,'' he said. ''Without it we would be back in Auvers.'' He gave a short laugh. ''Believe me, I am delighted that we have only used the riding lessons so far. If you had a pistol, I suspect you would already have demonstrated your mastery of that subject on me.''

"I thought about it," she admitted. "The other night. When I first saw—when I came into the library. Fortunately, I didn't have a gun, because I realized later that you were telling the truth. That you had pushed her away before you knew I was there.''

He almost lost his grip on the reins. This was the first sign that his many fumbling attempts over the past few days to explain his last meeting with the countess had made any impression. "Does that mean there is a chance you might reconsider what you said then?''

"Don't," she said, biting her lip. "Let's not talk about it until you are safe.''

"It's not my safety which is worrying me at the moment," he said bitterly. "You've put a price on your head for my sake, and look how I repay you." They were leaving the orchard now and turning into a narrow path which led north through some pastures.

To his surprise, she twisted around so that she could see him. "There's a price on *my* head?''

He nodded.

She looked pleased.

"I don't find it a matter for congratulation," he informed her tartly. "Especially when the two of us—together now worth the price of twenty orchards in this district—are currently in plain sight of at least three farmhouses, on a horse who has only two gaits: slow and slower. My only hope is that no one could imagine any fugitive in his right mind would ride this animal.''

"I find it rather romantic to have a price on my head," she said. "Like the Lady Marian.''

If she thought of herself as Marian to his Robin Hood, he certainly wasn't going to discourage her. "In that case, on my next trip to France I'll try to pick up one of the broadsheets for you," he promised. "As a memento.''

At this she turned around again, appalled. "You mean you're coming *back*?"

"Of course. It's my job." He saw her incredulity turn to anger and said defensively, "It's not nearly so dangerous as it seems. All this"—he waved vaguely at the horse and their carefully muddied clothes—"is very unusual . . ." His voice died away as he realized he had been about to tell her that it would have been easy for him, once he was recovered, to reach the coast. Easy, that is, if he hadn't been encumbered with her. She *was* slowing them down—as if that mattered, when you considered why they were in this mess in the first place.

Luckily, she was so angry at the thought that he meant to return to France she didn't notice the obvious conclusion to his sentence. "It's a good thing we won't be married much longer, then," she announced stormily. "I don't see how your sister can bear it."

"It's no different than being a soldier's wife," he argued.

"Yes, it is." She leaned her head into his chest.

"Why? Why is it different?" he asked finally when she said nothing more.

"Because you're alone," she said into his neck. "Soldiers have each other. Other men in their unit, other units in their regiment, other regiments fighting alongside theirs. Their wives can hope, when they first hear of an engagement, that their husband's regiment was not there, or that his unit was in the rear, or that he is safe and the losses in his unit are some other women's husbands. And if the worst does happen, she imagines him with friends around him, comrades who have shared his danger and grieve when he falls. She doesn't picture him all alone in the dark facing a firing squad in the ditch at Vincennes."

There really was no answer to that, because he had spent plenty of time picturing himself in that same ditch during his stay at Vincennes. And although he had told himself that getting shot in the moat of a prison was no different than getting shot on the battlefield with his regiment, he had known it wasn't true. For one thing, battlefield casualties were not scheduled in advance and announced to the victim. And for another, he wouldn't have felt, on the battlefield, that his death was both utterly pointless and richly deserved.

Twenty-seven

Eloise felt as though the entire world had slowed to a crawl. There should have been a sense of urgency, of haste, in their flight. Instead every part of it seemed suspended in some sort of thick liquid. This might have been understandable for some portions of their stop-and-start journey: that long first day in the wagon, the endless waits in cellars and sheds and haylofts for Bourciez to return from his scouting expeditions. But all of it seemed to leave her with the same feeling of lethargy, even the bits which involved galloping, or running in the woods. And there had been a lot of that since that sickening moment when she saw the salesman's eyes widen and his mouth drop open. A mad race through the twilight on horseback when they had learned that the militia were headed towards the cellar where they were hiding. Fortunately, by that time, they had exchanged the cart horses for proper mounts. A bent-over scramble through a ditch by the side of a field while soldiers rode by, shouting to each other in the dark. Their most recent dash through the heavily patrolled outskirts of the harbor and down to the beach. She had hated that one in particular because they had to go one by one. But even as she sprinted across the muddy strand, gasping for breath, it had seemed as though each foot took ages to land, then rise, then land again.

They were in another hidden compartment now, this one on the boat which had been pulled up on the beach. She could feel it rocking under her; it had been pushed gently into the water and was nudging up against the piles of seaweed at the edge of the cove. If the world had not obligingly become so sluggish, the rocking would have made her sick. But now it was so slow it did not bother her. A very good thing, since they had lain here for hours. Bourciez had explained, when he had introduced them to the "fisherman" who would take them out to sea, that they could not leave until dawn. All the fishing boats must leave together at the normal time. Even James, feverish with impatience, had seen the sense in that. Any boat trying to slip out in the middle of the night would be highly suspect. It was odd enough that some half-dozen boats were to venture out on a raw January morning; normally, regular fishing did not resume until a month from now. But Bourciez had friends who had friends who had cousins, and a little fleet of decoys would sail out with them some time soon.

She couldn't guess how soon, of course. Not only was her own sense of the passage of time completely gone, but she and James were inside a hollow space in the stern of the boat. Not one glimmer of light penetrated their hiding place. It was cleverly built beneath the rear portion of the deck over a foreshortened rudder and concealed by a long, shallow box designed to hold bait, which dripped every once in a while onto the back of her neck. James had been very impressed. Storage for contraband, he had told her, was usually in the bows. This boat even had a small, easily found "hidden" compartment in the expected place to satisfy the curiosity of veteran customs officers.

In the darkness beside her, James lay quietly, seemingly relaxed. It was uncanny how long he could lie still. They were on their sides, squeezed together to avoid pressing up against the rough boards of the hull, and she had scarcely felt him move the whole time, even though her head was right up against his chest.

"Still there?" he asked lightly when he felt her turn a bit to give him more room. "Not much longer now, I think."

As he spoke the boat suddenly bobbed more fiercely, and the thud of booted feet moving across the deck came echoing down into their hiding place. With a scraping sound, the tray which formed the ceiling of their chamber suddenly tilted slightly, and they heard Silvio's voice, very low.

"Signor, can you hear me?"

"Yes," said James, equally quiet.

"They still have the boom across the harbor. They are searching every boat as it leaves."

"We're fine," James said.

Eloise wasn't sure whether that was an answer to an unasked question, or authorization to go ahead and take their place in the queue of exiting boats. In any case, it seemed to satisfy Silvio. The tray was lowered back into place, and a *plop* followed by a sudden shower of drips announced that the box had been filled with fresh bait. Then came a flurry of strange noises she couldn't identify, but which presumably involved rigging or anchors or something of the sort. And then they were underway, and the gentle rocking turned into a lurching series of lifts and falls, each fall punctuated by a huge slap.

"Can we still talk?" she said, suddenly feeling very frightened. "Or must we be quiet?"

"Probably no one could hear us," he said. "Still, it's safest not to once we're out of the cove. Just in case. You're not feeling sick, are you?"

"Not yet," she said. But her protective shell was fading. The slaps did not seem slow or filtered through honey any longer. She began to suspect darkly that whoever had named the boat the *Douceur* had been making a grim joke.

"I promised you a real ship on the way home," he said bleakly.

"Compared to those wagons, this is very comfortable," she reassured him. "At least we can be together." She hadn't meant to say that. She felt him move now, a startled jerk.

"Does that mean—" he started to ask.

"It doesn't mean anything," she interrupted hastily, trying to remember when, in the two days since they had left Paris, she had abandoned her resolution to stay as far away from James Meyer as possible for the rest of her life. She had been compelled to share a mount with him the first night, but the second time she had agreed without a murmur, and the third time, just a few hours ago, she had been offered a properly saddled horse and had still elected to ride with James. It was not, she admitted, qualms about her ability to handle her own horse, although there was certainly justification for those qualms. No, it was one more excuse to be with him for just a bit longer before they were safe at home and she returned to being Miss Bernal.

The boat swung violently to one side and then settled again.

"That was the captain, going about. We're out in the harbor," James whispered, sounding very disappointed that he could not press her further on her inadvertent revelation. Was it her imagination, or was he holding her more tightly? Perhaps that was simply to protect her as the boat slewed around onto the other tack. She wished she knew more about boats. If she did, she could interpret the motions, as James apparently could, and tell what they were doing and when they were approaching the boom, with its accompanying inspection.

She realized within a few minutes that she didn't have to know how to read boats. She could read James. While they scudded along after the first tack, he lay quietly. No danger yet. When they tacked again he took her hand. That meant they were approaching the boom. When the boat slowed, then turned sharply and rolled sideways, he gripped it very hard. They were there. And then even she could interpret what was happening, could feel the boat shifting as several people came on board, and hear the feet above them. The sense of unreality came back. She had no idea how many minutes, or hours, they lay there, waiting for the cover to be wrenched open and their hiding place laid bare under the winter sky. She began to regret cutting off James's question. *Yes,* she wanted to tell him. *It did mean what you thought.* Why hadn't she said something? All she could do was peel off her gloves and grip his hand in return, lacing her fingers through his.

James had discarded his gloves long ago. If that cover came off, he wanted access to his dagger. Daggers, rather. He had stuck an extra one into the wooden sides of the hull right beneath the opening. Now he was listening, listening hard. He did know boats, and he knew inspections, as well. Three men had come on board. One had come to the stern and was now standing right in front of the bait tray. Two had moved to the front of the boat. There were faint tapping sounds as they tested panels. He couldn't hear voices at all, but he could tell from the regularity of the taps that they hadn't found anything yet. The taps were getting farther and farther away. Now a pause. Then harder, repeated taps. They had found the bow compartment. Two pairs of feet moved forward: the third official, and, presumably, Roulard, the master. A very long time with no footsteps and no taps. Then many footsteps, moving towards him. He put his hand on the dagger, careful not to move in a way which would tell Eloise what he was doing. She was curled slightly in front of him, her side resting on his other arm, her back up against his chest. He could feel her shoulder blades, rigid with anxiety. The footsteps were moving again. For a moment he couldn't tell in which direction. Towards the side. The boat dipped sharply, once, then twice more, as the patrol climbed out of the boat and then more moving feet, running now, and a sudden lift as the sails filled.

Thank God, thank God, he thought, letting his hand drop from the hilt of the dagger onto Eloise's shoulder. One hurdle crossed, the biggest one. They were still in sight of the patrol crew manning the boom, of course, and there might be other patrols sailing nearby. It was too soon to feel triumphant. The boat tacked again, and he grabbed Eloise to keep her from slamming into the hull. He saw no reason to let her go again, even when Silvio cautiously lifted a corner of the bait tray and told them they would be able to come out in less than an hour, once they had rounded the point. No other French military craft were in sight.

It was not clear when the tension of waiting and listening turned into a different kind of tension. When the two bodies, taut with anxiety, began to press against each other in a different and more purposeful way.

She acted first. They were still tangled together against the keel boards, and she pulled away slightly to free one arm and turn so that she was half facing him. He felt the arm steal over his head and around the back of his neck, and then her breath, warm and yearning, as she sought tentatively in the dark for his mouth. There was one sweet, rather innocent kiss—innocent on both sides—and then she gave a little sob, and suddenly both were grappling madly, banging elbows and knees against the rough sides of their prison, seeking each other with a fierce urgency.

He had a brief moment of lucidity where he realized what she wanted to happen.

"Eloise, no," he said helplessly. "Not here, in this reeking hole."

"Yes," she insisted, holding him so tightly that he could feel her nails through his coat. "Yes. I don't care. It doesn't matter."

And he abandoned his resistance, returned kiss for kiss and caress for caress, pillowing her head on one arm while he pushed her clothing aside with the other, more impatient now than she was. Part of him knew that they would both regret this: relief and exaltation were urging her on, not love. But another part, a little voice, was telling him that this was his chance to make her his wife—indisputably, permanently. Annulments were almost never granted once the marriage had been consummated.

Through the layers of damp wool he could feel her slender shoulders straining towards him; under his hand the muscles of her thighs trembled eagerly as he shoved her skirts higher. She was kissing him everywhere: his neck, his ear, anything she could reach. Her hunger fed his own; he drove into her in a haze of desperation and desire, as though it were a race, and barely paused even when he realized with a shock that she was a virgin. All the better that she had never lain with another man, he thought fiercely. This would bind her; this would bring her back to him. And she clung to him, drew him on, equally determined, equally reckless. The boat was tossing him sideways, and it didn't matter; it was almost as though gravity had lost its hold on him. He was caught up in a crescendo of insistent motion, his breath coming in great gasps, his head burrowing into the side of her neck.

And then it was over. The haze receded. Gravity returned, and the smell of fish, and the sharp press of her collar buttons on the side of his face. She stroked his hair as though he were truly her lover, but he knew better. Remorse mingled with the triumphant little voice, which was repeating over and over: *Now you have her; now you have her.* The only thing he could think of to do was kiss her again, so he did, very softly—her mouth, her forehead, and both eyes. To his surprise, she was not crying. He, on the other hand, was dangerously close to tears. He rolled sideways so that he could be underneath her and pulled her up to lie on his chest.

"I'm sorry," he whispered.

"Sorry for what?" She pushed up slightly on one elbow and smoothed her skirts back down. He wished desperately that he could see her.

"I didn't want it to be like that," he said painfully, easing her down into his arms again. "I was going to wait, hoping you would forgive me, hoping you would let me have another chance. I'm not a very experienced lover—it's not easy to

practice the arts of dalliance when you're disguised as a
priest most of the time—but what just happened is not what
I had wanted for you. For us.''

''I told you, it doesn't matter.'' She leaned her head
against the hollow of his shoulder. ''I'm not sorry.''

He thought about their wedding, and all the mistakes and
evasions and absences piled in a great heap starting at the
door of that bedchamber in Ramsgate. If only he could go
back, walk in that room again, see Eloise as she really was,
sit on the bed with her and laugh at the herbs on the pillows
and the stiff, brand-new furniture. They would still have
been nervous, unsure of themselves, of the marriage, so that
perhaps that night they would not have made love—but he
suspected they would have. Certainly soon afterwards, if
not then. And now, because everything had been poisoned
and tainted and skewed by his delusions, she had just had
her wedding night jammed up against bilge-soaked planks
underneath a trough full of fish bait.

It was time for honesty, although there might be a price.
''I did not realize you were a virgin.'' She stiffened, but he
stumbled on. ''I would never have allowed that to happen
had I known. It should be gentle and careful, the first time.
Not—not some savage frenzy.''

She was not interested in the etiquette of deflowering
maidens. ''What do you mean, you did not realize I was a
virgin?'' she demanded, enunciating every word.

There was going to be a price. He could hear her locking
him out again with every consonant. ''When you told me
you were not with child, I understood that and I believed
it.'' He shivered at the memory of her fury, of her hands
flattening out her gown over her flat belly and her tiny
breasts. ''But for some reason, it never occurred to me that
the other part of my assumption was also wrong. I still
believed you must have had a lover. That you married me
thinking you were carrying his baby, and then discovered
you had been mistaken. I spent so many hours brooding

about him, imagining him, hating him, that I suppose he became real to me.''

He thought she would pull away from him now, but instead, she reached up to touch his face.

''Why?'' she said, sounding more puzzled than angry. ''Why? Why did you ever think such a thing? What had I done or said to make you believe it?''

''Why was the wedding pushed through so quickly?'' he countered. ''Why was it in Ramsgate, of all places? I was amazed there were any guests at all. Why was your grand-mother not there?''

She jerked her head up. ''Is that what made you think I was spoilt merchandise? That the wedding arrangements were a bit irregular?''

''*Novio lo kiero, presto lo kiero.*'' He pronounced the proverb as a Spaniard would, rather than as her mother would have. ''I want a bridegroom; I want him right now.''

''James,'' she said with an exhausted sigh, ''didn't you believe what my father told you?''

''No one told me anything.'' Then he remembered how he had moved through the betrothal process in a stupor, and corrected himself. ''Or rather, I don't recall your father telling me anything.''

''It was my grandmother,'' she explained patiently. ''She fell ill, with what she thought was her last illness, and wished to see me settled. She asked my parents to arrange a match for me at once. The wedding was held in Ramsgate in case she was well enough to travel, so that she would not have to endure a long carriage ride to London. Your uncle offered to arrange passage for her from France, but as it turned out she was not able to make the trip.''

''That is the truth?'' he said incredulously. ''That is all?''

Exasperated, she snapped, ''You have met my grand-mother, have you not? What part of this story seems implau-sible to you?''

None of it, he realized. Indeed, Madame Carvallo had virtually described this exact scenario to him when he had been presented to her. He had simply not been paying attention.

She pushed away from him and sat up, her head bumping the panel above them. "You Meyers," she said angrily, "are so accustomed to prevarication and deceit and manipulation that you see it everywhere. We are not all like you, you know. Some of us tell the truth most of the time."

She was gone again, he realized, back on the other side of the chasm. Their wild and awkward union already seemed like a dream, but it was real, and it had saved him. He had time now. He could win her back. He could make her believe that he loved her.

Suddenly, the panel tilted back above Eloise's head. The relative quiet of the cubby vanished in a confused roar of sound, and daylight stabbed down into their hiding place, revealing with painful clarity the disordered state of their clothing and hair. Blasts of spray assaulted them; the violent motion of the boat was no longer a giant disembodied rocking but the logical consequence of gust after gust of freezing, sleet-filled wind.

"Come up at once," shouted Silvio over the noise of wind and water. "Trouble."

Twenty-eight

The captain of the *Douceur* was waiting for James in the bow of the boat. "See that?" Roulard pointed grimly at a black shape looming out of the waves some distance ahead. "That's a British frigate. And she's seen us." He punctuated this remark by spitting emphatically over the lee rail. "In one minute, she's going to signal us to heave to." As he spoke, a puff of smoke emerged from one side of the ship, followed a moment later by the delayed *boom* of a cannon. A ball sailed lazily through the air and splashed down some hundred yards ahead of the *Douceur*. "Now," Roulard continued, "in lighter air I could just turn downwind and reach up away from her, land you farther north. But in this muck, I daren't let the waves hit me broadside. That's asking to be capsized. And I can't get past her on this point of sail; not with a reef in my main. So our only choice is to turn around and run back to France. She won't pursue us; we're no great prize and we've a fair start on her."

This didn't sound like trouble to James. It sounded like a godsend. Head back to France? Was the man insane? He gave Eloise, who had trailed after him to the foredeck, a reassuring squeeze on the arm. "You're forgetting something," James told the master. "I'm a British officer in distress. Answer her signal; stand to, let her come alongside. She'll take me and my wife up, and you won't have to risk going all the way into Eastbourne."

Roulard shook his head. "You may be a British officer," he said, "but I've no mind to put my helm over and let that frigate near me. Your captains are all the same: a prize is a prize, and more than likely I'd end up with my boat confiscated and my men and myself in irons—or worse, pressed into the Royal Navy."

"Heave to," said James tersely. "I give you my word you'll sail off unharmed afterwards." He looked down at the shivering Eloise, now folded in his arms for shelter against the wind. "I'm not taking her back to France. She's been through enough." His eyes met Roulard's, and the Frenchman nodded grudgingly.

The *Douceur* turned upwind and slowed to a halt with a great flapping of sails and swinging of spars. "Get down, both of you," shouted Roulard, as he bawled orders. James half carried, half dragged Eloise back and huddled next to the rail near the stern.

"Ahoy, lugger!" came a bellow in English, amplified by a speaking-trumpet. "Stand to!"

"Ahoy!" James shouted back, but his voice was lost in the wind.

"Do you have a British flag?" he asked Roulard, who had come up behind him.

The creased face split into a smile. "But of course." A moment later, the flag was being run up the mizzen, and within five minutes a very skeptical group of Navy seamen were tying the *Douceur* alongside the frigate. Their scornful glances at the ragged red-and-blue cloth now flying over the stern were reinforced by six marines with muskets trained on the crew of the French boat.

"*Intrepid*, under Captain Francis Newton," was the hail

from the deck of the frigate. "And if you're a British ship, I'll eat my drawers."

"The ship isn't British, but I am," James shouted back. "Captain James Nathanson, Ninety-fifth Rifles, currently returning from special leave. I've been in a French prison. My wife is with me, and my batman." He indicated Silvio, who was thankfully pulling off the stained fisherman's smock he had been wearing. "Can you take us on board, or do I have to pay these gallows-birds extra to sail me in to the coast?"

The crew at the rail were replaced by a young lieutenant, who peered down at James doubtfully.

"We're headed to Portsmouth," he shouted. "Take it or leave it."

"I'm not choosy," called James. "So long as it's an English port, we'll be delighted."

More officers appeared, and after a brief consultation a rope ladder was lowered and Silvio was grudgingly allowed to ascend. There were still muskets trained conspicuously on both James and the French sailors, but these wavered a bit when James stepped over to the rail, carrying Eloise.

"I can walk," she said faintly.

"No, you can't," he said roughly. "Besides, you're my olive branch. They won't shoot me while I'm carrying you."

"I'll take her up, sir," volunteered a young seaman, starting down the ladder. But James was determined to carry her up the ladder himself, injured ankle or no, and to his own surprise he managed it quite neatly, swinging himself onto the deck as he helped her over the side. She was looking more feverish and dazed every minute, he saw, and he said into her ear gently, "We're safe. This is a British ship, and she'll take us down to Portsmouth." She nodded and leaned against him with an exhausted sigh.

"You're not in uniform," said the lieutenant suspiciously.

"Imagine that," said James sarcastically. "I'll just go back to France properly dressed and see if they put me in prison again."

"Don't be more of a fool than you can help, Potter," said a square-jawed man who had come up. "Francis Newton, captain of this vessel. I gather you claim to be a British officer."

"I am a captain in the infantry, yes."

"What are you doing with this lot of ruffians?" He jerked his head towards the French boat.

"They took me off the coast this morning just ahead of pursuers from the *Sûreté*."

Newton raised his eyebrows at the mention of the feared French surveillance unit. "For a fee, I assume?"

"As a matter of fact, they asked no fee. But I paid them; they are poor men who risked a great deal." As he saw Newton eyeing the French boat speculatively he added firmly. "And you will release them, of course, now that my wife and I are safely aboard."

"Oh, no," said the captain. "That's an enemy craft, and I'm entirely within my rights to confiscate it."

"You've a mighty convenient definition of 'enemy,' " said James, eyes flashing. "What if it had been one of your naval officers they had rescued?"

"It wasn't," replied Newton laconically. "Mr. Potter, prepare to bring the crew off and tie the boat astern."

"I gave them my word they could sail off unmolested," objected James furiously.

"Well, I didn't give my word," said the captain, unruffled. "And those fellows look to me like a pack of roguish smugglers who would be better off without that boat." He nodded to his officer, who stepped over to the rail. The marines suddenly raised their muskets again, and Roulard looked up at James with a cynical sneer which said, *I told you so.*

"I wouldn't give that order if I were you," said James, very softly.

"And why not?"

"Because if you do, you will never be able to secure a loan again, even with the biggest prize ever captured as security. Which means you will not be able to refit your ship." His eye swept over the patched rigging. "And every debt you or any member of your family now have outstanding will be called in, with interest, the minute I am ashore. I am Eli Roth's nephew."

"I thought you said you were an officer in the Ninety-fifth?" said Newton suspiciously.

"I am."

Muttering in disgust, the captain signaled his second officer to cast off the lines holding the *Douceur*.

"Thank you," said James ironically as the French boat scudded off. "And now I'd like accommodation for my wife, if you don't mind. She's ill." Eloise was barely upright; he was supporting nearly her whole weight on his arm.

"And who is she?" asked the captain sarcastically. "The sister of Rear Admiral Schomberg?" Two of the officers, recollecting that the Schombergs were converted Jews, permitted themselves a snicker at this witticism.

"No, the daughter of Samuel Bernal."

There was a sudden silence. Bernal owned four shipyards.

"Clear your cabin at once, Mr. Reynolds," said the captain sharply to the most senior of the three officers on deck. "And find Dr. Fry." He turned to James. "Where would you like to be put ashore? Dover? Eastbourne? We could take you up the river to Chatham."

"Dover will do," said James, lifting Eloise up. She had closed her eyes again and was trembling like a leaf. "I wouldn't want to inconvenience His Majesty's Navy."

By the time they landed in Dover, James was frantic. The ship's physician had declared that Eloise was suffering from nothing more than a severe chill, combined with exhaustion and nerves. James told him to his face he was a fool and banished him for the duration of the trip. He and Silvio took turns trying to warm Eloise, swaddling her in hot cloths and urging her to sit up and drink a powerfully spiced steamed wine the bosun had sworn was a sovereign remedy for the

ague. He had even bullied the crew into bringing a bathtub
and several gallons of steaming water into the cabin. Eloise
emerged from a long soak, clean—but still cold. As he had
watched her lying in her bunk, shivering convulsively, he
cursed himself for giving in to temptation on the *Douceur*.
What if that had brought this on? He should be drawn and
quartered.

The result of his anxiety and guilt was that he somehow
fixed it in his mind that the only thing to do was to take
Eloise to Rachel, and he would not be swayed from this
opinion even when it turned out that they were not put
ashore until well after sunset. Silvio pointed out that traveling
through rural Kent after dark was a risky proposition. He
held stubbornly to his plan. The valet then raised the horrible
possibility that Rachel might no longer be at Knowlton. She
had promised her husband, after all, to remove to London
at the first sign that she might need medical attention.

"Then we'll go on to London," James said grimly.

"I think a warm bed at an inn in Dover will do the signora
more good than hours in a post chaise in the dark," muttered
Silvio. "No matter who is waiting at the end of the journey."

"We're taking her to my sister," he repeated obstinately.
"If I have to carry her there myself on foot."

The object of their concern raised no objections to any
of these plans but sat huddled in the only chair at the livery
stable's office, still shivering. She shivered in the carriage,
too, no matter how many hot bricks James stuffed under
her feet. Even when she fell at last into an uneasy doze, she
still seemed to him to quake slightly with cold, like an ash
tree in a very light breeze. She was certainly agreeable
and obedient. If James led her somewhere, she followed
unprotesting; if he set her in a chair, she did not move until
he lifted her out again. Her illness was offering him, in
effect, a temporary reprieve from the angry distance which
had threatened him again after their conversation on the
boat, and it did once occur to him that if he wrote out a
statement pledging not to seek an annulment she would

probably sign it. He wondered if *he* had been like this in the weeks leading up to the wedding. Very likely he had, minus the shivering.

At the last inn before Knowlton he had hired a horse for Silvio and sent him on ahead, and when they pulled up to the house, the door was wide open and the front drive was blazing with light. Still, he saw no sign of recognition on her face when he lifted her out. She looked up at the white stone facade as though she had never seen it before in her life. Only when Rachel came hurrying out to meet them did she seem to realize where she was. Her face brightened, and she even managed a stammered greeting.

"Go away," Rachel told him after he had set Eloise down in a bed piled high with quilts. And as he opened his mouth to protest, she pushed him towards the door. "Go away," she repeated. "I'm inclined to agree with that doctor on the ship. There's nothing serious wrong with her. She's exhausted, that's all. Maria and I will sit up with her, and if I'm mistaken, I'll come and wake you. But you need some sleep, and I'll wager that is what she needs as well."

"She can sleep just as well if I stay," he argued.

"No, she can't." Rachel pushed harder. "You look like a hawk about to pounce on a rabbit. No one could sleep with you hovering like that. Not without having nightmares, at any rate."

He would just take a short nap, he told himself as Silvio folded his clothes and turned down his bed. Then he would go back and make certain Eloise was no worse. If she was, he would ride into Canterbury for a doctor. But after the servant had turned down the lamp and withdrawn, he found that tired as he was, he couldn't sleep. Finally he pulled his clothes back on and tiptoed down the hall to the sickroom. Rachel looked up as he pushed the door open.

"She's fine, James," she said patiently. "Look." She nodded at the bed. Eloise was sleeping, sleeping deeply, one hand curled up under her cheek, the other flung out across the stack of quilts. She was sweating lightly, and the hair at her temples was damp when he brushed it with his hand. His heart eased a bit. She wasn't shivering or tossing. She looked like herself again. Perhaps the doctor had been right after all.

"You should be in bed yourself," he said, remembering, now that he was calmer, that she was in no condition to mount midnight vigils.

But she smiled at him and shook her head. "Maria will come in soon," she said. "I can't lie down for very long these days." She looked down in mock reproach at her belly. "He won't let me. You go and sleep for me and your nephew. Uncle, sleep."

He did.

When he woke, it was late afternoon. He had slept for over twelve hours. Silvio was nowhere in sight, and James did not ring for him. He was content to lie in bed savoring the knowledge that they were safe, that Eloise was well, that Rachel was well, that the Drayton baby was well—he felt like a town crier from some old book. *Four o'clock of the afternoon and all is well!* True, Eloise had not yet retracted her promise to seek an annulment, but he felt optimistic on that score. Had she not eventually accepted his help during that terrible flight from Paris? Had she not turned to him when fatigue and exposure left her temporarily helpless? Had she not pledged with her body that she was his wife?

The door inched open, and his valet appeared. "You are awake, signor?" he asked in an oddly subdued tone. He avoided James's eye and swerved around to the far side of the bed to open the shutters. "Your sister would like to see you when you are dressed."

"What's wrong?" asked James, who knew his servant very well. His optimism vanished into thin air. "Is it Mrs. Meyer? Is she worse again?"

"The signora is very well. Nearly her old self," said

Silvio, still careful not to look at James. "A good night's rest appears to have worked wonders." He laid out a clean shirt and began to brush James's pantaloons, apparently forgetting that he had already cleaned them the night before.

"My sister?"

"Also well." Silvio had his head bent over James's boots.

James tried to catch the valet's eye in the mirror as he helped James dress, but somehow he was always looking down. Finally, he twisted away as Silvio held out his jacket and swung around.

"Stop sliding away from me," he ordered, beginning to feel angry as well as worried. "You know I can always tell when you're in a pucker over something. What is it?"

There was a knock at the door, and Silvio gratefully hastened over to open it. "It's your sister," he announced, a statement which proved to be both the answer to James's question and the herald of a very, very angry Rachel.

At the sight of her face he backed instinctively towards the window.

"What did I do?" he asked.

"A very good question," she said, glaring at him. "What did you do?"

"Eloise is awake," he said, suddenly understanding.

"Indeed she is."

"And she told you what happened."

Rachel bit her lip. "No, she didn't provide any details."

"Then who—?" He looked at the half-open door, through which Silvio had suddenly vanished.

"I asked him," said Rachel, moving hastily to block James from pursuing his treacherous valet. "I asked him once I had spoken with her. She woke up, you see, and I said I would go and fetch you at once, and she told me not to."

He sank down onto the sofa under the window and buried his head in his hands. So much for optimism. "What did Silvio say?" he said, his voice muffled by his neckcloth.

"He wouldn't look at me, and he mumbled something

about the countess. So now I am asking *you*. What happened?''

He told her. He told her the whole story from the night of the wedding, not leaving anything out, not sparing himself, but not omitting the confusion and despair which had distorted his judgment.

''Do you think there's any hope?'' he asked miserably when he had finished. The expression on her face, when he had reached the description of that last night in Paris, suggested the answer was no. This was Rachel, his beloved and only sister, who had forgiven him sins beyond measure, including one episode where he had shot her accidentally. If she was that horrified, he couldn't begin to imagine what Eloise must be feeling.

''Let me put it this way,'' said Rachel. ''Eloise did not merely say that she was not feeling well enough to speak with you at the moment. She said three things. One, she loved you. Two, she did not want to see you. At all. Three, she was planning to seek an annulment. And when a woman says those three things at the same time, without crying while she says them, she means every word of all three statements.''

So she did love him. That was not much consolation in the face of her resolution to purge herself of that love. The episode on the boat was beginning to take on a different coloring. It was not, as he had thought, the instinctive promise of a woman to her mate. Rather, Eloise had allowed herself one desperate, farewell taste of a dream which was now too painful to pursue any longer.

Twenty-nine

James had a wary relationship with God. On the one hand, he had seen too much pain and brutality on the Peninsula to give God the sort of unquestioning trust he envied in some of his more devout relatives. On the other hand, he was forced to admit that he himself had not exactly been the most obedient of God's servants. His observance of faith was limited to a sincere attempt not to break too many of the Ten Commandments, and even there he was forced to make numerous compromises. For example, lying and stealing didn't count when he was in enemy territory.

He was well aware that his bargains with God were often self-serving, and now he was confronting another example of his underhanded dealings with the deity. He had prayed constantly since his arrest for one thing and one thing only: Eloise's safety. He had promised God that if only she could return to England unharmed, he would ask nothing further. Well, she was here, safe, and he was reneging on his promise. He wanted her back. And he didn't really have much left to offer God in return.

Perhaps that explained why, thus far, his attempts to win

her back had met with nothing but failure. He had been back in London for nearly three weeks. Every day it was the same: twice a day, morning and evening, he called at the Bernals' house in Kennington. Mrs. Meyer was never at home to her husband. He had tried asking for her parents; they were not at home, either, even when visitors were brushing by him on the stairs as the butler repeated the lie. Once he had gone to Samuel Bernal's place of business. Mr. Bernal could not receive him, the clerk said, giving him a stare so hostile that James wondered if Bernal had sent out a memorandum to all his employees: *The iniquitous and reprehensible behavior of one James Roth Meyer, otherwise known as James Nathanson.* He was too proud to ask his father to intervene, but he did make the long trip back down to Knowlton to beg for Rachel's help.

"I don't think it will do any good, James," she had said gently. They were sitting in the drawing room, waiting for Maria to bring in tea.

"She won't see me; her family won't see me; she returns my letters unopened," he said despairingly. "How can I reason with her if I can't talk to her or write to her? She'll receive you; I know she will."

"She probably would," Rachel conceded. "But if I 'reasoned with her,' as you put it, that would not serve your cause very well."

"Why not?" he demanded wildly.

"Because reason is on her side, not yours." His sister directed Maria to put a heavily laden tray down in front of her. "Passion and mercy. Those are the weapons you can bring to bear against reason. But to do that you need to see her. A visit with me will not summon up more than a faint trace of the feelings you need as your allies."

"Could you try?" he pleaded.

Rachel sighed and poured for him. "If another week goes by and she still won't receive you, write me."

Maria, Rachel's maid, was giving James a pointed look which meant he had plagued her mistress enough and should gulp his tea and leave. But James was still hoping for some miraculous new piece of advice, and he wasn't particular about its source. Here came Lady Ingram, for example. She gave him a stare very similar to that of Bernal's clerk, and he abandoned the idea of consulting her. Behind her was Caroline, looking unusually clean and neat. After a slightly wobbly curtsy to both ladies, she darted happily over to his side. This was more promising.

"Good afternoon, almost-Uncle James," she announced cheerfully. "Aunt Rachel said I could come to tea today since you were here." Apparently, the memorandum about his iniquitous behavior had reached Lady Ingram but had not yet arrived in the schoolroom. Caroline was not unobservant, however. She read Lady Ingram's stiff posture and her aunt's clouded face instantly.

"You're in trouble," she said with a hint of satisfaction in her voice.

"I am, rather," he admitted.

Her eyes grew round. It was not often that adults admitted fault. "Did you kill someone?" she asked solemnly, clearly hoping for a dramatic revelation.

He smiled in spite of himself and shook his head.

Rachel started shooing Caroline towards a chair to forestall more awkward questions. But he stopped her.

"Caroline," he said, hoping for at least one vote in his favor, "if you did something very wrong, something which hurt someone you cared for, what would you do to make it right?"

"Apologize?" said the little girl doubtfully. She looked quickly at Rachel to see if her answer was acceptable.

"What if they won't see you or read your letters? So that you cannot apologize?"

She frowned. "Is it someone rude? Or someone nice?"

"Someone nice." He moved from the hypothetical "you" to the actual "I" to make it easier for her. "Don't you think this someone should give me a chance to say I'm sorry?"

"Why did you hurt someone nice?" she demanded, not cooperating with his plan.

A very good question.

But she wasn't finished twisting the knife in the wound. "You know," she advised him kindly, "if you hurt someone nice, they're probably afraid of you now. That's why they don't want to see you. Like Mr. Abbot's mare, after his groom beat her. She wouldn't let anyone come near her for a very long while."

"What did they do with her?" he found himself asking, still hoping for a crumb of comfort. An oracle. Something along the lines of *They waited patiently and offered her apples every day, and at last one day, she came cautiously over and took an apple*.

She stared at him. "With the mare? Nothing. They dismissed the groom, of course."

Well, he had asked for an oracle. This one was less ambiguous than most. He had driven back to London, reflecting glumly that he had just damned himself in Caroline's eyes as well. Her farewell comment had been the anxious question, "You didn't beat a horse, did you?" Which in Caroline's world was far worse than killing someone.

Burying himself in work would have been a good way to pass the time until Eloise relented—had he been allowed into the Tower. When he had reported in upon his return to London, White had informed him that he was relieved from his duties and on half-pay pending an investigation.

"An investigation into what?" he said, feeling the blood draining from his face.

"What do you think?" White snapped.

James made a list silently in his head. Lying to a superior officer. Unauthorized dealings with French counterintelligence. General stupidity, incompetence, and recklessness. "Sir, did you know before I left that I requested an assignment to France in order to see—her?" he had said at last.

"I had my suspicions, yes."

James grimaced. "Why didn't you stop me?"

"Because I thought perhaps if you saw her again you would come to your senses." White's voice grew harsh. "And even if you didn't, it never occurred to me that you would manage to put your uncle at risk. Don't you realize he is, for the army, the most important man in France at the moment? We are marching north on the gold he is smuggling into Gascony." He paused. "You did come to your senses, at least?" he asked finally.

"Yes, sir." James gave a bitter smile. "After she humiliated my wife and had me carted off to Vincennes, even I saw the light."

"Well," his colonel said gruffly, "I wouldn't lose too much sleep over this investigation. Your father returned with some very useful items, one of which we would never have laid hands on without your ill-advised decision to walk into Meillet's trap. And you did send over that warning. That will count in your favor."

"Sir, couldn't I do *something* while I'm on half-pay?" James had pleaded. "Transcribe reports? Copy maps? Unofficially?"

"I think you've been involved in quite enough unofficial activities lately," White had said with asperity. "You're dismissed, Captain."

Since then his days had become very monotonous. Get up, get dressed, call at the Bernals'. Wander around London, avoiding any locations where he might see his father, his uncle, or any of his fellow officers. Call at the Bernals' again. Write another letter to Eloise. In the intervals, he was attempting (with some success) to read a very long, very technical Prussian treatise on firearms which White had silently handed him on his way out the door. Since it was the first sign that anyone he knew might actually believe he was redeemable, he kept it by his bed and studied each tiny, labeled spring on each diagram until he was sure he understood the mechanisms.

Today was different, though. Today he was actually going to see someone who had spoken with Eloise. He consulted the letter again and looked at the number of the house. 15 Goodmans Fields. Only half a mile north of his own flat, the neat houses around the green offered a silent indictment of his failure to provide adequate lodgings for his new bride. The letter requested that he call on a Mr. Joshua Lindo with reference to the petition of his wife for an annulment of their marriage. His first reaction, of course, had been to tear the letter in half. Luckily, he had stopped there and not destroyed it any further, because a moment's reflection convinced him that this communication might actually be a good sign. It meant, at the very least, that all was not proceeding smoothly with her quest. And this Mr. Lindo might be a reasonable man. He might be willing to carry some word from James to Eloise. He might even persuade her to see him. More than that, he did not allow himself to hope.

He tried to read clues to the character of his host as he was shown into a small sitting room facing the street. An elderly maidservant—that argued prudence and respectability. Brittle, old-fashioned furniture. No paintings on the walls. Not likely to sympathize with an errant husband, he thought, and when Lindo came in, that impression was only strengthened. He was a frail man, slightly stooped, with a long white beard and spectacles. James knew the type. Scholarly, pious, ascetic. His hopes of using him as an intermediary vanished instantly.

"Mr. Meyer," Lindo said in a reedy voice. "Do sit down. This will just take a moment. A rather simple legal matter. A point of information, shall we say."

James perched gingerly on a chair which looked slightly less ancient and warped than the others.

"I am a friend of the Bernal family," Lindo explained, shuffling over to another chair. "And also, at the moment, an advisor to the *Mahamad*, the governing council of the Bevis Marks synagogue. I have explained to your wife that it is pointless to seek an annulment. The legal precedents are very clear: even if there is an irregularity in the marriage vows, as there appears to be in this case, the wronged spouse surrenders their right to have the marriage declared void if they, er, accept the offending party fully as their husband or wife *after* they have become aware of the irregularity.''

James understood not one word in ten of this, but he grasped the important point: Eloise could not obtain an annulment, because of what had happened on the boat. His guess about the consequences of that unthinking frenzy had been correct. For all the wrong reasons, he was being given a second chance. And he would treasure it, nurse it. He wouldn't let it escape him.

''That is very good news,'' he said, standing up again because he suddenly had too much energy to sit still. ''Presumably, my wife wanted you to explain the legal details to me, but I assure you I am not interested. And you can tell her, from me, that I understand she will need some time to recover from—from our rather painful journey to France. I do not expect her to return to my home immediately. Indeed, I would like to find more suitable accommodations for us. But perhaps she would be willing to see me now?''

The older man looked at him sadly without saying anything.

''Just briefly?'' James said desperately. ''With others there? Her mother?''

The awkward silence told its own tale. ''She isn't coming back, is she?'' he whispered, sitting back down.

''She wants a divorce,'' said Lindo gently.

''No!'' James shouted, jumping up again.

''She wants a divorce,'' Lindo repeated, as though James had not spoken, ''and unfortunately, under our law, wives may not divorce their husbands.''

James blinked. ''What does that mean?''

''It means,'' said Lindo, still in that same gentle voice, ''that your wife is asking you to divorce her.''

The jumble of words was beginning to form itself into something that made sense. ''I beg your pardon,'' he said cautiously, ''but are you telling me that I can divorce Mrs. Meyer, but she cannot divorce me?''

"Precisely." Lindo looked very pleased with the success of the legal lesson.

James was pleased, too. "Excellent," he said calmly. "I am delighted to have these matters clarified. Good day, Mr. Lindo."

"Wait!" called his host as he headed for the door. He struggled out of his chair. "Mrs. Meyer—due consideration for her difficult situation—perhaps some time for reflection—"

"Please tell Mrs. Meyer from me that she may take all the time she needs for reflection," James informed him. "If it takes her six months to forgive me, I will wait six months. Or a year. Or more." He hoped fervently it was not more. "I suspect I could legally compel her to return to my house, but I will never do so. But I will never divorce her, either. I will not compound the lies I told at our wedding with another lie which says I don't want her as my wife."

"I meant reflection on your part," said Lindo weakly.

"I know you did," said James. "I don't need to reflect. I know a completely undeserved piece of good luck when I see it."

Two days later he received a fatherly missive from Lindo, full of quotations from various long-dead sages. Enclosed inside it was a short note from Eloise. This was a very stiff and self-conscious composition; he could see that her pen had stopped several times. There was a deep indentation before the *D* of *Dear,* for example. Had even that conventional phrase struck her as impossible? And he noticed that she had originally started to sign it formally, *Your most obedient* and then changed it to the *most affectionate,* which would be normal between husband and wife. The note itself said just what he expected it to say: she asked him, as a man of honor, to respect her wishes in this matter.

"Man of honor, hah!" he muttered, crumpling the letter. "Were I a man of honor I wouldn't be in this pickle." But he didn't burn the note. He left it sitting on a corner of the bookshelf, and Silvio, who brazenly smoothed it out and read it, warned Nan and Peg not to throw it in the grate.

A week went by. His initial satisfaction, his feeling that now he held the cards, began to fade. What if she never came back? What if it wasn't one year, or two, but ten? If he could only see her, he was sure he could show her that she was wrong. He wrote and requested a meeting to discuss the divorce. She wrote back that it would be best to conduct their business in writing. This was some progress, at least. She was answering his letters. He replied asking her to clarify her reasons for requesting the divorce. This was not one of his finer hours; he worded the letter in such a way that there was a very definite implication that he was considering her request and needed the information to prepare the writ. Her answer consisted of three sentences:

You never intended to marry me. You continued the marriage believing me to be something I was not. Your fitness as a husband is not proven.

That last phrase sent him out into the streets in the blackest mood he had known since their return. What did she mean, *his fitness as a husband?* Each explanation that occurred to him, from the crudest to the most philosophical, was more damning than the one before. He raged over to Kennington and stood glaring at the Bernal house until the frightened glances of passersby brought him back, a little, to himself. He walked over to the Tower and scowled at the stairway to White's office. He even walked over to his uncle's house. There was smoke coming out of the little corner chimney which served his father's study. He toyed with the idea of confronting his father but eventually turned away without ringing the bell. He began to walk simply for the sake of walking, without a destination, wishing he were still studying boxing. He had a strong desire to hit someone.

It was under these unfortunate circumstances that he did, for the first time in a month, actually meet Eloise face to face. She was turning onto Bond Street with Evrett, her arm tucked comfortably into his, and they were laughing and talking in a way which made him grind his teeth. He forgot that Evrett was one of his oldest friends. He forgot, too, that he had had the same reaction when Eloise kissed Bourciez on the cheek in farewell, and had been very ashamed of himself once he calmed down. The contrast between his own loneliness and misery and Evrett's sparkling good humor was an insult. Eloise's obvious health and spirits, which he had prayed for only a few weeks ago—another insult.

"What an odd coincidence," he said acidly, stepping in front of them so that they stopped, startled. "I have been hoping to see my wife this age. I should have realized I had only to follow my good friend Evrett to come up with her."

Eloise lifted her head and looked at him, a long, sad look. He had thought so long about what he would say if fate did grant him some chance meeting, and now it had all flown out of his head. He remembered he had settled on something very gentle and penitent. There was a demon inside him right now, however, which was not interested in penitence. It was interested in violence. Preferably violence right in front of Eloise.

"James!" Evrett actually looked delighted to see him, the fool.

"Do I know you?" James said coldly. "Ah, I had forgot. Amongst the nobility it is customary for the cuckolded husband to cry friends with the adulterer. Shows good *ton*."

Evrett dropped Eloise's arm, looking shocked. "Good God, man, what is wrong with you?" He pushed Eloise behind him and took a few steps away from her, as though protecting her from contamination. James followed him happily. He could have free rein now, without the constraint of her presence. Her bewildered expression as the two men moved out of hearing was like a goad, pricking him on.

"What is wrong with me? I should rather ask you that question, my lord. I am not the one in the habit of pursuing other men's wives." This was a cruel and very unfair allusion to Evrett's former courtship of the woman who was now Mrs. Southey.

"Elizabeth Southey was not even betrothed when I proposed to her," Evrett said. His expression was the patient, wary expression of someone trying to humor a madman. "And I am not pursuing Mrs. Meyer. We merely struck up a conversation at the bookstore, and I offered to escort her to Kennington."

He couldn't take any chances of Evrett wiggling out of this, so he made sure to insult Eloise as well.

"Of course, she's better suited to you than Elizabeth Southey, isn't she? Now that I've trained her to take a cripple into her bed."

Evrett stared at him and shook his head in disbelief.

"Have it your way," he said at last. "Name your friends. If you have any left." Then he turned on his heel and limped back to Eloise.

James's last glimpse of her was meat and drink to the demon. She was no longer laughing. She looked pale and upset. She was turning, again and again, to look back at him, and when Evrett bent over and said something to her she shook her head, pulled her arm out of his, and hurried away with her maid trailing behind her. James could have gone after her, of course. But the demon was far more interested in Evrett. He swung around and headed for a tavern where he knew he would find some young officers to act as seconds. Tomorrow. He would see if he could arrange it for tomorrow. He wanted blood.

Thirty

The demon was riding high. With a speed and ease which suggested divine assistance, the meeting had been set for tomorrow, in Regent's Park. Pistols, of course, since both he and Evrett lacked the sure footing required for swordplay. He was sorry now that he had spent so much time reading the Prussian book on firing mechanisms. It had brought home to him with devastating clarity how completely unreliable most guns were. He would have to hope that the demon could take care of that, too.

Once the duel was arranged and the sense of urgency on that score had abated somewhat, a slightly more reasonable part of him had actually had a brief quarrel with the demon. Why, he had demanded as he climbed the stairs to his attic room, did the demon stop him from speaking with Eloise? This was the first chance he had been granted since their return to London. He could have goaded Evrett into fighting him later. The demon had laughed.

"Why wait for chance to bring her to you?" the demon had said. "Has your patience, your forbearance made any impression on her? Do you need permission to see your own wife? What is keeping you from her? Servants? Locks? Not much of a barrier for someone in your line of work.''

So here he was, at midnight, on the roof of the Bernals' house, carefully prying up the bolt on a skylight. Someone was still working in the kitchen; he knew that. He had peered in from the cellar steps. And lamps were burning in the central hallway on each of the upper floors. The Bernals were rich; they did not have to grope for a candle and tinderbox should they choose to get up in the middle of the night. But most of the house was dark.

Eloise, in particular, had gone to bed quite early—nearly two hours ago. It had taken every ounce of self-discipline he possessed to wait until the rest of the household retired and then allow a good twenty minutes after the last flurry of activity in the upper rooms. Only then had he climbed up the side of the house and onto the lowest of a series of roofs—a task made easier by numerous odd additions to the original structure. The particular roof he was on right now was not the highest one. It did, however, have a skylight which gave access to a sitting room on the same level as her bedroom.

His many vigils outside the house in the past month had not been in vain. And he had spent some money, discreetly. He knew where she slept. He knew that she had not yet replaced Danielle, but had ''borrowed'' one of the upstairs maids and was using her in combination with her mother's dresser. No one, therefore, was sleeping in the maid's chamber which adjoined her room. He knew that the ordinary maidservants were housed in an attic two floors above Eloise's rooms; the men on the lower floor by the pantry. Whoever was working in the kitchen would not be able to hear him. Still, he held his breath as he pulled up the rusty frame of the skylight. It gave a faint, metallic screech, but that was all. He counted to thirty. Then he lowered himself down and hung by his hands until his eyes could adjust to the dark room. He was above a table. Very convenient. With a small thud he dropped gently onto it; both his ankle and the table teetered for a moment, then held.

Take off his boots? He decided against it. The door to the central hall was already open, and the extravagant all-night lamp beckoned him right over to the door of Eloise's room. He extinguished it, lest the light wake her when he opened the door.

He needn't have worried. There was a small lamp burning in here, too. Perhaps she had been reading and had fallen asleep. From where he was now, he could just make out a series of bumps under the quilts: she was on her side, her legs slightly bent, her face nearly buried under a dislodged bolster. He moved quietly over to the bed. There was indeed a book, wedged up against the headboard. It was a recently published description of the Peninsular campaign of last year. He hadn't been the only one reading about guns.

"Eloise," he said softly, leaning over and shaking her by the shoulder. She stirred slightly. He pulled away the pillow over her face and stood frozen for a minute. She was a study in dark and light: dark hair, dark lashes, dark brows, fair skin—her skin wasn't white, like the starched pillow-cases, but some sort of cream with a glow behind it that made it look healthy in spite of its pallor. Her hair was coming out of its braid, of course, as it always did. One strand was curling into the corner of her eye, and he carefully pushed it away. "Eloise," he repeated.

She turned her head, her eyes still closed. Perhaps he shouldn't wake her. He could stay here and look at her, stock up for the lonely months ahead. If he were very careful, perhaps he could even kiss her. Her face was turned up now. He pulled back the covers partway, climbed onto the bed next to her, and brushed her lips very gently. She made a little sound and reached up drowsily to touch his shoulder. Suddenly, he didn't want to be careful. He slid his arms around her, besieging her sleep with embraces and broken endearments, and felt her come to life. First slowly and dreamily, then ardently, matching every advance with an attack of her own. For one glorious minute it was the boat all over again: deep, eager kisses, smooth hands stroking his face, her neck arching up as he turned his head sideways and breathed her name into her hair. This time it would be the way he had pictured it, he was thinking—and then it all came crashing down, of course. He felt her go rigid, pull desperately away. He let her go at once, but she still struggled frantically until she realized that it was the bedding, not James, trapping her feet. Then she sat, staring wide-eyed at him, one hand covering her mouth.

"You're not a dream," she said faintly. "I thought you were a dream." Her voice got stronger, took on a bitter edge. "Although I have been expecting you. I assumed sooner or later the spy would show his colors."

"You wouldn't let me into the house," he said defensively. "I needed to see you. I was forced to take some rather questionable measures as a result."

She surveyed her loosened braid and half-unbuttoned nightgown. "Questionable indeed," she said scornfully. "What was your plan? Impregnate me in my sleep? Shouldn't you have drugged me first?"

"I merely wanted to talk to you," he said, trying to stay calm. She hadn't screamed or rung for a servant. That was a good sign, wasn't it? Not to mention the obvious implication that she was dreaming about him.

"This," she said, pointing to the buttons he had unfastened, "is not talking."

"It just happened," he said helplessly.

"Very well," she said, folding her arms. "You have two minutes, and then I ring for help. Talk."

"I love you." That wasn't what he had meant to say; it had just burst out of him.

"I am honored to learn of your regard," she said with exaggerated courtesy. "But that has nothing to do with what I assume you came to talk about. If you did indeed come to talk."

"This annulment—"

"Divorce," she reminded him.

He made an impatient gesture. "What does the language matter? Divorce, annulment: the result is the same. We won't be married any longer."

"Something you yourself proposed as a very desirable state of affairs, on our wedding night."

"Eloise," he said sternly, "if we only have two minutes I don't want to talk about all my errors on the wedding night. I want to talk about what I consider a desirable outcome *now*."

"Which is?"

"We remain married. I confess that I have been an imbecile and a blackguard, you forgive me, and we get on with our lives."

"What about what *I* consider a desirable outcome now?"

He had the uneasy feeling that she, too, had been rehearsing for this long-postponed conversation and that she had done a much better job of preparing than he had. "And what is that?"

"We dissolve our marriage, which has brought me nothing but heartache, is probably illegal, and was at the very least a sham from the first night on."

He scrambled off the bed and stood in front of her. "But what if it isn't a sham any longer? What if it became real?"

She shook her head. "It couldn't."

"Why not?" He was nearly begging now.

"You can't build truth on lies."

"Eloise, I love you. I would die for you. That's a truth. And it grew out of a lie."

She sat all the way up and looked at him fiercely. "It's not a truth. You don't really love me. If you did, you wouldn't keep me imprisoned in a marriage I don't want. You would value my happiness, not your own."

This struck him as a dangerously plausible argument, and he stood speechless for a moment. Then he fought back, rallying. "You can't tell me you don't love me. You can't tell me that you don't want me. Look at what was happening just now. Look at what happened on the boat.'' He was shouting, forgetting all about the need for privacy and caution.

She stood up in the bed, so that she was looking down at him, and shouted back. ''Yes, I want you! Go ahead, congratulate yourself! But I don't want you as a husband! Can't you understand that? Let me go! When I'm married again you can be my lover.'' She stepped onto the pillows and tugged at the bellrope. ''Your two minutes are up,'' she said, her voice shaking.

''Eloise,'' he pleaded, ''you can't expect me to explain myself, to persuade you about something of this magnitude, in two minutes.''

''We have been married for three months,'' she said coldly. ''You were not very persuasive during that time.''

And then the door opened, far too soon for anyone who was responding to the bell, and he saw three grim faces in the doorway: A large man he recognized as the night porter, Samuel Bernal, holding a pearl-handled pistol, and Silvio. His soon-to-be former valet.

''Very well,'' he said, looking up at her. ''I'll go. But I won't divorce you. You will just have to hope for an early widowhood. Don't despair; my occupation should offer you numerous chances. Not to mention my engagement with Lord Evrett in a few hours.'' He stalked to the door and addressed Silvio. ''Are you coming with me, or have you changed employers?''

''With you, signor,'' said the Italian. But he bowed to Eloise before he closed the door behind James.

After the fuss had died down and everyone save her maid had left, Eloise stood unmoving for several minutes, staring at the floor. Her argument was a good one, and she knew it. James knew it as well. She had shaken him deeply; that was obvious. But some nagging instinct told her that there was something she had overlooked—some flaw in her logic.

The maid was fluttering around the room, twitching the coverlet and pillows back into place and pretending not to stare at her. She should get back in bed and let the poor woman go back to sleep. Impatiently she dismissed her, refusing two offers to fetch a tray from the kitchen and one to warm her sheets again. It was true; they were cold. She lay shivering while the bed gradually thawed around her, and tried to think of what she had missed when she had told James that if he loved her he would value her happiness, not his own. What was wrong with that? Had he not claimed, extravagantly (but probably quite sincerely), that he would die for her? Wasn't that simply the most extreme case of what she had proposed: that love was selfless?

It took her twenty minutes, lying there with her eyes wide open in the dark, to realize what the problem was. There was, in fact, no error in her argument. If James loved her, he *would* prefer her happiness to his own. The error lay in her assumption about what constituted happiness. Divorcing James was not going to make her happy. It was going to make her just as miserable as he was. It was time to face facts: her argument had not really been based on logic, or even on some instinctive feeling about what would be best for the two of them. It had been based on wounded pride.

"Now what?" she whispered, as the consequences of her miscalculation opened out before her. "Now what do I do?"

"I take it I am dismissed," said Silvio as they climbed out of the boat which had brought them back downriver to the City. "I'll go back to your rooms and pack up my things."

"No, you're not dismissed," said James wearily, realizing that his resolution to fire his servant had lasted approximately two minutes. "I think ruining my life is quite enough for one evening. I needn't ruin yours as well. I can't blame you for following me over there after the way I've been behaving today." Then a thought struck him. "Or do you want to leave? My father would be glad to engage you. I'm going by there now; I can leave him a note."

"I'll stay," said Silvio. "If you don't mind." He took this somewhat literally, walking with him right up to the door of his uncle's house. Only then did he bid him good night and turn back towards their own apartments on the other side of Tower Hill.

James had a key to the house, but he knocked gently at the rear door in case any servants were still awake. To his surprise, he heard movement, and the door opened a crack to reveal the familiar bald head of Bullin, the Roths' porter.

"Master James," he said, as though James were keeping an appointment. The door swung wide, and he stepped in. "Your father has not yet retired. I believe he is in his study."

Another surprise, although his father often kept very odd hours. Still, it was nearly two in the morning.

"Go off to bed, Bullin," he said roughly. "I can let myself out."

The servant handed him a candle and shuffled off obediently towards the kitchen, then paused. "Your father said to tell you your bed is made up in your old room, should you wish to stay here, sir."

Frowning, James made his way through the dark and silent back rooms to the corner where his father's study lay tucked underneath a staircase. Light was shining out through the half-open door. He pushed it open, half expecting to find his father standing there ready to scold him; Meyer would have heard Bullin greet him, heard his footsteps coming through the breakfast room. But when he went in, his father was sitting in a chair by the fire, staring at his hands. He did look up at the sound of the door, but made no other movement.

"It seems I am expected," James said.

"I did not know it would be tonight," his father admitted. "But yes, you were expected."

"I went to see her."

Meyer sat up straighter and said eagerly, "She changed her mind, then, and agreed to receive you?"

"No."

His father sighed. "The window?"

"The roof."

"And?"

"She had me thrown out." He added bitterly, "By Silvio, among others."

Reading his son's face, Meyer reached over and dragged a small stool across the hearth towards his own chair. "Have a seat."

Scarcely noticing what he was doing, he sank down next to his father. It was a low stool, and when he bowed his head he found himself staring at his father's ankles. The view wavered and blurred, and reemerged. He realized that he had tears in his eyes.

"Papa, I had her," he said in anguish. "I had her, and I threw her away. And now I can't get her back."

"I know," said his father softly. There was no condemnation in his voice, only pain and sympathy. His hand rested tentatively on James's shoulder, as though expecting a rebuff.

Perhaps it was the low stool, or the dreamlike quality of the dying fire and the silent house. Perhaps it was something in the way his father had spoken, or that awkward touch on his shoulder. He laid his head in his father's lap like a small child and wept, silently and hopelessly.

His father talked to him—about what, he could never remember afterwards. He was grateful that he didn't say any of the obvious and useless and false things: that it would all turn out well in the end, that he was not to blame, that there would be someone else to take her place in time. Eventually, his father got up, put James in the chair—he nearly had to lift him in, he was so weak and disoriented—and disappeared for a few minutes. When he returned he had evidently been to the kitchen; on the tray he carried there was a pot of hot tea, which had spilled slightly, teacups, two glasses, a bottle of claret, a large slice of cheese, and half of a currant loaf.

"I know it's a rather odd assortment, but I was hungry," said Meyer apologetically as he saw his son's eyes rest on the currant loaf. "And I didn't want to wake any of the servants. I just grabbed a few things which seemed expendable." He set the tray down on his desk. "Tea or wine?"

"Tea, please," he said. "I wouldn't mind some cheese, if there's enough."

He followed the tea with a small glass of the wine. His head had cleared; he felt very alert and calm. He saw now that at some point while his father had been speaking he had crossed the border between frustration and resolve. Resolve was much more comfortable.

"I gather you have an engagement early tomorrow," said his father. "Today, rather. Should I be worried?"

"No," he reassured him. "Not at all." The demon had vanished. He wondered suddenly how many of his duels his father had known about, how many times he had woken at dawn and lain there hoping that his son would emerge unharmed. He had probably fretted about the safety of the opponents, as well.

"I must drive you mad," James said ruefully, leaning back in his chair. "Don't you wish sometimes that I had listened to my uncle and become a scholar? No duels, no false names, no midnight sails to France. Just a nice, peaceful library."

"You know, after your mother died and I began traveling for the army, he was very angry with me," Meyer said slowly. "Your uncle, that is. He was angry when I left you and Rachel; he was even angrier when I decided to take you with me into Spain. He said it was bad enough for me to take foolish risks myself because I was crazed with grief, but involving you and your sister was criminal.'' He looked at his son. ''I don't think it was a mistake.''

''Nor do I,'' said James.

''But,'' continued his father, ''I cannot expect a quiet, dutiful son. Not after I trained to him to lie in three languages, forge papers, pick locks, and steal horses.''

Thirty-one

He got back to his rooms at four and slept for two hours. Then he got up again. His attempt to shave and dress without waking Silvio failed, as it usually did, but the valet, surprisingly, did not offer his usual lecture or even scowl at him. Perhaps he was grateful that he still had his job, after last night. An offer to accompany him to the ground was refused, but gently. His quarrel was not with Silvio. For the first time in many months, the only person he was angry with was himself, and even that anger was blunted by the memory of his father's unquestioning welcome last night.

No one else was there when he arrived at the half-thawed patch of grass they had designated for the meeting. He sent his hired carriage off, set his pistol case down on a relatively dry patch of ground, and simply paced back and forth, careful not to go near the spot designated as the actual location for the duel. He was not impatient. He was confident that what he was about to do was completely right.

His seconds, two brash young officers from the Ninety-fifth, drove up together. He had selected them deliberately as being very unlikely to propose a reconciliation—normally the first duty of a second. They were not friends; their presence here was not due to admiration for a fellow officer or even regimental solidarity. In fact, he suspected that if he tried to call at their lodgings or greet them in a public place they might cut him dead. He had calculated that they would consent to act for him out of morbid curiosity, and he had been correct. They nodded to him affably and hurried over to the field to begin the ritual inspection for rabbit holes and hummocks.

When Southey arrived, James assumed that Evrett had named him as a second, and did not approach him. A few minutes later, however, a carriage pulled up and disgorged Evrett, LeSueur, and a vaguely familiar figure—Winters, he thought the man was called—who headed in a purposeful fashion towards his own seconds. James stared at Southey for a moment and then walked slowly over to the slight rise where his fellow courier was standing. Southey looked down at him warily.

"You're not with Evrett?" he asked, just to make certain.

"No." Southey added in a low voice, "He didn't ask me, thank God. I wouldn't have known what to do."

"Then why are you here?"

"I don't know. Hoping for a miracle, I suppose."

"Your prayers have been answered. Go tell him I wish to apologize. I can't go over myself; they're on the ground."

He had expected astonishment, but what he saw instead was relief: relief and a flicker of something that looked like affection. Embarrassed, he lowered his eyes and stood staring at his boots while Southey hurried over to the other men.

His seconds would be disappointed, he knew, and might well try to paint him as a coward, but his record as a successful duellist would give the lie to that, and in any case he was not concerned with his reputation at the moment. He was concerned with not making yet another mistake.

Footsteps were approaching; he straightened up and lifted his head to see his opponent, looking puzzled, standing about two yards away. Behind Evrett were LeSueur and Winters, who seemed slightly stunned. His own men were clearly outraged and were glaring impartially at both him and Evrett. They placed themselves conspicuously far away from him. As if in reply, Southey moved to stand by his shoulder. He gave him a grateful glance.

"My lord, we have not yet taken our ground, and I am therefore still at liberty to apologize to you in the presence of these gentlemen," he said loudly, making certain everyone could hear. "If you choose to continue, that is your right, but I wish everyone to understand that I offered you the grossest insults, insults which were completely false and unfounded. I am prepared to make this same statement to any audience you designate, at any time."

LeSueur, shaken, muttered to Winters, "By God, he doesn't do things by halves, does he?" But James ignored him. His attention was focused on Evrett. He realized suddenly how much it meant to him that his friend should understand, should forgive him. It would be an omen. If he could make it right with Evrett, perhaps someday he could make it right with Eloise, also. He was careful to keep his face completely expressionless. A smile might be interpreted as an attempt to trade on their old friendship; a frown as an indication that the apology was not sincere.

There was a very long pause, and he saw nothing in Evrett's mien or bearing to give him much hope, but he waited.

"I was going to aim over your head," said Evrett finally. "And pray I didn't stumble at the wrong moment and end up hitting you." A momentary gleam of the famed Weyland family twinkle appeared in his dark eyes, and James realized he had been holding his breath. He let it go.

"Apology accepted." Evrett stuck out his hand. "I owe you a small one myself. I should have known a man in your situation would be easily provoked by the sight of a reprobate like myself in the company of your wife."

James shook the extended hand, hoping that no reply was necessary. He did not trust himself to speak.

"You know, she only puts up with me for one reason," Evrett added. The two of them and Southey had started walking towards Southey's vehicle, slightly ahead of the other four men.

James's voice came back. "What's that? Your title?"

"No, you clunch. The same reason she seeks out my redheaded friend here." He gave Southey a wry look. "Because we can tell her stories about you. That's all she wants to hear about—Captain Nathanson and his doughty deeds." He put his hand on his friend's shoulder. "Just be patient, James. Give her some time."

He shook his head. "It's too late."

"Don't tell me it's too late," said Evrett, exasperated. "My God, the woman is besotted with you! Didn't you see the way she looked at you yesterday?"

"I spoke with her last night," James said, his face bleak. "She made her feelings very clear. I wrote her this morning before I came here to tell her I will grant her a divorce."

Shocked, Evrett started to protest further, but Southey gave him a sharp dig in the ribs and said quickly, "May I offer you a ride home, Your Humbleness?"

"A ride, yes, but not home," he said, grateful for Southey's intervention.

"Where, then?" And then, in a slightly incredulous tone, "Not White's office?"

He shook his head. "I'm suspended at the moment, remember? Could you set me down near there, though? I'm going to consult the rabbi at Bevis Marks."

James arrived at the very end of the morning service and stood in silence at the back of the synagogue as the congregation dispersed. The great arched windows sent pools of thin sunshine into the room, and the faces of the men who hurried past him seemed half in light, half in shadow, caught between the serenity of the austere sanctuary and the bustle of the day's business which awaited them.

Seeing a stranger looking hesitantly around, a black-garbed man approached—an officer of the congregation, James surmised. He did not seem surprised at the request to speak to the rabbi; he merely nodded.

"The *haham*? Wait here," he said. After ten minutes or so, the man returned, requesting that James follow him. Out the door they went, down the narrow lane which gave access to the synagogue, and into a house which stood a few doors away. "Wait here," the man said again, ushering him into a study.

James wasn't sure what he had pictured, but the disorder here was comfortingly familiar: piles of papers, books weighted open with other books, half-finished letters. It looked just like White's office, save that the books and papers were largely in Hebrew. When the rabbi came in, however, he looked nothing like White. No scowl, no bristling mustaches. Raphael Meldola was a mild-looking man with large dark eyes and a slightly melancholy air.

"Senhor Meyer," he said, closing the door. "I have been expecting you. Please sit down."

So here, too, he was expected. James wondered if everyone in London knew what he was going to do these days before he did. At least he had surprised Evrett this morning. He sat, as directed, on a bench next to the study table. "You know who I am?"

"I met with your wife twice," explained the rabbi as he sat down opposite him. "Regarding her petition to annul your marriage."

Suddenly, James knew that he had been wrong. That an annulment, with its simple declaration that the marriage had never happened, was infinitely preferable to a *get*, which would state forever in writing that he repudiated Eloise.

"And what Mr. Lindo told me is true, that an annulment is not possible?" he asked. "Even if I do not contest it?"

"That is correct, yes. To dissolve the union, you will have to divorce your wife."

There was a long silence, and James realized that although the rabbi knew perfectly well what came next, he was not going to help him. "I have decided to grant my wife's request and release her from the marriage," he said at last. "I'm sorry, but I have no idea how these things are done."

"Naturally not," said the rabbi agreeably. "Divorce is, fortunately, very rare in our community."

James caught the implication: he was not a member of that community. No wonder the marriage was a failure.

"Now, in theory," the rabbi was saying, "the process is very simple. The husband sends the wife a piece of writing announcing that he divorces her. The end. The marriage is over. But over many centuries it has been agreed that it is preferable to have the *get*—the husband's declaration— prepared by a scribe in consultation with a rabbi, just as you did in the case of your marriage contract. There have been cases where the husband deliberately included errors in the *get*, because he wished to be able to resume the marriage later, or because he was granting the divorce under duress and hoped the wife would eventually change her mind."

"I see," said James, wondering if the rabbi's sharp glance at him was a result of something Eloise had told him or the result of his own involuntary grimace at the last phrase.

"I could give you the address of one of the scribes normally employed in such matters," the rabbi went on. "But perhaps, as I will be consulted in any case, you would be willing to entrust me with the particulars required? The scribe will then notify you when the document is ready for signature."

"That would be very kind."

This was real, then. He understood only now that he had secretly hoped the rabbi would offer him advice, some untried strategy, some way to extricate himself from the pit. Instead he was bowing James into the abyss, with a gentle smile on his face.

The rabbi rummaged at the bottom of one of the piles of paper and extricated a clean sheet. "Your name?" he asked, dipping his pen in the ink.

"James Roth Meyer."

"Parents?"

"Nathan Meyer and Miriam Roth."

"Other names you are known by? Nicknames, names used for school, or employment?"

James blinked. "Names I am known by? All of them?"

Something in his tone made the rabbi look up.

"You'll need more paper," James said. "In the last year alone I have used more than two dozen names."

"You have to understand," Southey told her earnestly. "James *never* apologizes. Or almost never. And certainly not when he is already engaged in an affair of honor."

Evrett nodded emphatically, seconding his remarks. "He was notorious in the regiment. Never backed down. Seemed to go out of his way to accept challenges, in fact."

Eloise looked from one to the other. She still hadn't grasped why, at the unconventional hour of half past one, James's friends had suddenly appeared on her doorstep and demanded to speak with her urgently. "He apologizes to me," she said. "Constantly, in fact. I just received another one this morning." The letter had also said that he had changed his mind, that he would set her free. But she didn't want to think about that right now.

"That's quite a different matter," said Southey, looking uncomfortable.

"But surely it's a good thing that the duel was averted?" Frowning, she turned to Evrett. "One of you might have been hurt. Or even killed. When your cards were sent up, in fact, I thought something had happened to James; he had let it slip last night that you were engaged to fight this morning." She didn't want to think about that terrifying misunderstanding, either, or her embarrassment when she had gone flying down the stairs and confronted what she had believed to be messengers of tragedy, only to find them placidly sipping sherry in the second-best drawing room.

Everett flushed and mumbled something about inexcusable thoughtlessness.

"Let me begin again," said the harassed Southey. "Lord Everett and I went out to breakfast after the duel. We had a long conversation. Our conclusion, at the end of that conversation, was that we should call on you."

"To tell me that he apologized?"

"Yes. Among other things."

"But why?"

"We thought it was a sign," Everett said slowly. "A pledge. A sacrifice. His seconds were appalled, you know. The normal thing to do if you wish to avoid hurting your opponent and are willing to acknowledge fault is to fire in the air. You then avoid the charge of cowardice, because you offer your opponent the chance to hit you. A public apology by someone like James is virtually unprecedented. It will be all over London by this evening. And he has plenty of enemies who will be only too happy to crow over his embarrassment. We thought he was doing it for you, and you might never even know of it."

"I see," said Eloise, although the niceties of the dueling code were still unfathomable to her. James had done something odd, something which would cause him great embarrassment, because he had decided she would think it right. And she did. It was mystifying to her why otherwise reasonable young men made a habit of trying to kill each other before breakfast in London's larger parks. Her visitors were still sitting there, looking uncomfortable, and she remembered the phrase "other things." "Was there something else, then, that you wanted to tell me?"

Southey looked at Everett.

"We don't mean to pry," said Everett awkwardly. "We know this is really none of our affair, but James did tell us he had written you this morning. That he was granting your request. In fact, he went off to consult with a rabbi right after the meeting."

"He did?" said Eloise, feeling suddenly a bit queasy.

"We thought—before it was too late . . ." The normally eloquent peer faltered into a helpless silence.

"Can't you give him another chance?" said Southey, cutting to the heart of the matter. "We've known him for years, Evrett and I. He's not always an easy friend to have. He's infernally proud, and he has a terrible temper, and he doesn't confide in people very often, and he has a tendency to jump to conclusions—" He broke off and turned to Evrett. "He sounds dreadful. Why do we like him?"

Eloise knew why they liked him. For the same reason she loved him. Because it was easy to describe the negative things about James, and very difficult to describe the positive ones, but they weighed so much more. His quick, rare smile. His loyalty. His wit. His unexpected gentleness. How many men, believing their new bride to be carrying another man's child, would have taken on that burden so unhesitatingly? And qualities that his friends had never seen, but she had: the strange combination of passion and restraint, of mastery and helplessness, which had marked their turbulent marriage and which she recognized only now as the signposts of his feelings for her.

"Where is he right now?" she said, standing up suddenly.

"I'm not certain," said Southey. "Not at the Tower; he's suspended on half-pay at the moment, as you may know."

She hadn't known, but she didn't care. In fact, she was glad. If he was suspended, he couldn't be ordered back to France. And she didn't have to face the inquisitive gaze of dozens of soldiers. She had had enough of stone castles full of guards at Vincennes.

"I'm going to our apartments to look for him," she told them. "Would one of you be willing to escort me?"

* * *

James had returned from Bevis Marks in an unusually quiet mood.

"What happened?" Silvio inquired cautiously.

"They're preparing a document for me to sign," he said heavily. Then he realized that the question had probably referred to the duel. "Oh—the meeting. Nothing. I apologized."

Silvio had never mastered the art, proper to a gentleman's gentleman, of remaining completely impassive in the face of astounding revelations by his master. He dropped the boot he had been polishing and stared.

James picked it back up and handed it to him. "Pack my bag for three days," he ordered. And, forestalling the next question, "You will not be accompanying me."

With a not-quite-suppressed sigh, his valet excavated the battered cloak bag from the bottom of the wardrobe and began to lay out linens. "Will the signor be dressing for dinner, or will he only require spare shirts?"

A legitimate question, on the face of it, but James knew what the real object was: to determine where he was going and what he would be doing. It suddenly occurred to him that Silvio had every right to that information. Should he be needed, Silvio would have to know where to reach him. Only since Vienna had he begun to mistrust everyone, to lie and hide and run away. It would have to stop. He had vowed that it would stop.

"I am going to Ramsgate," he said carefully.

Startled, Silvio looked up, a half-folded shirt dangling from his hands.

"I only expect to be gone for two days or so. A message sent to the Red Lion will reach me." He was not staying at the Red Lion, and they both knew it.

He held out a sealed note. "Deliver this later today. No need to wait for a reply." It was addressed to Mrs. James Meyer, in care of Samuel Bernal, Kennington Terrace.

"Is this it? The paper for the divorce?" Silvio looked at it as though it were poisonous.

"No, just a letter advising her that I have requested the paper."

Silvio took the note reluctantly. Then he burst out, as though he could not help himself, "Master James, why are you going down there? It will not help anything."

"Penance," he said, his face remote.

Thirty-two

The Bernal home was suitably dark and lonely when he walked up to it late that night. A gleam at an upper window in the gatehouse next to the drive told him the Murdocks had already retired to their lodging. The house itself was his for the night. He could have picked any of the locks except the one on the massive front door, but broken glass seemed appropriate, so he pushed in a pane on one of the terrace doors and reached in to unlatch it from the inside. It was petty, and it did not make him feel better. After some reflection, he decided he ought to sweep up the glass. It took him twenty minutes of hunting with a lantern to find a broom in a storeroom off the kitchen, and another ten minutes to find an old tray to use as a dustpan. But this was all delay. Eventually, he climbed up the stairs and opened the double doors to the little suite.

He had expected it to look the same, and some of it did. The crimson and gold window-hangings were still there, with not too many cobwebs, and the little table where they had eaten their soup. The divan was shrouded in a coarse white cover, though, and looked like a deformed sarcophagus with its black lacquered feet sticking out from beneath the lumpy white top. The chest with the sphinxes had been pushed into a corner and turned slightly sideways—presumably when they had pulled up the carpet, which was rolled up beside it.

The bedroom was worse. The smaller chairs had been stacked against the wall and covered; he could only tell what they were because the cloth had fallen away from the side of one chair, revealing a walnut armrest. The bed had been stripped, of course, and the hangings taken down from the circular canopy overhead. The gilt eagle looked rather ridiculous on the naked iron hoop. There were no drapes at the windows. His lantern shone back at him, glaring in a sea of shiny black and casting harsh shadows on the drawn face reflected in the glass.

The side table where Eloise had taken refuge that night was in front of the armoire; he moved it very carefully over to the chairs, opened the upper cupboard, and unpacked his bag. After a moment's thought, he went back out into the anteroom and took the cover from the divan to use as a sheet. Then he removed his boots, wrapped himself in his coat, and climbed into the bed. There was a giant lump under his hip, so he sat up again, took off the coat, and emptied the large outer pockets. The pistol he had known about, also a small set of picklocks and about a half-dozen keys. What he hadn't remembered was the silver flask he had filled with Bourciez's cognac.

"Your health," he said, saluting the eagle perched above his head.

He woke, very late, to the improbable smell of coffee. Surely the caretakers could not have heard him last night? He kept his eyes closed for a minute, trying to think of some tale to explain to Mrs. Murdock why he had broken into his father-in-law's house and gone to sleep wrapped in holland covers. She couldn't be too angry if she had brought him coffee, he decided. He opened his eyes. It wasn't Mrs. Murdock. It was Silvio, holding out a steaming china cup.

"I thought I made it clear you were not accompanying me," James said, closing his eyes again.

"I'm not accompanying you," retorted the valet. "I'm with the signora."

That took a minute to penetrate the fog of sleepiness and brandy residue. Then he opened his eyes again, very cautiously, and found himself looking at Eloise. She was sitting right next to him on the bed, quite composed, in a deep-red dress which was nearly the exact color of the missing bed-hangings. He had actually seen her out of the corner of his eye when he first woke and had filed her mentally under "drapery."

"I was going to wake you myself," she informed him. "I gather you are normally rather a light sleeper, and I thought this might be my only chance to pay you back for your visit to my bedchamber the other night. But Silvio said you would need coffee."

"I do," he said, seizing the cup and taking a large, scalding gulp. "I wouldn't have minded, however, if you had brought it to me instead of him."

"Your conduct of late has been a bit erratic," said the servant coldly. "I felt it best to make sure you were in a rational mood before you spoke with the signora. If you don't mind, I will just put sheets and pillows on this bed. Most people use them, as you may recall. Then I will go down and assist Mr. Murdock. He is replacing the glass you broke."

He knew that broken window had been a mistake. He climbed out of bed and sipped coffee while his valet converted bed-making into a sustained exercise in silent reproach.

"There's hot water," Silvio said at last, indicating a covered basin on the table. "And your kit is laid out." He withdrew.

James sighed. "That was the ultimate snub," he told

Eloise, walking over and exchanging the coffee cup for his razor. "He never lets me shave myself if he can prevent it. I'm in his black books."

"Why?" asked Eloise, sitting back down on the newly made bed.

"Ostensibly because of the broken pane in the door, which was admittedly rather childish. But in fact because of you. Because I lost you."

She didn't reply, and the silence stretched out until it became awkward.

"Did you get my second letter?" he asked finally, when he had shaved every inch of his face three times over and had no further excuse to ignore her.

"Yes, I did."

"Is there something else I need to do? Some additional legal matters which need my attention? Is that why you came down here to find me?"

"No," she said.

He rinsed his face and took another gulp of coffee. He was getting the distinct impression that the brandy last night had not been a good idea, although he hadn't had that much. Something odd was going on, and he was too thickheaded to understand what it was.

"May I ask why you are here, then?" he said after another long silence. He saw her bend her head, and the telltale glint in the corners of her eyes gave her away. "No, don't cry!" he said, horrified. "You're well out of it. You were right all along, I came to see that. I wasn't much of a husband."

"I know," said Eloise. "It seems very unfair that I should want you back anyway."

He was sure he had misunderstood her.

"Would you mind saying that again?" he asked cautiously.

"I want you back," she repeated stubbornly. "I love you. I'm miserable without you. It's completely unreasonable and unfair and unfathomable and every other word commencing with *un* I can think of."

"Unfortunate?" he said, sitting back down beside her. "Uncanny?" He picked up her hand and kissed it softly. "Unworthy?" She was starting to smile through her tears. "Unregenerate?"

"Oh, James," she said, half laughing, and he knew that in his current condition he would run out of vocabulary fairly quickly, so he tried her mouth this time. "Undesirable," he added between increasingly long tastes. He tried to think of an *un* adjective which meant happy, since he was so intoxicated with joy it seemed wrong to be uttering all these negative words, but he couldn't find one. "Unyielding." She felt anything but unyielding at the moment. "Unattached."

It was meant to describe the floating sensation which enveloped him at that moment, but it was a very poorly chosen example. She pulled away and stood up. "Stop kissing me," she said, blushing. "We need to talk about the divorce. About what to do afterwards."

"Afterwards?"

"Yes, afterwards," she said patiently. "After the *get* arrives."

He slid off the bed and stood next to her. "You still want a divorce?" he asked incredulously.

She nodded.

He sank down into one of the shrouded armchairs, shaking his head in disbelief. "I suppose I deserve this," he muttered, closing his eyes and leaning back until he was nearly swallowed in the white slipcover. "I beg your pardon for spoiling your sport. Pray continue. Come over here and kiss me again and then tell me how you despise me and cannot wait to be free of me."

"I don't despise you," she said with dignity. "I am quite fond of you. I thought I had made that very clear."

He erupted out of the chair and waved his hands in the air in frustration. "Nothing is clear!" he shouted. "You refuse to see me for a month; my sister and Silvio have nearly disowned me; I yield at last to what seems to be universal agreement that I am not fit to kiss your little kid slippers, and consent to the divorce. *You*"—he pointed at her—"*you* follow me down here, escorted by my own treacherous servant, who proceeds to lecture me until I feel like a schoolboy." His voice dropped and became ragged. "Then you announce that you love me, and proceed to demonstrate same, quite convincingly. So convincingly that I am on the verge of locking the door and joining you in this ridiculous bed where I botched it all on our wedding night. I thought we could begin again, go back and try to do things properly. And now you tell me you want a divorce after all!"

"But that is precisely the point," she insisted. "To begin again. This marriage was ill-omened from the start. We both agreed to it for the wrong reasons. The wedding ceremony was a disaster. Your stumble with the goblet, your false accusations, my cowardice—is that what you want to tell our children when they ask us about our wedding?"

At the word "children" his shoulders relaxed infinitesimally. "Are you saying," he asked cautiously, "that you wish to proceed with the divorce and then remarry?"

"Not quite." Then, seeing his expression, she added hastily, "Well, yes. But if we are to start fresh, I want to start from the beginning. No *kasamentero*. No uncles. No edicts from my grandmother. I want to be courted. I want you to call for me and take me riding in the park. I want you to escort me to concerts. I want you to take me to Hatchard's and buy me books and write my name on the flyleaf with a little epigram underneath. I want—" she groped for something which would represent what they had not had, something that shy and tentative young couples would do. "I want you to pay a morning call and sit and look at your boots."

"I did that," he pointed out.

"You did not," she retorted. "Some *danyador* wearing your body sat in my mother's drawing room. I was married by proxy to a man possessed by a demon, and I want a real ceremony with my real husband."

"You realize," he said in mild tones after a moment, "that this is completely absurd."

"Not as absurd as marrying a naive, trusting girl when you believe you are in love with someone else."

He winced. There was a long silence. "Very well," he said finally. "After all, I gave you my word in writing yesterday that I would grant the divorce. We will dissolve the marriage."

She looked startled rather than triumphant. Presumably, she had not expected such an easy victory.

He shifted at once to the attack, pressing his advantage. "It will take several days to prepare the document. You do understand that?"

She nodded. "You said so in your letter."

"And until you receive the *get*, we are married."

"I suppose so." She was looking more nervous now.

He took a step towards her and watched, amused, as she hastily stepped back. "Does this courtship, as you call it, begin now, or only after the marriage is dissolved?"

"Afterwards," she whispered.

"Good," he said, reaching her in one long stride and catching her by both elbows. "Because what I have in mind at the moment would cause quite a scandal in, say, the concert rooms at Hanover Square. Luckily we are well situated, in a house amply provided with brand-new beds, thanks to your mother's forethought. And no boxes of fish bait in sight."

"Oh," she breathed.

There was a resounding tattoo on the half-open door, and they sprang apart. Silvio appeared, and James was about to tell him in three languages just how untimely his interruption had been, when a stocky boy of about eighteen appeared behind him. A boy in uniform, carrying a messenger's bag. James's heart sank.

"Captain Nathanson?"

"Yes," he said wearily.

"I've had quite a time coming up with you," said the

messenger cheerfully. "Luckily, I ran into Major Southey and he told me you had gone to Ramsgate. Then I inquired of various people in the town until the ostler at the inn directed me up here." He was clearly very pleased with himself, but James, who had a fairly accurate idea of what came next, was wishing he had been slightly less enterprising.

"It's good news, sir," added the young soldier, pulling a sheaf of orders out of his bag. "You've been reinstated. With back pay," he added impressively.

Eloise's face lit. "Oh, that is good news," she said, relieved.

"No, it isn't," James said grimly. "You don't know Whitehall. Once you're reinstated you're called up for duty immediately."

"Oh, not immediately, sir," the messenger assured him, handing over the packet. "Not until eight tomorrow morning."

"I stand corrected." James gave a short laugh. "If I ride like a madman and have no trouble at the posting stations, I could enjoy my wife's company until at least midnight."

"You'd be better advised to start back this afternoon, sir," the messenger said earnestly. "It's snowing on the Downs."

"What is your name, if I may?" he asked the soldier.

"Abell, sir. William Abell. Corporal, Twenty-fourth Foot."

"Corporal, has anything of great moment happened since I left London yesterday? Anything which requires an urgent military response?"

"No, sir," answered the puzzled messenger.

"Well, something has happened here. I have just asked my wife to marry me, and she has said yes."

The corporal tried to make sense of this for a moment, then gave up. "I'm sure I wish you very happy, sir."

"I would take it as a personal favor," said James, "if

there might be some way to delay the delivery of these orders. Until, say, late tomorrow morning.''

The boy turned pink. ''That would be very irregular, sir.'' He looked at Eloise, who had slipped her hand into her husband's, at Silvio, who was scowling at him, and back to James.

''There is a ceremony,'' explained James. ''A family tradition. The Blessing of the Bedchambers. It would mean a great deal to me and my wife.''

The pink turned into red. ''I wasn't aware—in that case, sir, perhaps an exception could be made—''

James ushered him down the stairs and out the door, protesting his eternal gratitude, before the boy could change his mind. ''Don't forget these,'' he said, handing back the orders. ''I'll be delighted to take them from you tomorrow. Around eleven.'' He handed over something silver as well. ''To drink our health.''

''Yes, sir. My best wishes, sir,'' gulped the boy, saluting.

Eloise was waiting in the anteroom with folded arms. '' 'The Blessing of the Bedchambers'?'' she demanded.

''More like an exorcism, and it's going to begin right now,'' he promised her, a glint in his eye. He locked the outer door.

''At half past eleven in the morning?'' she said, scandalized.

''I know his type.'' He held open the door to the inner room. ''He'll get halfway down the hill and have a fit of self-righteousness. If I have to ride back to London later today, I'd like to have at least one pleasant memory of the beds in this house to take with me.''

She walked slowly over to the door and looked up at him. ''I did have a late breakfast,'' she conceded with a demure smile. ''I suppose we could postpone luncheon.''

He was pulling the pins out of her hair and tossing them on the floor when she suddenly said, ''James?''

''Yes,'' he said abstractedly.

''What if he doesn't come back? Until tomorrow?''

He smoothed the loosened strands back over her forehead. "Then we'll have time to bless some of the other bedrooms. Perhaps you should ask Mrs. Murdock to make them all up, just in case. How many of them are there?"

"Seven," she said faintly.

"Corporal Abell might even be indisposed tomorrow," he said thoughtfully. "One can but hope."

Her eyes narrowed. "What did you do?"

"Oh, nothing much," he said. "I merely gave him the rest of Bourciez's brandy. And there was quite a bit left."

Historical Note/Acknowledgments

An Englishman in Paris during the winter of 1814 might well have ended up in the dungeon at the Château de Vincennes—even if he did have a safe-conduct. Factions were competing for control of Paris from the moment Napolean left to join his troops, and the secret royalist organization (the Chevaliers de la Foi) was beginning to be a serious threat. The royalist plot mentioned in the book is real. The mayor of Bordeaux did indeed declare for the Bourbons in March, handing over his city to Wellington's troops, and Lyons was lost shortly afterwards by what some now consider purchased incompetence.

On a more domestic front, the strained détente I described between the two Jewish communities in London also reflects the actual situation at the time. Intermarriage between the well-established Iberian Jews and the newer immigrants from eastern Europe was rare until the period of my story, when a few powerful families began defying tradition.

I made up the *Sûreté,* the sinister French counterintelligence unit, as well as its heroic English counterpart, the courier service. Both are exaggerated versions of the loosely organized and partly unofficial military intelligence services under Napoleon and Wellington. Sometimes, however, you make something up and it turns out to be true. I wrote James's escape from the coast, including the attempt of the Royal Navy to confiscate his rescuer's boat, thinking it was fiction. I later discovered a virtually identical incident in a biography of Colquhon Grant, Wellington's premier intelligence officer.

For more information about the historical background and about earlier books in this series, please visit my Web site (www.nitaabrams.com). It includes photos of various places in the books and a mail link (nita@nitaabrams.com). I always enjoy hearing from readers.

Finally, thanks to Nancy Kobrin, Ph.D., Professors Jonathan Paradise and Ellen Umansky, and the staff at the Château de Vincennes and Bevis Marks Synagogue for their help with everything from Ladino to original architects' drawings to Jewish marriage law. And special thanks to my amazing research crew: Mom, Dad, MK, and, of course, Rachel.

Thrilling Romance from
Lisa Jackson

More By Best-selling Author
Fern Michaels

__Kentucky Rich	0-8217-7234-1	$7.99US/$10.99CAN
__Kentucky Heat	0-8217-7368-2	$7.99US/$10.99CAN
__Plain Jane	0-8217-6927-8	$7.99US/$10.99CAN
__Wish List	0-8217-7363-1	$7.50US/$10.50CAN
__Yesterday	0-8217-6785-2	$7.50US/$10.50CAN
__The Guest List	0-8217-6657-0	$7.50US/$10.50CAN
__Finders Keepers	0-8217-7364-X	$7.50US/$10.50CAN
__Annie's Rainbow	0-8217-7366-6	$7.50US/$10.50CAN
__Dear Emily	0-8217-7316-X	$7.50US/$10.50CAN
__Sara's Song	0-8217-7480-8	$7.50US/$10.50CAN
__Celebration	0-8217-7434-4	$7.50US/$10.50CAN
__Vegas Heat	0-8217-7207-4	$7.50US/$10.50CAN
__Vegas Rich	0-8217-7206-6	$7.50US/$10.50CAN
__Vegas Sunrise	0-8217-7208-2	$7.50US/$10.50CAN
__What You Wish For	0-8217-6828-X	$7.99US/$10.99CAN
__Charming Lily	0-8217-7019-5	$7.99US/$10.99CAN

Call toll free **1-888-345-BOOK** to order by phone or use this coupon to order by mail.

Name_____

Address_____

City _____State_____Zip_____

Please send me the books I have checked above.

I am enclosing	$_____
Plus postage and handling*	$_____
Sales Tax (in New York and Tennessee)	$_____
Total amount enclosed	$_____

*Add $2.50 for the first book and $.50 for each additional book. Send check or money order (no cash or CODs) to: **Kensington Publishing Corp., 850 Third Avenue, New York, NY 10022**

Prices and numbers subject to change without notice. All orders subject to availability. Check out our website at **www.kensingtonbooks.com**

The Queen of
Romance

Cassie Edwards